When the
Stars Sang

BOOKS BY CAREN J. WERLINGER

Novels:
Looking Through Windows
Miserere
In This Small Spot
Neither Present Time
Year of the Monsoon
She Sings of Old, Unhappy, Far-off Things
Turning for Home
Cast Me Gently
The Beast That Never Was
When the Stars Sang

Short Stories:
Twist of the Magi
Just a Normal Christmas
(part of *Do You Feel What I Feel? Holiday Anthology*)

The Dragonmage Saga:
Rising From the Ashes: The Chronicles of Caymin
The Portal: The Chronicles of Caymin
The Standing Stones: The Chronicles of Caymin

When the
Stars Sang

CAREN J. WERLINGER

CORGYN
Publishing

When the Stars Sang
Published by Corgyn Publishing, LLC.

Copyright © 2018 by Caren J. Werlinger
All rights reserved.

e-Book ISBN: 978-0-9982179-1-8
Print ISBN: 978-0-9982179-2-5

E-mail: cjwerlingerbooks@yahoo.com
Web site: www.cjwerlinger.wordpress.com

Cover design by Patty G. Henderson
www.boulevardphotografica.yolasite.com

Cover Photo: Hendrik Mandla

Interior decoration: Can Stock Photo/Red Koala

Book design by Maureen Cutajar
www.gopublished.com

This is a work of fiction. Names, characters, places, and incidents are the product of the author's imagination or are used fictitiously, and any resemblance to actual persons, living or dead, businesses, companies, events, or locales is entirely coincidental.

For Beth, *mo chroi*

Acknowledgements

This story has been years in the making—inside my head. It's a story I've wanted to write for a long time, but it never came together until recently. Inspiration came from many places.

Thanks to Shannon for her stories about her great-aunts. I want to thank the people of Eigg—who don't know me at all—for their inspiring fight to save their island and make it self-sustaining.

Thank you also to Lisa T, my editor, and to my spouse, Beth, for her constant support and encouragement.

And thank you to my readers. Without you, I'd probably still be writing, but it wouldn't be nearly as much fun!

"Her voice was like the voice the stars had when they sang together."

DANTE GABRIEL ROSSETTI
The Blessed Damozel

Chapter 1

A BLAST OF COLD WIND hit Kathleen, nearly knocking her over and misting her glasses with sea spray so that she could barely see. She couldn't recall ever having such a rough crossing before, but she'd never made it at this time of year. She tried to ignore the little voice telling her this was a sign—a sign that she'd made a huge, impulsive mistake.

She jumped when a door slammed behind her.

"You should come inside."

She held to the rail of the ferry and turned to the man who had shouted at her over the wind. "I'm okay. We're almost there."

She pointed to a hump of land only just visible through the gloom.

The man bent over at the waist, laughing so hard he nearly lost his balance as the deck heaved. "That's Big Sister Island. We got nother hour before we get to Little Sister. Maybe more in this chop. It's wicked cold. You'll be froze by the time we get there."

1

Her heart sank while her stomach rose uncomfortably. She followed him back into the little cabin. One bare bulb illuminated the interior. Two steps up, in the pilothouse, sat the ferry's captain, his hands firmly gripping the wheel and the throttle.

"Aren't there any other passengers?" she asked.

She took off her damp jacket and sat on one of the hard plastic benches that lined either side of the cabin. Using the hem of the T-shirt under her sweater, she wiped the droplets off her glasses and put them back on.

"Nope." The man who had invited her in held out a cup of coffee in a dented enameled cup. "Just you and supplies."

With a nod of thanks, she accepted, trying not to grimace at the dark stains that dyed the interior of the cup. The black coffee itself was so thick, it was in little danger of sloshing over the lip, no matter how the ferry pitched. She turned the cup so that the handle was away from her, telling herself no other lips had touched this part of its chipped rim.

"Fred," the captain called, holding out an empty mug of his own.

Fred obliged by refilling it with more thick coffee and handing it back up before taking a seat across from Kathleen.

"So you're Maisie Halloran's granddaughter."

Kathleen, who had just taken a sip of scalding coffee, could only nod through watery eyes as she tried to swallow the bitter sludge. She forced it down. "How did you know that?"

Fred shrugged. "Small island. Not much happens everyone don't know about."

Up in the pilothouse, the captain raised his own cup in a kind of toast. "We were sorry to hear about Maisie's passing," he said over his shoulder. "Not many left like her. Kind lady."

Kathleen nodded again, cradling the cup in her chilled hands. She decided it worked better as a hand warmer than a beverage. Below them, the ferry's engine vibrated as it churned them onward. "You both knew my grandmother?"

"Oh, we know most all the islanders. Not too many folks live there. Bobby here," Fred pointed to the captain at the wheel, "he was born and raised on Little Sister. Still got family there."

He nodded toward the rear of the ferry where Kathleen's car was now thoroughly drenched in seawater. "Good thing you got to the landin' when you did. We was late pushin' off or we'd've already been underway."

"I could have caught the next ferry," Kathleen said.

Fred bent double and guffawed again. She wasn't sure what she'd said that was so funny. He gestured with his cup, proving her wrong by slopping some coffee onto the stained linoleum tiles of the cabin.

"You'd've had a long wait. Ferry don't run again for a week. We'll probably have to put in overnight 'fore we go back."

She frowned. "But the ferry schedule had lots of ferries listed."

"Yup." Fred nodded again, rubbing the backs of his fingers over the gray stubble bristling along his jaw. "For Big Sister. Only boat goin' to Little Sister is this one. State ferry runs once't a week once the season is over. Once't a month come winter, and that's weather permittin'." He turned to look out the droplet-covered windows, but Kathleen couldn't see anything through them. "Tons o' folks go to Big Sister. Not many wants to go the extra to get out to Little Sister. Get some tourists in high season, but usually the only passengers we carry this time o'year is just the islanders goin' to the mainland for a few days and back home."

Kathleen watched a rivulet of spilled coffee run toward her feet as the ferry rolled with the waves. She clutched her coffee cup, trying to keep the semi-liquid inside from splashing onto her jeans.

Fred tilted his head as he regarded her. "Weather's gonna be turnin' soon. When you plannin' on goin' back?"

"I'm not."

"Not what?"

"I'm not planning on going back." She pretended to take a drink from her coffee cup. "I'm moving to Little Sister to stay."

Fred's bushy gray eyebrows rose as he lifted his cup to his lips. His silence clearly communicated his surprise. *And his doubt,* she realized when he scrutinized her over the rim of his mug.

Just as quickly, his eyebrows scrunched together in a puzzled frown. "If Maisie was your grandma, how come you didn't recognize Big Sister?"

She turned to gaze out the window behind her, though the only thing she could see in the harsh glare from the naked bulb was her own pale reflection staring back. "It's been a long time. Almost twenty-five years."

If he was waiting for further explanation, he was going to be disappointed. A moment later, she heard his heavy boots clomping and then the cabin door opening and closing with a gust of wind.

She took advantage of his absence to quickly dump her coffee in the little sink near the coffee pot, grab her jacket, and slip out the rear door of the cabin. Grasping railings and crates to keep her balance, she made her way to her car. She got in and closed the door just as another heavy gust of spray washed over the windows. The cabin's yellow glow floated in and out of focus through the wet windshield.

She pulled her phone out of her jacket pocket and opened the last text she'd received as she'd sat on the ferry dock.

"Don't do this to us. I know we can work things out. I didn't mean what I said. Please call me. Please come back. I love you, Suze"

She powered the phone off and put it back in her pocket. She closed her eyes and drifted into a restless sleep.

It was dark when a rap on the window scared the life out of her.

"We're here," Fred called through the glass.

She knuckled the sleep from her eyes and turned the ignition. Following his hand signals, she drove off the ferry and onto the island.

The sweep of her headlights sliced through a heavy fog, and she realized she hadn't the first clue where she was.

"It's a small island," she muttered to herself. "It can't be hard to find one little cottage."

But she hadn't been here since she was ten, and it all looked turned around in the dark and the fog. She crept down what she remembered was the main street of the island's only town. She supposed things could have changed in twenty-four years. A trash can appeared out of nowhere, and she jerked the wheel away from the curb.

Cursing under her breath, she put the car in park and got out. Most of the shops along this stretch of the street were dark, but there, like a beacon from a lighthouse, was a larger building with lights glowing a welcome. She got out, locked the car, and made her way toward the lights.

She peered through the glass door into a cozy dining room. About a dozen people were seated at tables and along the counter. Every single one of them turned at the tinkling of the bell on the door as she entered.

Kathleen stood there a moment until a rosy-cheeked woman bustled from behind the counter, the lights glinting off the streaks of silver running through her dark hair.

"Land sakes! What a cold night!" she said, taking Kathleen by the arm. "Table, dear?"

Kathleen nodded even as she was being propelled to an empty table.

"You'll want something hot," said the woman, her fists propped on her wide hips. "Coffee or tea? Or hot chocolate maybe?"

"Coffee, please."

The others all watched her with open curiosity as the woman hurried back behind the counter and returned a minute later with a white mug filled with coffee.

"Thank you," Kathleen said.

The woman slid a menu in front of her, pulling a pencil out of the bun at the nape of her neck. "You look that over and let me know what you want. We still have a little of the chicken and dumplings left."

"That sounds wonderful," Kathleen said, not even bothering to look at the menu.

"My name is Wilma. You just holler if you need anything." Wilma stuck her pencil back in her hair and hurried off.

The bell on the door tinkled again, and Fred and Bobby came in.

"Hey, Wilma," said Fred loudly. The locals all nodded in their direction. "See you already met..."

He looked in Kathleen's direction. "She's Maisie's granddaughter we heard, but never got her name."

Kathleen felt like a zoo specimen as the curious glances intensified. The heat rose in her cold cheeks. "I'm Kathleen Halloran," she said, apparently to the entire diner. "And you never really said. How did you know I'm Maisie's granddaughter?"

Fred chuckled as he and Bobby took stools at the counter. "Sadie, at the ticket window, told us."

Kathleen remembered now, the nosy young woman wondering why anyone would go to Little Sister Island this time of year.

Her eyes widened in alarm as chairs scraped and stools swiveled. Every person in the dining room got up to come to her table and shake her hand, some with murmurs of condolence and others of welcome. A few people mentioned remembering her from when she was a girl.

Wilma shooed them away as she bustled back over with a steaming bowl. "Let the poor thing eat. She looks half-froze."

"Thank you," Kathleen said.

The coffee—she wondered if Fred noticed the difference as he gulped his down—and the chicken and dumplings were all delicious. With hot food and drink and the cozy warmth of the diner, she began to feel drowsy.

"Can you tell me how to get to my grandmother's house?" she asked when Wilma brought the check.

"Land sakes," Wilma clucked. "You can't go out there tonight. We didn't know you were coming. No one's been out to start up the furnace."

6

Kathleen hadn't even considered that there might be things that would need to be tended at the house after sitting empty in the months since Nanna's death.

"Well..."

"How about a room here tonight," Wilma suggested. "And we'll call Mo Cooper to meet you out at the cottage tomorrow and set things right."

Kathleen hadn't planned on spending money on a hotel, but she supposed it was the smart thing to do. She went out into the cold night and tugged one bag loose from the crammed back seat of her car, trying not to cause an avalanche of boxes and suitcases.

Wilma led the way through a door at one end of the dining room, up a wide staircase padded with a faded Persian runner with old-fashioned brass rails holding the runner in place. Upstairs, the long hall had crisp white woodwork and a series of rooms with open doors.

"You're our only guest at the moment," Wilma said. "Do you like morning light?"

"Sure," said Kathleen, following Wilma into one of the rooms.

"We keep the doors open to air them out this time o'year." Wilma switched on a bedside lamp. "You can flip the bolt to lock up. Breakfast starts at six. Welcome home."

She pulled the door shut behind her, leaving Kathleen alone in the clean, simple furnishings. She stepped into the bathroom and groaned when she saw her reflection in the mirror.

"I look like a drowned cat," she muttered, staring at her lank auburn hair, courtesy of the dried sea spray from the ferry. "Nice first impression."

She rinsed her glasses under the tap to wash away the salty film coating the lenses and dried them before stripping to take a quick shower.

A short while later, she lay under clean sheets, covered with a heavy quilt worked in nautical patches of cloth. She stayed stiffly on the left

7

edge of the mattress, listening to the continued howl of the wind outside. She swept her arm out over the empty mattress beside her and shifted to lie sprawled across the middle.

"Welcome home," she whispered to the dark room. "If only."

※※※※※※※※※※

KATHLEEN SQUINTED AT THE beam of sunlight insistently piercing through the opening in the curtains. She yanked the covers over her head, wondering why in the world she'd said she liked morning light.

It was no use.

With a heavy sigh, she flung the covers off and sat up, rubbing her eyes. She climbed out of bed and padded across the room to squint again at the sun hovering just above the treeline. The storm had passed, leaving the skies calm, the sunlight shining directly into her face. Everything sparkled. She turned back to the room, temporarily blinded.

A hot shower rinsed away what remained of her drowsiness. She took some time with the blow dryer, hoping to present a bit better appearance than she had the previous evening.

"Only a bit," she said to her reflection.

She dressed in jeans and a long-sleeved T-shirt with a fleece vest, then repacked her bag. She found her phone and powered it on, but was surprised to see no bars. She held it up and walked to the window. Nothing. She tucked it into her pocket and went down to the dining room where Wilma was apparently waiting for her. A mug of fresh coffee was pressed into her hand while Wilma ushered her to the same table.

"Land sakes, you needed a good night's sleep, Katie."

"It's Kathleen."

But Wilma wasn't listening as she set a menu down on the table and bustled off to fill other coffee mugs.

Kathleen got a couple of nods from the men seated at the counter—mostly faces she recognized from the evening before.

She gave Wilma her order and closed her eyes as she inhaled the coffee. Fred really needed to take a lesson from Wilma. She was startled by a jostling of the table as Wilma sat with a cup of coffee for herself.

"Nels will have your breakfast cooked up in a jiffy," she said, laying a motherly hand on Kathleen's arm. "Bobby and Fred told me you're planning on moving here. Living here."

"Yes."

"Then you'll want to be seeing Rebecca."

"Rebecca?"

Wilma nodded. "Rebecca Ahearn. Bobby's sister. She's the island Keeper and historian now. She'll do your Passing."

Kathleen frowned. "My passing."

Wilma nodded and patted her arm as a bell dinged from the kitchen. "That'll be your breakfast."

A moment later, she slapped a plate of corned beef hash and fried eggs down on the table as she expertly sloshed more coffee into the half-empty mug. Kathleen had her mouth open to ask more questions, but Wilma dashed off to fill more coffee cups and clear empty dishes.

Kathleen shook her head and dug into her breakfast. This was a taste she remembered from her summers here on the island with Nanna. She hadn't had corned beef hash in years, not since—

"Good morning."

Kathleen jumped at the unexpected appearance of a woman at her table. "Good morning," she said uncertainly.

"I'm Rebecca," said the woman, holding out a hand.

Kathleen shook it, surprised by the firmness of the grip as Rebecca studied her with eyes that were a surprising light blue-green against her black hair and bronze complexion.

"Kathleen."

"I'll let you finish your breakfast." Rebecca nodded toward the counter. "When you're done, I'll be waiting."

She moved away to where Wilma had a cup of coffee waiting for her. They put their heads together, whispering as Wilma glanced over Rebecca's shoulder in Kathleen's direction.

Kathleen's enjoyment of her breakfast was pretty much gone as she ate the last few bites and gulped what remained of her coffee.

No sooner had she stood than Rebecca slid off her stool.

Kathleen motioned toward Wilma. "I just need to settle…"

"Of course." Rebecca zipped her jacket. "I'll be out front."

Wilma led the way back out to the lobby of the hotel, which Kathleen hadn't paid much attention to the evening before. Furnished with comfy-looking sofas and chairs scattered about, with bookshelves lining the walls, it had the feel of a family room. The check-in desk actually had an old-fashioned guest ledger.

"Would you mind signing?" Wilma said, holding out a pen. "We've kept track of the hotel guests going all the way back to the 1880s."

Kathleen signed and paid for her room and meals.

"Thank you so much," she said. "I was more tired than I realized last night."

Wilma came around from behind the desk and surprised Kathleen with a hug. "It's good to have you back."

Startled by the unexpected gesture, Kathleen simply nodded and turned for the door.

Outside, Rebecca was waiting for her.

"How far are we going?" Kathleen asked, her breath puffing in the cold air.

Rebecca pointed vaguely. "Not far."

Kathleen stashed her bag inside her car and joined Rebecca, pulling her jacket on as she walked. Everything was washed clean in the clear, cool air of morning. Overhead, not a single cloud littered the blue sky. The trees were still brilliantly colored for autumn. Her head swiveled as she walked, taking in the buildings lining the main street, mostly painted clapboard, but some shingled, weathered to a dove-gray. It was still early, not yet nine, but most of the shops were open and a good many people were out. They waved to Rebecca.

"Has it changed much?" Rebecca asked.

"Yes and no." Kathleen stopped to look down the hill toward the bay and marina where the ferry was still docked, apparently being unloaded, judging from the bustle of activity there. "It all feels familiar, but it's been so long..."

"Nothing changes too much here."

Rebecca led the way across the street and around a corner to a small clapboard building sheltered among a stand of oak trees. It had a front porch, framed by white railings, with two rocking chairs, empty and inviting.

A carved and painted sign was fastened to the railing: Little Sister Library.

Rebecca opened the door and stood back, allowing Kathleen to precede her inside.

"I remember this," Kathleen said, her eyes lit up as she took in shelves crammed with books. "Nanna brought us here."

"That would have been when Naomi was librarian and Keeper," Rebecca said.

Kathleen turned to her. "Keeper of what?"

Rebecca didn't answer, just walked around the librarian's desk into the back room. Kathleen followed her. This room, too, was lined with bookshelves containing row upon row of books, but these books were different. They were bound in leather, very old, with no visible titles that Kathleen could see. Rebecca, however, seemed to know exactly which was which. She went to a shelf and pulled two heavy tomes down, plopping them on the table that occupied the center of the space.

"Have a seat," Rebecca said, taking a chair herself.

Kathleen sat beside her as Rebecca flipped open one of the books. Kathleen leaned closer to see what looked like the lines of a family tree.

"We just need to verify your line," Rebecca said, slipping on a pair of reading glasses.

"I don't understand."

"Surely you know the story of Little Sister."

"Well, I know there was a shipwreck in the seventeen hundreds, and the Indians rescued—"

"We're not Indians," Rebecca said sharply. "We were the First Ones. We lived on both the island and the sea. When the ship went down in 1760, our ancestors rowed out to save those they could."

She frowned at the blank look on Kathleen's face. "Didn't your grandmother or your father tell you this story?"

Kathleen shook her head. "My parents... after my brother died, we never came back here, and they never spoke of the island. Nanna and I wrote a few times, but then she stopped. I hadn't seen her since that summer."

"Oh." Rebecca's expression softened. "Of course. We were all saddened by your brother's death. People still talk about it. We've lost others in boating accidents, naturally, but none so young as him."

"What does any of that have to do with this?" Kathleen gestured toward the book.

"The ship's survivors were all Irish, fleeing poverty and landowners who worked them to death. Most of them settled here, the ones who were willing to live by First Ones' laws."

"What laws?"

"No one on Little Sister Island owns any land. It's written into the island's charter. The houses are leased, and passed down along family lines." She pointed to the book. "If you don't come from a lineage that can trace itself back, you can't live here."

Kathleen stared at her for a moment and then gave a little laugh, but Rebecca wasn't smiling.

"You're serious."

"That's why this island has stayed our home. Over at Big Sister, the First Ones' and early islanders' descendants have had to move away while strangers came and bought up the land to build bigger and bigger houses, pushing the islanders out. Most of the islanders couldn't afford to live there any longer. That hasn't happened here and never will. That's my job as Keeper of the Records. And why you must go through the Passing if you intend to live here."

Kathleen's mouth opened and closed a couple of times as she considered whether this was worth the trouble. *Where else are you going to go?* she asked herself.

Rebecca seemed to sense the internal debate. She waited patiently.

"Okay," said Kathleen at last. "What do I have to do?"

"We need to update your family line." Rebecca pulled the book closer. "Your father, Michael, married Christine Turnbull. Bryan died at age fifteen?"

Kathleen nodded. No one in her family discussed Bryan. Ever. It felt weird to be discussing his death so casually. Rebecca must have felt her discomfort.

"I'm sorry. I know this must be hard. Are there any other siblings? Anyone after you?"

Kathleen shook her head.

"And your father's sister, Moira? Where is she?"

"My aunt is in California somewhere."

Rebecca sniffed. "Got as far away as she could. Is she married? Any children?"

"I don't know. We haven't heard from her in years."

Rebecca gave a small "hmphh" noise and made tiny notations at the bottom of the page. She closed that book and flipped the other one open, leafing through pages until she came to the one she sought. Kathleen leaned closer to see line after line of signatures dating back to 1812.

"This is the list of lessees of the Halloran cottage," Rebecca said. "Your ancestors."

"The cottage is that old?"

"More or less. The island council grants permission for remodeling and rebuilding. Houses have burned down over the years or been damaged by storms. And indoor plumbing was a nice thing when it came along. Every now and then a family line dies off or moves away, and then that house is let to someone from another family."

Kathleen squinted at the page. "What are these dark blotches?"

"Blood." Rebecca's brow furrowed at the look on Kathleen's face. "It's just a drop. This is a blood pact. Signed by your blood before you."

She held out a pen and a knife. "Your signature and a drop of blood, please."

When Kathleen didn't take them, Rebecca's expression went carefully blank. "Of course, if you only want to spend some time visiting with us and then leave, that's up to you."

Kathleen let out a shaky breath and picked up the knife. Biting her lip, she gingerly dragged the blade across the pad of her finger three times without drawing blood before Rebecca huffed and took the knife from her.

"Here." Grabbing Kathleen's hand, she jabbed the point of the blade into her finger.

Kathleen yelped and yanked her hand away. "How clean is that knife?"

"Guess we'll know if your finger falls off. Now squeeze," Rebecca said unsympathetically.

Kathleen squeezed her finger until a drop of bright red blood welled up. She pressed her bloody finger to the page.

Rebecca handed her the pen. "Your signature."

Kathleen sucked on her finger and signed.

"That will be one dollar."

Kathleen laughed again. "One dollar?"

"Your yearly lease payment."

"And how long is this lease?"

"Ninety-nine years, if you live that long." Rebecca stared with those fascinating eyes. "Welcome back to Little Sister."

Chapter 2

K ATHLEEN DROVE SLOWLY. She had nearly gone back into the hotel diner to ask Wilma for directions, but changed her mind.

"It's an island; how big can it be?" she said as she got behind the wheel of her Altima. Everything looked familiar and different at the same time. She'd never realized how little attention she'd paid as a child when her father drove them off the ferry to Nanna's.

She followed a hard-pack road out of town, climbing so that the glimpses she got of the ocean gave her an incredible view. She passed other houses—neat, painted in cheerful yellows and blues and grays or else clad in weathered shingles. She drove past a stand of trees and caught a glimpse of blue. Slamming on the brakes, she backed up to a winding drive and took it.

Unexpected tears filled her eyes as her grandmother's cottage came into view. She sat with her hand pressed to her mouth as memories came flooding back. This had been her refuge—a place of summer magic for the first ten years of her life. Carefree days wandering the trails down to the rocky beach with its narrow strip of sand, nights spent reading or lying curled up with Nanna as she and Bryan watched the stars with her. And then...

An engine rumbled behind her. In her rearview mirror, she saw a battered SUV pull up. She blotted her eyes on her sleeve and got out of her car as the SUV's driver also climbed out. Kathleen got a quick impression of a slender figure wearing a baseball cap with faded jeans and T-shirt as the stranger walked to the back of the SUV and opened the tailgate.

"Wilma said you needed to get your furnace cranked up."

"Um, yes." Kathleen realized the driver's door had a faded star painted on it. "Wilma said she was sending someone named Mo, not the sheriff."

"She did."

"She did what?"

"Both." The driver stepped back around the vehicle, carrying a toolbox in one hand and a long pole in the other.

Kathleen found herself staring into blue-green eyes very much like Rebecca's.

"I'm Molly Cooper. Part-time sheriff, part-time everything else."

"The island has a sheriff?"

"Part-time. Usually only need one when a tourist gets drunk and does something stupid. The rest of us know how to behave. Hard to live on a rock in the ocean with people who don't follow the rules."

Molly's gaze swept down to Kathleen's feet and back up again. "And you're Katie. Maisie's granddaughter."

"Kathleen. Halloran."

"Mmm." Molly tilted her head, peering hard from under the bill of her cap. "I think I remember you. You used to have redder hair when you were little. Always chasing around after your brother and mine."

Kathleen flushed, tucking her hair behind her ear. "You have a good memory."

18

Molly turned to the house. "Let's see about this furnace. Probably hasn't been fired up since the cold weather in the spring used up the last of Maisie's—"

She stopped so abruptly that Kathleen nearly walked into her. "I'm sorry about Maisie, by the way. She was one of the kindest people I've ever known. We all miss her."

Kathleen felt the prick of tears again. "Thank you."

Molly opened her mouth to say something further, but seemed to think better of it and made for the side of the house. Kathleen followed her to where a large metal tank sat.

"Kept telling Maisie she should add solar as a backup," Molly said as she set the toolbox down and unscrewed the cap on the tank. She stuck the pole in until it clunked hollowly against the bottom, echoing a little. She sighed. "That's what I was afraid of. Empty."

She pulled the pole back out.

"Our supply tank is empty. Everyone filled up over the past month. The tanker won't be back out here for a week." She looked Kathleen up and down again. "You sure you can get by a week with no heat? Nights are getting cold."

Kathleen drew herself up. "I'm not helpless. I'll get by. I remember a fireplace." She pointed to a large stack of firewood wedged between two trees and covered with a tarp. "I'm sure I can light a fire."

"Okay." Molly picked up her toolbox. "I'll give them a call to make sure they're coming and then I'll bring some oil to get the furnace started for you. She'll belch like a chain-smoker at first, but at least you'll have heat then."

Kathleen went to the porch while Molly put her gear into the back of the SUV. She turned the knob on the front door, but it was locked.

Behind her, she heard Molly getting into her vehicle and starting it. She'd just declared that she wasn't helpless, but...

"Hey!"

Molly rolled the window down and stuck her head out.

Kathleen jerked her thumb over her shoulder toward the house. "I don't have a key."

Molly stared. For a moment, Kathleen thought she might just drive away, but she turned the ignition off. "Most folks don't bother locking up at all. Probably the last ones to leave the house did it when they came to get Maisie."

She poked around, tipping over flowerpots and looking under stones near the porch. "Got it."

She held up a dirt-encrusted key. She wiped it clean with a rag she pulled out of her back pocket and handed it to Kathleen.

The key jammed partway into the slot in the doorknob.

"Wait here."

Molly jogged back to her SUV and rummaged around in the back, returning a few seconds later with a small bottle. "Graphite." She inserted the bottle's nozzle into the lock and squeezed, releasing a small cloud of fine black dust. "You'll want to have a bottle handy. Nothing metal lasts too long in salt air."

She slid the key in and out a couple of times to work the graphite into the internal mechanism, and then the key turned with a soft click. "There you go."

She twisted the knob and pushed the door open for Kathleen. "See you next week when the tanker gets here. If not before then. It's a small island."

Kathleen bit her lip, peering into the dark interior of the house. Behind her, Molly started the SUV again. Kathleen watched her back out and returned Molly's wave before stepping inside.

MOLLY PULLED UP TO a somewhat rambling house, cobbled together over decades of additions jutting out here and there.

"Miss Louisa, Miss Olivia, anyone home?" she called as she got out of the Toyota.

She lifted the tailgate of the 4-Runner and loaded the pouch of her tool belt with nails. The screen door slapped.

"Molly, how are you this morning?"

She grinned at the prim woman standing on the porch, her housedress wrapped tightly around her bony frame, with big, fuzzy slippers on her feet. Her silver hair was pulled back in the bun she'd worn for as long as Molly could remember. A delicate silver chain looped from the glasses perched halfway down her nose.

"I'm going to take care of those missing shingles today, Miss Lou," Molly said, buckling her belt around her waist.

"Oh, you shouldn't bother—"

"Sure it's no bother," Molly said, reaching back inside the cargo area for a stack of cedar shingles. "The northers'll be blowing soon. You and Miss Olivia will have real problems if we don't get those shingles taken care of."

Louisa turned back to peer through the front door's glass. "But we can't—"

"Don't you worry about paying me." Molly pulled a ladder off the roof rack of her vehicle. "You just make an extra loaf of your orange cranberry bread for me next time you're baking. That'll be payment enough."

She was adjusting the extension ladder when the front door opened and the screen door slapped again.

"You're up early, Molly Cooper," said Olivia, also in fuzzy slippers and a red-and-black-checked flannel bathrobe, but with her silver hair in a short bowl cut. A leather eyeglass keeper was looped around her neck, with her glasses bumping against her heavy bosom.

"Not so early." Molly said from up on the ladder where she was sliding a new shingle into place. "Already been up to Maisie's place."

"Why?" both sisters asked in unison.

"Her granddaughter's come. Claims she's going to live there."

"Really?" Olivia rounded on her sister. "Lou, we must go and pay her a visit."

21

"I wouldn't bother," Molly said, though her voice was muffled by the nails she held between her lips. "She won't last."

"What makes you say that?" Louisa asked.

Molly shrugged as she tapped the nails into place, being careful not to split the shingle. Louisa and Olivia waited until the nails were out of her mouth. "Just a feeling. She's not an islander. Bet you at the first big blow, she'll pack up and wait for the ferry to take her back wherever she came from."

"But she's one of ours," Olivia said. "She used to come and spend summers here."

"Ages ago," said Molly, now prying out another broken shingle. "Where's she been? Where've any of them been? Never came to see Maisie, did they?"

"Well, after the boy died..." said Olivia.

"Molly has a point, Ollie," said Louisa. "Maisie was alone. They should have come. None of them did."

"Maisie had us," Olivia said stoutly, snugging the flannel collar of her robe under her chin. "Let's get baking, sister. Then we'll take Daddy to see the girl. It's a nice day. He'd enjoy the ride."

The sisters had just started inside when Louisa stopped. "What was her name, Ollie?"

Olivia frowned. "Kathy? No, that's not right."

Molly pulled a nail out of her mouth. "Kathleen."

"Oh, that's right. Remember, Ollie? Little Katie."

"No," said Molly. "Kathleen. Made that very clear."

"Oh, phtt," Olivia said with a flap of her hands. "Maisie always called her Katie to us."

Molly opened her mouth to argue, but the screen door slapped shut, cutting her off. She shook her head and reached for another shingle. "Good luck with that."

THOUGH THE SUN HAD warmed the air outside, the house had a definite chill. Sheltered as it was by the trees, even though they were starting to lose their leaves, it was cold and still and musty inside.

It looked exactly as Kathleen remembered. There in the living room was Nanna's rocking chair, by the fireplace. A big, overstuffed chair sat near one window with an equally overstuffed ottoman. Both sagged in the middle now. It had been Kathleen's favorite reading chair. On the fireplace mantel was an old clock, still and silent now. Inside the little door on the back, she recalled, was the key for winding it.

She went from room to room, opening the windows to let in fresh air. Most of them stuck, and it took a little wiggling and a lot of pounding with the heel of her hand to get them to lift.

A thick layer of dust coated everything. She found a closet off the kitchen with buckets and rags and mops and brooms. She pulled the string attached to the light bulb. Nothing. It hadn't occurred to her that she might not even have electricity. She stood on tiptoe and twisted the bulb a little further into the socket. This time when she pulled the string, the bulb lit. She heaved a sigh of relief and turned to the ancient turquoise refrigerator. Holding her breath, she opened it to find it cold. The small freezer above held two aluminum ice trays that were frozen solid.

The kitchen faucet, when she turned the handle, coughed and sputtered. Below her, she heard the hum of a pump. A moment later, an asthmatic stream of water gurgled through the pipes. Rusty at first, the water soon ran clear.

She filled a bucket with soapy water and set about wiping down all the counters and woodwork. She quickly warmed up and stripped off her vest. With her T-shirt sleeves pushed up to her elbows, she scrubbed and rinsed, working her way through the kitchen.

She muttered as she worked, carrying on a one-sided conversation in which she told Molly Cooper off.

"Like I can't light a damned fire in the fireplace. Or can't live without heat for a few days." She slammed the toaster down after wiping the counter. "I'm sick and tired of people telling me what I can and can't do."

It bugged her that Molly remembered her when she couldn't remember Molly. But then, she'd tried hard not to remember. Here, in this place, the memories pushed their way in... Wind and pelting rain, standing in the wet with Nanna's arm around her while the men, nearly every man on the island, put out in boats in the storm as the women gathered round, willing them all to return...

Her eyes flew open at the sound of car tires crunching on the drive. Two car doors creaked open. Kathleen paused her cleaning and went to the front door.

"Hello, dear!" said one of two old women who were getting out of a rusty Ford sedan.

The smaller one carried something wrapped in a red and white gingham towel while the taller one who had driven reached into the back seat for a basket.

"We heard you were here and had to come by to welcome you," said the woman carrying the basket. "I'm Olivia Woodhouse and this is my sister Louisa."

"Maisie was our dear friend," said Louisa, reaching the porch steps.

Kathleen stepped down to take her elbow. "I remember you. Weren't you the island schoolteacher?"

Louisa beamed. "Yes, I was! Oh, how I loved teaching. It's sweet of you to remember, Katie."

"Kathleen."

Olivia followed up the steps. "We brought you a few things, Katie. Figured you hadn't gotten to the market yet."

Kathleen opened her mouth to correct the nickname again but gave up. "Oh, thank you."

She was about to invite them in, but Louisa opened the door and charged inside. Olivia did the same, leaving Kathleen to follow.

In the kitchen, Louisa was unwrapping the gingham towel from around a fragrant loaf of bread, while Olivia opened the flap of her basket and pulled out butter, coffee, milk, eggs, and bacon.

"Glass bottles of milk?" Kathleen asked, picking one up.

"Oh, yes." Olivia nodded. "You have a compost bin out back for egg shells, food scraps, coffee grounds, anything that can be composted."

"We all make a pledge to keep garbage to a minimum," Louisa said, her hands clasped as if she were lecturing a class. "The market has big bins for everything that can be recycled, and one for what absolutely has to be thrown away. The ferry takes them and brings us empties." She pointed at the milk. "Wash the empty bottles when you're done and take them down the market. They get sent back to the dairy to sterilize and re-use."

"Can't poison our own island with garbage if we want to live here," Olivia said.

Without asking, the sisters began putting everything away in the refrigerator that hummed along as if happy to have a purpose again.

"Don't put the eggs there, Lou," said Olivia. "That's where the butter goes."

"No, it isn't. The butter goes here."

Kathleen stood by as they bickered about what went where.

Olivia spied Kathleen's cell phone sitting on the counter. "Those won't work here, either, Katie."

"What do you mean?"

"We never had one of those big antennas installed on the island."

"Ugly old things," Louisa said with a shake of her head. "Ollie's right, dear. You need to call in down John's Market and they'll get your phone hooked back up."

She pointed to the old black wall phone whose partially coiled cord was so stretched out it dragged on the floor.

She turned in place. "We can help with this."

"Oh, you don't have to—"

"I'll get the vacuum," Olivia said, disappearing into the pantry that doubled as a kind of mudroom and led to a back porch. "Lou, did you bring Daddy in?"

"Oh, for heaven's sakes! Katie," Louisa said to Kathleen, "would you mind going out to the car and getting Daddy. He loves to go for a ride, but we don't like to leave him there."

"Of course," Kathleen said, hurrying outside, picturing a frail old man expiring in her drive. She became more frightened when she didn't see any heads visible in either the front seat or the rear.

"Jeez, don't let him be dead," she whispered as she peered into the empty front seat and then opened a back door.

There, seat-belted securely, was a wooden box. She leaned in and read, *Walter Woodhouse*, carved into the box's top. She nearly laughed out loud but clapped a hand over her mouth, certain Louisa and Olivia would disapprove.

She reached in to unbuckle the seat belt. She'd never held anyone's ashes before. Carrying the box well out in front of her as if it were a bomb that might explode, she brought it back into the house.

"Oh, thank you, dear. Just set him down here in the sun," said Louisa, who was now dusting the lampshades. "He always loved the sun on his face."

Kathleen set the box on a table in the sunlight as requested but, before she could say anything else, the vacuum roared to life as Olivia began cleaning the sofa and pillows. With a shrug, she went back to her bucket of water and started wiping down more of the woodwork around the windows.

⁂

JENNY COOPER LOOKED UP from where she was chopping potatoes for soup as Molly clomped up the back steps to the kitchen door. She toed off her boots on the rug inside the door, leaving them to join all the others piled up there.

"Hey, Mom."

"I heard we got a new islander today."

Molly's mouth twitched. News spread on Little Sister faster than gulls finding chum in the water. And they were usually just as noisy as they gossiped over whatever the news was. A loaf of orange cranberry bread sitting on the counter told her everything she needed to know.

"So?" Jenny prompted when Molly didn't say anything.

"So, Maisie's granddaughter thinks she's going to live in Maisie's house."

Jenny scraped the potato chunks from the cutting board into the pot. "Why wouldn't she? Rebecca did her Passing this morning."

Molly went to the sink to scrub the grease and dirt of the day off her hands. An orange tabby jumped onto the counter and came over to bat her paw at the stream of water. "She hasn't been here since she was a kid. Even then, she was a summerer. Never really lived here, did she?" She shook her head. "She won't last. Had to order oil for her. Bet she won't be here long enough to use it."

"You never know. That old place probably needs a lot of work." Jenny slid her daughter a sidelong glance.

"That's enough, Minnow." Molly turned the tap off, and the cat glared at her. She felt her mother watching her. "I've got better things to do."

"A house falling down does none of us any good."

Molly grabbed a towel. "I'll do what I can."

"I know you will." Jenny smiled and held out a peeled carrot. "What does she do for a living?"

Molly accepted the carrot and munched on it. "No idea. She hadn't even unpacked her car when I was there."

"What?" Jenny turned, another carrot in one hand and a knife in the other. "You didn't offer to help her?"

"What for? I told you, she won't be here long enough to unpack."

"Molly Ahearn Cooper." Jenny's lips tightened into a thin line Molly knew only too well. "She probably has a million things to see to.

27

You will take a pot of this soup to her when it's ready. Poor girl will at least need a hot meal if there's no furnace."

Molly opened her mouth to argue, but thought better of it. "Right."

She peered out at the sun setting low in the sky. "Is Dad down the marina?"

"He had to take a boat to Big Sister today. Aidan was going to meet him over there and bring him home. They've been gone all day. No idea when they'll be in."

Molly leaned against the kitchen counter. "Then Aidan doesn't know."

Jenny's lips pursed again. It was a moment before she said, "No. He doesn't."

Molly threw what was left of her carrot into the sink. "Why the hell did she have to come here?"

"She has as much right to be here as any of us," Jenny said quietly.

"Her being here is only going to dredge up the past."

Jenny chopped the remainder of Molly's carrot. "The past has a way of doing that all on its own. It's not her fault."

<hr>

KATHLEEN SAT HUDDLED NEAR the hearth as dusk gave way to full night. Despite her indignant insistence that she could light a fire, it had taken a lot of old newspapers and several matches before the wood actually began to burn.

The musty smell was gone from the house. In the dancing light of the fire, the floorboards gleamed, thanks to a good mopping and waxing by Olivia.

The two sisters had spent nearly the entire day helping her get the house clean. Upstairs, the linens on the bed were freshly laundered, though she hadn't been sure the washer would last through an entire wash cycle as it banged and groaned. The bathroom was scrubbed, and the kitchen fairly sparkled.

"I can't thank you enough," she'd said as Louisa took a break to fry them all some eggs and bacon, followed by thick slices of their delicious orange cranberry bread.

"It's our pleasure," Olivia said, shifting the box of their father's ashes to a new window as the sun moved around the house. "Maisie would have done the same for us."

They regaled her with tales of their days growing up on the island, the three of them getting into all kinds of shenanigans as girls.

Their stories had brought her grandmother to her in a way she'd nearly forgotten. Even the way they spoke, with a slight Irish lilt, reminded her of Nanna. She reached out to trace a finger over the faded embroidered upholstery on Nanna's rocker, remembering her laugh, the way she always smelled of spring flowers.

She hugged her knees to her chest, listening to the little noises of the house. She was alone, but it was funny... she had felt more alone growing up at home—her father away as often as he could arrange it on business trips; her mother, whether drunk or sober, shut away in her room. After she'd met Susannah, she'd clung to her, like a life preserver, afraid of what being alone might mean, but she'd begun to drown in that relationship the last few years as things got uglier and she realized nothing was going to change.

Kathleen shut her eyes, willing those memories to stop, pushing them away.

Headlights suddenly shone through the windows as tires crunched in the drive yet again. Kathleen got up and went to the front window. Pulling the curtain aside, she peered out to see a familiar SUV.

She flipped on the light and opened the door as Molly stepped up onto the porch.

"Hello," Kathleen said.

Molly looked different without her ball cap, her dark hair brushed back off her forehead to hang just shy of her shirt collar. She held up a stainless steel pot with a lid clamped on top. "My mother sent you some soup. She wasn't sure you had anything hot to eat in the house."

"Thank you."

Kathleen stepped back to let her by. Molly strode past her to the kitchen, apparently familiar with the layout of the house. She set the pot on the stove.

"You'll want to warm that up." Crooking a thumb at what remained of the loaf of bread, she said, "I see Miss Olivia and Miss Louisa have been here."

"Yes. They helped me clean the house. They're really sweet."

"They are." Molly glared at her as if she'd insulted them.

Kathleen looked down at herself. "Is... is there something wrong?"

"No." Molly walked by and straight out to her vehicle. "Oil will be here next Monday," she said over her shoulder.

The engine roared as she turned the key.

"Thank your mother for me," Kathleen called. She wasn't certain Molly had heard.

As the SUV backed up, the headlights swept through the darkness. A pair of eyes glowed out of the bushes near the house.

Kathleen nearly hollered for Molly again, but something made her stop. She reminded herself that she wasn't helpless as Molly's vehicle disappeared down the road.

Everything was quiet. She stood still, listening. A faint whine came from the direction of the bushes. She had no idea what wildlife lived on the island. Foxes? Possums? Skunks?

She went into the house to hunt for a flashlight, but by the time she got outside and aimed it into the bushes, the glowing eyes were gone.

"Great." She swept the flashlight's beam back and forth. "Watch me have a skunk living under the house."

She shivered in the cold night air. Once inside, she locked the door and went to sample the soup.

KATHLEEN WOKE EARLY, NEARLY every blanket she could find in the house piled on the bed so that she was weighed down as she curled up with the covers drawn over her head. Her breath helped warm her a little, but her feet were freezing, despite her socks. Outside, she heard gulls mewing.

At last she gave up and braced herself as she crawled out from under the covers. She swore she saw a frosty puff of breath.

"If it's this cold just barely into October, what will December and January be like," she said to the room, her teeth chattering as she dashed down the hall into the bathroom where an old-fashioned claw-foot tub stood with a shower curtain suspended by a ring.

The black and white basketweave tiles on the floor shone from the scrubbing they'd received the day before.

She turned on the tap in the shower, deciding not to take off her pj's and socks until there was hot water to jump into. She sighed as the steamy spray chased away the chill. She washed her hair and soaped up, staying under the shower until the water was no longer hot.

Her teeth chattered again as she stepped out of the tub into the cold bathroom. She toweled off as quickly as she could and got dressed before drying her hair.

Back in the bedroom, she hurriedly made the bed, smiling as she touched a finger to the chipped white cast iron bedframe—the same bed she'd slept in as a girl. Everything was the same. Nanna hadn't changed a thing. Even the quilted comforter was the same—shells and starfish.

Down the hall was Bryan's room, overlooking the front porch. That summer, he'd figured out how to climb out the window and shimmy down an overhanging tree to sneak out with the island boys. He'd made Kathleen promise not to tell, but maybe if she had...

Last night, she'd gone into Nanna's room. On the bedside table were framed photos—her father and aunt when he was about sixteen and she maybe fourteen, another of her parents proudly holding baby Bryan, and one taken that last summer of her and Bryan sitting with Nanna on the front porch of this cottage. She couldn't recall who would have taken it. Bryan at fifteen was already handsome, tan and lean, with a carefree grin. She looked almost the same as now, except Molly was right, her hair had been redder. But the blue eyes behind her glasses and the freckles were the same. Nanna was beaming, an arm around each of them.

It was a larger bed and room, but Kathleen couldn't bring herself to sleep there. Not yet.

Downstairs, she realized with something of a shock that there was no coffee maker, only Nanna's old percolator.

She groaned and then remembered the hotel diner. The clock showed just shy of six a.m. She shrugged into her jacket and grabbed her keys.

Outside, a heavy blanket of fog covered the island, forcing her to drive slowly. Her car was just barely warming up by the time she had driven the few miles down into town and parked. Inside the diner, the same people she'd seen yesterday nodded in her direction. Apparently, breakfast at the diner was part of the daily routine for them.

"Good morning," sang Wilma, automatically bringing a cup of coffee to her table. "All settled in?"

"Getting there," Kathleen said. "No coffee maker."

Wilma chortled. "Miranda and Tim can take care of that. You can do pretty much all your marketing there."

Kathleen tilted her head. "I thought it was John's Market."

"That was her great-grandfather. Miranda has the store now. Corned beef hash and eggs?"

"Yes, please." Kathleen closed her eyes and sipped her coffee, letting the hot liquid warm her from the inside. She figured she'd have to find a way to kill a couple of hours before she could do her shopping.

When Wilma brought her breakfast, Kathleen asked, "What time does the market open?"

"Land sakes, they're already open." Wilma refilled her coffee. "Most everybody on the island gets an early start to the day. Early to bed and early to rise. That's us."

"This is so good," Kathleen said, pointing at her breakfast with her fork.

Wilma beamed. "That's because the eggs are all fresh from the island. Mostly Miranda and Tim's chickens."

Kathleen ate quickly and paid for her breakfast. She moved the car to the market's lot and went inside.

This, too, was familiar. It was like stepping back in time twenty-some years. She remembered the candy counter, a tall, old-fashioned thing made of oak, with a glass front. She supposed that's where she'd spent all her time, because the rest of the market was crammed with things she'd never really noticed: tools, building supplies, groceries, household items. Just about everything anyone could need was somewhere in here.

"Good morning," whispered the woman behind the counter. She pointed to a baby asleep in a bassinet on the floor.

"Hi," Kathleen whispered back.

The woman wasn't much taller than the candy counter. Her blonde hair caught the light as she came around to shake Kathleen's hand.

"You must be Maisie's granddaughter."

"Kathleen." She nodded. "The house is kind of empty. Need to get a few things."

"I'll bet you do. I'm Miranda Shannahan. My husband, Tim, is around here somewhere." Miranda reached for a small cart, pushing it toward Kathleen. "I'll let you look around. Just holler if you need any help." She glanced at the sleeping baby. "Well, whisper if you need help."

It took no time at all to fill the little cart with a coffee maker and electric blanket. Kathleen got a second cart for groceries.

"I don't mean to pry," Miranda said, passing her with a case of toilet paper to restock, "but there may be a few tools you'll need, too. A hammer, some nails and screws, grease and household oil. Maisie probably had all of those things. Check her closets and cupboards. Anything you can't find, we'll have. Oh, I set you up with a post box and I connected your phone to the switchboard. Hope that was okay."

By the time Kathleen got everything loaded in the car, the sun was scrubbing the fog away. She drove back to the cottage and put everything where it belonged. Once the bed was remade with the electric blanket, she folded the extra quilts and blankets and shoved them back into the linen closet.

With the house clean and the initial shopping done, she looked around. Her computer and monitors sat idly on the dining table. She had backed up and downloaded enough work to keep her busy for a while until she could figure out an Internet solution, but the sun glinting off the trees called to her.

She went outside, locking the door behind her, and out to the road, deciding to walk rather than drive. The road wound, with driveways and some smaller trails forking off into the trees every so often. She took one trail that climbed in elevation to a bluff that gave her a wonderful view of the ocean. The trail looped around and began to descend back toward the road. She passed other houses. The few people she saw all waved and wished her a good morning. She figured they all knew who the stranger on the island was by now.

The last of the fog burned away under the autumn sun as she came to the island's cemetery. Situated in a sheltered copse of oaks and pines, the weathered granite grave markers stood among the cemetery's trees.

She hesitated a moment and then wandered in. Acorns crunched underfoot, and squirrels raced about, gathering as many as they could. She perused the names and dates on the tombstones, searching for Nanna. Expecting to find a grave that looked newer than the others around it, she was surprised to find it covered over with green grass and planted with a few small geraniums and a tiny rose bush with fragrant pink blossoms, still blooming in the reflected warmth from the granite. She had to remind herself it had been nearly a year.

Next-door was Kathleen's grandfather's grave. She had no memory of him at all. He'd died of a heart attack when she was a baby.

She knelt down and picked up a few scattered sticks that had blown across Nanna's grave.

"I'm so sorry I never came back to see you," she whispered. "I should have."

There were so many things she should have done. She should have stood up to her father. She should have come to see her grandmother while she was alive. She should have left Susannah long ago.

The wind murmured through the pine trees. It sounded like a voice, saying things she didn't want to hear.

Coward. You were never brave enough to stand up to any of them. You didn't tell Mom or Dad where you are. When you left Susannah, you snuck away without facing her. Coward.

Even as those thoughts ran through her head, she wondered how long it would be before her parents realized she was no longer in Philly.

She pushed to her feet. It was suddenly too crowded here in this lonely spot on a little island in the middle of the ocean.

Chapter 3

THE SUN WASN'T YET up as Molly swapped her ladder for her rowing scull. She secured it to her roof rack and slid the oars in through the tailgate. She drove carefully along the rocky track that took her down to the island's east side and parked.

A few minutes later, the scull was in the ocean and she was pulling with long, steady strokes. Her breathing settled into a rhythm that matched her rowing, and she quickly warmed up. Behind her, the sun peeked over the edge of the horizon so that she was watching her elongated shadow rippling over her wake. The chill of night gave way to the sun's warmth on her back. The swells were gentle, the air still. Overhead, gulls circled, hoping to steal a fish from the terns who were arrowing into the water. She rowed out for thirty minutes, and then turned the scull to head back. She was about halfway when she suddenly found herself surrounded by a pod of dolphins.

Grinning, she pulled her oars up and watched them watching her. They lolled sideways in the water, smiling back at her. A few flipped some water in her direction. She reached down and slapped some water at them. That seemed to be the signal for tail splashes and leaps that soaked her. As quickly as they had come, the dolphins disappeared.

Her scull had drifted sideways to the island. The sun was fully up now, glinting off the rocky outcroppings of the bluff. The island's little harbor was luckily situated on its northern exposure. The Head, on the western end, was mostly granite, scrubbed down to bare rock by the constant wind and relentless storms. But it sheltered the interior of the island from the worst of the weather. Here, on the east side, was the island's only beach, a narrow ribbon of sand that filled the gap between the rocky sea wall and the water.

She squinted at the sole person walking along that skinny stretch of beach. She couldn't have said why, but she was certain it was Kathleen. She looked like a sandpiper, Molly decided, her arms wrapped tightly around her against the morning's chill, her head down and her legs churning along as if she had to be someplace in a hurry.

Aidan had reacted as Molly had feared he would to the news that she was here on the island. He'd been drunk nearly every night since. She had received a phone call every one of those nights from some person or other seeing her brother staggering toward his truck, and she'd gone out to pick him up before he could do something stupid.

You mean something stupider than what he's already done, Molly thought.

Bobbing in the water, she watched the source of her brother's pain. The fact that it wasn't Kathleen's fault only made her angrier. She was tired of being loyal, tired of picking up the drunken pieces of her brother's life.

Her other brothers told her to leave him be. "He'll work things out on his own," they'd said when she went to them. Joey and Matty helped her when he was falling down drunk and she couldn't lift him herself, but mostly, they left him alone to deal with his demons. She wasn't stupid enough to think her parents didn't know Aidan was drinking again, but nobody talked about it. And now, here was Kathleen Halloran, walking around like some fragile, wounded bird—

That thought startled Molly like a slap across the face. She watched Kathleen disappear from view, wondering where in the world that image had come from. Scowling, she hauled her scull around with one oar and rowed back out to sea.

⬚⬚⬚⬚⬚⬚⬚⬚⬚⬚

KATHLEEN PACED WITH A cup of coffee. Between Molly Cooper banging on the furnace down in the cellar and the satellite guy stomping around on the roof, it sounded as if the cottage was going to fall down around her. Next to the satellite guy's van, the oil truck—not much more than a modified pickup truck—was parked in the drive. With the tank filled, Molly had given her a curt nod and carried her toolbox to the wooden door leading to the cellar, disappearing down below.

From out the living room window, Kathleen saw the satellite installer climbing down his ladder. He knocked and came inside.

"Where's the TV?"

"Don't have one." Kathleen pointed at the two computer monitors set up on the dining room table. "Just need Internet."

He nodded and got to work connecting cables and routers and modems. "Lucky you called when you did. This is a hard island to get to."

"Hey!" came Molly's voice from below. "Turn up the thermostat."

Kathleen looked around and found the thermostat on the wall. She turned the dial and heard a muffled roar from the cellar.

A few minutes later, the satellite guy said, "Try that."

She powered up her computer, and he stayed until she had set up her password and accessed various accounts.

39

Caren J. Werlinger

"You're good to go now," he said, reaching for his tool bucket.

By the time he had packed up and left, Molly was letting the cellar door slam shut.

She, too, knocked, but waited for Kathleen to answer the door before entering.

"The furnace is clean and running fine," she said. She went to the thermostat and turned it down. "Radiators will be warm soon. This should get you through Christmas."

"Only through Christmas?"

Molly shrugged. "Depends how warm you keep it. It's but early October. We've plenty of cold weather coming. My advice is to keep this as low as you can stand it, especially during the day. Might want to keep an electric blanket on the bed."

"I already bought one."

"Makes the nights more comfortable." Molly pointed upward. "You might also want to check on the insulation in this cottage. I doubt Maisie ever upgraded it."

"Thank you." Kathleen lifted her cup. "Would you like some coffee?"

Molly eyed her for a moment. "Sure."

She followed Kathleen into the kitchen, pausing in the dining room to stare at the computer setup.

"Are you doing surveillance? Spying on Canada?"

Kathleen gave a half-laugh as she poured another cup of coffee. "Nothing that nefarious. I'm a book editor. Come to think of it, my authors might call that nefarious. I also do some cover design and formatting. The wonder of the Internet. You can work from anywhere."

"As long as it doesn't storm." Molly pointed skyward again. "We always lose satellite reception when it storms."

"Milk? Sugar?"

Molly shook her head. "Black is fine." She accepted the cup and joined Kathleen at the little table in the kitchen. "So why are you doing your work from here?"

40

Kathleen took a sip before saying, "Why not from here?"

Molly set her cup down and leaned forward, her elbows braced on the table. "You haven't been here for decades. Neither of Maisie's kids ever came back here after—"

Kathleen bit her lip, staring at her coffee.

"She said Michael blamed her," Molly said, an accusing edge to her voice.

"He did," Kathleen said quietly. "That's why I was never allowed to come back here again."

"Bad things happen," Molly said, a little more gently. "It wasn't your grandmother's fault."

"I tried to tell my father that, but he wouldn't listen."

"Okay." Molly sat back. "That accounts for maybe ten years. Where've you been the other fourteen?"

Kathleen felt the heat rise from her neck to her cheeks. "Why are you interrogating me?"

"Because the whole island was affected by what happened. Because you didn't even know your grandmother. Because part of her died that day, too, and none of you ever came back to be with her. Because your coming here has dragged things up. Things the folks here haven't had to deal with for ages."

Kathleen bristled at this assault. "And that's my fault? That the islanders haven't dealt with what happened?"

This time it was Molly's turn to blush. "You don't know—"

She set her cup down and stood abruptly. "Thanks for the coffee. I need to get going."

"I still have to pay you," Kathleen said, carrying the cups to the sink.

"Pay my father down the marina."

She heard Molly's footsteps and the front door open and close—almost a slam. She went through the pantry and yanked the back door open. Standing on the covered porch, she rubbed her neck where she could feel the tension building up and took a couple of deep breaths.

41

She just touched a frayed nerve.

She might have been able to blame her parents for not bringing her back to Little Sister to spend childhood summers with Nanna after Bryan died, but she had only herself to blame for all the years since.

A sudden rustling in the bushes near the house startled her. She grabbed a broom propped in the corner and, holding it like a weapon, descended the porch steps. As she neared the bushes, she heard a faint whine and saw the outline of a dog's partially upright ears.

"Are you the one I keep seeing?" she asked in a soft voice. "Are you my skunk?"

The dog whined again and backed away. Kathleen moved slowly around the bushes and saw a skinny brown and black dog, its ears pricked in her direction, the tips flopping. She crouched down and held her hand out, but the dog tucked its tail and refused to come any closer.

"I'll bet you're hungry."

She went inside the house and chipped up some turkey she had in the fridge, but by the time she got back outside, the dog had disappeared. She set the plate down near the bushes.

"It'll be here when you're ready."

She went back inside to catch up on a couple of weeks' worth of emails.

⬚⬚⬚⬚⬚⬚⬚⬚⬚⬚

THE CRIES OF GULLS and the soft lapping of the water against the pylons under the boathouse lulled Molly into a meditative state as she sanded. Antique wooden boats and reproductions had become a status symbol for the rich people on Big Sister and a steady source of income for Joe Cooper. Molly helped when she wasn't busy sheriffing—which was most of the time—or doing handyman jobs around the island. Her brothers were out on the lobster boat and probably wouldn't be back until after dark.

Her dad had left her to work on this antique Runabout while he went over to Big Sister to give an estimate on another. If it was seaworthy, he'd tow it back, and they'd have another project to see them through the winter. The boys would be home after they dropped off the day's catch to the restaurants they supplied. Her mom never knew for sure when they'd be in, so she had learned early on to make vats of soup and stew and things that could be kept warm for hours if need be.

Usually, Molly welcomed these days working alone with time to think, but today, she felt restless.

A gull flew in through the open bay of the boathouse. He fluttered to a landing on the deck and squawked as he tilted his head, eyeing her.

"Hello, Cap'n Jack," Molly said, tossing him a bit of bread she'd saved from her lunch.

He hopped on his one leg to snatch the bread and settled with a rustle of his wings. She guessed some seal had tried to grab him, getting only his leg for its trouble. He was an amiable bird, often keeping her company when she was working here at the marina. She had the feeling he preferred human company to that of other gulls.

She switched to a finer grit sandpaper and resumed her patient sanding.

Islanders, she mused, were a funny lot. They fell into one of two camps: the ones who couldn't wait to get away—"couldn't wait to escape," she supposed they would have said—and the ones, like her, who maybe left for a while, but always felt pulled back and never really wanted to live anywhere else.

Maisie's children had escaped. Kathleen's dad, Michael, had come back long enough to drop Kathleen and Bryan off every summer until Bryan died, but he'd never returned after that. The other one, Kathleen's aunt, had never returned at all after she left. Maisie had been stoic about it, always cheerful when Molly had seen her, but she

heard Miss Lou and Miss Ollie talking about how much it hurt her that they never called or came to visit.

Molly paused, running her hands over the curved boards of the boat's hull. Not smooth enough yet.

She wondered how Kathleen was doing up at the cottage and then sat back, irritated that Kathleen Halloran was in her thoughts so often lately. It was annoying. Molly still expected to see her back at the ferry landing, her car packed up, ready to run back to wherever she'd come here from.

"Maybe I need to take a few days," she said to Cap'n Jack, who was the only one listening.

It had been a while, over a year, she realized with some surprise, since she'd gone to the mainland for any kind of holiday. She wasn't looking for an entanglement, just a night or two at a Portland bar, some dancing, maybe something more if she met a desirable woman. Sometimes, she missed being around more women. Other than Siobhan, the only women her age on Little Sister were married with families. Dorm life had definitely had its perks, she reminisced with a smile.

Miss Louisa had hounded her into applying for scholarships, working with her late into the nights to make sure she aced her SATs. When she got accepted at Vassar, the entire island had celebrated, had raised money to help cover what the scholarships didn't. Those four years had been magical—not just for the academic world that had opened before her, but everything else she'd discovered about herself.

Everyone at Vassar had assumed she would be attending graduate school and making a brilliant career in the field of political science or law, but... she'd begun to feel the island calling to her. More and more, she had felt restless and homesick until it became a physical ache.

She clenched her jaw and scrubbed harder with the sandpaper, trying to sand away the memory of the disappointment in Miss Lou's eyes when she'd returned—one of Miss Lou's last students, her last chance to show something for all her years of teaching.

"And here you are, thirteen years later, repairing boats and fixing damned furnaces and picking up your drunk brother while you waste away on this rock."

Cap'n Jack gave a little squawk.

"Shut up."

※※※※※※※※※※

KATHLEEN TOOK HER GLASSES off and rubbed her eyes. The amount of mark-up on this manuscript was making her head hurt. Even a sunrise walk on the beach couldn't make this project palatable. She wasn't sure who had accepted this pile of gobbledygook, but it should have been rejected and sent back for a rewrite. There were plot holes as big as the Grand Canyon; characters changed names halfway through the story; the author had no sense of how not to switch point of view in the middle of a scene.

She shoved her glasses back on. No amount of editing could make this presentable. She wasn't sure she wanted her name associated with it at all.

She pulled up her email and dashed off a message to the acquiring editor who had palmed this garbage off on her, telling him she would be charging triple if they insisted on trying to get this in publishable form.

She absently raised her coffee cup to her lips to find it empty. She got up and stretched, taking the cup back into the kitchen for a refill. The windows were open, allowing a wonderful breeze through the house on what was probably one of the last warmish days of the fall. Other work called to her but...

"I just can't."

She pulled a light jacket off a hook by the door and stepped out onto the back porch. She smiled when she saw the licked-clean plate. The dog had eaten every bit of food she'd put out over the last few days. She'd gradually been moving the plate closer to the house, last night leaving it on the porch.

She sat down on the top step. "Blossom, are you out there?"

It was silly to give the dog a name, but ever since her scare that the unknown critter was a skunk, the name Blossom had stuck. She had seen only enough of the dog to know it was a male. A shadow moved beyond the bushes, and she knew she was being watched.

"Want to go for a walk?"

She kept talking as she headed toward the bluff, taking a path she'd discovered behind the cottage that meandered through the woods. Blossom trailed behind her. The wind made a light rattle as it blew through the dried leaves still dangling from the trees. The smell of salt air mixed with the bite of autumn. Kathleen breathed deeply as she tromped along.

When she got to the head of the bluff, she sat, taking in the vista below. Sitting with her arms wrapped around her knees, she heard the dog behind her. She patted her thigh invitingly, but Blossom stayed just at the edge of the trees, hiding under a bush.

Kathleen turned back to the ocean. She felt… It was such a potent mix of emotions that she didn't really have a name for it. The island felt like home—a feeling she realized only now she'd never had before, at least not since before Bryan's death. But it came tainted with sadness and regret. She bitterly regretted never defying her father—*or Susannah,* said a voice in her head—to come back here while Nanna was alive. She'd slowly come to accept that not wanting to confront her father was part of why she hadn't. Even after she was grown and could easily have come here on her own, she'd known without being told that her father would have been furious. She hadn't been willing to face his rage. He had never stopped punishing his mother for letting Bryan out of her sight, for letting him pal around with the boys on the island, for letting him die.

As for her mother, she'd never forgiven any of them.

Her parents still didn't seem to realize she was here. *Or maybe*, said that voice, *they just don't care*. There'd been no emails. No phone calls, though she wasn't sure how they'd get her number. The only messages she'd received had been emails from Susannah—pleading messages, asking where she was, how she could just disappear with no explanation, why she wasn't answering her phone, what had happened between them, begging her to come home so they could go on from here.

Normally, those messages would have torn at Kathleen's heart. But she wasn't sure she had a heart any longer. She tapped her chest, half expecting it to sound hollow, like the Tin Man.

When she had met Susannah, caught her first glimpse of the laughter in Susannah's beautiful dark eyes on the stairwell of their dorm, she had instantly fallen for her. Susannah seemed to feel the same—at least Kathleen had thought so for a while. Susannah trusted her enough to confide much of what her father had done to her, to all of her family, and it had broken Kathleen's heart to listen to it. But then, Susannah had become afraid—afraid of how close they'd become, afraid of what her father would say if he found out. When she began to push back, saying she was tired of having Kathleen following her and hanging on like a puppy, Kathleen had only clung more tightly. When Susannah ignored her calls and went out with others, Kathleen camped outside her door until she got back, whenever she got back. She knew the other girls in the dorm had snickered, but she didn't care. Susannah always came back. Always. When she told Kathleen to get the hell out of her life, Kathleen had known it was only a test of her love. When she refused to leave, and Suze eventually apologized and said she loved her, it was confirmation that Kathleen's loyalty was what Susannah needed.

Kathleen wasn't sure when it began to change. Fourteen years of clinging to an emotional tornado had worn her down, hollowed her out. Now, Susannah's messages left her cold. It was such a foreign feeling, she wasn't sure what to do with it. She hadn't responded to the messages, but she hadn't deleted them, either.

She froze at the soft sound of a snuffling breath at her back. She hadn't realized that she'd been sitting with her forehead pressed to her knees. She opened her eyes and peered under her arm to see Blossom, lying as flat as he could, his ears back and his neck stretched out to sniff at her.

She didn't reach for him, but saw him watching her, his brown eyes wary and concerned.

"I'm okay. Just some unpleasant memories."

When she lifted her head to look out over the ocean again, he stayed behind her rather than scurrying back to the bushes as she expected. She slowly set a hand on the ground beside her and, a moment later, felt a cold, wet nose probing it.

Blossom belly-crawled a bit closer. He cringed but didn't run when she lightly scratched his neck. She smiled when she allowed her to rest her hand on his back.

"Well, that's progress, isn't it?"

Chapter 4

THE WIND HOWLED, AND the skies looked like something out of a Biblical end-of-days scene. Kathleen was grateful she'd taken the time to enjoy a walk earlier as she put the soup pot in the back seat of her car along with two wrapped plates of oatmeal pecan cookies. She'd found Nanna's old cookbooks and remembered these cookies as a special treat when she was little. To her delight, they hadn't turned out half-bad.

As she drove to town, though, she realized she still didn't know where anyone lived on the island. She smiled to herself as she headed to the diner. She was a passable cook, but nothing she made compared to Wilma's husband, Nels. Funny name for a man descended from Irish or Ind—First Ones blood, she corrected herself.

It was only mid-afternoon, but she'd skipped lunch working on that damned manuscript, so she was starving. Expecting to find the diner to herself, she was surprised to be greeted by cries of, "Hello, Katie!"

Louisa and Olivia were seated at a table, waving to her as if she could possibly miss them.

Giving up on any thoughts of a quiet meal, she threaded her way through the tables to theirs.

"Join us, dear," Louisa said.

Kathleen pulled one of the empty chairs back before she saw the carved box sitting there.

"Don't sit on Daddy," Olivia said.

"Of course not." Kathleen partially slid the chair back under the table and took the fourth seat.

Wilma appeared with a mug of her wonderful coffee, not even bothering to ask. "Gonna be a big one. Good thing you're getting out now. Should be here before nightfall."

"Did you watch the weather radar?" Kathleen asked.

The other three women looked at one another in bewilderment and then all burst out laughing.

"Don't need radar to know that," Wilma said, pulling a menu out of her apron pocket to place in front of Kathleen.

"Still have any of the beef stew?" Kathleen asked, scanning it quickly.

"That's what we're having," Olivia said.

"I'll make it a third," Wilma said, picking the menu up and bustling off to the kitchen.

Kathleen watched her give the order to her husband. His blond head bobbed as he worked.

"What's their last name?" Kathleen asked. "Wilma and Nels."

"Greatneck," said Louisa.

"But that's an island name," Kathleen said, remembering other Greatnecks. "How does someone who looks Scandinavian have that name?"

"Island names carry, dear." Louisa nodded primly as she took a sip of her tea.

"Excuse me?"

"Any offlander who marries into an island family takes that name," said Olivia. "So the island names pass down."

"The First Ones, naturally, didn't have last names," Louisa said, sounding very like a schoolteacher. "After the shipwreck, they took names, like the Irish had—Woodhouse, Greyeagle, Greatneck, Cooper, and others. Of course, the Irish kept their names. When the island charter was established, it was decided the family names would carry, whether it was through the wife or husband. This made sense to the First Ones, who traced their lines matrilineally anyway."

Wilma brought a big tray with their bowls of beef stew at that point. She set down a plate of hot rolls and, without being invited, pulled up a fifth chair to join them. Olivia scooted over to make room.

"I don't understand," Kathleen said.

Wilma must have overheard their conversation. "When Nels and I got married," she volunteered, buttering a roll for herself, "he took my family name. Tim took Miranda's down the market. Others have done the same. Anyway, it's just the way it's done here."

"Really?" Kathleen thought about this as she ate a few bites. "What about the First Ones? What you said about matrilineal."

"Oh, well." Louisa blushed. "When the Irish were rescued, they found themselves among non-Christians." She cleared her throat delicately.

"The First Ones didn't have marriage," Olivia said bluntly.

Wilma jumped in, leaning in to whisper, though there wasn't anyone else in the diner to overhear. "And women weren't property, so they didn't belong to just one man. When a woman got pregnant, they sometimes didn't know who the father was, but of course, they always knew who the mother was. Made sense to trace their lines back through their mothers."

"Wow."

"You really should talk to Rebecca if you want to know more," Louisa said. "She knows the history of every island family going all the way back."

"Speaking of Rebecca," Kathleen said, her curiosity getting the better of her, "she and Molly Cooper have very similar eyes, kind of light against dark complexions."

"Well, that'd be because Rebecca is Molly's aunt," said Wilma. "Like most of us, their family line has First Ones blood in it, more than some of the others. Rebecca is an Ahearn, one of three: Bobby you met on the ferry, her, and Molly's mother, Jenny."

"But you said island names carry," Kathleen said. "So why isn't Molly an Ahearn?"

The women chuckled, and Kathleen felt as if she were a young child being patiently lectured to.

"Because Joe Cooper is an islander, too," said Olivia. She nudged Wilma and grinned. "Jenny caught his eye early on, but she couldn't see it. She didn't want to stay. For the longest time, we thought Jenny would leave us, and she did for a while. But she came home and married Joe."

By the time Kathleen left the diner, with a takeout container of more beef stew and a bag of rolls that Wilma insisted on sending with her, her head was swimming with new information about the island families.

She opened her car door, hoping she had enough time for a quick trip to the market before the storm hit, and saw the cookies.

"Wait," she called to Louisa and Olivia. She jogged to them with one of the covered plates. "I made these for you. They're probably not as good as Nanna used to make, but I wanted to thank you for helping me get the cottage cleaned up."

"You didn't have to do that, dear," Louisa said.

Olivia was leaning through the back door, seat-belting the wooden box in place. She closed the door and reached for the plate.

"We were happy to help." Olivia peeled back the foil and sampled a cookie. "Not bad." She nodded. "Maisie would have approved."

"Can you tell me how to find the Cooper house?"

"SIOBHAN?" MOLLY KNOCKED AND let herself through the door at the back of the gift shop into Siobhan's private living quarters.

Siobhan was on her yoga mat—nude—holding a tree pose with a dozen candles burning around the room.

"Sorry," Molly said, moving into the kitchen to wash her hands. She grinned, glad she hadn't walked in on downward dog.

She scrubbed the oil from her hands as Siobhan came in behind her, tying the belt of a robe.

"I replaced the pump on your boiler," Molly said. "Should purr now."

"Thank you," Siobhan said, leaning against the counter. Her fall of red hair spilled down her back, loosely gathered in a scrunchy tie. Her robe fell open a bit, revealing the soft white curve of her breast. Molly cursed herself when her eyes drifted down.

"You're embarrassed by the memory of our time together," Siobhan said. Her tone was amused, but a hint of hurt lingered in her eyes.

"No," Molly said quickly. "Not embarrassed. Exactly."

Siobhan turned to put the kettle on. "We found each other when we each had need, Molly. I was mourning my mother. You were lonely, that first winter back here with no one like you. There's no shame in that."

Molly frowned as she rubbed a thumb against a callus on her palm. "I know."

Siobhan smiled and came to her. She ran her hand down Molly's waist to her hips. Pressing her whole body against Molly's, she kissed her lightly. "I would still take you to my bed, willingly, but you're not built like that." She moved her hand to press it against Molly's chest. "You have to feel it here first."

Molly lifted one shoulder in a half-shrug.

Siobhan laughed and caressed Molly's cheek. "I have a feeling the one who can do that to you is already here."

Molly puzzled on her words as she drove home. The first fat raindrops began to splatter as Molly pulled into the driveway. She braked abruptly when she saw Kathleen Halloran's Nissan parked there. She slammed the door of the SUV and ran for the back porch where she stopped at the sound of laughter.

Peering through the glass of the back door, she saw her mother talking with Kathleen, who was sitting at the kitchen table, laughing at something, with Minnow curled up on her lap. It was the first time Molly had heard her laugh. It was as if she were watching a completely different person. Molly stood there for a long time, trying to figure Kathleen out. She had come back here, apparently for good, after years and years of being away, not even returning to see her aging grandmother. She didn't seem to know the first thing about living on the island, which Molly found frustrating. She was going to get herself into trouble and need help, and yet, Molly had been driving by the Halloran cottage more often than she needed to, wondering if she should stop in to see if everything was okay.

This laughing Kathleen was so at odds with the image Molly still had of her as wounded somehow. She'd seen her other mornings, walking the beach while Molly was rowing. In fact she'd started looking for her... It really was annoying.

She opened the back door, just barely hanging on as the wind gusted through. She had to lean a bit to close it.

"Storm's almost here," she said by way of greeting.

"Hello." Kathleen stood, forcing the cat to jump down. "I brought your mother's soup pot back."

Jenny pointed at the table. "And she brought some cookies. An old recipe I remember Maisie making. You should try one."

"Later." Molly peeled off her jacket and hung it up. "Dad should be finishing down the marina. Any word from the boys?"

Jenny nodded toward the radio sitting on the counter. "They're putting in now."

"Just in time."

"I should go," Kathleen said.

"Nonsense," Jenny said. She poured another cup of coffee and set it on the table. "Molly, sit down, have a cookie. Dinner's all made. Just waiting on the guys."

Reluctantly, Molly pulled out a chair and sat. An awkward silence filled the space between her and Kathleen. Minnow meowed and jumped into Molly's lap, sniffing at the cookies on the table.

"Things okay at the cottage? Your furnace is working?" Molly asked to fill the void.

"Yes. Thanks so much for that. By the way, I haven't paid your father yet. I went by the marina, but no one was there."

"Dad comes and goes. You'll catch him at some point."

Molly waved a dismissive hand, but Kathleen said, "No. I need to pay him. That's your business. Speaking of which, how do you bank here?"

"What do you mean?" Jenny asked, joining them at the table.

"I have a checking account and a debit card, but I'm almost out of the cash I brought with me. Where's the nearest bank?"

Jenny laughed. "We forget how strange it must seem to an offlander who's not used to island life. Miranda and Tim can handle anything small. They send their deposits and checks with my brother, Bobby, when he comes on the ferry, and he brings cash back to us."

"That seems very trusting," Kathleen said.

Molly and her mom exchanged a puzzled glance.

"Why wouldn't we trust one another?" Jenny asked.

Kathleen didn't reply as she took a gulp of coffee. "So I can start paying with a check at the market?"

Molly nodded. "Yeah. There's a bank on Big Sister, if you need anything done in between ferry runs. Someone can always take you over."

"By boat."

"Yes," Molly said slowly. "That's kind of how we do things on an island."

Kathleen flushed a blotchy pink from her neck up to her cheeks. "Thanks. Good to know."

A heavy stomping of feet on the back porch made all three of them turn as the back door opened again, and her father and the boys entered.

"Get in here," Jenny said, immediately jumping up to start dishing dinner out.

"It's going to blow up big tonight," said Joe. He glanced at the table and did a double take. "You're Maisie's granddaughter."

Kathleen stood to shake his hand. "Kathleen. Nice to see you, Mr. Cooper."

"I'm Joe. This," he said, turning to the others, "is Joey, Matty, and Aidan."

Kathleen shook hands with each of them, but Molly saw the tension in their faces as the others pointedly didn't look at Aidan.

"I remember you," Kathleen said to them. She held to Aidan's hand for just a few extra seconds before he pulled away, wiping his hand on his jeans.

Molly nearly jumped between them, but Aidan cleared his throat and said, "I have to go get cleaned up. I'll eat later, Mom."

"And I really need to get going," Kathleen said. "It was nice to see you all again."

Molly followed Kathleen out into the gathering darkness. She grabbed one of the tattered umbrellas stuck in an old concrete planter on the porch.

"I'll walk you to your car."

She sheltered Kathleen with the umbrella, walking close enough that their arms brushed. It was funny, how she kept thinking of Kathleen as small, but she was only an inch or two shorter than Molly's five-eight. She reached her free arm out and almost wrapped it around Kathleen's shoulders before catching herself and pulling back.

"If you haven't refilled Maisie's oil lamps, you'll want to do that."

Molly held the umbrella a bit higher as Kathleen opened her door. "We almost always lose power in bad storms. It's not usually out for long, but you'll have to get used to it."

"Thanks."

Kathleen paused, standing close under the umbrella, looking into Molly's eyes. "Aidan was the one..."

Molly stepped away so that rain pelted her exposed back. "You should get back before this gets worse."

Kathleen got in and closed the door. She stared through the window at Molly as she turned the ignition. Putting the car in reverse, she backed around and drove off.

Molly stood there, the rain running in a steady stream off the edges of the umbrella as she watched the taillights disappear into the darkness. Upstairs, the light glowed in Aidan's dormer window.

She jogged to the back porch and flapped the umbrella before jamming it into the planter with the others. At least he was home, and she wouldn't have to go out in this mess to pick his sorry ass up after he got drunk.

⬛⬛⬛⬛⬛⬛⬛⬛⬛

AS PROMISED, THE STORM was fierce. The rain slashed in waves with the gusting winds. Kathleen crouched on the back porch, one hand shielding her eyes as she searched the darkness behind the cottage.

"Blossom! Blossom, come." She shook a bowl of the dog food she'd picked up at the market. She had no idea if the dog had ever had actual dog food. When there was no sign of movement, she set the bowl down and went back inside.

She searched the pantry and found Nanna's three oil lamps, filled and ready. Apparently, her grandmother knew what the other islanders knew. She got the lamps out and, just as she was fiddling with the wicks, the power went out. She fumbled with a match but got the

57

lamps lit, turning the metal dial to adjust the height of the wicks on all three. She had already taken the precaution of powering off and unplugging all of her computers and monitors, not willing to trust her work to a surge protector.

She left one lamp burning on the kitchen table and carried the other two out to the living room where she snuggled into the over-stuffed chair, sitting sideways with her legs drawn up and a blanket on her lap as she listened to the wind whistling around the house, drowning out any sounds from the ocean waves she knew must be battering the island's rocky cliffs and little beach.

Drowning.

She gave an involuntary shudder as she stared into the blue-gold flame of one of the lamps. She didn't really remember what Aidan looked like and wouldn't have recognized him, but he clearly knew who she was. It had turned into a night very like this one—the storm blowing up out of nowhere it had seemed; Nanna sending her out to bring Bryan home; the gradual realization when she couldn't find him that he and Aidan had both gone out in their boats to race; darkness falling before Aidan made it back with the searchers, but no Bryan...

Kathleen wiped the wetness from her cheeks.

Molly and her brothers took after their dad, dark-complexioned with black hair, but only Molly had those curious eyes. She wasn't beautiful or even pretty. Not in the usual sense, but she was... striking, Kathleen decided. High cheekbones, strong features. Must be the First Ones blood in their family. If she hadn't been told Rebecca was Jenny's sister, she would have guessed she was Joe's sibling. Jenny looked to have more Irish or mixed blood, with her lighter skin, blue eyes, and honey-brown hair.

Kathleen chewed absently on a fingernail. Molly was a puzzle. Sometimes she was downright hostile, challenging Kathleen's right to be on the island and then other times, she was kind, like tonight, walking her out to her car, sheltering her with the umbrella. For just a moment, Kathleen had had the crazy urge to burrow in against Molly's side, seeking her warmth.

But she'd done exactly that with Susannah—reaching out and clinging tightly. *Too tightly,* she thought now. *I won't be that gullible again.*

A scratching sound from the kitchen roused her from her thoughts. She went in, listening. There it was again. Peering through the glass on the back door, she saw Blossom, wet and bedraggled, nosing at the empty food bowl, scooting it across the porch boards.

When she opened the back door, the dog bolted.

"Blossom," she called quietly. "Come here. Come here, you silly dog."

She got another handful of food and dropped some on the porch floor, leaving a trail as she backed toward the kitchen. She retrieved an old towel from the cupboard above the washer and sat on the floor, waiting. It took a few minutes, but Blossom crept onto the porch, his pink tongue reaching out to pluck up the kibble, his wary eyes on her. He hesitated at the threshold, but she waited, not facing him directly. He belly crawled inside, still following the trail of food until he was close enough to touch. Just as Kathleen reached out to drape the towel over him, he shook, showering her and everything else in water droplets. She flung the towel over him and pushed the door shut with her foot. He crouched, his ears flat against his head, trembling.

It broke her heart to see him so frightened. "I will never hurt you," she murmured.

She kept talking in a low voice, reaching out to rub him with the towel. Slowly, he stopped trembling and began to look around curiously. She got up and went to the sink. He followed, the towel still draped over him like a horse blanket.

"You can explore," she said, setting a bowl of water down on the floor. "Just don't pee anywhere."

He lapped up a bit of water and began to sniff every surface—floor, cupboards, table.

She went back to her chair in the living room. A few minutes later, Blossom was lying next to her, still draped in his towel, with his head resting on her foot and his eyes closed.

Smiling, she said, "Looks as if we're going to be housemates."

WITH A HARSH SCRAPE, Molly's scull slid over the skim of ice coating the wet sand. Her breath puffed from her mouth in steamy clouds, but she was warm. She sat for a moment, taking a drink from a water bottle as she let her breathing slow. The sun was peeking out from behind a heavy cloudbank to the southeast. *Might be the last row of the season,* she thought. She squinted at the sky. Smelled like snow. Probably wouldn't be a big one, but still, made it hard to get in freezing ocean water.

She stood up and dragged the scull farther onto the beach. She was glad the strip of sand was empty. She wasn't in the mood to see Kathleen this morning, not after getting a call at two a.m. from Patrick Flaherty that Aidan had just left the pub and was stumbling toward his truck, having refused all offers of a ride home from Patrick.

She grunted a little as she hoisted the scull onto her roof rack and secured it.

It made her even angrier that she could no longer really muster up any resentment toward Kathleen. Aidan's problem was his. Just because the trigger was named Kathleen didn't make it her fault.

She got into the 4-Runner, tossing her knit hat and gloves onto the passenger seat as she let the engine warm. What was it about Kathleen that made Molly want to hold her and protect her? It was crazy. And what was with the dog she'd seen tagging along with her the last couple of mornings? So now, she was living here and had a dog. Damn.

She put the truck in gear and drove home to store the scull on its rack in the garage she and her brothers had converted into a gym, with a heavy bag, weight bench, Olympic bars, and dumbbell rack. And an indoor rower. She dusted it off, figuring it was now indoor time for the next few months.

She climbed the stairs into the kitchen where she was surprised to see Aidan sitting at the table, cradling his head, still in the same rumpled clothes he'd been wearing when she dumped him onto his bed.

She didn't speak to him, just went to the kitchen sink to rinse the sweat off her face.

"Don't say anything," he grumbled.

She pulled a towel from a kitchen drawer and pressed it to her face. Ignoring him, she poured herself a cup of coffee and stood leaning against the counter, sipping it and letting the warmth trickle down to her stomach.

When she didn't speak, he lifted his head enough to fix her with one bloodshot eye.

"Aren't you going to say anything?" he demanded.

She poured another cup of coffee and plunked it down in front of him as she joined him at the table. He winced at the sound.

"What do you want me to say?"

He scrubbed his hands over his face, his rough palms scratching over the dark stubble on his jaw. "You can tell me what a dumb shit I am."

"You are."

He glared at her. "You can tell me I owe you again for coming to haul my ass home."

"You do."

He lowered his hands. "You could tell me why you keep doing it."

Molly stared into his eyes. What she saw reflected in them hit her like a gut punch. She tore her gaze away and frowned at her coffee.

"I wish I could take it away, Aidan," she said softly. "I wish I could turn back time and undo what happened." She sat back. "I blamed Kathleen when she first came here. I don't anymore."

He scoffed. "You blame me."

She leaned forward and gripped his wrist. "I don't blame anyone. That's the difference. I don't blame you or Bryan Halloran or God or the weather or anything else. It was terrible, but it was an accident. You want someone to punch it out with. There is no one to blame so you keep punching yourself." She released her grip. "But until you believe that..."

Matty shuffled into the kitchen, yawning loudly. "Oh, good, you're already up."

He poured another cup of coffee and got down a box of Shredded Wheat. "I want to finish up early at the marina today. Got a date with Brandi, that hot waitress at the Lobster Pot on Big Sister."

He grinned as he plopped himself down at the table with his coffee and cereal. "With any luck, I won't be back tonight."

Molly caught Aidan's eye while Matty jabbered on, oblivious to anything but his impending night out. Aidan gave her a small nod and pushed up from the table to get changed for work.

⬚⬚⬚⬚⬚⬚⬚⬚

BLOSSOM SNORED SOFTLY FROM his new bed near the fireplace. To Kathleen's relief and delight, he hadn't messed once in the house. He'd let her bathe him in the big tub, though she had ended up as wet as he was. With the dirt washed off him, she realized he actually had white hairs marled into his coat, including a white tip to his tail that waved like a flag when he wagged it. His ribs weren't quite as prominent with regular feeding.

The first few times she'd let him out to do his business, only to watch him disappear into the woods, she'd been certain that was that— she'd only catch glimpses of him around the island from that point on. But after a half hour's romp, he'd scratched gently at the back door, trotting inside when she opened it for him and settling with his

62

head resting on her foot. He was always either touching her or lying where he could see her. He accompanied her everywhere—on her walks, into town, shopping at the market—where Miranda gave him too many dog treats.

"Well, I don't suppose he's had many of these," Miranda said, scratching him under the chin after he delicately accepted the biscuit. "He must have stowed away on a boat or the ferry." She held the baby who gurgled and reached for Blossom's ear with his chubby fingers.

"How do I get him to a vet for a checkup?"

"Oh, there's a vet on Big Sister," Miranda said. "Anyone can take you over."

When Kathleen had seen the dog bed—the only one in the market—she'd bought it. At first, Blossom hadn't been too sure of what it was for. He nosed it, pushing it around, but the first time he crawled into it and lay down, his unabashed joy made her laugh. He rolled on his back, feet kicking in the air as he wriggled and rubbed. At night, she carried the bed upstairs to her room so he could be near her.

His snores blended with the soft music that played on her computer—Irish pipes, mournful and breathy, suiting the book cover she was designing. She sat back, chewing on a fingernail as she studied the proof.

"Wrong font," she muttered aloud.

She kept working, trying to find just the right font to match the image. Editing was steady income, and she was good at it, but it involved polishing someone else's work, oftentimes arguing with a stubborn author who thought his every word was golden and shouldn't be messed with. But cover work, this was her opportunity to create something of her own from nothing more than a nebulous idea. It was nice to see books she'd edited do well in terms of sales or awards and to know she played a part in that, but when her covers won awards, that really floated her boat.

She sat back, thinking of boats. She'd seen Molly out in hers when she was walking most mornings. She knew people in Philly who sailed, others who enjoyed powerboats, but until she got on the ferry to come here, she'd never been back on a boat since that summer. Watching Molly's strong pulls on the oars, the way she skimmed over the water, rising and falling with the swells, it had awakened her curiosity. That was the same kind of rowboat—she knew it wasn't technically a rowboat, but she couldn't remember what they called it—Bryan and Aidan had been racing. They'd only found splintered pieces of Bryan's... and then a day later, his body.

Blossom lifted his head, his ears partially up, the tips flopped over. "What did you hear?"

A moment later, she heard the sound of a car coming up the drive. He scrambled to sit at the front door, whining and tilting his head.

From the front of the house, there was a call of "Yoo-hoo, dear!"

There was a loud bang and an "Oof!" as Louisa and Olivia both tried to enter the locked front door before Kathleen could get there. Blossom backed out of the way as she turned the lock and swung the door open. For a moment, Kathleen felt a flash of irritation.

Louisa must have seen it. "We're so sorry, Katie," she said, grabbing her sister's shoulder to pull her back. A canvas tote bag swung from her other hand. "We're so used to coming and going from here without giving it a thought."

Olivia, her hands holding a slow cooker, looked back and forth between them. "Oh, yes. Maisie did the same at our house for years. Sometimes we forget."

They seemed so contrite that Kathleen felt herself blush. "No, it's okay. Really. I'm just—I come from a city where everyone keeps their doors locked all the time. No one just walks into anyone's house."

"Oh, that must be awful," Olivia said, walking past her into the kitchen. "We made a big batch of chili for tonight and thought you might like some as leftovers."

"With a fresh loaf of bread," Louisa said, reaching into her bag and pulling out a towel-wrapped object.

"You shouldn't have done that," Kathleen said. "What's the occasion?"

"For tonight," Olivia repeated, as if it should be obvious.

"What's tonight?"

The sisters stared open-mouthed at each other. "Has no one invited you?"

"Um..." Kathleen tried to recall an invitation.

"It's Samhain," said Louisa.

Kathleen's brain raced, trying to place the word in some kind of context. "You mean Halloween. But I didn't figure anyone here goes trick-or-treating."

"Not Halloween for us, dear." Louisa tucked the edges of the towel around the bread. "When the Irish were rescued and some of them settled here, they brought their traditions with them. One of them was Samhain. We've carried on ever since. We'll have a big bonfire on the beach tonight at sunset. Everyone brings something to share. And then we all bring a bit of the Samhain fire home with us."

"This is very important," Olivia said solemnly. "You must light a fire tonight from the Samhain fire. Have your kindling and logs built up, ready to light. It brings a blessing on the house for the coming year."

"But I don't have anything to bring," Kathleen protested.

"Don't you worry about that." Louisa patted her arm. "There's always more than we can eat. Just be at the beach before sunset."

Olivia noticed the dog for the first time. "Who's this then?" She crouched down with a loud creaking of her knees. "Come here," she said, holding a hand out to Blossom who peered at them from behind Kathleen's legs. "What's his name?"

"Blossom."

"Blossom? What kind of name is that?"

He crept cautiously forward and let Olivia pet him.

"Well, I thought he was a skunk at first, and... Never mind."

65

"Oh," said Louisa with a smile. "*Bambi* is one of my favorite movies."

Olivia pushed to her feet with a groan and more loud cracks from her knees. "Come on, Lou. We need to get Daddy home and rest up for tonight."

Kathleen followed them out of the kitchen and almost ran into Louisa when she stopped suddenly.

She pointed at the computer. "Did you do that?"

Kathleen blushed and nodded.

"We didn't know you were an artist," Olivia said, bending to get a better view of the book cover on the monitor.

"I'm not."

"Oh, but you are," Louisa said. She beamed at Kathleen. "Maisie would be so proud."

"We'll see you tonight," Olivia said. "Don't be late."

They hurried out the door and got into their car. Kathleen stood on the porch and waved them off as Blossom sat and leaned against her leg.

"Guess we have a date tonight," Kathleen said, scratching his ears. "With the entire island."

Chapter 5

THE BEACH WAS ALREADY in shadows as the sun set over the Head on the far side of the island. Overhead, the sky was a deep indigo as Kathleen and Blossom made their way down the path. She carried a fresh batch of cookies. Blossom darted after a rabbit and returned a few minutes later, his tongue lolling and his tail held at a jaunty angle as he trotted at her side.

It seemed to her when she arrived at the beach that the island's population had tripled. She had no idea this many people—over eighty were gathered—lived here.

Olivia made a beeline for her, taking her by the arm and guiding her to where blankets were spread on the sand and a few portable tables were set up, already loaded with platters and casserole dishes and covered crockpots. Louisa scooted a platter over to make room for Kathleen's cookies.

"We're so glad you joined us," she said. "Have you met everyone?"

Without waiting for an answer, she hooked her arm through Kathleen's, her other arm cradling her daddy's ashes, and took her around to introduce her to people. Many of the faces she recognized, but the ones she hadn't met knew who she was. Her head was soon spinning, trying to remember all the names.

A few people held babies, she noted. "Why are there no children?"

Louisa's nostrils flared for a moment. "When the powers that be decided I was no longer fit to teach, we couldn't find another teacher willing to live on the island. The children go to boarding school on the mainland. They'll be home for a month over solstice and Christmas."

Sunset turned to dusk turned to full darkness. A thumbnail of moon rose over the edge of the ocean.

"It's time," Louisa said, guiding her back to where everyone was gathered around the wood stacked in a pyramid on the sand.

Rebecca stepped forward and, immediately, all conversation ceased. Only the soft sound of ocean waves lapping at the beach filled the night.

She knelt next to a torch that had been stuck in the sand and, with a few strikes of a flint on steel, ignited the torch. It flared in the darkness. She stood with the torch and walked a circle around the bonfire, speaking words that sounded to Kathleen like a mixture of Irish and something else.

"What is she saying?" she whispered to Louisa.

"It's a prayer," Louisa whispered back. "To the spirits of our ancestors and to the gods who watch over the island, asking them to protect us through the coming winter storms."

Someone began beating on a drum. Kathleen looked around and recognized a bodhrán in someone's hand. The beat was hypnotic, with the ocean as background noise. One woman, the torchlight glinting off her mane of brilliantly red hair, wearing flowing robes and shawls and bangles that jangled as she moved, danced in a circle around the fire.

"Isn't that...?" Kathleen whispered again.

"Siobhan Greyeagle."

"Who owns the gift shop in town?"

Louisa nodded. "She's a witch."

Kathleen waited for Louisa to laugh at the joke, but she didn't.

Everyone began swaying in rhythm to the drum. The islanders linked arms. Olivia took one of Kathleen's elbows, Louisa the other, and led her in a slow circle dance around Rebecca and Siobhan and the bonfire. Rebecca stuck her torch into the base of the pyramid, and the wood caught. The flames leapt into the night, sending a shower of sparks skyward to join the stars.

In the sudden flare of light from the fire, Kathleen saw Molly on the other side of the circle, watching her. Her eyes burned with an intensity that hit Kathleen in the belly. Olivia handed her a bottle, pushing it to her lips. Before Kathleen could complain about germs, Olivia tipped some of the liquid into her mouth.

Kathleen coughed and gasped as the liquid burned its way down her throat while the bottle passed to Louisa and the next after her. She'd barely been able to catch her breath when a pipe came around. It looked very old, with its scarred wooden bowl and clay stem.

Olivia took a couple of deep drags and then held it out.

"Just two or three puffs, dear. And be sure to inhale."

Whatever was in the pipe set off another bout of coughing. When she stopped coughing, she realized that all of Siobhan's clothing had been shed. Her bangles still jingled as she continued to dance in the nude.

Kathleen tried to look anywhere but at Siobhan. When she glanced toward Molly again, she was whispering in her brother's ear—Kathleen couldn't tell which brother.

The dance continued. Kathleen shuffled around the fire with the others. The bodhrán sounded as if it were beating inside her head and chest. She closed her eyes, listening to Rebecca's chant as her feet moved of their own accord.

This seemed a very odd ceremony for people who were Christian, and she suddenly thought of stories she'd heard of pagans dancing naked at solstice and other celebrations. She supposed that was what Siobhan was doing if she really was a witch. For a brief moment, she thought it might be nice to take her clothes off and dance with her. She giggled as a picture of all the islanders naked on the cold beach flashed through her mind.

"What are you laughing at?"

She opened her eyes to find Molly standing beside her where Olivia had been. "Nothing."

Was it the beat of her heart or the beat of the drum that was pounding so loudly in her chest as she stared into Molly's eyes?

"Time to eat." Louisa yanked on her other arm, dragging her toward the tables.

Soon, everyone was seated on blankets around the fire, balancing drinks and plates piled high with food. Kathleen lost track of where Molly had gotten to. She took a few bites.

"Oh my gosh, this is delicious!"

Olivia grinned and nodded.

Kathleen decided it must be the combination of eating outdoors in the cold air warmed by the huge bonfire that made everything taste so good. Blossom squeezed in, pressing himself against her thigh. She fed him a bit from her plate.

Her belly still burned from whatever had been in that bottle, but it was a pleasant burn. With food on top of it, the fire warming her, and her new friends gathered around, she was content. A moment later, she was mortified to find her eyes filling with tears.

She lowered her gaze to her plate, trying to swallow past the sudden lump in her throat.

"Are you all right, Katie?" Olivia asked.

Kathleen nodded, but didn't trust herself to speak. What could she say? She didn't understand it herself. She'd been among these people for less than a month, but they had accepted her as one of them. She hadn't felt that kind of belonging in so, so long...

"Walk with me."

Rebecca stood over her, holding out a hand. Kathleen allowed herself to be pulled to her feet. Rebecca took her plate from her, passing it to Louisa, and led her by the hand, out of the circle of warmth and conversation, along the beach to where it was just the two of them and the stars and the ocean. And Blossom, tight to Kathleen's side. Rebecca smiled at his inquisitive expression.

Kathleen gestured back toward the bonfire. "What a curious mix of traditions."

Rebecca fixed her with an intense gaze. "It should be a mix. None of us is just one thing, complete in and of ourselves. For us, First Ones and Irish blended together to make us who we are. We are the island, and the island is us. If it's injured, we're injured. If we thrive, it thrives."

She tilted her head to look at the stars. Kathleen followed her gaze and realized she had never seen a sky like this since she was a child. She'd forgotten how many stars there were when there was no other light. The night was black as velvet, the stars so bright, with only a sliver of moon, that she felt she could see forever into the universe.

"You're open tonight."

Kathleen opened and closed her mouth, unsure how to respond. "Open to what?"

"Tonight, anything is possible," Rebecca said. "It's said, on this night, the veil between worlds thins."

"What does that mean?" Kathleen realized Rebecca was still holding her hand. She tugged it free.

"Just try to remain open."

Rebecca went back to the fire, leaving Kathleen staring after her. She glanced down at Blossom who was gazing up at her.

"What the hell does that mean?"

⬚⬚⬚⬚⬚⬚⬚⬚⬚⬚

PATRICK HAD PULLED OUT his fiddle, and someone else had produced a pipe. Some nights, down the pub, impromptu sessions of traditional Irish music broke out. Tonight, they played on the beach.

The bonfire was burning low, and the islanders began to disperse, calling out to one another as they left. Molly had no idea what time it was, but knew it was well after midnight. She hoped everyone would just go home and sleep in, leaving her alone tonight—and that included her brother. She still wasn't exactly certain how she'd been talked into the sheriff job.

For months after she'd graduated and returned to Little Sister, she'd been restless, rudderless, unable to decide about grad school or jobs on the mainland. "You were a pain in the ass," she knew Aidan would have said. When she was away from the island, she missed it like an amputated limb, but when she was there, she was unsettled, irritable. Finally, the island's elders stepped in and suggested the sheriff's position.

"It's only part-time," they said. "We'll send you for training, and you can see how it goes. If you don't like it, you don't have to continue."

So she went to the academy. Those few months away had been hard, but she'd relished the physical training, pushing her body to the breaking point.

"You won't have to do anything, really," they said upon her return.

For the most part, it was true. The sheriff position on Little Sister was mainly administrative, filling out police reports for insurance forms after homes and boats were damaged, or filling out the rare death certificate.

The actual sheriffing on the island mostly consisted of rounding up rowdy tourists speeding along the island's roads or taking boats out while intoxicated. The island didn't have a jail. She just escorted them back to Wilma's hotel to sober up. A few had been disinvited to return to the island. The job paid a small monthly salary that supplemented the fix-it work she'd started to pick up here and there.

That was thirteen years ago. Tonight, all she wanted was a peaceful night with no need for a sheriff.

On the far side of the fire, Kathleen was saying goodnight to Miss Louisa. Molly had watched as Rebecca pulled her away into the darkness, curious as to what her aunt wanted with her. Kathleen had looked a bit shaken when she returned. Miss Olivia pushed a plate of leftovers into Kathleen's hand as she waved to Wilma and disappeared into the darkness with the dog at her side.

"I'll see you at home," Molly said to her mother.

She grabbed one of the wooden torches stuck in the sand and lit it from the bonfire. Jogging to the rocks that edged the beach, she made out Kathleen's figure climbing the path through the woods. The dog heard her first. Kathleen stopped when it did, turning to see what the dog was staring at.

"Oh. It's you."

"You forgot one of these." Molly held up the torch and put out her other hand for the dog to sniff. "You have to light a fire tonight with flames from the Samhain bonfire. It's tradition."

Kathleen tilted her head, her features lit by the dancing flames of the torch. "What happens if you break the tradition?"

Molly hesitated. The question had never occurred to her. "Don't know. No one's ever done it. Not a good idea. It might bring catastrophe down on the entire island, and then how would you feel?"

Kathleen gave a half-laugh and reached for the torch. Molly pulled it back.

"Thought maybe I'd walk you home."

"Do I need to be walked back to the cottage?"

Molly flushed at the amusement in Kathleen's voice and knew her excuse was flimsy. "Depends. I need to make sure you light this fire. And how much did you have to drink? I am the sheriff here."

Kathleen smiled and nodded in the general direction of the cottage. Molly fell into step beside her as the dog trotted ahead of them.

Molly pointed. "Your new sidekick?"

"He was a stray, but I guess we belong to each other now."

"What's his name?"

"Blossom."

"Blossom. You sure you didn't have more to drink when I wasn't looking?"

"I haven't had anything to drink since that bottle got passed around," Kathleen said, picking her way over roots and rocks in the trail. "One sip of that stuff was enough. And then the pipe. I still feel woozy. What was that?"

"Island moonshine and…"

"Pot." Kathleen glanced in her direction. "Isn't that illegal?"

Molly shrugged. "The law looks the other way for this one occasion."

Kathleen stopped. "Meaning you look the other way."

"It's part of the tradition. The *poitín* opens us."

Kathleen threw her hand up. "That's what Rebecca said. What does that mean?"

"A lot of people have visions on this night."

"Visions."

"Visions."

Kathleen stomped up the path a few steps and then stomped back. "You're serious. You can't be serious."

Molly shrugged again. "You didn't grow up here. You can't be around all of this…" She held up her empty hand, looking to the skies. "… and not believe in things like visions."

Kathleen shook her head. "You're crazy."

She headed up the path. Molly caught up to her.

"You're the one who wanted to live here," Molly reminded her.

"I didn't think…" Kathleen slowed her pace. "Did my grandmother buy into all this spiritual stuff?"

Molly shifted the torch to her other hand. "I think so. Especially after..."

Kathleen bit her lip and then resumed her march up the path. Molly followed her.

"She needed something to help her deal with it, I think." Molly couldn't see much of Kathleen's features, obscured by her curtain of hair as she kept her head lowered. "Didn't you?"

She waited for a response.

"I didn't," Kathleen said so quietly Molly wasn't certain she'd heard correctly.

"Didn't what?"

Kathleen slowed. "I didn't deal with it."

"Ever?"

Kathleen came to a halt, one hand shoved into the pocket of her jacket while the other balanced the plate. The dog whined and hurried back to sit beside her. She raised her head and, in the torchlight, tears shimmered in her eyes behind her glasses.

Molly nearly reached out to brush her fingers over Kathleen's cheek. She stuffed her own fist in her pocket.

"This next summer will be twenty-five years," Kathleen said softly. "In all the years since Bryan died, I've not felt the urge to come back here. Even wanting to see Nanna wasn't strong enough to overcome what kept me away. But lately... there's been this pull back to the island. I had to come." She sighed, her breath forming a cloud in the cold air.

She walked on. Molly followed her to the cottage. She kept her mouth shut as Kathleen fished a key from her pocket, deciding this wasn't the night to tease her for locking her door.

"You really didn't have to walk me back," Kathleen said, holding a hand out for the torch.

"Well, I have to protect the island." Molly walked past her into the house where she was surprised to find wood stacked and waiting in the fireplace.

"Protect the island."

Molly heard the bite in the words. The dog trotted over and curled up in a dog bed, watching them with bright eyes as she knelt to stick the torch under the fireplace grate, letting the flames ignite the newspaper and kindling laid under the logs. They caught right away. Molly laid the torch on top of the logs and watched as the flames licked around it.

Kathleen sat cross-legged beside her as the logs crackled and popped.

"Yeah," Molly said. She shifted to sit on the floor and pointed at the fire. "The whole tradition thing. What if you bring some kind of curse down on us? Plus, you came here all mysterious, leaving your old life behind. I mean, for all I know, you might be a serial killer."

Kathleen held a hand out to the warmth of the fire. "Hmmm. A serial killer."

"Or," Molly continued, "maybe you faked your death to escape from an abusive husband or something. And now he's on his way here to find you."

Kathleen laughed. "Yes, people confuse me with Julia Roberts all the time."

Molly grinned. "I mean, if I ran a background check on you, would I find that you didn't exist until three months ago? And you've been working your way across the country as a truck stop waitress to escape him?"

Kathleen shifted to hug her knees to her chest. The mantel clock ticked as she stared into the fire. "No," she said at last. "What you would find is that I worked for a publisher with offices in Philly and New York before leaving them six months ago to start freelancing. And you'd find I have lived in Philadelphia for the past twelve years with a woman named Susannah Moore, whom I left to come here."

The only sound was the crackling of the fire as Molly absorbed this confession.

"I can't believe you said that," she said at last.

"What?" Kathleen's expression when she turned was guarded, wary.

"Whom. You said whom. Who says whom?"

Kathleen stared at her for a moment and then snorted. The snort turned into a giggle and the giggle into a full-blown belly laugh. Molly watched her, her face lit by the firelight as she rocked with her laughter.

The laughter faded, and Kathleen met Molly's eyes. Molly heard her heartbeat pounding in her ears and felt herself leaning toward Kathleen. She drew back and cleared her throat.

"Well, you've got your Samhain fire lit. The island is safe. That's my job done." She pushed to her feet. "I should go."

Kathleen followed her to the door. "Thanks for seeing me safely here."

Molly simply nodded, not trusting herself to speak. She almost ran down the porch steps into the starlit night. Halfway down the drive, she turned and looked back. Kathleen was on the porch, watching her.

Molly stood still for a moment. *Go back to her*, urged a part of her. She lifted a hand and jogged out to the road.

※※※※※※※

KATHLEEN SAT AT THE kitchen table, cradling her head, while the steam from her coffee cup rose to fill her nostrils with a scent she usually loved. She had a damned hangover. From one sip of that moonshine—*poitín*, Molly had called it—and whatever had been in that pipe. She pushed the cup away.

Blossom looked up from his food bowl. Leaving his kibble, he came to her and sat with his head resting on her thigh. She smiled and patted him, playing with his soft ears. He closed his eyes contentedly.

But Kathleen felt no sense of contentment.

"It was all those suggestions of stupid visions," she mumbled, rubbing her fingers against her forehead.

The whole night had been filled with dreams so that she felt she'd hardly slept. Dreams of Nanna and Bryan, but not the Bryan she'd seen in her nightmares after that summer. It had been months and months before she stopped having those nightmares—of his body, the way it had looked when the ocean finally gave him up. She still had them occasionally, but mostly, she'd stopped dreaming of him at all. *Not just dreaming. You haven't let yourself think of him for years.*

Last night had been different. Bryan and Nanna, sitting and laughing together on the cottage's front porch. They stopped when she approached.

"Hey, squirt," Bryan had said, grinning.

Nanna held out a hand, more gnarled and arthritic than Kathleen remembered. "We've missed you."

She sat down with them, it seemed for the whole night. Nothing happened, just talking and laughing and... *they were happy,* she realized.

Kathleen rubbed her eyes now, pressing her fingers hard to them. And what was up with Molly Cooper?

God, her face last night, first around the bonfire and then here at the cottage, the way Molly's eyes burned into her, as if they could see straight through her. And then she had just blurted out her relationship with Susannah, and Molly had practically run from the house. What the hell did that mean?

"It was just the pipe and the moonshine," she said aloud.

Blossom's tail thumped on the kitchen floor. She patted his head.

"Go finish your breakfast. I'm going to shower."

By the time she came back downstairs, her head felt a little clearer. She warmed up her coffee and forced herself to eat a piece of buttered toast.

She went into the dining room and stared balefully at her computer. She had work to do, but she reached for her jacket.

"Let's go for a walk."

The cold air felt wonderful—the sharp bite of autumn, the sky a brilliant blue with just a few puffy clouds.

Blossom raced down the drive and back, jumping playfully at her. She laughed and followed him out to the road. As it meandered, she came to an overlook where she could see Big Sister in the distance. Blossom sat to bite at his haunch. Miranda had said there was a vet on Big Sister. Maybe she should see about getting Blossom checked out. He lifted a back leg to scratch.

"Let's add neutering to the list of things to talk to the vet about," she said, averting her eyes.

She walked on and circled around to the cemetery, pausing there to clean Nanna's grave of leaves and sticks.

"Were you really visiting me last night?"

There was no answer but the sigh of the breeze through the trees.

Kathleen shivered and decided she needed to be among the living. She brushed her knees off, whistling to Blossom who was sniffing around the grave markers.

Together, they followed the island's ring road.

"Yoo-hoo!"

Kathleen turned to see Miss Olivia hailing her from outside a rambling house that seemed to be a hodgepodge of additions. The wooden shingles covering different sections of the house were varying shades of gray and brown, as they clearly hadn't all been exposed to the weather for the same amount of time. The roof also was a patchwork of black and gray shingles.

Olivia was wearing faded dungarees with muddy Wellies and a red and black flannel jacket. Kathleen smothered a laugh at Louisa, wearing a similar pair of Wellies under her flowered cotton dress with a heavier wool coat against the morning's chill. Her outfit was set off by the floppy straw hat on her head.

"What are you doing?"

"Just gathering the last of the potatoes and carrots and turnips," said Louisa, pointing to three overflowing bushel baskets. Nearby was the wooden box of ashes, sitting in the sun.

"We've already canned our tomatoes and beans," Olivia said.

"And put up strawberry jam and rhubarb and a few peaches," Louisa said.

"Sure we got that done ages ago," Olivia said with a dismissive wave.

"I didn't say we just did it," Louisa argued.

"Well it sounded as if that's what you were saying," Olivia countered.

"Looks like you've been busy," Kathleen said to interrupt them.

"We must give her some, Ollie." Louisa brushed the dirt off her hands.

"Oh, no, you don't have t—"

"Stuff and nonsense," Olivia said. "We've more than we can eat, and you can't do better than home-grown and canned in the middle of winter."

"Can I at least help you here?" Kathleen asked.

"Oh, Katie, you are a dear," Louisa said. "I think we've got everything dug up, but if you could help carry these baskets to the house while we put a few things together for you."

Kathleen went to pick up the basket of potatoes and felt a fresh pounding in her head as she bent over. "Aren't either of you feeling the effects of last night?"

Olivia cackled. "Got a bit of a head this morning, do you?"

"Oh, we've just the thing for that." Louisa picked up the box of ashes. "I'll take Daddy inside. You come on in with that basket, Katie, and we'll get you taken care of."

Kathleen lugged the heavy basket up onto the porch and through the house into the kitchen. She looked around curiously at the mishmash of antique furniture scattered about, and paintings covering almost every inch of wall space. There was even a piano, its top occupied by an array of framed photos.

"Do you play?"

Louisa glanced over. "Oh, yes. Just for Daddy and Ollie now, but we used to have the gayest parties."

She stopped abruptly, sweeping the straw hat off and patting her hair. "I suppose I shouldn't say that nowadays."

"What?"

"Gay. People might get the wrong idea."

Kathleen felt her heart drop to the vicinity of her stomach as she followed Louisa into the kitchen, painted a cheerful butter-yellow. "And what idea might that be?"

"Just set that down here," Louisa said, pointing to the kitchen floor next to the sink. "That we care about such things."

Kathleen straightened. "You don't?"

"Oh, heavens no," Olivia said, coming in behind them carrying the basket of turnips and carrots, Blossom on her heels. "The First Ones always had those who preferred to be with their own sex. Some never had children. Others wanted children, so they, what do they say now, hooked together? Just until they got the job done and then went back to their loves."

"We've never been bothered by that here," Louisa said from the pantry where she was up on a step-stool, plucking jars off the floor-to-ceiling shelves and putting them in an empty cardboard box.

"Love is love." Olivia found a smaller basket and filled it with onions and turnips and carrots and potatoes.

"Life's too short and this island too small to make a fuss about such things," Louisa said. She held up a jar filled with something pink. "Do you like rhubarb?"

"I don't know," Kathleen said, her heart much lighter than it had been a moment ago. "I never remember having it."

"Well, you take a jar. And this jar of strawberry preserves. Look for Maisie's recipe for strawberry-rhubarb pie. There's nothing like it."

"Now," said Olivia, going to the stove. "Let's get your head cleared up for you."

81

She ladled some pale green liquid from a pot simmering there. She pushed the cup into Kathleen's hands. "Drink this down."

Kathleen stared at it dubiously. "What is it?"

"Our island brew for the morning after," Louisa said. She carried her box filled with canning jars and set it on the table. "We've already had ours. Some make their own, but most come by here for ours." She winked. "We add a few secret ingredients that make ours better."

Olivia tipped the cup to Kathleen's mouth, just as she had the bottle of *poitín* last night. Kathleen took a cautious sip, expecting something bitter and medicinal, but it was cool and refreshing.

"This is good."

"Well, of course it is," Olivia said with a chuckle. "Wouldn't do to drink something awful to make the aftereffects go away."

Kathleen took another drink. "It tastes of... spring. Flowers and sunshine."

Louisa beamed. "That's my doing."

"It is not," Olivia said. "I thought of adding the elderflower."

Louisa sniffed. "It's the lavender, not the elderflower that gives it sunshine."

Kathleen drained the cup and closed her eyes. "Oh, that feels better already."

"That's just what Molly said." Louisa closed the flaps of her box.

Kathleen's eyes flew open. "Molly was here?"

"Oh, yes. She came by early before she left."

"Left? Where did she go?"

Olivia glanced up from where she was stirring the liquid that remained in the pot. "She said she was going to the mainland for a few days."

"Come, Katie," Louisa said. She handed Kathleen her box of preserves. "Ollie, you get the potatoes and such. We'll drive her home with these."

MOLLY SAT AT THE bar in a dark club in Ogunquit, nursing a cold Sam Adams. She normally liked these clubs better than the ones in Portland. The problem was, she didn't seem to like any of them at the moment. This was her third stop tonight. The music pulsed, the bass vibrated in her gut, and the dance floor was full of people, mostly guys, gyrating and grinding.

"Hi."

Standing beside her was a cute young woman with short, spiky, pink hair.

"Hi."

"Want to dance?"

"Uh... not tonight." Molly decided she looked like a fairy escaped from some animated movie.

The fairy pointed at her beer. "Can I buy you another?"

"How about I buy you one?"

"Sure. I'm Caitie, C-A-I-T-I-E." She hopped up onto the next barstool.

Molly felt her face freeze. "Of course you are."

"Sorry, didn't hear that." Caitie leaned closer. "What did you say?"

"Nothing." Molly waved a hand in the bartender's direction.

"Gin and tonic," Caitie said to the bartender. "And you are...?"

"I'm Mary." Molly forced a smile as she shook Caitie's hand.

The gin and tonic appeared, and Molly slid a bill across the bar.

"Let's find a table," Caitie said, nearly shouting to be heard. She took Molly by the hand and tugged her off her stool, weaving through the tables to an empty one.

"So what do you do?" Molly asked to make conversation.

"I'm a waitress," Caitie said. "But I'm saving up to go back to school in January. I moved back in with my mom and her boyfriend, but I have to get a place of my own." She sipped from her gin and tonic, draining nearly the entire drink while she went on and on about how her mother's boyfriend kept hitting on the women she brought home with her, and how her last girlfriend had actually hooked up with him. Molly had stopped listening a long time ago so almost missed it when Caitie asked, "What about you? Where do you live?"

Molly quickly congratulated herself on having the foresight to lie about her name. "I live in Freeport. Just visiting up here for a few days." She chugged her beer and set the bottle down.

Pointing to the rear of the club where the restrooms were, she said, "Be right back."

She made her way through the crowd to the dark corridor where she had to squeeze past couples kissing and groping each other. She passed the restrooms and almost ran out the back door into the cold night.

She scanned the parking lot, nearly panicking when she couldn't find her Toyota, and then she remembered. She dug the keys out of her jeans and had to inspect the key under the parking lot's light. A Ford. She was driving Bobby's extra car he kept at the ferry landing in case one of them boated over and needed a vehicle while they were here. She found the blue Escape and jumped in, starting the little SUV and peeling out of the parking lot before the fairy could come looking for her.

"God, what was I thinking?"

She quickly dismissed the thought of going to another club. Three in one night was enough. So were the three possible women she could have gone to bed with. *What is wrong with you?* She'd come here hoping for some fun, maybe some sex. She could have had it with any of the women she'd met tonight, but she'd run from each of them.

"I must be getting old," she said to no one but herself.

Only that wasn't the problem. Siobhan was right. The problem was back on Little Sister Island, living in her grandmother's cottage with a stray dog she'd adopted.

"Shit."

She drove through the dark streets of Portland toward the ferry landing. No sense in wasting money on a motel room. She parked in the nearly empty parking lot and reclined the seat, making herself as comfortable as she could. She'd grab a few hours' sleep, then go to where her boat was docked and be back on the island not long after dawn. Not exactly the night she'd had planned.

Secured in the cargo area was the new reciprocating saw and drill bits she'd bought for herself, along with some flannel shirts her mom had asked her to pick up for her dad and the boys for Christmas. She reached over to the passenger seat and picked up the dog collar and leash she'd bought at the last minute. Green with pink blossoms woven into the nylon. For a dog named after a cartoon skunk. Adopted by a woman she didn't understand—a woman who admitted she'd left her last relationship, who had basically run away from her old life.

There were so many reasons to stay away from Kathleen Halloran. She fingered the collar. *Since when have you done what you should?*

She wriggled into a more comfortable position and closed her eyes.

Chapter 6

THE COTTAGE WAS FILLED with the homely scents of garlic and onion and tomatoes. Kathleen breathed deeply, her stomach growling hungrily, as she stirred the sauce simmering on the stove. She was only a recreational cook, but she'd begged this family recipe for spaghetti sauce from a co-worker years ago, and it had become her go-to choice when she craved comfort food. Miranda and Tim didn't stock Italian sausage at the market, so she'd had to make do with ground steak and regular sausage but... She spooned up a bit. Not bad. She adjusted the heat on the burner and went back out to the dining room. Blossom followed dutifully.

Hands on her hips, she decided there was no way she could clear the dining table of all her gear. It was becoming obvious that she was going to have to set up a real office in one of the rooms upstairs. She sat down to try and finish one more chapter of this edit. Thankfully, this author knew the mechanics of good writing, and her job was much easier as a result. Working on this manuscript was a delight, more of a polishing than a total rewrite.

She got so absorbed in her work that she lost track of time and was startled by Blossom's low woof when a car came up the drive.

"Crap."

She saved her work, powered off her computer, and went to open the front door just as Louisa and Olivia climbed the porch steps.

"This was so nice of you, dear," Louisa said as she entered, carrying a towel-covered pan.

"Well, you gave me most of the ingredients for tonight's dinner," Kathleen said. "So it seemed like you should get to share it. Hope you like spaghetti."

"Oh, we like anything," Olivia said, sniffing. She carried the box of ashes. "Mmmm, smells good."

"Come on in the kitchen."

Louisa held up her pan. "We brought brownies for dessert."

Kathleen put a pot of water on to boil while Olivia deposited the box on a chair and set the kitchen table. Blossom scratched at the back door to go out. Kathleen opened the door for him.

"Won't he run away?" Louisa asked as she got water glasses down from the cupboard. She spied the bottles of wine sitting on the counter and got wine glasses down as well.

Kathleen smiled, remembering how annoying it had been at first for them to charge in and take over. "He hasn't yet. I think he's learned to like it here. A warm bed and plenty of food. Speaking of which, he'll expect dinner when he comes in."

She scooped some kibble into his bowl.

A few minutes later, the spaghetti was draining and Kathleen had the sauce poured into a blue and green ceramic bowl.

"I remember when we gave this to Maisie," Olivia said, admiring the bowl as Kathleen set it on the table. "For Christmas, wasn't it, Lou?"

Louisa nodded. "It was 1989."

Kathleen glanced at her. "How do you remember that?"

"Oh, I've a head for dates." Louisa chuckled. "Can't say many of my pupils did."

A scratching at the back door announced Blossom's return. Olivia opened the door, and he trotted in, trailing a leash hooked to a collar around his neck.

"Where in the world—?"

Molly's face peeked around the doorjamb. "I don't mean to interrupt your dinner party."

Olivia pulled her inside. "Of course you're not interrupting. Get in here."

For a moment, Kathleen locked eyes with Molly. Something in that gaze felt physical. Kathleen's face flushed, and she fished for something to say.

"We didn't expect you back on the island for a few days," Louisa said. She went to the cupboards to get down another set of glasses.

"Me either."

Kathleen squatted next to Blossom who was busily eating. She twisted the collar around to look at the shiny new tag attached to it. Etched into the metal heart was "BLOSSOM".

"What is this for?"

Molly shuffled her feet, looking distinctly embarrassed. "Saw them at a store on the mainland. Embroidered blossoms. Just seemed like they should be his."

Kathleen held her gaze for a few heartbeats and then smiled and unclipped the leash from the collar. "Thank you."

Molly pointed toward the door. "I should go."

"Nonsense," Louisa said. "We've plenty to go around. Molly, pour the wine. Ollie, get another plate and move Daddy."

89

THE LITTLE COTTAGE RANG with light and laughter. Two empty bottles of wine sat on the table.

Louisa drained her wine glass. "I can't remember the last time we had such a nice evening."

Olivia dabbed her eyes with her napkin. "It's almost like Maisie's here with us."

"Oh, don't cry, Ollie," Louisa said, patting her arm.

"I am not crying. I had something in my eye." Olivia snatched up her plate and Louisa's. "Let's clean up, sister."

"You don't have to do that," Kathleen said.

"We are not leaving you with a dirty kitchen," Louisa said firmly. "You cooked. We clean."

Molly washed while Louisa dried. Olivia helped Kathleen spoon the leftover sauce into containers.

"Are you sure you don't want to keep some?" Olivia asked.

"I still have enough for two more meals here." Kathleen wrapped some of the leftover garlic bread for them. "You take this."

"I can drive you home," Molly said.

"We can drive ourselves," Louisa said.

Molly folded her arms. "When was the last time you had two glasses of wine, Miss Louisa? And it would be awkward if I had to arrest my teacher for driving under the influence."

"She's right, sister." Olivia scooped up the wooden box from the stool it had been sitting on. "Let Molly drive us."

Kathleen held a container out for Molly. "Some sauce for you, too."

As Molly took it from her, her fingers covered Kathleen's. It felt as if the space between them was suddenly devoid of air. Somewhere behind her, Kathleen was aware of Louisa and Olivia gathering their things and talking but, for that moment, there was only Molly's eyes and the touch of her hand.

Kathleen caught herself and pulled her hand free. "Thank you again. For Blossom's collar and leash." She smiled and nodded at him.

He was using one back foot to gently scratch at the collar, turning it in circles around his neck, making the tag jingle. "I think he likes it."

Molly backed away. "You're welcome. Thanks for dinner. And this." She lifted the plastic container. "Mom will be happy to have a meal she didn't cook."

Kathleen and Blossom walked them all out. He trotted off into the trees while she waved goodnight.

Olivia hung out the back window. "Good night, Katie!"

The headlights swept through the darkness as Molly backed the car around and drove away.

Kathleen shivered in the cold, watching the taillights disappear in the darkness. She looked down at her hand, almost expecting it to glow from the heat she'd felt at Molly's touch.

She called for Blossom, who galloped out of the woods and bounded up the steps, his new collar and tag tinkling.

"I'll know where you are now."

He followed her inside. She locked the door—a habit she wasn't sure she would ever lose—and adjusted the thermostat back down a little, mindful of Molly's warning not to use up all of her oil too quickly.

The house might not be toasty, but her insides tingled with a warmth that had nothing to do with the furnace.

"WHERE THE HELL ARE YOU? Why aren't you answering your phone? Give me a call asap or I'm calling the police."

Kathleen read the terse email several times. It hadn't occurred to her that anyone might assume she was missing. Or that they might contact the police. She remembered Molly's wild theory about her having faked her death and snorted.

"Love, Dad," she muttered.

This was just like him. He could go for months and months with-out knowing or caring if she was alive, breathing, or sucked down a well. When he wanted something, then it became a matter of urgency. It was all about control with him.

The message felt as if the real world had just dropped down on top of her—jarring and unwelcome. She clicked Reply and typed:

"I'm on Little Sister. No cell phone. Do not call the police."

She hesitated, her cursor hovering over the Send button. If she didn't send a reply, things would only escalate. If she did, her life here would change. She knew it. Reluctantly, she tapped the button and got back to work.

Within an hour, there were more messages—two from her father and one from Susannah. Apparently, they'd been in communication.

The ones from her father were expected—*"What the hell are you doing there? Why would you ever go back to that godforsaken rock?"*

But the lengthy email from Susannah had shaken her—*it shouldn't have*, she reminded herself. *You knew this was coming.*

Susannah had gone from "let's make up" to "how could you do this to me?" over the course of her messages. Kathleen could feel the seething build-up, the resentment, as it apparently was sinking in that Kathleen had left and wasn't coming back.

"You said you'd never leave me, Kath. You promised we'd be together al-ways, and that you would be there no matter what."

Kathleen pushed away from the table. She grabbed a coat and scarf and stormed out the front door, Blossom on her heels. The air, when she inhaled, was like little icicles stabbing her lungs, but the sting felt welcome. She breathed deeply as she walked the path through the woods toward the bluff.

Knowing that Susannah would sooner or later get to the point of guilting Kathleen about breaking her word didn't make it any easier to swallow that she had done just that. As she walked, she argued with herself.

"How many times did she tell you to get out or to go to hell?"

"Doesn't matter. I said I'd never leave her."

"But you stayed, for fourteen years, through everything—her father, her sister, her caving every time they put pressure on her to come home and leave you behind."

She knew she must look crazy, her hands flying about, carrying on both sides of the conversation as she tromped along, but she didn't care. There was no one else to talk to about this, about the punch-in-the-gut ache in her belly of knowing Susannah's family hated her and, worse, knowing Susannah would never confront them to acknowledge Kathleen as her partner.

So preoccupied was she that she didn't realize there was someone else at the bluff until Blossom gave a low woof. Startled, Kathleen saw Rebecca sitting on a boulder, patting her thigh. Blossom went to her cautiously and allowed her to scratch behind his ears.

"Hello," Kathleen said. "Sorry to disturb you. I didn't know anyone was here."

Rebecca swept her free arm toward the sea. "The view's big enough for three of us. Come sit down."

Kathleen sat beside her on the rock, not sure what to say.

"I come here to pray," Rebecca offered.

"You... pray?"

"There are many entities one can pray to. I pray to the ones that speak to me." She nodded back down the trail. "You sounded upset."

Kathleen felt the heat rise in her cheeks.

Rebecca smiled. "I talk to myself all the time. Don't be embarrassed." When Kathleen didn't respond, she asked, "How are you adjusting to life here on Little Sister?"

"It's been really nice here." Kathleen kept her gaze focused on the ocean. "Until I got some messages from my father this morning."

"Ah." Rebecca nodded.

"What? All I said is I got some messages from him, and you sound as if you know what they were."

93

Rebecca looked at her—those eyes so like Molly's—and gave her a tight-lipped smile. "It isn't difficult to figure out that Michael isn't pleased you're here. I could feel the cloud over you before you got anywhere near the bluff." She sighed and returned her gaze to the ocean. "I grew up with your father. He wasn't happy when he lived here. In fact, I've never known him to be happy, or even content. And those aren't the same thing, are they? Never came back except to drop you and your brother off and then pick you up. And after Bryan died, he never came back at all."

Kathleen bit her lip, thinking. "I have felt more at home here than I have anywhere since Bryan died. I don't want to leave."

Rebecca turned to her, her mouth open. "Why on earth would you leave?"

Kathleen flushed under her scrutiny. "I just... It's always been easier to do what he wants than to argue. No one ever wins an argument with my father."

Rebecca scoffed. "I beg to differ. Maybe Michael has gotten used to having his way, but that doesn't make him right."

Kathleen turned back to the vista below them. The knot in her gut eased a little, and she felt her jangled nerves calm.

"It doesn't make him right," she murmured.

⬛⬛⬛⬛⬛⬛⬛⬛

CAP'N JACK WAS ROOSTING, his feathers fluffed against the cold, under the shelter of the boathouse where Molly was planing a new mahogany board to replace a rotted one on the boat's deck. The whisper of the plane as it shaved paper-thin curls of wood from the edge of the board blended with the soft lapping of the water and the shimmering reflections of the sunlight to create a dreamy, drowsy atmosphere. The gull's eyes were half-closed.

She heard voices—her father's and another that sounded familiar. She set the plane down. Cap'n Jack opened his eyes and watched her as she went to the door of the boathouse and saw Kathleen Halloran talking to her dad inside the marina's little office. Her father was nodding and writing something down. He said something and gestured toward the boathouse. Molly ducked out of view.

She went back to where her board was clamped in the workbench and resumed her planing. A moment later, Blossom trotted through the open door. Cap'n Jack spread his wings, but the dog ignored him, coming over to greet Molly.

The voices drew nearer.

"Molly?" said her father as he and Kathleen entered the boathouse. "You available to boat over to Big Sister tomorrow?"

Molly paused her work to glance up. "Why?"

Kathleen laid a hand on Blossom's head. "Miranda told me there's a vet over on Big Sister, and I just talked to your dad about getting over there. They can see him tomorrow."

"If you're busy, I can get one of the boys to take her," Joe said.

Molly considered quickly. She was supposed to put a new kitchen faucet and sink in for Wilma and Nels, but that faucet had been dripping for months. It wasn't an emergency. "I should be able to do that. Just need to make a call."

"Good. See you tomorrow then," Joe said with a nod to Kathleen before he went back to the office.

"What time do you need to be there?" Molly asked.

"Early. They're going to do a check-up and..." Kathleen made a snipping motion with her fingers.

"Oh." Molly grinned at Blossom, whose tail thumped against the boathouse floor. "Going to get tutored, is he?"

"They only need to monitor him for the day and said I could pick him up by three."

Molly nodded. "We'll be on the water early and late then. Better dress warm."

"I will." Kathleen glanced around. "I didn't know you built boats, too."

"My dad has always done boat restoration. My brothers and I learned along the way."

Kathleen went to the boat, braced on a system of wooden blocks. She ran a hand over the hull. "This wood is so smooth."

Molly's mouth twitched into a half-smile. "It is now." She pointed to the sanding block. "That represents about twenty hours of hand-sanding so far. And a lot of work yet to do."

"Wow. That's a lot of time."

"You've no business working on wooden boats if you're impatient." Molly caressed the wood herself. "You have to coax them along, get the boards to bend without breaking."

"Kind of like people, I guess."

"Maybe."

"You don't think so?"

Kathleen locked eyes with her, and Molly realized how blue they were. She broke eye contact. "I think boats are probably more pliable."

Kathleen stepped back and slid her hands into her jacket pockets. "We'll see you in the morning."

"Six o'clock."

Kathleen nodded and patted her thigh. Blossom led the way as they left the boathouse.

Cap'n Jack settled again with a ruffling of his feathers. He stared at Molly with his bright, black eyes.

"What are you looking at?"

The gull just shook his head and closed his eyes.

A HARD FROST GREETED Kathleen and Blossom when they stepped out the front door the next morning. She had his new leash coiled in her jacket pocket, along with a hat and gloves. A warm scarf was snugged around her throat, her backpack slung over one shoulder.

He peed and trotted back up onto the porch to stand at the door, clearly reminding her they needed to go back inside for the breakfast he hadn't had.

"Not today." She opened the rear car door, and Blossom leapt inside. She put her backpack on the passenger seat.

She had to scrape the windshield while the defroster blasted air from inside. Once she could see, she drove into town, careful on curves as the headlights pierced the darkness, and the road twisted and wound. The lights were on at the diner and the market as she drove past them to the marina.

Molly was already there. She waved a greeting from the deck of a medium-sized boat, its engine idling. The marina's office door opened, spilling an elongated rectangle of yellow light into the darkness. Joe stepped out with all three of his sons, almost walking into Kathleen. Aidan nodded curtly and immediately went to a larger fishing boat.

"Morning," Joey said.

"Good morning," Kathleen said.

"Hey, Mo!" Matty called. "Be sure to tell Brandi I'll be over to see her as soon as I can."

"Be careful," Joey said. "She might like Mo better." He slapped his brother on the back.

Matty frowned, apparently thinking about this. "On second thought," he said, "stay away from her."

"Not my type, Matty," Molly said.

"How do you know?"

"If she likes you, she's not my type."

Joey doubled over, guffawing.

Even Joe chuckled. "She's got you there."

Kathleen and Blossom walked down the wharf toward Molly's boat.

Joe supervised Joey and Matty loading their gear while Aidan finished fueling the boat. "Be careful out there."

"He says that to them every morning," Molly said.

Blossom jumped into the boat, sniffing everything. Kathleen hesitated.

"Anything wrong?" Molly asked.

"No."

Kathleen steeled herself and stepped onto the boat's side. Molly reached a hand up to steady her. Without thinking, Kathleen took it. She hopped down, and Molly released her hand slowly.

"You look kind of pale," Molly said. "You sure you're okay? You don't get seasick, do you?"

"It's just... except for the ferry here, this is the first boat I've been on since..."

"Oh."

"Mo," Joe said.

She went to the rail. He pulled his wallet out and handed her some money, speaking in a low voice.

"I will," Molly said, pocketing the bills.

"Have a good day." Joe gave Blossom a rough rub. "Sorry, old man."

Blossom wagged his tail in response as Joe untied the line from the cleat and gave the boat a shove with his foot.

"Be safe."

"I will, Dad."

Molly pointed toward a short set of stairs leading down. "You'll be warmer inside the cabin. It's small, but there are a couple of bunks. And I promise, I'll be careful. We should have calm water."

Kathleen gave a self-conscious laugh. "I trust you. And I'll stay up here. If you have to be in the cold, we can, too."

Molly watched her for a heartbeat and then nodded. "Okay. I have extra blankets under that seat. You two can wrap up. I figured Blossom might be chilled coming out of his procedure this afternoon."

Kathleen was touched that she had thought of that. "Thank you."

She stowed her backpack and settled into one of the seats, pulling on her hat and gloves. Blossom roamed from one side of the boat to the other as Molly eased the boat away from the dock and out into the island's small bay. Kathleen kept hold of his leash, afraid he might get spooked and jump into the water, but he soon curled up on a folded blanket at her feet. She covered him with another blanket, and he propped his head on her foot.

Kathleen took a deep breath. *If he can relax, so can you.*

As if she could sense Kathleen's anxiety, Molly turned to her from where she stood at the wheel.

"There are life jackets just there." She pointed to a stack of orange life vests Kathleen hadn't noticed. "And Mom packed us a basket of food—muffins and cookies. I could use some coffee if you don't mind."

"Sure."

Kathleen tugged her gloves off and opened the basket to find a couple of covered travel mugs full of hot coffee. She handed Molly a mug. "What do you want to eat?"

"Anything. I'm not fussy."

Kathleen plucked a muffin from the basket. "I think this one's blueberry."

"That's great. Thanks."

Kathleen took her seat with a cookie and a mug of coffee. She watched Molly guide the boat past a buoy marking the entrance to the bay. Once past, Molly sat down and slid the throttle. The boat picked up speed. Overhead, the stars still winked down at them.

"How can you see?"

Molly glanced back. "I've got GPS, but I've been doing this trip my whole life. All of us have. Sun won't be up for an hour. If you want to take a nap, go ahead."

Kathleen finished her cookie. Clamping her coffee between her knees, she slipped her hands back into her gloves and wiggled back in her seat. Her gloves hid her white knuckles as the boat bounced gently over the swells. Behind them the sky began to lighten, and the stars faded.

Molly looked back again. "You okay?"

Kathleen gave a tight nod.

The sun broke over the horizon behind them, bathing them in golden light. She watched Molly, her knit cap pulled over her head, a hooded sweatshirt snugged around her neck with a down vest over top. Scarred leather gloves warmed her hands, and faded jeans hugged her thighs. It couldn't have been more opposite the way Susannah would have dressed, she realized. Kathleen caught herself admiring the lean curves.

There was something about Molly's quiet confidence, her ease at the wheel, her slight adjustments of speed to smooth the roughness of the ride, the firm set of her jaw—Kathleen felt herself relax into the seat. Some of the questions she'd had about Molly seemed to have been answered that morning.

"So, you're into women, and your family is okay with it?"

Molly glanced back at her. "Yes and yes."

When she didn't offer anything further, Kathleen wondered if that meant she didn't want to talk about it. She really had no right to pry, so she was surprised to hear herself ask, "When you went to Portland a couple of weeks ago, was it to meet someone?"

She thought maybe Molly was smiling, but she didn't turn around this time, so it was hard to tell.

"Well, not a specific someone," Molly said. Kathleen had to listen hard to catch her voice over the loud hum of the motor and the wind in her ears. "I went to try and meet someone but... It didn't work out."

For some reason, that made Kathleen happy. She sipped her coffee, thinking about what Olivia and Louisa had told her about the islanders' acceptance of those who preferred their own sex.

As the sun rose fully, Big Sister came into view. Kathleen sat up a little straighter.

"Are those all hotels?"

Molly shook her head. "Houses."

"Houses? They're huge."

Molly half-turned toward her, keeping an eye on the water ahead of them. "That's what happens when you let offlanders buy up all the land. They try to claim all the beaches and prime building sites, make them private. It's disgusting."

Kathleen shifted forward. The enormous east-facing windows reflected the sun. "Your ancestors were so wise, to keep this from happening on Little Sister."

"Our ancestors."

Kathleen blinked. Molly was right. She sat back again, her throat suddenly tight. She pressed a hand to her chest where something now burned, a realization that chased away the morning chill. *I'm one of them.*

Chapter 7

THE SHOPKEEPERS OF BIG SISTER Island were beginning to stir as Kathleen and Molly left the marina with Blossom trotting between them. Kathleen's head swiveled as she looked from side to side of the main street.

"Is this the only shopping area?"

"No." Molly checked for traffic, and they crossed the street. "This island is probably three times the size of Little Sister. They've got a dozen developments with shops and restaurants all over the island. Seems like every year there's a new one."

She led the way through a little maze of side streets to a neat white building with a sign out front announcing it was the Big Sister Veterinary Clinic. She opened the door to allow Kathleen and Blossom through. Kathleen introduced herself to the front desk staff. They all cooed over Blossom, who grinned up at the attention. She filled out the paperwork.

"He was a stray," she said as she got to a space on the form for age. "I don't know how old he is."

"Dr. Steve will examine him and give you some idea," said the receptionist. "Hi, Molly. How's Minnow?"

"She's fine," Molly said. "Mom will probably get her over here for a checkup in the spring."

One of the techs came out to take Blossom's leash. Kathleen dropped to one knee to plant a kiss on his head.

"Don't worry. We'll take good care of him." The tech pulled gently on the leash, and Blossom followed her through a door into the back.

Kathleen stood staring after them. Molly tugged on her sleeve.

"Come on. He'll be fine."

Kathleen followed Molly back out into a brilliant fall morning.

"What would you like to do?" Molly asked. "We've got several hours to kill before you can pick him up."

Kathleen hooked a thumb at her backpack. "I brought a laptop and a book. I figured you would have friends or customers you need to see while you're here."

Molly shook her head. "The only thing I need to do is get a few gifts for Mom. Since everyone on Little Sister sees the same stuff in our shops, it's hard to surprise anyone. So if one of us is going somewhere, she asks us to pick up a few things. Come on. No work today. Besides, I need help." She pulled a list out of her pocket. "I have no idea what to get Olivia and Louisa."

"Your dad gave you money, too."

"Yeah," Molly said. "He wants me to pick something up for Mom."

"Don't sound so glum. That's nice." Kathleen smiled. "Your folks are really sweet."

"I guess they are. I'm just not much of a shopper." Molly glanced over hopefully. "So you'll help?"

Kathleen shrugged her backpack straps higher on her shoulders. "A shopping holiday then."

"Good." Molly gave an exaggerated sigh of relief. "There's a cool lighthouse here, too. I haven't been there in years."

Kathleen fell into step beside her. "Why doesn't Little Sister have a lighthouse?"

"The waters around us have sharp underwater rocks. Big boats and ships have to take a wide detour around us or they'll founder and sink."

"Like the ship our ancestors came from?"

"Yeah. There are lighted buoys now to warn them."

"Let's go to the lighthouse first, then. Before we're loaded down with packages."

Molly led the way, pointing out various points of interest as they walked. Kathleen enjoyed playing tourist, making note of some shops they should visit later. The hike, combined with the sun's thin November warmth, was enough to have them soon yanking off hats and gloves, and unzipping jackets and vests.

"Here," Kathleen said, shrugging off her backpack. "We can put everything in here."

"Okay, but I'll carry it now." Molly tugged against Kathleen's grip on the straps. "I promise I'll take care of your laptop, but you shouldn't have to carry everything."

Kathleen surrendered, and Molly slid the straps over her own shoulders as they made their way toward a rocky promontory with a squat, round lighthouse perched on it. The red brick was painted with two white stripes wrapped around it horizontally.

"It looks like a rook," Kathleen said.

"A bird?"

"No, a chess rook. Like a little castle."

Molly stopped and tilted her head. "I guess it does. It's not the highest lighthouse, but it has stood here for over a hundred fifty years. A lot of lighthouses have been lost or had to be moved as their base is eroded by the sea."

Nearby was a quaint, white clapboard house.

"That was the keeper's house. Now it's the gift shop." Molly handed the backpack to Kathleen. "Be right back."

She returned a moment later with two tickets.

"You didn't have to do that," Kathleen said.

"You can buy me a drink later." She slipped the backpack onto her shoulders.

They entered the lighthouse and climbed its spiral staircase, the cast iron treads and rail coated in many layers of black paint. Kathleen was out of breath by the time they got to the top. Molly wasn't breathing hard at all, despite the weight of the backpack.

"I may have to start working out harder," Kathleen said ruefully.

"I could teach you to row," Molly said. She immediately looked stricken. "I am so sorry."

She followed Kathleen out onto the lighthouse's balcony.

"It's not your fault," Kathleen said. "You don't need to watch every word you say around me."

"I know, but..."

"I've watched you." She flushed as she realized what that sounded like. "Rowing, I mean, and wondered what it's like."

"I love it. That feeling of being out on the water by myself. No one needing anything from me, no phones, just me and my body providing the power."

For several minutes, they stood shoulder to shoulder, looking out at the ocean below them. A light breeze blew, playing with their hair.

"Before, when we were talking about my parents," Molly began hesitantly, "you sounded... I don't know, kind of wistful. Sad."

Kathleen didn't respond right away. "I would give a lot to have a family like yours."

"I know you lost your brother, but aren't you close to your parents? I would think they'd hang on even tighter to you after..."

From the corner of her eye, Kathleen saw Molly watching her. She wandered around the lighthouse, taking in the views of the island. Molly followed.

"I've been on Little Sister for over a month," Kathleen said. "And they just noticed."

Molly opened her mouth and closed it, clearly at a loss for what to say.

"Don't get me wrong," Kathleen said. "Part of it's my fault. I don't call or go to see them very often, so there's nothing unusual about us going months without speaking."

"What about the woman you were with? You said you left. That must have been rough."

Kathleen sighed. "You'd think so, wouldn't you?"

"Wasn't it?"

"Not as hard as it should have been."

"What did she do to you?"

"Who said she did anything to me?"

"Well, someone did something. That's a lot of years to walk away from."

Kathleen's cheeks burned. "Maybe it wasn't her. Maybe it was me."

Molly studied her with narrowed eyes. "No."

"No what?"

"She cheated. Or lied. Or both."

Kathleen walked away around the lighthouse. *It's like my life. I can walk away, but I keep circling back to the same place.*

Another couple climbed up to the balcony, his arm around her as they looked out over what probably was a really romantic view, Kathleen realized. Molly kept her distance. The couple ambled around the balcony, smiling and nodding at Kathleen, and then descended the spiral stairs again.

Molly came to her. "Sorry. Didn't mean to pry."

"It's not you," Kathleen said. She shook her head. "Love can die a slow death. It doesn't always come in a huge blow that breaks your heart. It can die a little at a time, small pricks to your heart that leave you bleeding until, one day, it just stops. And you can't remember if you ever had a heart."

Molly leaned with her back to the balcony railing, her arms crossed. "But what was the source of all those pricks?"

Kathleen bit her lip. She scuffed the toe of her sneaker over the grid of the balcony floor. "Have you ever thought you could save someone? If you could just love her enough, you could make everything else better?"

Molly waited without answering.

"I met Susannah in college. I fell for her immediately, and I just never went away. She tried to push me away. But I knew, that's not what she really wanted. It was a test, of how much I cared. So I stayed. No matter what she said or did, or what her family said or did, I was always there. But after fourteen goddamned years..."

"I thought you said you lived with her for twelve years."

"Two in college, twelve after."

Kathleen turned away, lifting her glasses to wipe her sleeve across her eyes. Molly was still studying her.

"The other person has to want to be saved," Molly said softly. "You can't do it for her."

Kathleen tried to smile but couldn't quite pull it off. "And she doesn't want it. She told me, for the hundredth time, to get the hell out, but when I did..."

"Now she wants you back."

Kathleen nodded.

"For what, if nothing has changed?"

Kathleen snorted. "Good question."

Molly was quiet for so long, Kathleen risked a glance in her direction.

"What are you going to do?" Molly asked.

Kathleen felt trapped by those eyes staring into her, into her soul it seemed...

Voices echoed from inside the lighthouse. A moment later, four children erupted from its staircase, racing around the circular balcony, shouting and chasing one another.

Kathleen turned and led the way back down the stairs.

⬛⬛⬛⬛⬛⬛

MOLLY DELIBERATELY KEPT THE conversation light as they roamed more of the island. She let Kathleen buy her an ice cream cone, and they had lunch at The Lobster Pot, where they did meet Brandi.

"My brother, Matty, says hi," Molly told her as she brought their drinks and took their order.

"Oh," Brandi said, her eyes lighting up. "Is he by any chance coming to Big Sister any time soon?"

"Depends on the catch," Molly said. "He said he'd come when he can."

"Cool." Brandi snatched up their menus. "Be right back with your food."

"So," Kathleen said in a low voice as Brandi sashayed away to place their order, "is she your type?"

Molly choked on her Coke. "You heard that?"

Kathleen grinned.

"Well..." Molly pretended to eye Brandi studiously. "She's not bad. Pretty face, nice smile, firm..." She paused and grimaced at Kathleen, who was trying not to laugh. "But she's so perky. If I had to listen to someone that happy every day, I'd go mad."

Kathleen did giggle, covering her mouth with her napkin.

They sat for a while, enjoying the harbor view through the restaurant's windows. Colorful sailboats bobbed in the water, while other boats, including some enormous yachts, sat moored at the marina.

Kathleen's attention seemed to be focused on the scene outside, but she asked, "What is your type then?"

Molly busied herself rearranging her silverware. "Um, I don't know that I really have a type."

"Isn't there anyone special?"

Molly felt heat rise from her neck to her cheeks. "Not now. I had a girlfriend when I was in college, but when I came back to Little Sister, we lost contact. There hasn't been anyone steady since then."

"That's a long time to go without having anyone in your life."

Molly forced her gaze upward to meet Kathleen's. She opened her mouth to respond when Brandi returned with their food.

"Crab cakes for you," she sang, setting a plate in front of Molly, "and clam chowder for you." She set a steaming bowl in front of Kathleen along with a plate of cheese biscuits. "Enjoy."

Molly hoped Kathleen would forget where the conversation had left off, but she spooned up some of her chowder, letting it cool, and said, "You were about to answer, I think."

Molly ate a bite of her crab cakes before saying, "I have people in my life. A whole island of them."

Kathleen searched her face. "It's not the same."

"Maybe," Molly acknowledged. "But it's true. Islanders don't get divorced. No one in my lifetime has. We don't marry young as a rule, because anyone we pair up with has to buy into living by Little Sister rules."

"Is that why all four of you still live with your parents?" Kathleen tilted her head. "That must be a little weird."

Molly had to smile. "I guess it is. But none of us want to leave the island, and until a house comes available..."

"Like Louisa and Olivia's?"

Molly nodded. "It's not something we talk about, but they don't have anyone to pass it to, so it's kind of an open secret that when they're gone, the house will be available."

"And how does that work?"

"If there's family, we have to wait a year to see if they claim the house."

"Like I did?"

Molly nodded.

"Why don't you just build more houses?"

"They did," Molly said. "In the beginning. But within two or three generations, they realized they'd run out of room quickly. You have to clear more trees, now we'd need more septic and water and electricity. We'd be completely out of balance. They decided to cap the houses to what existed at that time."

"I'm amazed how forward thinking they were."

Molly tore a cheese biscuit and popped a piece in her mouth. "It's basically our population control. If there is no family, then a house doesn't have to wait to be rehomed. Anyone who wants it can apply for it. If there's more than one, then the islanders hold a lottery in front of everyone."

Kathleen shook her head. "It's just so strange. I've never been around people who take care of one another like that."

She sounded so sad as she said it that Molly nearly reached across the table to take her hand. She caught herself in time and reached for her glass instead.

Kathleen ate her chowder, lost in her own thoughts, and Molly decided to let her be.

When Brandi brought the check, which Kathleen insisted on paying, she elicited one more promise from Molly to have Matty come see her soon.

Kathleen signed the slip and said, "What about that shopping list?"

They left the restaurant, and Molly pointed the way to a women's clothing boutique. A little bell announced their entrance. Kathleen wandered in one direction, Molly the other.

Kathleen held a lacy, sheer negligee high over the clothing racks. "How about this for your mom?"

Molly closed her eyes and held her hands up to block the view. "I don't even want to think about what my parents would do with that. I think I'll stick to her favorite perfume."

"Coward." But Kathleen smiled as she said it.

They spent a couple of hours going through several shops. One of Kathleen's favorites was a bookstore where she picked up five new books. When they had completed their shopping—including a new multi-tool for Joe—they made their way back to the vet's office. Molly waited in the lobby while Kathleen was taken to an exam room to speak with the vet.

She and Blossom emerged a little while later. Molly held his leash while Kathleen paid the bill.

"You're a little drunk, aren't you, buddy?" she asked as he leaned against her leg.

He grinned up at her and wagged his tail sluggishly.

They took their time walking back to the marina, letting Blossom set the pace. Kathleen carried a small inflatable vinyl ring.

"No cone of shame?" Molly asked.

Kathleen held the ring up. "Just this, if he needs it. The vet said he's probably about a year old."

Molly gave him a pat. "We can make today his birthday. Not a very nice birthday present, was it?"

She glanced at Kathleen. "When's your birthday?"

Kathleen's cheeks turned pink as she pointed to a shop they hadn't gone into. "Too bad we didn't have more time."

Molly decided not to press the point about the birthday. When they got to the boat, she picked Blossom up.

"Just steady the boat for me," she said to Kathleen. She carried him on board and down the steps into the tiny cabin.

She laid him on one of the bunks. Kathleen followed her down with a blanket.

"Are you sure?" she asked. "He can lie on the floor."

"Oh, not this time," Molly said, rubbing his head as his eyes closed. "He's had a rough day. Shots and—whatnot. He doesn't even know the whatnot isn't there anymore."

They knelt side by side next to the bunk, both of them stroking his soft coat. He sighed deeply.

"This has been the nicest day I can remember in a very long time," Kathleen said in a low voice.

She looked at Molly, her eyes soft and unguarded. Without thinking, Molly leaned toward her. All she knew was the warmth of Kathleen's breath on her face as she met soft lips. She took her time, savoring the feel, the taste of Kathleen's mouth.

When she pulled away, Kathleen's eyes searched her face. Molly felt frozen in place, held there by the ache in her own heart. Kathleen reached up to place gentle fingers on Molly's cheek, drawing her in. Kathleen's lips parted, pressing hungrily to Molly's.

Molly was breathing hard when the kiss broke. She rested her forehead against Kathleen's.

"Stay down here where it's warm," she whispered. "I'll get us home."

※※※※※※※※※※

KATHLEEN SAT IN FRONT OF her computer monitor and realized she'd been staring at nothing for the last fifteen minutes. She grabbed her coffee cup only to find it empty.

Blossom opened one eye when she stood.

"Want to go out?"

He curled into a tighter ball in his bed. She smiled.

"Okay. You stay comfortable. You went through enough yesterday."

She went into the kitchen to refill her cup. Outside, everything was dripping and sodden, thanks to a storm that had blown through during the night. She was glad to have an excuse to stay in. *To avoid Molly, you mean.*

She stepped out onto the back porch and closed her eyes, feeling a tingle in her stomach at the memory of that kiss.

What the hell were you thinking? Why did you kiss her?

But oh... the things that kiss had done to her, body and heart. It was the last thing she'd expected.

But exactly what you hoped for, that nagging voice forced her to admit.

She pressed her fingers to her lips. She hadn't been kissed like that since... Her eyes flew open. She'd never been kissed like that. Every kiss with Susannah had been rushed, furtive, as if she expected her bastard of a father to walk in on them at any minute. And sex—it was always sex, never lovemaking, she realized as she thought about it—like two horny teenagers sneaking a quick grapple and getting it over with as quickly as possible, rarely even getting completely naked with each other.

But with Molly, Kathleen wanted to make love with her. Wanted her naked. Wanted to explore that wonderful body, wanted to take her time, touching and kissing and tasting every inch of her. A powerful throb between her legs had her half-ready to grab her car keys and go in search of Molly, right then and there.

Her telephone jangled, startling her out of her preoccupation. She went back inside. This phone hardly ever rang. It was probably Olivia or Louisa, wanting to bring something by.

She picked up the receiver. "Hello?"

"Hello, yourself."

Kathleen collapsed onto one of the kitchen chairs, her legs suddenly too weak to hold her. It was a moment before she could speak. "Suze. How did you get this number?"

"The nice lady here at the market connected me."

Despite the "nice lady" comment and the surface politeness, Kathleen heard the ice underneath. It took a second for the implication to sink in.

"You're here? On Little Sister?"

"I am. I've got directions. I'll be there in a few minutes."

Chapter 8

MOLLY CURSED UNDER HER breath as she lay on her back under Wilma and Nels's kitchen sink, connecting hot and cold water hoses to the new faucet she'd installed in their new stainless steel bowl. Their small house was an extension off the back of the hotel, giving them their private space, but keeping them close enough to heed calls from guests.

After she'd canceled on them to take Kathleen to Big Sister, she'd felt obligated to get to this job at the first opportunity.

Part of why she was cursing was that her mind was more on Kathleen than on what she was doing. She couldn't stop picturing Kathleen's face, remembering the feel of Kathleen's lips on hers...

The telephone rang, and Molly jumped, cursing more loudly when she banged her head on the U-bend.

Wilma bustled into the kitchen and answered the phone.

"Oh, hello, Miranda."

Molly rubbed the lump already forming on her forehead and went back to work.

"You're kidding," Wilma said.

Molly shook her head. More island gossip. She adjusted her wrench and slipped it over the nut to tighten it.

"Really? On today's ferry? And Katie didn't know?"

Molly froze.

"But she's going there now?"

Molly held her breath.

"Okay. I'll talk to you later."

Wilma hung up and immediately dialed another number. "Olivia, you'll never guess. Katie Halloran's *friend* showed up unannounced on today's ferry. She's on the way to Maisie's house now."

Molly listened hard, her heart thumping.

"Okay. You and Louisa meet me at the diner."

Wilma hung up and trotted off toward the hotel and diner. Molly wriggled out from under the sink. With a regretful glance at the unfinished plumbing, she abandoned her tools. She scribbled a quick note to Wilma before dashing to her SUV to race home.

She skidded to a stop in the drive and ran up the back steps. Flinging the door open, she shouted, "Mom! Where are you? I need—"

She halted mid-sentence as Jenny walked out of the pantry and hung the phone up on the wall.

"You know," Molly said.

"Yes." Jenny gestured toward a kitchen chair. "Sit down."

Molly didn't want to sit. She opened her mouth to argue, but caught the look in her mother's eye. She sat.

Jenny poured two cups of coffee and joined her. "Now, tell me what's going on."

Molly took a sip of coffee, trying to figure out just how to start. She'd never actually come out to her parents, not in words. It had just been accepted without having to say it that Molly was gay. Why did this suddenly feel so hard?

"Kathleen, when she came here, left a relationship," she began. "From what she says, it wasn't a good relationship."

"And now the other woman has come here," Jenny said.

Molly nodded. "I guess so." She jabbed her chin at the phone. "You probably know more than I do."

Jenny smiled. "Wildfire. The island hasn't had this much excitement in years."

"Mom..." Molly frowned at her coffee. "We have to help her."

"Help her? I would have thought this would solve all your problems."

Molly hesitated, thinking hard. "What problems?"

"Weren't you the one who kept insisting she didn't belong here?" Jenny reminded her casually.

That seemed so long ago, Molly could barely remember when she felt that way.

"And, if she leaves, the cottage will most likely be available to another. You or the boys could enter the lottery if that's what you want."

Molly struggled to find the words to say everything she was feeling. "Kathleen is just starting to set anchor, to feel she belongs somewhere. The island is her home now. We can't let this woman drag her away."

She felt her mother's probing gaze—that "mom-stare" she'd hated growing up—and forced herself to meet her mother's eyes.

"What if this is what she wants, Mo?"

Molly stared helplessly at her mom. "If it's what she wants, then she should go with her. I won't say another word."

Jenny reached out and grasped Molly's hand. "Do you love her?"

"What? No, of course not." Molly pulled her hand away and stood. "I've only known her, what? Six weeks? Why would you ask that?"

Jenny sipped her coffee, her eyes following Molly over the rim of the cup as she paced the kitchen. Wordlessly, she waited.

Molly stopped, her eyes closed as she remembered that kiss. She ran both hands through her hair. "I don't know."

Jenny set her cup down. "Go to the marina. Get your uncle to keep the ferry here a few extra hours."

"How?"

"I don't care." Jenny stood and went to the phone. "Take the damned engine apart if you have to. Just keep that ferry here until we're ready."

※※※※※※※※※

KATHLEEN STOOD ON THE porch, her arms wrapped tightly around herself, as she watched for Susannah's car. She briefly considered locking herself inside and not answering the door, but that was ridiculous. Her heart pounded so hard, she could hear it thumping. When Susannah's white Lexus pulled in behind her Altima, she found herself holding her breath. She leaned against the porch pillar, as much to prop herself up as to try and appear nonchalant.

Susannah got out and stood looking at her. The sight of her almost took away what breath Kathleen still had—but not the way it used to. Not in the *God, she's so beautiful, what does she see in me?* kind of way, though she was still beautiful. It was more *Now you have to face the consequences of your decisions. No more running away.*

Her silky dark hair framed her face, falling just short of the collar of her camelhair coat. Designer jeans and expensive-looking boots completed what Kathleen was sure had been a carefully chosen look. Her eyes moved down Kathleen, taking in her baggy sweater and faded jeans. Kathleen fought the impulse to apologize for how she was dressed.

She didn't say anything as Susannah pulled a suitcase from the back seat of her car and walked up to the porch steps. Kathleen couldn't read her face. A smile was firmly fixed on her mouth, but it didn't quite match the coolness in her eyes.

118

"Aren't you going to welcome me?" Susannah asked.

Kathleen had a sudden vision of how she would normally have been stumbling down the steps to take the bag from Susannah, to hug her, to escort her inside. She saw a flicker of irritation in Susannah's eyes as she did none of those things.

Blossom, who was still moving gingerly, hid behind Kathleen's legs, his tail tucked between his legs.

"What is that?" Susannah asked.

Kathleen laid a calming hand on his head, realizing he must be feeling her tension. She hadn't even thought about how Susannah would react to him—*I didn't have time to think about anything*—given that Susannah had always adamantly refused to allow them to have any kind of pet, claiming she was allergic. Funny, she never seemed to be allergic when she was interacting stiffly with friends' pets, a fact she refuted whenever Kathleen pointed it out to her.

"This is my dog."

"Your dog." Susannah stared up at her, and Kathleen could almost see the wheels turning as she quickly recalibrated how to deal with Kathleen. "You've been here a month and you have a dog."

"It's been a month and a half, and I have a dog."

If Susannah had any criticisms of that decision, she swallowed them as she climbed the steps, clearly waiting to be invited in.

Kathleen opened the door, following Susannah inside. She held the door for Blossom, but he dropped to his belly, his ears flat against his head.

"It's okay," she murmured.

She watched warily as Susannah walked through the ground-floor rooms, looking around. She took her coat off to reveal a form-fitting sweater that showed off her curves.

"This is charming," Susannah said. "Why didn't we ever come here?"

Kathleen stared at her. "This was my grandmother's house, remember? You never wanted anything to do with my family, and I—"

She stopped.

Susannah turned around, her perfectly groomed eyebrows raised in question. "You what? What were you going to say?"

Kathleen found herself breathing hard considering she wasn't doing anything but standing there. Her jaw worked back and forth for a moment. "I was too afraid to go against you, to come without you."

Susannah nodded slowly. "So you're blaming me?"

"No." Kathleen released the breath she'd been holding. "I'm blaming me. For being too afraid to start an argument. With you or my father. For hiding behind that all the years I never came to see my grandmother before she died."

Susannah opened her mouth, but just then, another car pulled into the driveway with a honk of the horn.

Kathleen went to the front door to find Wilma reaching into the trunk of her car and retrieving...

"A slow cooker," Kathleen said with a smile.

"Yoo-hoo," Wilma called.

Kathleen stepped onto the porch as Wilma climbed the steps. Blossom's back end wagged in greeting.

"Katie, Nels is trying a new recipe, and I heard you had unexpected company," Wilma said as she pushed past Kathleen into the cottage. "Oh, hello, dear," she said to Susannah. "Well, aren't you a pretty thing?"

She walked past Susannah into the kitchen. "Land sakes, I completely forgot. Katie, there's a basket of rolls in the back seat. You go get that, and I'll dish out some of this stew."

"We don't want stew," Susannah said, but Kathleen was already jogging out to Wilma's car.

Behind her, she heard Wilma saying, "Oh, tut. It's a bit early for supper, but you haven't had my Nels's seafood stew. Best cook in Maine, he is."

When she came back inside with the rolls—Blossom followed her and made a dash for the safety of the dining table—Susannah glared at her. As Kathleen sailed by her toward the kitchen, she realized how that glare would have cowed her once upon a time.

"Here are the rolls, Wilma. Oh, that stew smells wonderful."

Wilma, who obviously knew her way around the kitchen, was getting three bowls down from the cupboard. "I knew you didn't have time to prepare anything for your guest."

She pointed to another cupboard and said to Susannah, "Would you be a dear and get three glasses down?"

Susannah hesitated, and Kathleen knew she was waiting for her to send Wilma home. Instead, Kathleen said, "I'll get bread plates and butter."

Left with no choice, Susannah poured three glasses of water and set them on the table where Wilma was settling herself into a chair with the aromatic bowls of stew.

"It's freezing in here," Susannah complained as she dropped into a chair.

"I'm fine," Kathleen said, tugging on the collar of the shawl sweater she wore.

"Got to dress warm in November, dear," Wilma said cheerily. "We're not in Florida."

She turned to Kathleen. "Now tell me if you think it needs anything. We're thinking of putting it on the menu and want to make sure it's right."

Kathleen took a few bites, ignoring the harsh vibes almost bouncing off her from Susannah's direction. "I think it could use a bit more pepper and maybe not so much onion. What do you think?"

Wilma smacked her lips as she took another spoonful. "I think you may be right."

She chatted merrily as they ate, trying to draw Susannah into the conversation. Susannah grudgingly answered Wilma's questions.

When they were done eating, Wilma carried the bowls to the sink. "Nels will be delighted to hear you liked it. I'll leave you two to visit now. You don't have long, after all."

"What does that mean?" Susannah demanded.

"Well the ferry will be leaving at three, won't it?" Wilma said with a chuckle.

"So? I can catch another ferry in a few days," Susannah said.

"There won't be another ferry for a month," Kathleen said.

"What?"

"How did you happen to catch it today?" Kathleen asked.

"I just called to make a reservation, and they said they had tickets for today. I assumed the other days were booked."

Kathleen left Susannah standing there, her mouth hanging open, to walk Wilma out the door. Wilma turned to her, placing her hands on either side of Kathleen's face. Without speaking, she gazed into Kathleen's eyes for a moment before giving her a tight hug.

Kathleen felt the tension leave her shoulders as she waved goodbye to Wilma and turned to go back inside.

⬚⬚⬚⬚⬚⬚⬚

A FIRE CRACKLED IN the grate. Kathleen had pulled the overstuffed chair and Nanna's rocker closer to its warmth. Blossom remained curled up under the dining table, watching them from behind the protection of the chair legs.

"You know I didn't mean the things I said," Susannah said, her voice choked with tears.

Kathleen kept her eyes glued on the flames. *Don't look at her. Don't, don't, don't...* How many times had Susannah said that over the years? And how many times had Kathleen said, "I know you didn't." But not anymore.

"Then why did you say them?" she asked.

From the corner of her eye, she saw Susannah stiffen, and she knew that simple question had signaled a change in how this was going to work.

"You know how my family makes me crazy," Susannah said.

"I do." Kathleen leaned forward and poked the logs, sending showers of sparks up the flue. "When I met you, I thought I could take that away. I thought I could make up for what you need that they don't give you, but I can't. No one can."

"What does that mean?"

There were no tears now, no catch in Susannah's voice.

Kathleen had no desire to hurt her, even after everything that had happened between them. She took a deep breath and forced herself to look Susannah in the eye. "Your father does make you crazy. Your whole family does. We're thirty-four now. It's time for you to stop using them as an excuse. Obviously, no matter how much I loved you, it wasn't enough. You need to get counseling, Susannah. Or don't. Let them continue to yank you around. But either way, you're going to have to do it without me. I can't continue to be someone you're ashamed of."

Susannah stared at her, and Kathleen saw the emotions—the surprise, the disbelief—parading through her mind, reflected in her eyes.

"Kath, you can't mean that. I love you."

She shifted and came to kneel in front of the rocker, her hands on Kathleen's knees. A smile tugged on one corner of her mouth—that half-smile that had always melted Kathleen's heart.

"I know you love me back." Susannah reached up to caress Kathleen's cheek. "I'm sorry I hurt you. You know how much you mean to me. We can't throw fourteen years away. Please come back. I can't live without you."

Kathleen looked into her eyes and, just for a moment, tried to imagine what it would be like to go back.

From the dining room, Blossom whined. She turned to him as the mantel clock chimed two o'clock, and she knew the answer. Just as she opened her mouth, the telephone rang.

Susannah placed both hands on the arms of the rocking chair, blocking Kathleen in. "Let it ring."

A month ago, she would have, Kathleen realized. *A month ago, I'd already be packing.* The telephone shrilled insistently. She slid the rocker back, almost making Susannah fall as she lost her balance. Kathleen pushed to her feet and went into the kitchen.

"Hello?" She frowned. "Slow down. Miss Louisa, tell me again, what happened?"

After listening to a garbled account, she said, "I'll be right there." She slammed the handset on the hook. "I have to go."

Susannah gaped. "What do you mean, you have to go?"

"Someone is hurt. I have to go." Kathleen snatched a jacket from a hook near the door. "You're welcome to wait here until it's time to go to the ferry."

"I'm not going anywhere," Susannah said mulishly, her hands on her hips.

"Suit yourself." Kathleen patted her thigh, and Blossom came scrambling from between the dining chairs to bound out the front door.

"Wait for me!"

Susannah followed her out onto the porch, pulling her own coat on. She opened the passenger door of Kathleen's car and got in. Kathleen maneuvered around Susannah's Lexus and drove as quickly as she could to the Woodhouse sisters' home.

She skidded to a stop in the drive. Blossom jumped out of the back seat, and Kathleen ran to the front door, leaving Susannah to follow. Louisa met her on the porch, wringing her hands.

"Oh, Katie, thank you for coming," she said. "I didn't know what to do."

"Where is she?"

"Right in here." Louisa trotted ahead, taking her by the hand and pulling her into the living room where Olivia was lying on the sofa, her arms wrapped around her ribs, groaning. Blossom whined softly and gave her leg a tiny lick.

"What happened?"

"Ollie was on a ladder," Louisa said. "I've told her time and again, we're too old for that nonsense. But she was on the ladder and missed a step coming down. She fell ten feet."

"It was not ten feet," Olivia gasped through gritted teeth. "Maybe six."

"Have you called anyone else?" Kathleen asked, kneeling next to the couch, her hands hovering, unsure what to do or where it was safe to touch.

"Well, I called Molly," Louisa said. "She is the sheriff, but she was out somewhere. So I called you."

"She probably broke some ribs."

They all turned to Susannah, who stood there watching.

"This is Susannah," Kathleen said absently. "She's right. We need to get you to a hospital."

"No, no hospital," Olivia panted.

Kathleen took her hand. "You might have internal bleeding. You have to be examined by a doctor."

She stood and turned to Louisa. "We'll need help to get her to the marina."

⊠⊠⊠⊠⊠⊠⊠⊠⊠⊠

IT SEEMED HALF THE island had crowded into the sisters' living room. Everyone was talking at once as the islanders milled around. Little Sister didn't have anything that resembled an ambulance, but they did have a stretcher. It looked to Kathleen as if it was World War II vintage—olive-green canvas stretched between wooden poles. Someone had padded it with several blankets. They set it on the floor, and the four Cooper men gathered around Olivia to lower her to the stretcher. She let out a cry as they moved her.

Wilma stood with her arm wrapped around Louisa's shoulders as she dabbed at her eyes with a lacy handkerchief.

"This place is like something out of an Alfred Hitchcock movie," Susannah said in an undertone to Kathleen. "No hospital, no way to get help. You have got to get out of here."

Kathleen moved away to help cover Olivia with more blankets.

"Boys," Joe said.

Aidan, Matty, and Joey joined him at the four corners of the stretcher. Together, they picked it up and carried it outdoors to the bed of a pickup that Tim Shannahan had backed up to the porch. They eased the stretcher as gently as they could into the truck. Olivia let out another cry of pain. Joe and Aidan climbed into the bed with her as Tim maneuvered his way out of the drive.

"Katie." Louisa came to her. "I know I shouldn't ask, but would you come with me? I have to go with her, but I don't want to go alone."

Kathleen took her hand. "Of course, but wouldn't you rather..." She glanced toward Wilma and Jenny, who had their heads together with Rebecca. Something was odd.

Louisa squeezed her hand. "Please."

"Let me put a few things together," Kathleen said. "I'll meet you at the marina."

"Oh, thank you." Louisa gave her a watery smile.

The only person Kathleen hadn't seen was Molly. She didn't want to think about why that disappointed her so much.

Susannah followed her out the door to where she had parked. She called for Blossom, but he was nowhere to be found.

She had to wait for a few people to move their cars before she could drive back to the cottage.

"This is for the best," Susannah was saying. "We'll get back to civilization, and things will get back to normal. You'll see."

Kathleen felt cold and empty as she packed a small bag with a few things: a change of clothes and undies, pajamas, bathroom items.

She checked that her wallet was in her purse before she powered off all of her computers and monitors. In the kitchen, Blossom's food bowl sat. She filled it to overflowing and put it and his water dish on the back porch, along with his bed, hoping he'd be okay until she came back.

Are you coming back?

That thought hit her like a freight train. She felt she was caught in some kind of undertow that was pulling her away from her life here, dragging her away no matter how hard she fought the current.

"I'll drive us to the marina," Susannah said. She came to Kathleen and kissed her gently. "You'll see how much better things will be once we're away from here."

Kathleen's throat was tight as she locked the cottage and followed Susannah to her Lexus. She scanned the bushes and trees in the gathering dusk, looking for any sign of Blossom, but there was nothing.

She didn't say anything as Susannah drove back into town to where the ferry idled, waiting.

Fred was there, waving Susannah on board, guiding her to a parking place in between two large crates.

Kathleen got out of the car.

"Katie, Bobby said Miss Olivia is askin' for you," Fred said loudly, pointing to the pilothouse. "Bring your things with you," he added in a whisper.

"Miss," he said to Susannah as she also got out. "I need to have you move just a little further forward. It'll only take a minute."

Susannah frowned at him, but Kathleen pulled her purse and bag out of the back seat and left them to go find Bobby. He met her at the ferry's cabin.

"Where's Miss Olivia?" she asked, looking at the completely empty cabin where she'd expected to find Olivia's stretcher.

"Everything's going to be okay, Katie," he said, grinning at her. He put a fatherly arm around her shoulders and steered her toward the gangplank.

"But..." She stopped, pointing back at the ferry. "Miss Olivia..."

"Is waiting for you." He nodded toward the wharf, where Olivia stood with Louisa, Jenny, Wilma and Nels in his apron, Tim and Miranda, Rebecca, the Cooper boys—nearly everyone she knew on the island.

"But..." she said again.

"You'd best get going. This ferry's already over an hour late. I'm shoving off and won't be back for a month."

He gave her a gentle push. She trotted over the gangplank to the wharf. Joe pulled the gangplank as the ferry tooted its horn and began to chug away. Fred waved from the deck. Susannah appeared, and even from this distance, Kathleen could see the fury on her face.

She turned to Louisa and Olivia. "How...? Aren't you hurt?"

"Not a bit," Olivia said.

Kathleen stood with her mouth open. She looked from one of them to another. "You made it all up? Why would you do that?"

Rebecca gave her a cryptic smile. "You're one of ours now. We're not going to let you go without a fight."

People clapped her on the shoulders or gave her hugs. At the back of the crowd, she saw Molly watching her. For a moment, everyone else disappeared as they locked eyes.

"I think we all need to celebrate," Wilma said loudly. "Everyone come to the diner. Pie's on us!"

Kathleen paused to look back at the ferry as it chugged away. She knew she hadn't heard the end of this.

Louisa hooked her arm through Kathleen's. "Come with us, Katie."

Chapter 9

FROM HIS BED, BLOSSOM lifted his head at a particularly loud gust of wind that rattled the windows.

"It's okay," Kathleen murmured from her chair where she was sketching him. "You don't have to live in that anymore."

He looked at her, and she could have sworn he understood her. With a contented sigh, he curled up again.

She gazed out the window at the gray day. Turbulent clouds rolled across the sky, blocking all sunlight. It was only two in the afternoon, but it could have been five, it was so dark. She had a roast in the slow cooker with potatoes and carrots. The aroma was already spreading through the house. She set aside her sketchpad and pencil.

"Want to go for a walk before the rain gets here?"

Blossom was up in an instant, waiting for her to pull on a jacket and hat. Outside, he chose the trail that led down to the beach, and Kathleen willingly followed.

The wind tore the few remaining leaves from trees as the gusts whistled through the branches. Over it all, she heard the crashing of the sea.

At the bottom of the trail, there was no beach. The tide was up, and the waves were washing all the way up to the rocky sea wall. Out on the ocean, whitecaps rolled and spray flew.

Blossom chased gulls as they hopped around in the surf when the waves retreated, looking for anything edible in the foam. Kathleen stood watching them, warm inside despite the cold gale.

"You're one of ours now," Rebecca had said.

She hadn't felt that sense of belonging since she was ten years old. She'd come to realize over these past weeks that she could have had that long ago if she'd returned back here, back to Nanna. But she hadn't. Somehow, she had to find a way to live with that.

Blossom stopped, his ears forward, staring at something farther down the sea wall.

A figure stumbled over the rocks, falling to hands and knees in the surf. From the way his head was hanging, he appeared to be getting sick. Whoever it was sank back onto his haunches, raising his face to the sky, and Kathleen realized it was Aidan.

She stood for a minute, trying to decide if she should go to him, but she saw Molly clambering over the rocks. She knelt in the surf beside him, one arm around his shoulders. His head was hanging and his shoulders shook. Molly bent near, apparently talking to him. He shook his head and tried to push her away, but he toppled over just as a wave washed over him. She helped him to his hands and knees as he coughed. She stood and hauled him to his feet. With his arm draped over her shoulders and her arm around his waist, she helped him back over the rocks to her SUV and got him inside. As she came around to the driver's side, she saw Kathleen and stopped.

For a long moment, they looked at each other, the wind whipping Molly's hair. Then she got in and drove away.

Kathleen stood, letting the wind buffet her. She and Molly hadn't spoken since the day they'd gone to Big Sister, *since we kissed.* And then the whole thing with Susannah felt like a wall had been dropped between them. Kathleen hadn't called or sought Molly out. She didn't know what to say. But Molly hadn't come by, either. *Maybe we should just leave it at a kiss.*

She called to Blossom. He bounded in her direction, barking at the circling gulls. Together, they made their way back to the cottage as the first raindrops began to splatter.

※※※※※※※

THE STORM RAGED, THE rain turning to sleet and then to snow as the system intensified. Aidan was in his room, sleeping off his latest drunk. Molly had needed Joey's help to sneak him upstairs where they had dumped him on his bed and pulled his wet clothes off him.

"I'm not going any further than that," Molly said firmly when they had stripped him down to his boxers. She threw a blanket over him and left.

In her room—"Thank God I have my own room," she mumbled—she peeled herself out of her own soggy clothes.

She changed into sweats and flopped onto her bed. Switching on the bedside lamp, she opened the murder mystery she'd been reading and tried to get into the story. A few minutes later, she was lying with the book splayed across her stomach.

Kathleen.

Why did she rattle Molly so? What the hell was it about her that made Molly want to take care of her? She slapped the book shut and pushed herself up to sit on the edge of the bed.

She'd meant to go back out there and check the oil in Kathleen's tank. If the weather turned, there was always a good chance the oil tanker wouldn't get back here for a December run, though they tried

131

hard. But she hadn't made it, finding all kinds of excuses not to go by the Halloran cottage. Ever since the trip to Big Sister—*ever since you kissed her, you mean*—everything felt more awkward.

Almost forgotten in the crazy drama the day the ferry came—with Kathleen's girlfriend—Bobby and Fred had brought the Thanksgiving turkeys and fixings for the market, as well as some Christmas trees. Down in the kitchen, she heard her mom rattling around, probably baking more pies. Molly doubted they'd last the week between now and Thanksgiving, but she sure liked having pumpkin and apple and pecan pie in the house. She went to the window, staring out at the swirling snow.

Giving up on her book, she went downstairs. The scent of cinnamon and cloves and nutmeg filled the house.

"Can I help?"

Jenny looked up from where she was rolling out dough. "Yes."

The surprised tone of her voice shamed Molly that she didn't do this often enough. The boys never did, Molly thought resentfully, and it didn't seem to bother them one little bit.

Jenny put her to work peeling and slicing apples.

"How's your brother?"

Molly dropped her apple. She scrambled to pick it up before Minnow could bat it around the floor. She rinsed it at the sink.

"What do you mean?"

"Molly, I'm not stupid." Jenny kept her head down, leaning on her rolling pin.

"I know you're not."

"None of you have ever snuck by me." Jenny's mouth twitched. "Even when you thought you could climb down from your bedroom window without me knowing."

Molly gaped at her mother for a minute and then resumed peeling her apple. She dropped a curly strip of peel for Minnow to play with.

"You know about Aidan then?"

"It's a small island, Mo. Hard to hide anything here." Jenny wrapped the flattened dough around her rolling pin and laid it over the pie plate. "What set him off this time?"

"Who knows?" Molly heard the resentful edge in her own voice, but she couldn't help it. "The storm? He never says. Just promises it won't happen again. Until it does."

Jenny was quiet for a moment as she pressed the dough into the plate. She picked up a bowl of pumpkin mixed with spices and poured it into the waiting dough.

"Your father and I know it's kind of weird, growing up on this island. On the mainland, you and your brothers would all have moved out into places of your own."

"Maybe not Joey," Molly said.

Jenny chuckled. "Okay, maybe not Joey. But it's not normal for thirty-somethings to still be living under their parents' roof. We've tried to leave you to make your own decisions about coming and going, who you spend time with, and how you spend it."

Molly had never really thought of her parents actively deciding to let them live their lives. "We've tried to be respectful of you and Dad."

"We know that. We can't help but worry when the boys are out fishing, or when you're up on someone's roof, but for the most part, I think we've achieved a good balance."

Jenny smoothed the pie filling with a spatula before sliding the pie plate into the oven.

"But we have to do something about Aidan," she said quietly.

Molly bit her lip. "I've tried. I don't know what to do for him. Or with him."

"He's never stopped blaming himself."

Molly set her apple and knife down, bracing her hands on the counter, her head bowed. "If there was one day I could undo, it would be that one."

Jenny leaned against the counter, wiping her floury hands on a towel. "What did you have to do with it?"

Molly closed her eyes, picturing the way Aidan and Joey and some of the other boys had surrounded Bryan, taunting him, calling him "offlander", daring him to prove himself.

"We all knew the storm was coming," she said in a hushed voice. "I tried to stop Aidan, but Joey grabbed my arms and held me. They shouldn't have gone out, but they were calling each other stupid names, and neither one wanted to back down. I should have fought harder, made Aidan listen."

Jenny reached out to tuck Molly's hair behind her ear. "You're no more to blame than Aidan. It was terrible, and they were foolish. You were kids. Where were the adults? Why didn't we stop it?"

Molly looked into her mother's tear-filled eyes. "You couldn't keep an eye on us every minute. The island kids knew better. Aidan thought he could get out to the buoy and back before the storm got here." She swiped her sleeve angrily across her own eyes. "I told him I didn't blame anyone, but I'm sick and tired of paying for his stupid mistake!"

"No more," Jenny said, folding her towel and taking a deep breath. "We're a family. When one of us is hurting, we all hurt. We'll all step up more to help Aidan."

Molly picked her apple back up and began to slice it while Jenny sifted flour for a new piecrust. For a few minutes, they worked in silence. Molly felt a bit calmer.

"I'd like you to invite Kathleen for Thanksgiving," Jenny said.

"Mom, no!" Molly put her knife back down.

"Why on earth not? That poor girl is alone. Do you really want her to spend the holiday by herself?"

Molly opened and closed her mouth. She huffed as she picked her knife up yet again and concentrated on her apple.

"Molly Ahearn Cooper, you got the whole island to help her when she needed it. And you're afraid to ask her to join us for dinner?"

Molly ground her teeth. "I'm not afraid."

She heard the amusement in her mom's voice as she said, "Well, that's that then."

⬚⬚⬚⬚⬚⬚⬚⬚

KATHLEEN HAD TO HUNT to find Nanna's snow shovel buried in a closet off the back porch, hidden behind brittle, old, rubber galoshes and several rakes. Blossom launched himself into a foot of snow that had drifted against the house in the winds. She threw a few snowballs for him, laughing when he stood staring down into the snow, wondering where they'd gone. She shoveled a path around the house and out to her car. She was sweeping the snow off her Nissan when Molly's SUV pulled into the drive.

For a long moment, she stared at Molly through the windshield. Her heart was pounding, as it had the day Susannah had shown up—*but it's not the same at all*, she thought.

Molly got out, holding something. "My mom sent you an apple pie."

She trudged through the snow, bracing herself when Blossom came barreling toward her. She grinned and patted his snow-covered head. "Hello, little man. Looks like you've recovered."

"I think he likes the snow," Kathleen said. She gestured toward the house. "Want a cup of coffee to go with a slice of pie?"

"Let me help you clean your car off first." Molly set the pie on her warm hood and reached into the back seat for a scraper.

Together, they brushed and swept the car clean.

Kathleen stood staring at her drive. "I'm not really sure why I bothered. It's not like this car can go anywhere in this much snow. I don't suppose the island has a plow?"

Molly laughed. "Not officially. A few people have plows for their trucks. Give it a day or two, and they'll have the ring road plowed enough to navigate." She looked down the long drive to the road. "I'll talk to one of them about coming by to plow this for you."

135

"Thanks. Come on in and get warm."

Molly followed her, stopping on the porch to stomp most of the snow off her boots. Inside, they both took their boots off, leaving them on a towel Kathleen had placed there.

Molly hung her jacket up while Kathleen used another towel to dry Blossom. When she straightened, her glasses were so steamed up that she could hardly see.

"I'll be right back," Kathleen said. She disappeared upstairs and returned a minute later with clear glasses and a pair of thick socks, her own feet now sporting fleecy slippers. "Your feet will be freezing."

Molly was leafing through some pencil sketches—mostly of Blossom—lying on the ottoman. "Sorry, hope you don't mind."

"I... no."

"These are really good."

"Thanks." Kathleen blushed and held out the socks.

Molly sat down to pull them on over hers. "You're being careful with your heat." She followed Kathleen into the kitchen. "I'll check your oil while I'm here. Our supply tank is low. I placed an order for oil. They'll get here if they can."

Kathleen scooped coffee into a filter. "They might not?"

Blossom curled up under the table, resting his head on his toy rabbit as he watched them.

"Depends on the weather. They try. Bobby will do everything he can to get here. He'll have most of the Christmas presents people have ordered, and more Christmas trees. He and Fred are kind of Little Sister's Santa Claus."

"I saw some Christmas trees down at the market. Why are we bringing trees over on the ferry?"

"We don't cut trees on Little Sister," Molly said.

"Ever?"

"Not if we can help it. We're not big enough to rotate timber cutting, and we need the trees we have to stabilize the soil against storms. Not everything grows in the salt air and winds."

Kathleen got two plates down from the cupboard while the coffee maker gurgled. "The people on this island have thought of everything."

"We've had to make do for a long time."

Kathleen reached into a drawer for a knife and forks. She sat down and looked into Molly's eyes. "Like figuring out how to get Susannah off the island?"

"Ah, that." Molly gave an embarrassed chuckle and looked down at her hands.

Kathleen was hungry after all that shoveling. She cut two generous slices of pie. "How much did you have to do with that?"

"It didn't take much," Molly said ruefully. "Just a nudge. Wilma and Mom were mostly responsible." She snuck a glance at Kathleen. "Was it okay that we interfered like that? Did you want her to stay? Or did you want to go?"

Rather than answer, Kathleen got up to pour the coffee. Standing with her back to Molly, she said, "I didn't want to go. And I didn't want her to stay. I was trying to get her to understand that when..." She came back to the table and set a mug in front of Molly. "Let's just say Wilma and Louisa's timing was perfect."

Molly grinned and ate a few bites.

"Oh, my gosh," Kathleen mumbled around a mouthful. "This is so good."

Molly nodded. "My mom is a very good cook." She poked at her pie with her fork. "She's pretty. Susannah."

"She is," Kathleen agreed. "I always thought she was beautiful. And I always wondered why she was with me."

Molly shook her head. "You shouldn't have wondered that."

Their eyes met, and Kathleen felt a flutter in her stomach.

"Was it hard? Seeing her?"

Kathleen gripped her coffee mug, trying to figure out how to explain. "It was hard not doing what I've always done," she said at last. "I've always accepted her apologies and said it was okay and that I knew she didn't really mean it. I didn't say any of those things this time."

Molly was still watching her. "How did she take that?"

"Not very well. And that was when Miss Louisa called."

Molly choked back a snort, and Kathleen grinned. A second later, they were both laughing so hard they had tears running down their faces.

"You should have seen Olivia," Kathleen said when she could talk. "That performance was Oscar-worthy."

"I didn't know they were going to do that," Molly said.

"But it worked." Kathleen took another forkful of pie. "I don't know how I would have gotten her back on that ferry. And to have her here for a month..."

The silence between them shifted. Kathleen felt the change, the tension.

"We haven't talked about what happened on the boat," Molly said softly.

"No." Kathleen kept her eyes lowered.

"Are you sorry?"

"No," Kathleen said quickly, raising her gaze to Molly's. "I'm not sorry, but..."

"But what?"

"What I said a minute ago, about not doing what I've done before. I don't want to repeat my mistakes." At the hurt expression on Molly's face, Kathleen reached out impulsively and took her hand. "You're not a mistake. That's not what I meant. But I've never been on my own. This is new to me, and I'm still trying to figure out who I am on my own. Can you understand that?"

Molly flipped her hand over to intertwine their fingers. "I can. When you've figured it out, I'll be here."

For a moment, the contact between them was electric. Kathleen stared at their hands. They looked so natural, linked together. *What are you waiting for?*

Reluctantly, Molly pulled her hand away.

"By the way, I've been instructed by my mom to invite you to our house for Thanksgiving."

"Really? I'm kind of surprised Little Sister does Thanksgiving. You know, the whole Pilgrim and Indian thing."

Molly grinned. "Well, my aunt would school you on how that really happened, but we mostly like to feast. We're more Whoville than Plymouth that way."

"Well, I'd love to come. Tell your mom I'll bring Nanna's sweet potatoes. I found the recipe. For some reason, there's lots and lots of brandy involved. Alcohol seems to be an island staple."

The smile slid off her face as soon as the words were out. "Molly, I'm so sorry."

Molly gazed into her coffee cup. "You don't need to apologize. It's not your fault. Aidan is going to have to figure out how to live with his mistakes." She sighed. "I'm not going to let them dictate my life any longer."

※※※※※※※※※

BLOSSOM'S COAT GLEAMED, thanks to a thorough brushing and a wiping down with a damp towel. It was too cold to give him a bath, but Kathleen was determined.

"You can't go there smelling like a dog."

Blossom just thumped a back foot against the floor when she found a tickly spot on his flank with the brush.

She checked the oven. The sweet potatoes were about done. She'd lined one of Nanna's baskets with a heavy towel to carry the hot pan.

With nothing left to do but wait until it was time to go, she sat at the kitchen table and nervously toyed with the handle of her coffee mug. She'd thought briefly about calling her parents to wish them a Happy Thanksgiving, but had hung the phone up without dialing.

Her mother was probably shut away in her room. Her father was most likely trying to close some real estate development deal. The same things they did every day. Holidays didn't change any of that.

She'd only gone home with Susannah the one time—it had been like walking a minefield. Everyone had been on edge, waiting to see if her father would explode. Kathleen herself, her mere presence, had been enough of a trigger to set him off. He wasn't a drunk. Even Kathleen's mother would have behaved better than he did. He was just a controlling, abusive bastard, Kathleen thought bitterly now. An executive with a local bank, supposed pillar of the community. The entire family worked to hide their dirty little secret. Part of her ached for the fact that Susannah couldn't or wouldn't distance herself from that mess.

You tried, she reminded herself. *She made her choices.*

The oven timer startled her. She pulled the potatoes out and set them on the stovetop to cool for a few minutes while she went upstairs to finish dressing.

Brushing her hair, she realized she needed a haircut. Not that her hair was styled in anything fancy, just layers that had hung above her collar when she'd arrived on the island. It was past her shoulders now. It was actually long enough to pull into a tail. She gathered it in her hand, studying the difference it made in how open her face was and decided to leave it loose.

She hadn't asked Molly how people would be dressed, but decided she couldn't go wrong with khakis and a sweater.

Outside, fresh snow covered the ground. She figured this would be a steady thing until spring. Blossom hopped into the back seat, settling on another towel she'd laid there. She placed the basket in the front passenger seat to be safe.

"Not that you've shown any interest in sweet potatoes," she said to him as she backed the car around. "But you're too young for the brandy."

Winding her way down the ring road, she waved at the people she passed, gathering at neighbors' houses. When she arrived at the Cooper house, Miss Olivia was just pulling in ahead of her. Louisa got out, waving enthusiastically. She retrieved their daddy's ashes from the back seat while Olivia pulled an enormous picnic hamper from her side.

Blossom trotted over politely.

"Hello, Katie," Louisa said, bending to give Blossom a pat.

"Happy Thanksgiving," Kathleen said.

She followed them to the house, only remembering as they opened the front door that the Coopers had a cat.

"I'm sorry," she said to Joe, who was there to greet them and take the heavy basket from Olivia. "I can take him back to the cottage."

"No need," Joe said, giving Blossom a rub. "We've had dogs. Minnow can hide if she doesn't like him."

The inside of the house smelled like heaven—all kinds of cooking smells, apple and cinnamon candles lit everywhere, the smoky smell of the fire.

Louisa and Olivia dove in to help Jenny in the kitchen. Joey and Matty were sitting in the family room.

"Best to stay out of the kitchen," Joey advised.

Kathleen hefted her basket. "Need to get this in there."

"Good luck," Matty said with a grin, stretching out and crossing his ankles.

Joey saluted. "If you don't emerge unscathed in five minutes, we'll come to get you."

"I won't," Matty said. "I'm not going anywhere near that henhouse. They'll put us to work."

Kathleen shook her head and cautiously stepped into the kitchen. Louisa grabbed her by the arm and steered her toward the table. Rebecca was curling triangles of dough into rolls on a baking sheet. She slid the sheet over to make room.

141

"Kathleen, we're so glad you could join us," Jenny said, glancing up from the stove, where she was dropping lobsters into a huge pot of boiling water.

"Thank you for inviting me." Kathleen reached into her basket and took out her pan of sweet potatoes. "These might need to be warmed up."

"We'll put them in the oven when the turkey comes out," Jenny said.

Molly opened the back door and stepped into the kitchen with an armful of wood. The smile on her face warmed Kathleen through and through. She wound her way through the kitchen to carry the logs out to the family room.

"Can I help?" Kathleen asked. "I don't want to be in the way. Joey and Matty made it sound like..."

"Oh, don't you worry." Jenny chuckled. "The boys will be doing the dishes after dinner. You and Molly could set the table. We've got everything covered in here."

She found Molly kneeling in front of the fireplace—*who knew jeans and flannel could look so sexy?*—settling another log in place and playfully swatting at Matty. "Move your big feet."

He grudgingly shifted.

"Your mom asked us to set the table," Kathleen said when Molly got up.

Molly went to the china hutch and handed stacks of dinner plates, bread plates and platters to Kathleen. She retrieved water glasses and the nice silverware.

"These are beautiful dishes," Kathleen said, turning one of the plates over to check the marks on the back.

"They've been in Mom's family for a few generations. They would have gone to Rebecca, but since she never married, she insisted Mom should have them."

The table had been stretched to its max with two leaves, but they still needed to squeeze a couple of extra chairs in.

"Remember one for Mr. Woodhouse," Molly said.

"Already counted him," Kathleen said, sliding an eleventh chair up to the table.

And if she stopped for a moment to consider how weird that would have been a couple of months ago, it was soon forgotten as she was caught up in the laughter around the table. Even Aidan—after an initial awkward nod in Kathleen's direction—seemed to enjoy himself, reaching over to poke a hole in Molly's mashed potato moat and let her gravy run onto her bread stuffing. She in turn grabbed his lobster, holding it up in the air until he apologized.

"They do this every year," Rebecca said, leaning near as Kathleen watched with a bemused smile. "Probably seems silly."

Kathleen sighed. "It's wonderful."

She tucked her hair behind her ear as she bent over her plate. "Who styles hair here on the island?"

"Oh, you have to go to George," Joey said.

Kathleen noted the evil glint in his eye. "Isn't George the barber in town?"

"Everybody who's anybody goes to George," Matty said, trying to keep a straight face. "Just ask Mo."

Molly's cheeks colored as she ducked her head. "Shut up."

Aidan grinned and pushed back from the table.

Molly's eyes opened wide. "You wouldn't."

"There's a reason we call her Mo," Joey teased.

Kathleen frowned. "I thought it was short for Molly."

"Nope." Aidan reappeared holding a frame.

"I'm gonna kill you," Molly muttered as Aidan turned the frame around with a flourish.

Kathleen clamped her mouth shut, fighting the urge to laugh at the photo of a very young Molly with a severe bowl cut. "I remember you now."

"Great. This she remembers."

"How old were you?"

"Eight, but she had this cut until she was fifteen!" Matty crowed. He and Joey almost fell out of their chairs laughing.

"George scarred me for life," Molly said dramatically.

Kathleen giggled. "I'll never look at the Stooges the same."

Jenny tugged the photo out of Aidan's hands. "Sit down. Stop teasing your sister."

Olivia shrugged philosophically. "It's only hair." Her silver bowl cut glinted as she bent over her plate.

"It's not only hair when you're a kid," Molly grumbled. "George only knows two cuts—this or a crew cut."

Kathleen looked around at the Coopers. "But your hair looks great."

"Mom cuts it now," Joey said.

"I'll be happy to do yours if you want," Jenny said. "But you can't hold me responsible if you're traumatized."

Kathleen grinned. "I promise not to complain."

A few hours later, Molly accompanied Kathleen out to her car, her basket now loaded with leftovers.

"I'm really glad you joined us," Molly said, opening the back door for Blossom.

"Me, too." Kathleen took the precaution of putting the basket in the trunk. Blossom might have ignored the sweet potatoes, but she didn't think his restraint would extend to turkey.

She came around the car and stood looking back at the house. "This... this was so nice." Her throat was suddenly too tight to speak.

"Hey," Molly said, reaching out to place a gentle hand on Kathleen's shoulder.

"You just don't know..." Kathleen sniffed. "Your family is so great. I've never had a holiday like this."

"You mean you were never embarrassed by your older brother?"

Kathleen gazed out over the trees. "Bryan did tease. I'd forgotten. Our family used to be happy. Before."

Molly lowered her hand. "I guess it was hard on your parents, after he died."

Kathleen felt as if a stone had dropped into her stomach. "Yeah. I guess it was."

She opened the car door. "Thank your mom and dad again for me."

Molly opened her mouth, but Kathleen didn't wait to see what she was going to say. She started the ignition and pulled away, leaving Molly standing there in the cold.

Chapter 10

MOLLY SOFTLY HUMMED "God Bless Ye Merry Gentlemen" as she shifted her drop cloth. She carefully poured more paint into a smaller container and climbed her ladder to continue cutting in along the ceiling of Tim and Miranda's bedroom. She eased the brush along the ceiling edge, her hand steady as she drew the pale yellow paint in a straight line.

The image of Kathleen's face before she got in her car came back... Something had caused that wall to come crashing between them again. It happened every time they talked about Kathleen's family. Bryan's drowning was tragic, and Molly knew her own mom and dad would never fully recover if anything happened to her or her brothers, but there was something else there, something that made Kathleen shut down anytime they got too near it.

"Oh, this is wonderful, Molly."

She glanced down at Miranda, who was holding little Ellis. "I swear if he gets any chubbier, he's going to pop."

Miranda laughed. "He has a good appetite." She stepped farther into the room. "I love this color."

Molly twisted on the ladder to inspect the far wall and nodded. "It's pretty. Reminds me of spring."

"If only," Miranda said.

Outside, snow swirled in huge flakes.

"The snow's perfect for Christmas," Molly said, climbing down to shift her ladder.

"Next year, this one will be old enough to be excited about Christmas." Miranda gave the baby a little bounce. "He pulled up to stand yesterday."

"He'll be running before you know it." Molly climbed back up to work on a fresh stretch of wall.

"I'll leave you to it. Just holler if you need anything."

"Thanks, Miranda."

Miranda had just stepped out of the room when a thought occurred. "Hey, Miranda."

She came back into the room.

"Has Kathleen Halloran been looking at anything in particular when she comes into the market?"

A tiny smile played over Miranda's lips as she looked up at Molly. "Thinking Christmas present?"

"Well... yeah."

"The only thing she's been looking at lately is paint. I told her what we were doing. She said she's been sleeping in her old room, leaving Maisie's empty. She was thinking about painting it to turn it into her room."

"Really? She didn't happen to mention a color, did she?"

"As a matter of fact, she asked me to mix up a couple of samples for her. I told her we don't have the colors the big paint stores do, but she picked out three she liked."

Molly thought quickly. "Can you give me the samples instead?"

Miranda grinned. "I will. I'll make up some excuse if she asks."

"Thanks."

Out in the hall, Miranda smiled as she heard Molly singing, "We wish you a Merry Christmas..."

⁂

BLOSSOM WHINED AS HE sat at the bottom of the attic steps.

"It's okay," Kathleen called down to him. "I'll only be a few minutes."

In the dim light from the small windows in the gable ends of the cottage, she located Nanna's boxes of Christmas stuff. Tugging the flaps open, she found one box of lights along with a tree stand and skirt. Another was packed with ornaments wrapped in newspaper. She shifted them to the top of the stairs and looked around.

It was freezing up here. Molly was right. The house would be a lot warmer if she got this attic fully insulated.

"One more project for the list."

There was another stack of boxes under the eaves. She had to drop to her hands and knees to get to them and tug them free.

She opened the top box in the stack. Inside were old drawings Kathleen had done for Nanna. Every single one she'd done in the summers she'd spent here. There were the stories Kathleen had written, her imagination let loose on the island with stories of buried treasure and pirates. Bryan's old baseball mitt and ball were there. Kathleen picked them up, holding the mitt to her nose, inhaling the scent of old leather. She remembered Bryan and Aidan and the other boys playing baseball when they were here.

She shifted that box and opened the next. Inside were yellowed papers, curling and brittle. Scrawled across them were drawings and stories and school assignments by Michael and Moira. It looked as if

Nanna had kept everything Kathleen's father and aunt ever did for school.

"She saved it all," Kathleen whispered.

She hardly knew her aunt and could barely remember a father and mother who laughed and looked forward to coming to Little Sister. She knew that side of them had been there, before the accident, before Bryan died. She ran a tender finger over a drawing her dad had done in second grade and felt a sudden crushing weight, making it hard to breathe.

How lonely Nanna must have been, all those years without any of them.

Down below, Blossom whined again. Kathleen hurriedly closed the flaps of the box and carried the Christmas boxes down the attic stairs.

Blossom stood on his hind legs and nosed her, looking concerned.

"I'm okay."

She gave him a rub and lugged the boxes downstairs. She untangled the tree stand from the lights and took it out to the front porch, where a small Christmas tree sat in a bucket of water.

A few minutes and a lot of cussing later, she had the tree propped in front of the living room window where the snow was still coming down. She filled the stand with water and snugged the tree skirt around its base.

She turned to the box holding the tangled strands of lights.

"Hey!"

Blossom had pawed aside the tree skirt to drink out of the stand.

"That is not for you," she said sternly, wrapping the colorful skirt back around the tree.

She turned on her iPod and played a Christmas playlist while she strung the lights and decorated the tree. Nanna's ornaments were mostly handmade—some obviously made by her dad and aunt when they were kids that Nanna had carefully kept all these years; others Kathleen remembered were made by Bryan and her and mailed to

Little Sister when they were very young. There were several cross-stitched ornaments with the initials LW or OW on the back. She smiled. These looked like something Louisa or Olivia would make.

When she was done, she stepped back and inspected her work. It was a homely tree, one she knew her mother would never have approved of but—*it suits me perfectly*. Knowing this was the way Nanna decorated her tree added to its appeal.

The old-fashioned light bulbs glowed merrily as she went to her computer to get a few hours' work in on a manuscript she'd promised to have edited before the holidays.

It took her a few minutes to read back through three or four pages to get her mind into the story again. Just as she started to type a comment on a new section, the telephone rang.

Expecting to hear Louisa or Olivia on the other end, she went to the kitchen and picked up. "Hello?"

"When are you coming home?"

Her mouth hung open for a moment. "Dad."

"Obviously. So when are you coming home for Christmas?"

"Um... I'm not."

In the silence that followed, Kathleen heard her own pulse in the handset pressed to her ear. Something creaked and then there was the sound of a door closing, and she knew her father had shut himself in his study.

"You weren't here for Thanksgiving and now, you're not coming home for Christmas?"

Kathleen clamped her free hand over her mouth to stifle her initial impulse to laugh. When she could speak, she said, "Dad, I haven't been with you for Thanksgiving for years. And last year, you and Mom were in the Bahamas for Christmas. And Vail the Christmas before that. Why would I come back, even if I could get off the island?"

She could almost hear her father's frown at being contradicted in a way he couldn't refute.

"Well, we're here this year, and we'd like you to come. Your mother—"

"Don't."

The telephone line almost crackled with the tension.

"Don't even try telling me Mom misses me or wishes I would come home more often."

"Why can't you and your mother get along?"

Kathleen took her glasses off and rubbed her eyes. "You'll have to ask her that."

The ensuing silence pressed upon her, making it hard to breathe.

"Susannah said the islanders have basically kidnapped you."

This time Kathleen didn't even try to stifle her ridicule as she laughed. "So now you and Susannah are confidants?"

"I've always liked Susannah."

Kathleen waved a hand in the air. "Whatever. I won't be there for Christmas. I'm sorry that you and Susannah don't like it—"

She stopped suddenly. "You know what? I'm not sorry. I've spent almost every Christmas for the past twelve years by myself. The island is my home now. I'm where I want to be. Period. You can wish Mom a Merry Christmas for me. Or don't. It's up to you. Now I have to get back to work. Bye, Dad."

She hung up and stood there, her hand still gripping the phone as it took a few seconds for what she'd just done to sink in.

Where did that come from?

She had no idea, but it felt good. Really good. With a little skip, she went back to her computer.

⬚⬚⬚⬚⬚⬚⬚⬚⬚

THE ISLAND LOOKED LIKE a Currier and Ives print. Snow lay like frosting, coating every tree branch, softening the lines of roofs, and creating a hush, as if the entire island were hibernating.

That wasn't so, of course. With Christmas just a couple of weeks away, there was a flurry of activity. The scheduled arrival of the ferry came with the anticipation of a visit from Santa Claus. It was a feeling Molly remembered from when she was a child.

She couldn't go into any of the shops in town without someone casually spying to peek at what was in her canvas tote bags. She remembered too late how hard it was to pick things out for people who all knew each other and only had a handful of places to buy from. She wished she'd put more thought into her own Christmas shopping when she and Kathleen were on Big Sister. As it was, she'd relied largely on catalog shopping and hoped desperately that the ferry would come on schedule.

Everyone used Bobby's address as their shipping address. He and her aunt were such good sports about getting dozens of packages delivered to their house for all of the islanders.

After escaping the market, where Wilma was trying hard to see what she had in her cart, she ducked into Greyeagle's Gift Shop. "Hello, Siobhan."

Siobhan stood up from where she was restocking a shelf of candles. She could have been a model for a Christmas card, her magnificent mane of bright red hair held back by a dark green band. "Molly, how nice to see you."

She took a second glance at Molly's face. "Stressed?"

"It's just... trying to shop here."

"I know. They all turn into children," Siobhan said with a laugh. "Sure it's almost impossible to keep gifts a secret here, but that's become part of the challenge and the fun."

Molly strolled around, perusing the things packed into the little shop: crystals and incense, pottery and soaps, jewelry, dreamcatchers of all kinds. Cards and art prints filled stands and racks. She picked out a selection of the candles she knew her mother and Rebecca both liked.

She sniffed. "What smells so good?"

153

Siobhan pointed toward the back of the store. "I've been mixing herbs for more of my cold-weather salve."

"The hand cream? I need some."

Siobhan shook her head. "Sorry, can't sell you any."

Molly frowned. "Why not?"

Siobhan gave her a dry look.

"Oh."

"Don't worry. I have it on good authority you'll get at least a year's supply."

Molly chuckled. "Fair enough." She laid her candles on the counter.

Siobhan slid a boxed selection of scented bath salts and creams over to sit next to the candles.

"What's that for?"

Siobhan's sensuous lips curved in a sly smile. "I also have it on good authority that a certain book editor was eyeing this particular collection. She might even need someone to share these with."

Molly felt a furious heat rise in her cheeks. Siobhan laughed and kissed her lightly, rubbing her thumb over Molly's lips to wipe away the lipstick.

"Be happy, Molly."

THE DAY BEFORE THE ferry was due, Kathleen sat at the dining table, frowning at her monitor.

"Wonderful," she muttered aloud. "Just great. The editor actually injected an error."

With quick jabs of her delete key, she undid the last comment. She was only three chapters from having this job done and had been pushing hard to get through it, but she couldn't concentrate. This was stupid.

Giving up on getting any more editing done for the day, she saved her work and stood to stretch.

Blossom, who had found a way of propping himself upside down in his bed, somehow managed to twist upright and leap to his feet all in the same move.

"Shall we go for a walk?"

He'd learned the word "walk" quickly and bounded to the front door, dancing in place as he waited impatiently for Kathleen to tug on boots, jacket, hat. She hesitated a moment and took her camera out of its bag. Outside, Blossom launched himself off the porch.

"Who needs steps?"

She swept the steps clean of snow and then set off through the woods to the bluff. Blossom galloped around her, following rabbit tracks into the bushes for a few minutes before reappearing ahead of her on the trail, checking to make sure she was still coming. She stopped every so often to snap photos. She wasn't a professional photographer, but she never knew when images like these might come in handy for a book cover.

The view from the bluff was amazing. The sky was cloudless and blue, but the water was steel gray, the horizon a hard, unbroken line.

She worked her way through the woods and back out to the road. It had been plowed to make the hard-packed snow drivable for those without four-wheel-drive. Snowmobile tracks threaded along the snowpack.

She soon found herself nearing the cemetery. The stones were all topped with snow, the graves undisturbed except by bird or rabbit tracks. She took a few more photos, playing with the light.

The little rose bush on Nanna's grave stuck up through the snow, its bare branches loaded with rose hips.

She raised the camera to her eye, panning, and noticed something she hadn't before. A small, shingled building stood in the shadows at the rear of the cemetery, sheltered by a stand of pines. Off to one side in a large clearing was a circle of stones stacked taller than her head, with a small doorway set in the rock. It reminded her of photos she'd seen of ancient Irish circle forts.

She made her way to the building and cautiously tried the door. It was unlocked. Pushing it open, she stepped into a chapel. Blossom followed her inside, his nose twitching.

The interior was spare, with a low kind of altar made from a rough slab of wood supported by two pillars of stacked stone. It was quiet, austere. There were a few benches scattered around, with stacks of cushions here and there, and rocks at regular intervals along the walls with candles sitting on them.

She sat on one of the benches. The light slanting through the windows hit the altar, highlighting the bark left on the natural edge of the slab. She lifted her camera to her eye.

Behind her, the door opened, and Rebecca came in.

"I'm sorry," she said when Kathleen whirled around. "I didn't mean to disturb you."

"You're not." Kathleen stood. "I shouldn't have come in."

"Why not?" Rebecca carried a laundry basket full of pine greens. "This place is for all of us." She set her basket down. "I just came to decorate for solstice and Christmas."

"You celebrate both?"

"Of course." Rebecca raised her hands. "We come from both. We come from all."

Rebecca sat and patted the bench.

Kathleen joined her. "How do you celebrate?"

"We light a fire in the stone circle outside for solstice. If the weather isn't too blustery, some will stay all through the longest night. For Christmas, we gather in here."

"Do you have a priest come to the island?"

"We don't need a priest," Rebecca said a little sharply. "I'm an ordained minister. We've found it best to do things our way without outside interference."

"What are the cushions for?"

Rebecca nudged one of the cushions with her toe. "Most prefer to sit on the floor, but it gets cold. For the elders, the benches are easier."

"Will everyone fit in here?" Kathleen looked around dubiously.

"Some will choose to stay under the sky, but the weather can be unpredictable. So we try to be flexible."

Kathleen opened her mouth to say something but then hesitated.

"What is it?" Rebecca asked.

"I don't mean... this is awkward to ask," Kathleen fumbled. "You mentioned that the Keeper before you was Naomi."

Rebecca nodded. "She was Wilma's mother."

"Is it always a woman?"

Rebecca frowned. "Come to think of it, it has always been a woman. No particular reason. Why?"

Kathleen felt a warm flush creep up into her cheeks. "I just wondered who the next Keeper will be after you?"

Rebecca's eyebrows rose. "I'm not that old."

"No," Kathleen said quickly. "That's not what I meant. It's just, how is the next Keeper chosen?"

Rebecca considered. "We've always had someone who just stepped in. She usually began by studying the family lines for a few years under the guidance of the previous Keeper. I had hoped Molly would be the next, but she's never really shown any interest."

She gazed intently at Kathleen. "Are you interested?"

Kathleen's face burned. "I... I might be."

Rebecca nodded. "We should probably see how things go for you here first. You've only been back a couple of months."

Kathleen recoiled. It felt almost as if Rebecca had slapped her. "You think I won't stay."

Rebecca's face was carefully blank. "I think there are still things that you haven't put to rest. But if you're serious, you should start spending some time studying the books. You can begin after the New Year if you wish."

She stood. "Think about it." She gave Blossom a pat on the head and went to spread pine branches along the wood slab of the altar.

Kathleen got to her feet and left.

⬛⬛⬛⬛⬛⬛⬛⬛⬛

THE ARRIVAL OF THE last ferry of the year was a celebration for the whole island, and nearly the entire population of the island was in town. Kathleen knew most of the faces by now, even if she couldn't remember everyone's names.

There was an atmosphere of joy that was contagious. As the ferry drew nearer, the excitement grew. When Joe got the gangplank in position and the ferry gate opened, out poured a stampede of children.

She'd almost forgotten the islanders' children would be home for the holidays.

It was utter, happy chaos as everyone ran around, hugging and exclaiming over how much the kids had grown.

Kathleen found herself standing next to Olivia. "Do they stay home for a whole month until the next ferry?"

"Usually." Olivia paused to tousle the blond head of a little boy who ran up to hug her around the waist. "If the ferry can't make it, someone takes them back soon's the weather clears."

Kathleen watched the little boy who had hugged Olivia run on to hug Nels. "They're so young to be sent away."

"The wee ones are sent to live with relatives or host families on the mainland. They don't board at school until they're older."

"And then they're home all summer?"

Olivia nodded. "Best time o'year, when we're all here together."

"How crowded does it get with tourists?"

"We get a fair amount of traffic, but not near as much as Big Sister."

There was a parade of volunteers helping to carry boxes off the ferry. Fred was actually wearing a Santa hat as he used a forklift to move a pallet loaded with heavier items. A few people took charge of calling out names and handing out the boxes.

Kathleen searched the crowd and was disappointed not to see Molly. Olivia took her by the hand and dragged her to where Joe had just called her name, passing three large boxes her way.

"Oh, you hit the jackpot," Jenny said, coming over to them.

Kathleen grinned. "Well, they're not for me." She caught Olivia bending over the boxes, trying to read the labels to see where they were from. "No peeking!"

She snatched them up and put them in her car. She was opening her door to get behind the wheel when Jenny trotted over.

"You can't leave yet." She grabbed Kathleen by the arm. "Everyone's coming to the diner to have supper before Bobby and Fred have to shove off again."

"But I have Blossom—"

"Bring him."

Kathleen allowed herself to be dragged along to the diner. Blossom curled up under her chair while people thronged into the diner, filling every table. Apparently, most folks had anticipated this, as the counter was covered with casserole dishes and pans.

"This is kind of a pot-luck," Jenny said. "We can't expect Wilma and Nels to make supper for everyone."

"But I didn't bring anything," Kathleen protested.

"Don't you worry about that." Jenny swept her arm in the direction of the counter. "I don't think we're lacking."

Kathleen looked around. "Where's Molly?"

"Oh, she's somewhere," Jenny said vaguely.

She pushed a plate into Kathleen's hand and nudged her along the counter, spooning bits of this and that onto her plate. They sat down and were soon joined by Tim and Miranda. He left her at the table with the baby and went to fill a plate for her.

"Tim's growing a beard?" Kathleen asked.

Miranda checked to make sure he was out of hearing. "He's trying. It's his winter lumberjack look."

He was back in a few minutes.

"You okay by yourself?" he asked.

Miranda narrowed her eyes. "Why?"

Tim grinned through his patchy whiskers. "Nels did it. I want to talk to him about it. Be back soon."

He gave her a quick kiss and disappeared into the kitchen.

"Did what?" Kathleen asked.

Miranda smiled as she fed Ellis some of her mashed potatoes. "Nels ordered a solar panel kit for his greenhouse. He wants to experiment with having produce available for the kitchen all year round. Tim thinks we might be able to do the same and sell it at the market."

"That would be wonderful," Jenny said. "As much as I love preserves, fresh produce would be so nice in the winter."

Kathleen frowned as she ate some baked chicken. "Why don't more islanders use solar and wind turbines? We have plenty of both here. It seems natural."

"Molly has been pushing for us to do that for years," Jenny said.

Blossom crawled forward to lick up the bits of potato flying from Ellis's chubby hands.

Jenny reached over to take the baby. She held him as he bounced on her lap. "You exercise those legs." He rewarded her with a big smile.

Bobby pulled a chair up to their table. "Merry Christmas, little sister." He draped one arm around Jenny's shoulders.

Now that she could study them side by side, Kathleen saw the resemblance between them, with their lighter hair and blue eyes, while Rebecca, seated a few tables away, still looked as if she weren't related to them.

"Laurie sends her love," he said, reaching out to tickle Ellis's fat belly. "When you gonna have grandkids?"

Jenny sighed. "I keep waiting."

Miranda laughed, taking advantage of the opportunity to eat without Ellis grabbing her fork. "I think you might be waiting a while."

Bobby turned to Kathleen, his curious eyes searching her face. "We'll be shoving off soon. You staying? Last chance to get off this rock."

Kathleen glanced around—at Wilma going from table to table, pouring coffee and chatting while Nels added food to the overflowing dishes on the counter; at Louisa, sitting with a little girl on her lap, listening raptly as she told her about her school; at the islanders she'd come to know these last few months—all more of a family than any she'd ever known.

She grinned at him. "I'm staying."

※※※※※※※※※※

MOLLY LISTENED FOR THE sound of Kathleen's car as she brushed the third sample color onto the wall. When she heard it, she tapped the lid back on the paint can and went downstairs.

She stepped out onto the front porch, figuring it would not do to startle Kathleen inside her house, despite the fact that the Toyota was parked there.

"What are you doing here?" Kathleen asked.

Her puzzled frown was not lost on Molly.

"I have something to discuss with you," Molly said.

Kathleen reached into her back seat to retrieve a box. Molly hurried out to take a second box from the car.

"How did you get inside?"

There was a definite chill in Kathleen's voice.

"I actually have a spare key that Maisie gave me years ago in case she lost hers."

Kathleen deposited her box on the foyer floor. Molly set hers beside it.

"So I guess I can't have you arrested for breaking and entering."

Molly shoved her hands into the pockets of her jeans. "Technically, it isn't breaking and entering if I had a key. And I can't arrest myself. I am the law here."

Kathleen took her time hanging her jacket on a hook. "Okay. So are you going to tell me what you needed to discuss so desperately that you unlocked and entered my house when I wasn't here?"

She turned to Molly, clearly struggling to keep her face and voice neutral.

Molly's excitement went cold. "I'm sorry. I guess I shouldn't have... But I wanted to surprise you."

For a tense moment, Molly half-expected Kathleen to throw her out.

Kathleen lowered her head, her face curtained by her hair. When she looked up, her expression was contrite. "No. I owe you an apology for being so... I just have a hard time letting people in my space."

Molly exhaled. "I've noticed." She gestured up the stairs. "Come with me."

"Why?"

Molly took her by the hand. "Just come."

Blossom raced up the stairs ahead of them. Molly pulled Kathleen to a stop outside Maisie's room.

"If you don't like it, I'll make it right, I promise."

She pushed the door open and stepped back.

Kathleen's jaw dropped as she stepped into the room where Molly had painted a large swatch of each sample on each wall.

"The colors will change with the light," Molly said quickly. "So I thought you might want to see what they look like on each wall before you make your choice."

"How did you—?" Kathleen turned to her. "Miranda."

Molly smiled sheepishly. "She told me what you were thinking, so I thought maybe I could do this for you for Christmas."

Kathleen stared at her. "Why would you do that?"

Molly felt trapped. She couldn't tear her gaze away. "I want this house to feel like home for you. I want this island to feel like home."

"You know, I didn't think you wanted me to stay. When I first got here—"

"I didn't," Molly cut in, embarrassed to remember how hostile she'd been. "I blamed you for Aidan and his drinking but... I don't feel that way anymore."

Kathleen bit her lip and went to the window. She took her glasses off and pressed her fingers to her eyes. Uncertain as to what her reaction meant, Molly followed.

"Are you okay? I'm sorry if I overstepped."

Kathleen shook her head. "You didn't. No one has ever made me feel as wanted as you and everyone here."

Molly reached a tentative hand out to Kathleen's shoulder. Kathleen leaned her head to brush her cheek against Molly's hand. The tenderness, the vulnerability of that gesture nearly did Molly in. She stepped closer and wrapped her arms around Kathleen from behind.

Kathleen turned to face her.

For what felt like eternity, their lips hovered just a hair's breadth apart. Kathleen's eyes were hesitant, almost fearful. Molly leaned in and met Kathleen's mouth with hers. Lips parted, soft and yielding as Molly enfolded Kathleen in her arms, pulling her close. Kathleen reached out to encircle Molly's waist as their kiss deepened. Molly ran her hands over Kathleen's back and up to her hair. When they parted, Kathleen leaned against Molly, pressing her face into the crook of her neck. Molly held her tightly.

"Are you okay?"

Kathleen simply nodded.

They stood there, holding each other for ages. Blossom came over and sat, leaning against their legs. They both reached down to pat him.

Reluctantly, Molly let go. Kathleen quickly wiped her cheeks. Putting her glasses back on, she turned to look at the paint swatches.

She turned in place, studying the samples on each wall, and pointed to the swatch in the middle.

"I think I like that one. What's it called?"

Molly picked up the can. "Sea Foam Summer."

"Sea Foam Summer," Kathleen repeated. "That's the one."

Molly raised the can in a toast. "Merry Christmas."

Chapter 11

WITH A FLOURISH, KATHLEEN hit Send and, like magic, felt lighter. That manuscript gone, all pending book covers completed, she typed an "Out of Office" message on her email indicating that she would be unavailable until after the New Year. She did one last back-up—something she admitted she was a bit obsessed about ever since a computer crashed years ago—and powered everything off.

"We're going low-tech for a couple of weeks," she announced to Blossom, who thumped his tail in agreement.

They went outside where an early dusk was falling.

"Longest night of the year, Blossom. Might just be the best night of the year."

She stacked more wood on the back porch for the fireplace. Blossom chased a rabbit into the woods before trotting jauntily back, proud to have done his duty.

"You're full of yourself," she said.

She tossed a stick. Blossom just stared at her.

"Whatever."

She went back inside and lit the oil lamps, setting them around with bowls of Christmas potpourri.

"That looks and smells romantic, doesn't it?"

Blossom raised a back leg to lick himself.

"Why do I even ask you?"

He followed her upstairs where she smoothed the quilt on her bed, the scent of new candles from Siobhan's shop filling the room. She went down the hall to Nanna's room. She'd started dismantling it to get ready to paint. The linens were stripped from the bed, curtains down and dresser drawers emptied. It had been a little sad to bag up all of Nanna's clothes, her bottles of perfume and little bit of jewelry. She made a mental note to ask Jenny how to get donated clothing to a charity come spring.

She turned the lamp on and sat cross-legged on the floor in front of the nightstand.

The top drawer held reading glasses and a few books, including Nanna's Bible. She carefully boxed those items. Inside the middle drawer, she found more old photos, some framed, some in small albums. She amused herself flipping through the pages of the albums, chuckling at images of Nanna with Olivia and Louisa when they were all in their twenties. She set those aside and reached for the last drawer. It stuck. She had to yank hard to get it to open.

She was surprised to see that it was nearly empty, holding only a small bundle of envelopes, tied with a faded blue ribbon. She tugged on the ribbon, unfurling it. Leafing through the envelopes, they were almost all in Nanna's writing, unopened and addressed to her father, marked "Return to Sender".

The postmarks were all dated in the two years after that summer, and they were stacked in reverse chronological order. The bottom

WHEN THE STARS SANG

envelope in the stack was addressed to Nanna in her dad's small block letters with their Philadelphia return address. Her fingers trembled a little as she reached under the loose flap and pulled out the letter within.

Mother,
   Please stop calling. Your apologies mean nothing to us. Nothing you say or do will ever make up for your utter carelessness with the life of our son. Christine is devastated, and I am beyond words.
   We will not ever come to the island again. If I could, I would wish that place and all of you on it to hell for all time.
   Our boy, the light of our life, is gone forever, and that rests fully on your shoulders. We should never have trusted you with our son.
   Michael

Kathleen read the letter over and over. A faint buzzing sounded in her ears, and it was hard to breathe.

"Why couldn't it have been you?"

She clapped her hands over her ears, but the voice was inside her head, where nothing could stop it. She pushed to her feet, scattering the envelopes over the floor.

Rushing down the stairs, she paused only to grab her jacket. Outside, she saw dots of light. Candles and lamps. The solstice. People were walking to the cemetery and the stone circle. Dimly, she remembered that she was supposed to meet Molly there.

She turned to the woods behind the cottage. Her vision blurred by tears, she stumbled along the path. Branches scratched at her face and bare hands. A heavy layer of fog had moved in, obscuring the stars and moon, hiding the trail. Her foot caught on something and she tumbled headlong down a ravine.

Dazed, she lay there, crying, her head throbbing. When she pushed up to sitting, her vision was blurred. Her hand, when she touched it to her forehead, came away sticky. She knuckled the blood out of her eyes and felt around for her glasses. She couldn't feel them anywhere.

She staggered to her feet and pushed through heavy underbrush. She had no idea where she was or which direction the trail was, so she simply continued downhill, climbing over fallen trees and rocks.

The droplets of moisture from the fog condensed and were soon dripping from her hair. She had to keep wiping blood out of her eyes. Everything was blurry, but she couldn't tell how much was from the fog and how much was from her nearsightedness.

Some part of her realized she was disoriented and shivering, but her feet kept moving.

The woods suddenly thinned and she found herself on the path that led to the beach. A heavier layer of mist hung here near the water, undulating and swirling as if it were alive, a thing that could swallow her and take her away from here.

The sand crackled along the water's edge. Icy waves washed onto the beach, sloshing over her shoes.

She wasn't sure how long she stood there, her feet in the sea, the fog wrapping around her with its cold caress, when a voice spoke from the darkness.

"I tried that. Doesn't work unless you go all the way in."

She turned, squinting to see who had spoken. A figure moved near the boulders that formed the sea wall.

Aidan appeared out of the mists, a bottle in one hand. "What the hell happened to you?"

"Fell."

"No shit." He came to stand beside her.

She turned back to the ocean. "Why aren't you at the solstice thing?"

Aidan hoisted the bottle in a toast. "Kumbaya isn't my style."

For some reason, Kathleen found that funny. She giggled rather hysterically. "Mine either."

She eyed him as he took a long pull.

Aidan looked at her through bleary eyes. "You gonna lecture me on the evils of drink?"

"Nope." Kathleen took the bottle from him. "I'm going to join you." She tipped the bottle to her lips and coughed as the whiskey burned going down.

"All right then." He took her by the elbow and guided her back to the rocks where they sat side by side.

She held the bottle up, watching the amber liquid inside slosh around. "This was my mom's answer, too. My dad's drug of choice was work. As much as he could, as far away as he could. But my mom found hers right here. This and pills. Anything to make her numb."

Aidan didn't say anything, just took another swig before passing the bottle back to Kathleen.

She took a big drink. It wasn't so bad this time. Didn't burn as much. "No one remembers, but the day you and Bryan—It was my tenth birthday. So every fucking birthday since then has been just another reminder. As if anyone needed another reminder."

"I didn't know," Aidan mumbled.

Kathleen waved her hand, splashing a little whiskey from the mouth of the bottle. "That first summer after... My dad was gone, of course. I spent the day alone. I thought Nanna would remember and send a card. I was watching TV when my mom called me. I went to her room, thinking maybe she remembered it was my birthday, and maybe we would do something together."

Kathleen swiped her jacket sleeve across her runny nose. "But I was wrong. When I went in, the room was dark. She was sitting in her chair. I remember the only light was the glow of her cigarette. She took a drag, and the end lit up, and I saw her eyes. Her eyes, just watching me from the dark. You know what she said to me?"

She turned and looked at Aidan, though she was having a little trouble focusing. His eyes were locked on hers. She leaned over and bumped her shoulder against his.

"She said, 'Why couldn't it have been you?'"

Aidan's eyes were wide. "Jesus."

Kathleen nodded. "Yeah." She tipped the bottle back again. The burn felt good this time. "Why couldn't it have been me?"

"I think you've had enough of this." Gently, he tugged the bottle from her grasp. "You're cold and bleeding. Come with me."

He helped her to her feet and, together, they staggered into the dark.

❈❈❈❈❈❈

"WHERE'S KATHLEEN?"

Molly had been keeping an eye out for her as most of the islanders gathered at the stone circle. Centuries ago, the shipwreck survivors had found that the First Ones already had some stone markers for the solstices, but they had shown them how to build one—a bit like Knowth or Newgrange—with stone arches positioned to catch the first rays of the sun at each solstice. Every solstice of her life, Molly had celebrated here on this spot.

A fire burned brightly inside the circle, flames to chase away the dark on this longest night, to see them through until morning. As dawn neared, the fire would be extinguished and they would all sit in the dark just before the dawn broke over the ocean horizon, its rays piercing the darkness to bounce around the interior of the circle. Even on cloudy mornings, it was a humbling sight.

She'd been looking forward to seeing Kathleen's reaction.

Everyone she asked shook their heads. No one recalled seeing her this evening. Nervous now, Molly bent to crawl back under the low stone lintel.

"Mo?"

She turned to find her mother stooping to scramble out behind her.

"Do you think something's wrong?"

"I'm not sure." Molly searched the faces of the stragglers coming out of the mists. "I'm going to check on her."

She pressed against the incoming tide of people and made her way out to the road. She couldn't be sure this was the way Kathleen would come, but it seemed the most likely. The fog made everything seem surreal as trees loomed out of the murkiness. She worked her way toward the Halloran cottage and actually passed the drive before she recognized that she'd missed it. Backtracking, she trotted toward the cottage. She stopped abruptly at the mournful sound of a dog howling and sprinted the rest of the way to find the front door ajar, Blossom scratching frantically at the storm door. She burst inside, alarmed to see the oil lamps burning.

"Kathleen? Kathleen!"

She took the stairs two at a time and found the lamp lit in Maisie's old room, the envelopes scattered on the floor. She picked up the discarded letter, reading it quickly before tossing it on the bed.

As if he understood that they were going to search for his human, Blossom skidded back downstairs to the front door.

"Wait," Molly said, running to the kitchen, tearing drawers open, hunting for a flashlight.

She found one and quickly blew out the kerosene lamps before letting him out the door. "Find her."

He raced around the house, into the woods. She followed as quickly as she could, the beam from her flashlight cutting a jagged path through the fog as she ran. Blossom left the trail, his nose low to the ground as he veered into the woods. Molly raised one hand to shield her face from branches that whipped at her out of the darkness.

"Kathleen!"

She stopped to listen but there was no answer. Up ahead somewhere, she heard Blossom rustling through the underbrush. The ground suddenly disappeared from under her feet, and she slid down a ravine. The flashlight flew from her hand, landing a few feet away. Cursing, she reached for it. Something gleamed in its beam. Glasses. She picked them up, recognizing them as Kathleen's. She swept the flashlight back and forth, pausing when she saw a slash of red on a large rock. Dipping a finger into it confirmed it was fresh.

"Oh, God."

Ignoring the sharp pain in her knee, she pocketed the glasses and jogged on, limping after Blossom who was barking up ahead. The sound led her back to the beach trail. Relieved that Kathleen had found her way there, Molly played the flashlight around. She couldn't see anything. She called again, but there was only the sound of the surf washing up onto the sand. She aimed the flashlight at the sand and saw footprints. A small set—Kathleen's, they had to be. But there was a larger pair as well. For a second, her heart leapt in alarm, but she remembered where they were. No one here would hurt her. She studied them more closely and saw both sets of footprints angling toward the rocks. At the wall, she picked up a whiskey bottle that was almost empty.

Aidan.

Blossom was running in frantic circles around the beach, his nose down, trying to follow Kathleen's scent, but Molly knew where she was going now.

IN THE FIRELIGHT UP at the circle, the islanders huddled, their faces lit by the warmth as they cradled their children in their laps, just as their people had been doing for thousands of years. Soon, the stories would start—first the story of the shipwreck and the rescue. Every child heard that story every year on this night. It never grew old.

Jenny looked around restlessly. She hadn't expected Aidan to come. He never did anymore. But Molly hadn't returned, and she knew Kathleen had been anticipating this night.

She'd learned long ago that she had some extra ability to sense disturbances in the atmosphere of the island—as if it spoke to her. She'd known something horrible was happening the day Bryan Halloran died, the day they almost lost Aidan. She'd been the first to sound the alarm.

She tugged on Joe's hand. "Something's wrong. We need to go."

She whispered in Rebecca's ear, and Joe followed her out of the protective ring of stones.

"Where are we going?" he asked.

She closed her eyes for a moment. "Home, I think."

They hurried, taking shortcuts through the woods where they could. The fog slowed them, and Jenny's sense of foreboding grew. Almost all of the houses were dark, as was the custom. Everyone spent this night together, waiting for the break of dawn, heralding the return of the sun and the lengthening days to come. But when they got within sight of their house and saw lights on, they both broke into a run.

Aidan was sitting at the table, staring into a cup of coffee.

Jenny's sharp gaze took in everything—a smear of dried blood on his sleeve, a jacket hanging on a kitchen chair with more blood on it.

"What happened?" Joe demanded.

Jenny laid a hand on her husband's arm, as much to steady herself as to calm him. She pulled him toward a chair. She took the one on Aidan's other side.

"Tell us."

"I'm not drunk," Aidan said. "Kathleen might be, a little."

He looked upward. "Mo's upstairs with her now."

He rubbed his hands roughly over his face.

"What happened?" Joe asked again. "Whose blood is this?"

"Kathleen's. She fell, I think. Mom, you should go up."

Jenny rose slowly, trailing a hand over Aidan's hair.

Upstairs, she found Kathleen and Molly in the bathroom. Kathleen was sitting on the toilet lid, a towel wrapped around her shoulders.

Her face was deathly pale as Molly dabbed a wet washcloth over the blood covering one side of her face. Blossom had squeezed himself into the space between the toilet and the tub, resting his chin on Kathleen's thigh.

"Mom." The fear in Molly's voice kicked Jenny into calming mode.

"Let's see what's going on," she said.

Molly shifted out of the way. Jenny took the washcloth from her. Parting Kathleen's auburn hair, she found the cut. Already, the bleeding was staunched, oozing but not gushing, as it no doubt had.

"This will be fine," she murmured. "No worse than that time you gashed your chin when you were five."

She handed the washcloth back to Molly. "Rinse that for me, and I'll need a roll of gauze."

She placed a hand on Kathleen's cheek. "Kathleen? Katie, can you look at me?"

Kathleen's bloodshot eyes struggled to focus, and Jenny smelled the whiskey on her breath.

A few minutes later, Kathleen's face was clean and a gauze bandage was wrapped securely around her head.

"Let's get her out of these cold, wet clothes."

They helped Kathleen to stand and walked her into Molly's room. Molly went to her dresser and dug out a pair of sweatpants and a heavy sweatshirt. Together, they got her changed.

"Oh, no you don't," Jenny said when Kathleen tried to sink into the bed.

She and Molly propped her up against the headboard. Blossom hopped onto the bed, his ears back, waiting to be scolded and made to get down.

"We can't let you sleep just yet. Mo, go get a cup of coffee."

Molly stood, reluctant to leave.

Jenny smiled up at her. "She's okay. I'll stay with her. Go get the coffee."

With Molly gone, Kathleen's eyes filled with tears. Jenny sat on the bed beside her. She pulled Kathleen into her arms and let her cry. Whatever had changed on this night, she had a feeling it would be a sea change for all of them.

※※※※※※※※※

WHEN KATHLEEN BLINKED, everything was blurry. She lifted a hand to her pounding head and felt the gauze. Blossom licked her cheek.

"What are you doing on the bed?" she croaked, but as she struggled to focus, she wondered which bed they were both on.

Her mouth felt as if it were stuffed with cotton. She pushed herself upright and found herself in an unfamiliar room, what she could see of it. Twisting around to sit on the edge of the mattress, she almost stepped on someone lying on the floor under a blanket.

She pressed a hand to her head, trying to get the room to stop spinning, trying to remember…

Molly stirred and threw off her blanket when she saw Kathleen sitting up.

"What happened?" Kathleen asked, her throat feeling as if she'd swallowed broken glass.

Molly got stiffly to her feet. "I was going to ask you the same thing. Here." She handed Kathleen her eyeglasses. "Found these in the woods. Aidan said you were on the beach, bleeding from a cut on your head."

"Oh." Kathleen closed her eyes, swaying a little as everything came back to her. "Um… can I use the bathroom?"

"Sure."

Molly helped her to stand. Blossom hopped down off the bed as they made their way to the bathroom.

"You're limping," Kathleen said.

"Just twisted my knee in the woods last night." Molly pushed the bathroom door open. "You okay alone?"

"Yes."

"All right. I'm going to take the dog out. Be right back. Mom laid out a new toothbrush for you."

Kathleen closed the door and sank onto the toilet. When she was done, she flushed, tugged her pants up, and turned to the sink. Bracing both hands on the cool porcelain, she studied her reflection. She looked like hell. Her left eye and cheek were bruised, and she still had dried blood in her hair. She ran a hand over the sweatshirt and stopped. These weren't her clothes. Someone had undressed her. She groaned. How much more humiliating could this get?

She took her glasses off and washed her hands, splashing some cold water onto her face. She brushed her teeth, trying to scrub away the sensation that they wore sweaters. She toweled her hands and face dry and then combed her fingers through her matted hair before giving up. Shoving her glasses back on, she opened the door to find Molly and Blossom waiting for her.

"Mom is making breakfast."

Kathleen's stomach rebelled at the thought of food. Molly must have seen.

"You need to eat a bit. It'll help." She took Kathleen by the arm. "Come on."

Down in the kitchen, Jenny set a cup of black coffee and a plate with a piece of buttered toast in front of Kathleen.

"We'll keep it bland for now. You work on that."

Kathleen forced herself to nibble on the toast. Joe came in, followed by Joey and Matty as they talked about tearing apart a boat engine. Kathleen wondered why they had to shout. A heavy set of footsteps followed them into the kitchen, and she found herself gazing up into Aidan's face.

For a long moment, they stared at each other.

"You look a lot better than I feel," she said ruefully.

He gave her a sheepish grin as he ran his hands over his smoothly shaven face. "You're kind of a lightweight when it comes to whiskey."

She winced. "Yeah, I guess I am."

He pointed. "That knock on the head didn't help."

She nodded and held up a finger. "I'll remember that for the future. Don't rap your head against something hard and then drink whiskey."

He turned to Joe. "I'll come help you today."

"Really?" Joe clapped him on the shoulder. "All right. With all of us, we'll get this job taken care of in just a few days."

He kissed Jenny as the boys took their jackets off hooks and tromped out the back door.

"See you down the marina in a bit," Molly called after them.

"Well," said Jenny, joining them at the table with a cup of coffee. "Now that the men are out of the house..."

"Thank you, all of you," Kathleen mumbled. "I never meant to be so much trouble."

"You were no trouble," Jenny said. "You scared us, but you're safe, so that's all that matters."

An awkward silence fell, like a shroud. A buzzer sounded from somewhere else in the house.

"That'll be your clothes," Jenny said. "I'll see if they're clean."

She left Molly and Kathleen alone. Kathleen could feel Molly's gaze, and she kept her eyes on her coffee.

Molly pushed back from the table. "I'll get changed and take you home."

Bewildered, Kathleen rose. She supposed she deserved to be scolded. Everything she'd done the previous night had been stupid, so unlike her. She never lost control like that.

She left the kitchen to find Jenny and her clothes, and only then noticed how beautifully the house was decorated for Christmas. The tree's lights were on, the underside of the tree already piled with wrapped presents. There were garlands of holly and pine branches strewn along the fireplace mantel, which was hung with six stockings.

She met Jenny on the stairs. She beamed as she held up Kathleen's jeans.

"The blood came out. See? Just as if nothing happened."

⊠⊠⊠⊠⊠⊠⊠⊠

THE RIDE TO THE cottage was a silent one. Blossom restlessly paced from side to side in the back seat of the 4-Runner as Molly drove carefully on the snow-packed road.

When she pulled up behind Kathleen's car, Kathleen said, "Thanks again."

To her consternation, Molly didn't just let her out and drive away. This was all embarrassing enough. Why couldn't she just go away? Molly came around the SUV and accompanied her to the porch.

Molly gestured awkwardly. "You left the front door open and oil lamps burning last night. And you left Blossom inside."

Kathleen rushed inside.

"I blew them out and pulled the door shut before we went looking for you."

Mortified, Kathleen turned to her. "I am so sorry."

Molly stepped closer, her hands in her jacket pockets. "I found the letter. Upstairs. Is that what set you off?"

Kathleen blinked hard. "Aidan didn't say anything?"

"No."

Molly unexpectedly pulled Kathleen into her arms, squeezing hard. "You had me so scared," she whispered.

Kathleen wrapped her arms around Molly. "I'm sorry."

"When I found the house like that, and then found your glasses and the blood..."

"I'm sorry."

"Will you stop saying that!" Molly held her by the shoulders, staring hard into her eyes. "Just tell me you'll be all right here alone."

Kathleen nodded. "I will be. It was..." She closed her eyes. "I will be."

Molly pressed her lips to Kathleen's forehead, lingering for a long moment before rushing out the door.

Kathleen watched her go, the warmth and tenderness of that kiss spreading through her. It was almost enough to melt the cold place inside where the memory of her mother's words had long ago taken root. Almost.

Chapter 12

FLUFFY SNOWFLAKES FLOATED LAZILY as Kathleen and Blossom descended the porch steps. She carried a lit oil lamp in her gloved hands. Partway down the drive, she paused and turned. A single candle illuminated one of the windows of the cottage.

"Battery candles now," Miranda had told her. "Ever since Lizzie O'Shea's house burned down when the cat knocked her candle into the curtains, we made it island-wide."

"But why do we do this?" Kathleen had asked.

"Irish tradition. For *Oiche Nollag*."

"Christmas Eve," Kathleen translated.

Miranda's face split into a delighted smile. "You've been studying." She nodded. "One candle to light the night and welcome the Savior."

"*Oiche Nollag*," Kathleen murmured now, looking at the sky, covered with thick clouds, only a few stars peeking through.

She traipsed out to the road where others were all headed toward the cemetery as well. There, she found Molly waiting for her.

"Checking to make sure I'd come?" she asked.

Molly gave her a crooked grin. "Last time you were due to meet me, you stood me up."

"Tonight, I'm keeping our date."

They joined the others on their trek to the chapel.

Inside, the islanders were packed in, crowding the benches and sitting on every available bit of floor space. Children and babies were sitting on laps. The only illumination was the lamps set on high shelves along the walls.

"It glows," Kathleen whispered as she and Molly found floor space to sit down.

Molly nodded. "I've always loved this night," she whispered back.

Blossom curled up in Kathleen's lap.

The throng hushed as Rebecca stood behind the wooden slab of the altar. She was wearing a simple robe of white as she lit a row of candles, sprinkling some incense into the flames. Taking a ceramic bowl and a pine branch, she stepped down among the islanders, dipping the pine needles and spraying them all with droplets of water as she intoned prayers.

"Holy water," Molly whispered.

"Is she praying in Latin?"

Molly nodded, crossing herself as Rebecca sprayed them.

It had been years since Kathleen had set foot in a church, not since she was a child. She was bemused by the mix of Catholicism and paganism—what little she knew of such things.

Rebecca went back to the altar and nodded to a group of children, who got up to re-enact the story of the Nativity.

As the Nativity play ended, a trio, consisting of Patrick with his fiddle, the pipe player from Samhain, along with someone else playing guitar, led everyone through a few carols.

Kathleen was acutely aware of the pressure of Molly's thigh against hers. Molly reached over to pet Blossom and let her hand drop casually to Kathleen's knee.

Kathleen stared down at her hand, the graceful curve of those strong fingers. She raised her gaze to Molly's and was nearly bowled over by the feelings reflected there. She hesitantly placed her own hand over top of Molly's, her heart racing at the tenderness and intimacy of such public contact.

Her thoughts wandered in decidedly nonreligious directions for the remainder of the ceremony, so she was startled when Rebecca dismissed them with a loud proclamation of "*Nollaig Shona duit.*"

"*Nollaig Shona duit,*" everyone else intoned as they stood.

Outside, the islanders called out to one another as the light from their lamps scattered in the dark. Molly walked with Kathleen, neither speaking.

As they neared the driveway to the cottage, Kathleen's mind worked furiously to figure out whether this was the right time to—

"Santa!"

Joey and Matty ran up behind them, each grabbing one of Molly's arms. "Come on, Mo! Got to get to bed or Santa won't come."

Molly twisted to look back over her shoulder at Kathleen as her brothers jogged her home.

Kathleen stopped, watching them disappear into the darkness. Blossom trotted over to lean against her leg.

She sighed and reached down to scratch his ears. "You, too. Got to get to bed or Santa won't bring you anything. Come on."

<hr>

MOLLY WATCHED THE CLOCK anxiously, waiting until she could go without raising too much suspicion. They'd spent Christmas morning opening presents and having two rounds of breakfast—well, three for

Joey and Matty. She was wearing a new L.L.Bean sweater from her parents. Finally, she couldn't stand it any longer.

"Be back soon," she said to her mother.

She hurried outside to the SUV and drove to Kathleen's cottage, singing along with Bing Crosby. The front door was open, and Blossom was watching for her through the storm door. When she opened it, he bounded out, leaping off the porch to run into the woods for a romp.

"Hello?" she called as she stepped inside.

"Hi." Kathleen stuck her head out of the kitchen. "Come on in."

Molly looked around curiously. The night of the solstice, she had been so panicked, she hadn't really noticed anything else. She recognized Maisie's ornaments on the tree. A Christmas throw lay neatly folded on the ottoman, and a lone stocking embroidered with a dog bone hung from the mantel. Her heart sank when she saw no evidence of presents under the tree, no detritus from an unwrapping frenzy such as the one that had taken place in the Cooper house earlier. Three new-looking dog toys scattered about the floor were the only sign of gifts.

"It smells good in here," Molly said, walking into the kitchen.

"Thanks." Kathleen was plucking cookies off a cooling rack to put them in a plastic container.

"You didn't need to do that," Molly said.

"I don't like to come empty-handed."

Molly watched the way the light glinted off Kathleen's hair, catching reddish highlights. She noted the khakis and blouse under a thick, cable-knit cardigan.

"You look nice," Molly said. "You'll be way overdressed at our house."

Kathleen turned and smiled. "I like your sweater."

Molly grinned. "From Santa."

For a long moment, they stood there, neither seeming to know what to say. Molly cleared her throat and pointed.

"I didn't get a chance to ask last night. How's your head?"

Kathleen slid a finger gingerly under her hair. "It's better. Tender, but..." She closed her mouth and when she opened it again, Molly held up a hand.

"If you apologize again, I'm going to tell Mom you get nothing but coal."

Kathleen nodded. "Okay. No more apologies."

She snapped the lid on the container and carried it out to the living room. Blossom was at the door. She let him in and tied a Christmas scarf around his neck.

"Can you get that?" Kathleen asked, pointing to a bag filled with wrapped packages.

"You didn't have to do this, either," Molly said.

"I know." Kathleen shrugged. "I wanted to."

She pulled the door shut behind them. Molly noticed she didn't lock it.

Molly opened the cargo hatch, and Blossom jumped in. She deposited the bag inside and closed the hatch as Kathleen climbed into the passenger seat.

They drove on to pick up Louisa and Olivia, who were waiting for them. Olivia had a bag, while Louisa held the box of ashes. Molly and Kathleen helped them into the back seat. The wooden box was decorated with a red and green plaid ribbon wrapped around all four sides and tied in a bow on top. They secured it between them.

"Merry Christmas, Katie!" Louisa said. "And Molly, thank you for picking us up."

"You know it's never a problem," Molly said, smiling back at her in the rear view mirror. "That's what the sheriff is for."

Joe and the boys came out to help the Woodhouse sisters down from the Toyota and into the house. Molly handed them the bags from the cargo area. Blossom trotted inside as if he owned the house.

Molly held the door as Kathleen entered the house, stopping abruptly when she saw the fireplace. A seventh stocking was hanging from the mantel, embroidered with "Kathleen". She went to the fireplace and touched a finger to the bulging stocking.

Aidan glanced up from where he was setting her bag near the tree. "It's just a stocking."

Kathleen swallowed hard. "No. It isn't."

She spun on her heel and went into the kitchen, leaving Molly staring after her.

※※※※※※※※※※

IT WAS DARK AS they gathered up their things to leave.

"Thank you for the nicest Christmas I can remember," Kathleen said to Joe.

"Glad to have you," he said.

Jenny came over to hug Kathleen tightly. "Thank you so much for that painting."

Kathleen hugged Jenny back. "It's nothing."

Jenny held her by the shoulders, looking into her eyes. "It isn't nothing. You took the time to make something special for us." She glanced to where the watercolor sat on the mantel—a view of the beach and the ocean beyond. "We'll treasure it."

Rebecca chimed in, saying, "And the photo of the library. I love it."

Kathleen had managed to capture a moment where the sun was slanting through the oak trees, bathing the little library in golden light.

"And our home," Louisa said, holding the sketch of the rambling house. "Daddy would have loved this. It will have a place of honor on our wall."

Kathleen cradled her stocking and looked around for Blossom. He was lying with his head under the sofa, his tail wagging.

"I think we know where Minnow is," Molly said ruefully, going over to take Blossom by the collar and pull him toward the door. "Come on, little man." She shooed him outside.

"Ollie," said Louisa. "Time to go."

186

Olivia wrapped a scarf around her neck, a little wobbly on her feet.

"You okay, Miss Olivia?" Joe asked, taking her by the elbow.

"You shouldn't have poured me that last glass of wine, Joseph Cooper."

He grinned. "You didn't have to drink it."

She leaned toward him and whispered loudly, "But it was so good."

He laughed and wrapped an arm around her waist to guide her outside.

Louisa had Matty's arm as she, too, teetered down the porch steps.

"I haven't been on a young man's arm in ages," she said with a giggle.

Kathleen hid a smile as Matty said with a dramatic sigh, "Miss Louisa, you're too much woman for me."

"Oh, you flirt," she said, swatting him lightly.

He helped her up into the back seat of the 4-Runner while Joe did the same with Olivia.

"You sure you can get these two inside okay?" he asked Molly in a low voice.

"We'll be fine."

The island was dotted with lit-up houses as she drove—bits of warmth and joy as other families celebrated Christmas. Kathleen sat back, remembering when she was little, sitting in the back seat of the car as her father drove, wondering what other families were doing in their homes behind their glowing windows. She'd made up wonderful fantasies about how happy they all were.

Molly pulled up as close to the house as she could. She helped Olivia, who was carrying the ashes, and Kathleen took Louisa by the arm, guiding her up the porch steps and inside.

"I'll go and get their things," Kathleen said, jogging back out to the Toyota.

She retrieved their framed sketch and a bag containing new bathrobes from the Coopers along with some leftovers Jenny had packed for them.

"We'll be right back," she said to Blossom.

As she entered the parlor, Louisa was showing Molly something on the tree. She carried the leftovers into the kitchen where Olivia was standing, one hand rubbing her chest.

"Are you all right?"

Olivia straightened. "I'm fine. Just a little indigestion. Ate too much of Jenny's wonderful cooking." She reached for the bag. "Speaking of which, I'll put these in the fridge."

She quickly put the leftovers in the refrigerator and accompanied Kathleen back to the foyer.

"Merry Christmas," Louisa said, hugging Molly.

She hugged Kathleen as well. "Merry Christmas, Katie."

The sisters waved them out into the night, the stars bright overhead.

"We can walk from here," Kathleen said. "You don't have to drive us."

"I don't mind." Molly opened the door for her.

Kathleen hesitated a second and then climbed into the passenger seat.

They didn't speak as Molly drove them to the Halloran cottage. All day long, every time Kathleen had looked in Molly's direction, she'd caught Molly watching her.

She was aware of a shift in the atmosphere within the SUV. From the corner of her eye, she saw Molly's hands tightly gripping the wheel. Molly pulled up at the cottage and turned the ignition off. For a moment, they sat there, neither speaking, but then Molly got out to let Blossom jump down from the cargo space. He disappeared into the trees. She retrieved another bag of gifts and walked Kathleen to the house.

For the first time since she'd come here, the little cottage felt empty and lonely. After the warmth and laughter and companionship of the day, Kathleen didn't want it to end.

On the porch, Molly stepped nearer. Kathleen gazed into her eyes, wishing she could say just how much the day had meant.

"I had a really nice time today," Kathleen said, but further words were stopped by the crush of Molly's mouth against hers.

She still held her stocking in one arm, but her other was around Molly's neck, fingers tangled in her hair, pulling her closer as Kathleen's mouth opened to meet Molly's.

Molly pressed Kathleen's hips against hers, moaning a little into Kathleen's mouth.

She pulled her mouth away, breathing hard. "If I don't leave now..."

"Don't leave," Kathleen whispered, fumbling for the doorknob.

She pushed the door open, letting Blossom in. Molly shut the door behind them. They shrugged out of their jackets and kicked off their boots. They stood, looking uncertainly at each other. Kathleen reached for Molly's hand and led her upstairs.

MOONLIGHT STREAMED THROUGH THE window as Kathleen lay with her shoulder pressed against Molly's.

"That was..." Molly panted.

Kathleen nodded. Her hands clutched the sheet over her chest, but Molly lay with her torso exposed, her other arm flung over her head. Her breasts were beautiful, the nipples dark against the soft skin. Kathleen turned on her side and reached a tentative hand out to run it over Molly's stomach. The muscles tightened and quivered at her touch.

"I can honestly say I've never felt anything like that," Kathleen murmured.

Molly shifted her arm to slide it under Kathleen's head, pulling her close and cradling her. "I can say the same."

Kathleen snuggled into the crook of Molly's neck, inhaling her scent. She felt Molly kiss her hair. For a long time, they lay like that.

"You really don't know how much today meant to me," Kathleen said softly.

Molly squeezed. "I'm so glad you were with us."

"I noticed Aidan didn't have anything to drink."

"You know, I don't think he's had anything to drink since your little escapade on the beach. I know it's only been four days, but something feels different. As if he's completely with us. He hasn't been for a long time."

Kathleen's arm rose and fell with Molly's breathing. "I think part of him wished he'd died that day."

Molly's arm tightened around her. "I know."

Kathleen felt her hesitation.

"Do you?" Molly asked. "Is that what happened the other night?"

Under her arm, Kathleen felt the quickening of Molly's heartbeat. "It wasn't me."

Molly waited.

"I told him what my mother said. After."

"What was that?" Molly whispered.

Kathleen swallowed. It seemed easier to say, lying here in the protection of Molly's arms. "She asked why it couldn't have been me."

Molly's sharp intake of breath was her only reaction.

"I had never told anyone about that, until I told Aidan," Kathleen said.

Molly wrapped her other arm around Kathleen, holding her tightly. She kissed Kathleen's forehead, her nose, her eyes—tender, featherlight kisses. Kathleen raised her face to meet Molly's lips, open, ready to pull her in. She wanted this to go on forever.

Molly shifted onto her elbow, looking down at Kathleen in the moonlight. She tried to pull the sheet down, but Kathleen held on.

"Why are you hiding your body?" Molly stroked Kathleen's cheek, down her neck, to gently, but firmly, pull the sheet away, exposing Kathleen's breasts. "Don't you know how beautiful you are?"

She bent to take one nipple in her mouth. Kathleen couldn't hold back a groan at the exquisite sensations. Molly shifted to lie on top of her, all warmth and softness. So much softness. Kathleen felt she would never get enough of this.

"So beautiful," Molly murmured, lowering her mouth to Kathleen's.

<hr />

THE HARSH JANGLE OF the telephone jolted Molly out of bed. Confused for a moment as to where she was and why she was naked, she remembered as Kathleen sat up also.

Kathleen reached for some clothes while Molly scrambled to find hers.

"Jesus, it's cold."

"I know." Kathleen glanced over her shoulder. "I usually sleep with socks."

Molly grinned, pausing as she balanced on one foot to pull her jeans on. "That would have been practical, but not very sexy."

She saw the blush on Kathleen's cheek as she turned away. Molly got her other foot in her jeans leg and tugged them up.

Outside, they heard a vehicle pull up. Blossom barked from the hall. Kathleen shoved her glasses on her face and went to the window to part the curtain.

"It's your dad."

Molly froze for a second with her arms tangled in her T-shirt. "Something's wrong." She wrenched the shirt over her head and grabbed her socks, jamming her feet into them.

Without waiting for Kathleen, she ran for the stairs, nearly tripping over Blossom. They both raced down the steps to where Joe was banging on the front door.

Molly yanked it open. "What is it?"

"Olivia. We need you."

His eyes moved past her to where Kathleen was coming down the stairs. "Both of you."

He sprinted back to his truck, leaving them to follow. Molly tossed Kathleen her boots. They both sat on the steps to yank them on. Grabbing their jackets, they ran to the Toyota. Blossom jumped into the back seat.

"What must he think?" Kathleen said, her face a furious pink.

Molly gave her a sideways glance. "I think they all know what to think." She pointed to the glove compartment as she shifted into reverse. "There's some gum in there. That's the best we're going to do this morning."

Kathleen found the gum and unwrapped a piece for Molly.

Molly drove as quickly as she dared, the Toyota fishtailing a little in the snow. Almost a dozen other SUVs and trucks and snowmobiles were already parked at the Woodhouse place. Molly skidded to a stop and slammed the gearshift into park. She and Kathleen ran to the house, Blossom on their heels.

Jenny was waiting for them, tears running down her cheeks. "She's gone."

"What do you mean?" Molly grabbed her mother's shoulders. "Who's gone?"

"Olivia. Louisa heard her this morning. In the kitchen. Her coffee cup crashed, and she went down. When Louisa got to her, she was already dead."

Kathleen gave a little gasp. "Last night!"

"What?" Molly turned to her.

Kathleen looked stricken. "When we dropped them off. Olivia was in the kitchen, holding her chest. She said it was indigestion from too much food." She closed her eyes. "I should have said something. Done something."

Jenny hugged her. "There was nothing you could have done."

"But—"

"We don't have any kind of hospital," Molly said quietly. "No way to resuscitate. If she had a massive heart attack..."

"It's part of living here," Jenny said gently. "We all understand that. One bad accident or something like this. It's just the way of things."

Molly went into the kitchen where Olivia lay, still wrapped in her flannel robe, her fuzzy slippers on her feet, her eyes staring vacantly at the ceiling. Louisa sat at the table, cradling the box of ashes, her face pale and expressionless.

Molly crouched next to her, laying a hand on her arm. "Miss Louisa," she said softly, "I have to fill out the death report, and I'll need a statement from you. Later, okay?"

Louisa nodded numbly.

Molly got to her feet and went to Kathleen. "Stay with her, will you? I have to go get the papers."

Kathleen pulled a chair over to sit next to Louisa as Joe produced a sheet from somewhere and tenderly laid it over Olivia's body.

Molly went to her father and the others gathered around Olivia's still form. "I've got to go get stuff from the office," she said in a low voice. "You and Mom will stay?"

Joe nodded. "Yeah."

They both glanced back to where Kathleen sat with one arm wrapped around Louisa's frail shoulders.

"I'll call the state officials. Be back as soon as I can."

<hr/>

THE REST OF THE DAY was kind of a blur—for Kathleen and, she was sure, for Louisa, as well. The army stretcher was brought again. Kathleen's eyes filled with tears, remembering how Olivia and Louisa had helped cook up the conspiracy to get Susannah off the island.

"Where are you taking her?" she asked Rebecca in a low voice as they prepared to move the body. "Does the island have a funeral home?"

"No." Rebecca's retort was sharp, but then she said more gently, "We don't do funeral homes. We don't embalm or do anything artificial."

She took Kathleen by the arm and led her out to the parlor. "Mr. Woodhouse knew his girls would feel adrift without him. They've all made the decision to be cremated, and have part of their ashes interred in our cemetery, part dispersed into the sea."

Kathleen watched Joe and the boys carry the sheet-draped stretcher out the door. "But then where are they taking her?"

"The weather is turning," Rebecca said. "As soon as we can, we'll take her to the mainland to be cremated. In the meantime, she'll be in a wood casket in the storehouse at the cemetery. Even if she wanted to be buried, we can't do it now. Ground's frozen. Any funeral on the island has to wait until spring. There've been years past we've lost ten or twelve. When disease swept through us. Hasn't happened since my great-grandmother's time."

Kathleen sank down onto an ottoman, her shoulders shaking.

"Why are you crying?" Rebecca asked, sitting on the chair beside her.

"Sh-she's alone now," Kathleen stuttered between sobs. "Louisa."

"She's never alone. You should know that by now. She'll have all of us."

Kathleen hiccupped as she raised tear-filled eyes to Rebecca. "It won't be the same."

"No, it won't. Nothing stays the same for very long. Stop crying now."

Kathleen wiped her eyes and put her glasses back on. "I can't help thinking of Nanna. How lonely she must have been all those years."

Rebecca nodded. "It was hard for her, not seeing any of you again. But she knew."

Kathleen sniffed. "Knew what?"

"Life is drawn to life. Like you and Molly. You should know that."

"What do you mean?" Kathleen pulled away.

Rebecca simply looked at her for a long moment. "Life force is a kind of energy. Some energies are drawn to one another. You and Molly have been drifting toward each other, no matter how hard you both fought it. Bryan and Olivia were drawn to whatever lies beyond. There are some forces we can't resist."

Kathleen stared at her hands, tightly clenched in her lap. "You really believe that?"

"Don't you?"

Rebecca got up and went back to the kitchen.

Kathleen frowned after her. The house suddenly felt stifling, as if all the air had been sucked out of it. She called softly to Blossom, who was curled under the piano bench, out of everyone's way. They walked back, passing other cars and trucks, all on their way to the Woodhouse home. She waved vacantly, unable to shake the sadness that Louisa had lost her sister, her lifelong companion, thinking how empty that rambling house would feel now.

Back at the cottage, she went upstairs. The tousled sheets reminded her of the joy and wonder of the night she'd spent in Molly's arms. It seemed ages ago. She made the bed and showered, changing into clean jeans and T-shirt. As she headed back downstairs, she grabbed a thick fleece for warmth.

Her stomach growled, and she remembered none of them had had breakfast. She fed Blossom and made herself a piece of toast. Sitting at the table, she stared at the marmalade she'd spread on the bread. It felt wrong somehow to be feeding her body when Olivia's was lying in a cold storehouse in the cemetery.

She had no idea when she'd see Molly again. She knew she had a lot of official things to deal with to report a death on the island. Kathleen forced herself to keep moving. She cried softly as she dusted and ran the vacuum, which Blossom barked at as if it were attacking the house. She cried as she did laundry and scrubbed the kitchen floor and stacked more firewood on the back porch.

Briefly, she considered turning her computer on and checking her email, but there was no one she really wanted to hear from. *Or not hear from*, she figured would probably be more accurate. She doubted she'd received warm and fuzzy Christmas messages from her parents or Susannah, but she hadn't sent any, either.

Finally, exhausted, drained, cried out, she fell into her chair as dusk descended outside. The weather Rebecca had spoken of had arrived with swirling snow and gusting winds.

She was just wondering what to fix for dinner when headlights swept up the drive, beaming through the front windows. She went to the door to find Molly getting out of the SUV.

Wordlessly, Molly came in and wrapped her arms around Kathleen, holding her tightly. For long minutes, they stood like that.

"Are you all right?" Kathleen whispered.

"Yes. It's just been a tough day. Not the way I pictured our first morning together."

"No." Kathleen pulled away, turned away. "I'm sorry."

Molly came around to face Kathleen. "Why are you sorry?"

"Your father." Kathleen waved her hands in the air. "Finding us like that. Your family must be upset."

"Why would my family be upset that I've found someone I—" Molly shuffled her feet. "Someone I care about."

Kathleen stared hard at her, demanding the truth. "They're not angry? At me? With you?"

"They're not angry." Molly held her right hand up. "Honest Injun."

Kathleen grinned reluctantly.

"Don't tell Rebecca I said that." Molly glanced around the house. "Are you ready?"

"Ready for what?"

"The wake."

"What wake? What are you talking about?"

196

Molly angled her head. "The entire island will gather tonight. Down the diner. People have been bringing food all day."

The only funeral Kathleen had ever been to was Bryan's, and it had been horrible. Her parents had been a wreck, especially her mother. All of their friends and neighbors and country club acquaintances had come, everyone saying how tragic it all was. Kathleen's memories consisted of being left alone, sitting in a corner, while Bryan's body lay in an open casket on the other side of the room.

"People are celebrating Olivia's death?" she asked, aghast.

"No." Molly smiled. "We're celebrating her life. Bring something happy that reminds you of her."

※※※※※※※※※※

WHAT THE ISLANDERS CALLED "weather", Kathleen called a blizzard. She didn't even attempt driving as the snow swirled so densely that she couldn't see her car from the front porch. The gusting winds whistled and moaned through the trees. Blossom went out only long enough to relieve himself and then hopped through the deepening snow to come back inside.

"Bet you don't miss being out in this, do you?" Kathleen asked as she toweled him off.

The cottage was dark, as a perpetual twilight settled over the island.

Molly had warned her that they might have to cycle the available electricity—turning it off a few hours at a time in clusters of houses around the island. She kept her computer turned off, saving her electricity for the thermostat to keep the furnace running, and the ancient refrigerator, chugging along in the kitchen. And the slow cooker.

She chopped up potatoes, carrots, turnips, celery. In a separate pan, she stirred in a little tomato paste and a bottle of Guinness along with the chunks of beef she'd browned with a bit of flour. Adding it

197

all to the cooker with some broth and seasonings, she set the cooker on high.

"How did I survive without one of these before?" she asked Blossom.

Before.

Her life was firmly divided into Before Island and After Island. There had been no transition, no gradual move, and she found she didn't miss anything from her old life. She hadn't asked Susannah if she intended to stay in the apartment, but she assumed she would. The lease was in her name only. Susannah had never been willing to co-own anything in case her father asked too many questions. No buying a house together. No having a car titled in both their names. And no question, ever, of getting married once it became legal.

"Are you crazy?" Susannah had said at the mere suggestion, however timidly Kathleen hinted at it. "All of those things are public record! My family could see."

For years, Kathleen had been hurt by that. It was a constant source of tension that there was no sense of legality or permanence to their relationship.

Thank God, she thought now as she plunked down in the comfy chair. After their last fight, after Susannah left to spend the weekend with her family, all she'd had to do was to pack up her books, her computers, her clothes... Precious little to show for over twelve years living with someone, but the upside was no divorce, no attorneys, no mess.

She tried to read, angling her book toward the window, but she couldn't keep her mind on the story. Her thoughts kept drifting to Molly, wondering what she was doing out in this storm, hoping she was safe.

How did this happen? She closed her eyes. *You promised yourself you would never be weak enough to let yourself need someone ever again.*

Only... it didn't feel weak. It felt good. It had been so long, so very long since she'd felt this way, and back then, it had only been for bits of time—until the next time Susannah got angry and told her to leave, or the next time the Moores went off on why Kathleen was always around, and the heartache that always followed when Susannah didn't defend her.

A little something stirred in Kathleen's chest, sniffing hopefully. If Molly's family knew about them and was okay, if this turned into something real and not just a passing fancy, if... Kathleen was afraid to let herself ride that train of thought.

She went back into the kitchen and began to make a loaf of soda bread. Molly hadn't said she'd be back tonight, and Kathleen honestly wasn't sure even the Toyota's four-wheel-drive could handle this much snow, but she wanted to have a hot meal ready for her, just in case.

The wake last night had been nice, despite Kathleen's misgivings. She couldn't recall ever being at such a joyous celebration. She'd brought one of the old photos of Olivia with Louisa and her Nanna, an image of them when they were girls, wearing their old-fashioned swimsuits down on the little beach. That had brought laughter from everyone who looked at it.

At one point, she had stood off to herself, marveling at how, from such sadness, could come so much laughter and companionship. *What would my wake be like?* she wondered.

That had been a sobering thought. What could people possibly bring to her wake that would make them laugh or smile, or even remember her fondly?

Kathleen kneaded the dough, shaping it into a round, and then scored it deeply into quarters before placing the baking sheet in the oven.

She went around the cottage, lighting the oil lamps. Molly had told her the island's little electric generating plant was already running at near capacity with the increased hours of darkness and the demand for heat and light, even before the extra strain of the storm. Every little bit the islanders could do to lessen the drain on the system helped.

It was difficult to imagine the people she'd known in Philly voluntarily cutting their consumption of electricity or water or gasoline or anything else. The prevailing attitude was "if I can afford it, I should be able to use it." She was ashamed to admit how many times she'd thought the same thing during summer heat waves, with her AC cranked. She'd never lived among people who thought communally, who thought of one another as much as about themselves.

She went out to the front porch, her breath puffing out in frosty clouds in the cold air.

A twin beam of headlights cut through the murky twilight.

Her heart leapt as Molly climbed out of the Toyota and trudged through knee-deep snow, stomping her boots on the steps. Even bundled up in a knit cap and heavy down jacket, she was such a wonderful sight.

Wordlessly, she wrapped her arms around Kathleen, dropping her head wearily onto her shoulder.

"You've been out in this all day?" Kathleen asked.

Molly nodded without speaking.

Kathleen held her for a moment. "I've got Guinness stew almost ready and soda bread baking."

Molly picked her head up. "Really?"

Kathleen chuckled and took her by the hand. "Come on in and get warm."

She had a pair of thick wool socks waiting as Molly sat to take her snowy boots off.

"This place looked like a fairy tale cottage from outside," Molly said. "The snow coming down, the lamplight shining through the windows."

She stood and sniffed. "It smells so good. I'm starving."

"Come into the kitchen." Kathleen led the way. "Want some hot tea or coffee?"

"I don't suppose you have another Guinness that isn't in the stew?"

Kathleen smiled and opened the refrigerator. She reached for two bottles of beer and disappeared into the pantry where a bottle opener was mounted to the wall. "Do you need to let your mom know where you are? Will she worry?"

Molly accepted one bottle and took a long drink. "I told her this morning I probably wouldn't be home."

Kathleen felt a hot flush creep into her cheeks.

"What?"

"I'm not used to..." Kathleen turned to lean her backside against the counter, one finger picking at the corner of the label on her bottle. "Your dad coming here to find you, Rebecca talking about you and me, your mom knowing you're going to be here. It's just weird."

Molly came to her and kissed her gently. "Small island. No secrets here. Does it bother you?"

Kathleen looked into those fascinating eyes, seeing her own reflection among the flecks of green and blue. "No, it doesn't bother me."

Molly moved closer. "Good." She kissed her again, not so gently this time.

Kathleen felt her body respond as Molly pressed her against the counter.

"How long before the stew and bread are done?" Molly whispered when they came up for air.

Kathleen glanced at the timer on the oven. "Twenty minutes. More or less."

Molly grinned. "That's more than enough time. More or less."

She grabbed Kathleen by the hand and led her upstairs.

Chapter 13

THE ROOM WAS DARK when Molly woke. She peered at the bedside clock. The bedroom still smelled faintly of fresh paint. Stretching, she savored the extra room in this bed. She kissed Kathleen's shoulder, but she only turned over, burrowing further under the covers. Molly reluctantly crawled out of the warmth. Blossom watched her from his bed as she dressed quietly in the dark. Together, they crept down the stairs where she let him out and put the coffee on, knowing that aroma would wake Kathleen. She scooped some food for Blossom.

"Be good," she whispered when he came back in. "If she doesn't get up soon, go jump on her."

She put on her boots and jacket, and let herself out the front door. Everything was quiet as she drove. A couple of rabbits darted across the road, but nothing else moved.

The lights from the kitchen cast a soft glow onto the snow when she pulled into the drive behind her dad's truck. She needed some tools and supplies for the install she was doing of Nels's new solar panels for his greenhouse. The snow would complicate things, but he wanted to get the greenhouse cranking as soon as possible.

Though the sun wasn't yet up, the snow reflected enough light to show her the shoveled path to the back door. She scuffed her boots on the doormat and came into the kitchen.

"Morning," she said, kicking her boots off.

Jenny looked up from the stove where she was flipping pancakes. "Morning, Mo. How are things at Kathleen's?"

"We got Maisie's room painted and new curtains hung. I helped her get Bryan's old room set up as her office."

"That was a nice Christmas gift. To help her with those things."

"It'll make the cottage feel like home for her, I hope." Molly poured herself a cup of coffee and topped off her mother's cup.

She leaned against the counter and took a sip. "Is this weird for you?"

Jenny glanced over. "A little, if I'm being honest." She waved her spatula. "Don't get me wrong. We want all of you to have your own lives."

Molly grinned. "You mean, you and Dad want us out of your hair."

Jenny nodded noncommittally. "We've thought about changing the locks on the doors, but you'd just pick them." She sighed as Molly laughed. "Even though we want you to live your own lives, now that you're half-living at Kathleen's these days, you're the first to do it. It's going to take some getting used to."

Jenny slid the plate of pancakes into the oven to keep them warm and poured batter on the griddle for a new batch.

Molly planted a kiss on her mother's cheek. "Well, don't get too used to it. No telling how long this will last."

She headed toward the living room and the stairs.

"But you're happy, Mo?"

She turned to look back at her mom. "Yeah. I'm happy."

Molly paused in the living room and went to the fireplace where Kathleen's painting held pride of place. There, so small Molly hadn't noticed it at first, she had painted a tiny scull on the ocean, the sun reflecting off the oars. She smiled and took the steps two at a time, nearly colliding with Aidan.

He grinned. "No need to ask how you are."

Molly punched him in the arm. "Nope."

"What do you think about next week? For Miss Olivia? The weather should be calm."

She nodded soberly. "Next week. I'll make the arrangements and tell Miss Louisa."

He ran his hand through his hair. "I can tell her, if you want."

Molly didn't know what to say. "Uh... that would be great. Thanks."

"Okay." He started down the stairs. "Don't be too long. I'm not leaving any pancakes for you."

Molly stared after him. "Okay," she murmured, heading into her room to change her clothes.

<hr/>

KATHLEEN RAN HER HANDS over the timeworn smoothness of the wooden desk. She remembered spending hours at this desk as a child, drawing and writing stories.

By shuffling furniture around, she'd been able to set up a useable workspace in Bryan's old room. She'd hesitated about using it, but it got better light than her old room. Molly had drilled holes from the attic to run the cables for her satellite connections—something she would never have attempted on her own.

She saved the current manuscript she was editing. She'd been at it for over four hours and felt she was going cross-eyed.

Just as she was getting ready to turn off her computer, an email came through. She saw from the little bubble that it was from Susannah. She hesitated a few seconds before opening it. To her surprise, it was a nice message—saying she hoped Kathleen had had a good Christmas and that maybe this new year would see them start over.

Part of her wanted to believe she and Susannah could stay friends. Fourteen years—the two tumultuous ones in college and then twelve living together—"Who are you kidding?" she asked aloud. "They were all tumultuous."

Still, if there was a way to remain friends, maybe things could be different between them. She took a moment to type a cordial reply and hit Send.

Pushing away from the desk, she went down the hall to Nanna— "no, it's our room now," she said firmly to Blossom as he followed her.

She stopped, startled by that thought. *Our room.* That had never been the case before. At Susannah's insistence, they had always kept separate rooms for the sake of appearances. Their apartment had to look at all times as if they were nothing more than roommates. It felt a bit daring to openly create a space to share with Molly.

She loved this room. The newly painted walls were beautiful— depending on the light, sometimes green, sometimes blue, sometimes a kind of gray-sage.

Like Molly's eyes. She smiled as she realized why the color had appealed so strongly.

She smoothed the new comforter on Nanna's old bed—the bed they'd made love in almost every night for the past week. And it was lovemaking like she'd never experienced. Molly took her time, exploring, tasting, touching her in places she never knew could be so sensitive. Nothing was hurried or furtive. Slowly, Kathleen was learning to relax and open herself as she hadn't ever before.

The wonder of Molly's body in return was something Kathleen thought she would never tire of—lean muscles, smooth stomach, long legs that wrapped around her when she stretched out on top of Molly, luxuriating in their nakedness. Nights spent snuggled up together with their legs tangled. Just the thought of making love with Molly had Kathleen's body responding in ways that made her blush.

Molly hadn't officially moved in. Neither of them was ready for that, but Kathleen had set aside two of the four drawers in the dresser for Molly to bring some clothes over. The drawers were still empty, but...

Come spring, she planned to order a new bed and mattress. Her back ached a bit sleeping in this one, as it was saggy in places, but the extra room was nice.

She went downstairs to the kitchen to begin baking an apple pie. Molly and Aidan had left early that morning to take Olivia's body to the mainland. A group of people were gathering at the diner tonight for dinner to await their return. Wilma and Nels had insisted Miss Louisa stay with them at the hotel for the past couple of weeks, but she knew Molly had taken her by her house to check on things.

"It'll be tough on her to live there alone," Molly had told Kathleen. "That house was a lot for the two of them to keep up with, but now..."

While the pie was baking, Kathleen went upstairs to change the linens on her old bed, the one she'd been using since coming back to Little Sister. It might be a bit awkward to have Miss Louisa down the hall from her and Molly, but she intended to offer and wanted to have the room ready for her.

A couple of months ago, she realized, she would never have considered inviting someone else into her space. She had barely tolerated Louisa and Olivia coming by to bring her dinner or help her clean the cottage. Now she had Molly and maybe Louisa staying with her.

It was strange. She felt more complete, bigger somehow, as part of this community of people than she had trying to stand defiantly alone.

When the oven timer went off, she let the pie cool for a few minutes and then packed it up in a basket padded with towels. She and Blossom drove into town, where there were already several people inside the diner.

"Are Molly and Aidan back?" she asked Jenny as she set her basket on the counter.

"They radioed. They're about a half-hour out."

Kathleen helped Wilma set out stacks of plates and silverware, keeping one eye on the door. She spun at the tinkling of the bell, but it was just Joe, coming in with Matty and Joey. Siobhan arrived, and a few minutes later, Miranda and Tim came in with little Ellis.

She was setting out water glasses when the bell rang again. She turned around, and her heart quickened at the sight of Molly with Aidan. They both looked exhausted.

Everyone grew quiet. Louisa stood with her hand resting on her father's box of ashes.

"She's at the crematorium now," Aidan said. "The undertaker met us at the dock, and we followed to make sure everything was taken care of as you wanted. They'll call us when she's ready to be brought home."

Louisa's chin quivered, but she just said, "Thank you."

Molly went to her and gave her a long hug. Over Louisa's shoulder, Molly sent Kathleen a look that spoke of such sorrow that Kathleen longed to take her somewhere where she could just hold her.

"Let's get some hot food into these kids," Wilma said gently, guiding Louisa to a seat where several tables had been scooted together to make one long table.

Everyone filled plates and gathered. The conversation, Kathleen noted, carefully steered clear of Aidan and Molly's mission that day.

Nels brought a huge basket of rolls, walking down the tables from person to person to plop the fragrant bread on their plates.

"I tried a new recipe today," he announced. "Let me know what you think."

"Nels, Wilma," Louisa said. "I thank you for your hospitality, but tomorrow, I am going home."

Silence fell immediately.

"Louisa," Wilma began, but Aidan leaned forward.

"Miss Louisa, I have been meaning to talk to you about renting me a room."

Kathleen's eyes darted from Aidan to Louisa to Jenny to Molly and back to Aidan.

"What the—?" Matty started, but Joe elbowed him sharply.

"Renting a room?" Louisa asked.

"Yes. I'll be forty years old this year, and I think it's time I moved out of my parents' house. There aren't a lot of opportunities to get an apartment or place of my own on Little Sister, so I wanted to ask if you would rent me a room."

Louisa's mouth opened and closed a couple of times. "Well, Aidan..." She looked to Joe and Jenny.

Joe held up both hands. "Don't ask us. This is between you and Aidan."

"I can pay you a fair rent," Aidan said. "And to help out a little more, I can take care of some of the chores around your place. It's completely up to you."

Louisa blinked rapidly and cleared her throat. When she spoke again, it was in her teacher voice. "Aidan Ahearn Cooper, you'd just better put the toilet seat down."

Aidan grinned. "Yes, ma'am."

<hr />

LATER THAT NIGHT, MOLLY lay in Kathleen's arms.

"Was it hard?" Kathleen murmured.

Molly nodded against her neck. "My uncle took Mr. Woodhouse on the ferry when he died. This is the first time I've done it. We've had other burials, like your grandmother's, here on the island. It's never easy to lose someone you've spent your whole life with."

"Did Aidan talk to you about what he was planning?"

"No. Caught me completely by surprise."

"I think it caught everyone by surprise," Kathleen said. "What do you think?"

Molly considered. "Aidan's been different since Christmas." She shifted to look at Kathleen in the dim light of the bedroom. "Ever since you talked to him."

"You mean ever since the night when I hit my head and got drunk and spilled my guts."

Molly smiled. "Yeah. That." She snuggled into the crook of Kathleen's neck again, breathing deeply. "I think it'll be good. For both of them."

She closed her eyes and felt Kathleen's lips pressed to her hair. "And this is good for me."

She sighed and let herself drift off to sleep.

⸎⸎⸎⸎⸎⸎⸎⸎⸎⸎

KATHLEEN MUTTERED UNDER HER breath at the computer, reading aloud a section of dialogue that just felt wooden. She started typing a comment, asking the author to revise this section when the telephone rang.

Impatiently, she pushed away from the desk and ran down the stairs, nearly tripping over Blossom who raced down with her.

"Hello?" she said breathlessly.

"Is Molly there?" said the voice on the other end of the line.

"What? No. She isn't here. Who is this?"

"This is Neil O'Malley. My furnace went out. Tell her to give me a call."

"Why d—"

But there was a click as Neil O'Malley hung up. Kathleen glared at the phone in her hand for a moment before hanging the handset up and stomping back upstairs.

210

By the time Molly's SUV pulled up, she had finished three more chapters of the manuscript. She deliberately didn't get up when she heard the front door open. Blossom glanced back uncertainly before going downstairs.

"Hello?" came Molly's voice.

She didn't reply. She heard more noises as Molly took her boots and jacket off.

"Kathleen?"

Molly's sock-muffled footsteps came up the stairs. She peered around the door. "Hey."

"Hey, yourself," Kathleen said coolly, not taking her eyes off her computer monitor.

Molly stepped over the threshold and stopped. "Is everything okay?"

Kathleen didn't answer right away.

"What's wrong?" Molly asked, pulling another chair closer to the desk. "Did your father—"

"Why are people calling here looking for you?"

"What? What are you talking about?"

Kathleen swiveled around to stare at Molly. "Why did Neil O'Malley call here looking for you? Does the entire island know we're sleeping together?"

She saw the slight flush rise in Molly's cheeks.

"I doubt the entire island does," Molly said in clipped tones. "But this is what people do here. We don't have cell phones. If they need me, they call from place to place to track me down. If he called here, someone probably told him I might be here. I doubt it was anything more sinister than that."

She stood up and walked toward the door.

"Where are you going?" Kathleen asked.

Molly stopped. "Neil called. It probably means his furnace has conked out again. It's too cold to leave it until tomorrow." She paused in the doorway. "I'm sorry it offends you to think the people on this island might know we're sleeping together. Don't wait supper for me. I don't know how long I'll be."

Molly didn't slam the door, but the sound of it closing seemed to echo through the house for a long time after she left.

❈❈❈❈❈❈❈❈

THE ROWING MACHINE WHIRRED in rhythm with Molly's pulls on the handles. This trainer had been an extravagance, but it got her through the winter months when she couldn't get out on the water. Sweat dripped from her nose and chin.

Behind her, the side door to the garage opened, letting in a blast of cold air.

"You haven't been in here much lately, Mo."

Her dad sat on the weight bench, leaning his elbows on his knees. "Nope."

He watched her as she continued rowing. "What happened to your hand?"

She glanced at her bloody knuckles. "Neil O'Malley's furnace." Her breathing came in bursts in sync with her pulls. "Wrench slipped."

Joe nodded. "Any particular reason you're in here instead of with Kathleen?"

Molly continued rowing for a few minutes, but Joe just sat there, waiting. She stopped. He tossed her a towel, which she pressed to her face.

"You two have a fight?"

She snorted. "Not really. I think..." She bit her lip. "I think she's still trying to figure some things out."

Joe reached for a dumbbell and did some wrist curls as he considered. "You know, back in the day, when I knew I wanted a life here, I knew I wanted your mom to be part of that life. She wasn't sure how she felt. About me or the island. It was kind of tough. Trying to decide whether I should just wait her out and let her sort her own feelings, or whether I should try to tip things in my favor by telling her how I felt."

Molly studied him. "What did you do?"

He smiled. "Not gonna tell you. You have to figure that out for yourself. Just want you to know that I understand where you're at."

He set the dumbbell down and kissed the top of her head. "Don't leave without coming in to say hi to your mom."

He left with another gust of cold air. Molly sat there, her breathing slowing now. She slid a couple of weights onto the Olympic bar and pumped out a set of chest presses before grabbing her jacket and heading to the house.

"Hi, Mo," Jenny said from the stove where she was dishing chowder into four bowls.

"Hi, Mom." Molly went to the sink to rinse her face. She reached for the towel hanging from one of the cupboard knobs and mopped her face dry. Upstairs, she could hear Joey and Matty talking.

She eyed the chowder. "That looks good."

She opened another cupboard to get an extra bowl down, but Jenny shook her head.

"Don't bother. Kathleen called."

"Oh?" Molly's tone was wary.

Jenny nodded. "She said she's got dinner ready at home whenever you finish."

Molly's eyes narrowed. "She said that?"

"Said what? Dinner?"

"No. Home. That was the word she used?"

"Yes, why?"

Molly turned away. "She's never called the cottage home."

Jenny spun her around and pulled her into a hug. "Go home, Molly. But come by tomorrow to visit. I'd like to have more than a two-minute conversation with you."

She swatted Molly on the butt. "Now get going."

Molly ran upstairs to pack a gym bag with clean clothes and drove back to the cottage, where the porch light was on, like a beacon welcoming her.

She hesitated on the porch, wondering whether she should knock or just go in, but she was saved by Kathleen opening the door for her.

She stepped inside, sniffing appreciatively. "Smells good."

Kathleen stood, watching her cautiously, almost cowering, as if she expected to be hit. "It's chicken and dumplings. I talked Nels into giving me his recipe."

"Really?"

Molly toed off her boots and shuffled her feet awkwardly. She pointed upstairs. "I'm pretty sweaty. I should probably shower."

"Okay. I'll have everything waiting when you come down."

Molly hurriedly showered and changed into clean jeans and a sweatshirt. She stood for a moment in the bedroom and then opened one of the empty dresser drawers to put the rest of her clothes inside.

In the kitchen, Kathleen was ladling out two bowls of chicken and dumplings. Molly poured two glasses of water, and they sat at the table. Neither spoke for a few minutes as they busied themselves with eating.

"This is really good," Molly said.

"Not as good as Nels makes." Kathleen frowned. "He must have held back some secret ingredient."

Molly and Kathleen spoke at the same time, saying, "I'm sorry—"

Kathleen set her spoon down and reached for Molly's forearm. "Let me go first. I am so sorry. For the way I reacted. For the way I spoke to you."

She closed her eyes. "I left Susannah because she was too ashamed to ever stand up and acknowledge me, and then I did the exact same thing to you."

Molly covered Kathleen's hand with hers. "And I know that you've been very private, had to be private. It can't be easy, living in such a small place where everybody knows everybody else's business."

Kathleen gave her a wry smile. "You could say that."

Molly squeezed her hand. "But they really don't care. The ones who do know are happy for us."

Kathleen nodded. "I know. It's just... Be patient with me."

Molly placed her fingers under Kathleen's chin, drawing her near for a kiss, tender and lingering. "I know I should probably be taking your clothes off right now, but I'm really, really hungry."

Kathleen released Molly's hand. "Eat. The taking off of clothes will happen later."

Chapter 14

SUNLIGHT SLANTED IN THROUGH a window to splash across the pages of the book. Kathleen leaned over the heavy tome, her finger tracing the lines and names as she tried to memorize the branches of her family tree. She took her glasses off to bend closer and promptly sneezed. She wiped her nose with a tissue, the motes of dust from the book swirling about in the beam of sunlight. It was fascinating, learning where she came from. Her Irish ancestors had come from Mayo and Dhún na nGall, which she'd had to ask to realize was modern-day Donegal.

Another window let a warm pool of sunshine hit the floor, where Blossom took full advantage, stretching out on his side to nap.

She'd spent a couple of days each of the past few weeks with Rebecca, studying the island families and who was related to whom. The Keepers—whom Rebecca said went back to the first shipwreck survivors—had kept not just family trees, but short bios of each member of each family—only names and locations of the ones who left Little Sister—continuing with more detail on those who stayed or returned. This was a genealogical treasure. Without exception, everyone was related to someone else on this island; usually several family lines were connected.

"Well, it's inevitable, isn't it?" Rebecca had said when Kathleen commented on it. "Newcomers marry in, but over the centuries, people from all the island families have blended."

Kathleen's gaze followed one line of her grandfather's family tree back. One name caught her attention. She jabbed a finger at it, staring. She went to the bookshelves and pulled the Ahearn book out. Flipping through the pages, she found the one she sought.

Carrying both books with her, she went to find Rebecca, who was outside, sweeping a light dusting of snow off the library's porch.

"Molly and I are related?" Kathleen asked, holding the books out in front of her.

Rebecca paused her sweeping. "I've told you most of us are related to one another somehow. But yes, your great-great-grandmother on your father's side was sisters with Molly's great-great-grandmother on our side."

"But... but that makes us cousins, kind of," Kathleen sputtered.

"Yes." Rebecca resumed her sweeping. "That's part of what the Keepers do. Before any two islanders can bond, we have to make sure they're far enough removed to make procreation safe. It's part of why our work is so important."

"What happens if they love each other and are too closely related?"

"It has happened once or twice," Rebecca said with a shrug. She glanced at Kathleen. "It's not as if you and Molly are going to procreate."

Kathleen huffed in exasperation as she carried the books back into the genealogy room. It still felt weird, knowing that she was sleeping with a cousin, however distant, and knowing that everyone else knew about it.

218

And not just sleeping with, she was slowly beginning to realize.

Neither she nor Molly had spoken of anything more, of how they were feeling. Sometimes, the words were right there, reflected in Molly's beautiful eyes, ready to be spoken aloud, but... Kathleen could never bring herself to say them. She had said them—too early and too often—to Susannah, who rarely said them back, but always reminded her of them after one of their fights. Those three words had come to feel like a weapon, something to be used to chain her in place.

Lost in her thoughts, she returned the books to their place on the shelves and then went back outside. Blossom stirred himself to follow her.

"I'll see you Thursday," she said. "I told Louisa I'd come help her clean this afternoon."

Rebecca eyed her. "That's nice of you. Give her my best."

Kathleen drove to Louisa's house—it was odd not to think of it as the Woodhouse sisters' house—where the Ford sat, covered in the latest three inches of new snow. She was glad Louisa hadn't tried to drive in this. There was a clear path shoveled from the drive to the front porch, Aidan's work, she presumed.

Louisa must have heard her pull up. She stepped outside, an old cardigan over her cotton dress, her fuzzy slippers completing the ensemble.

"Hello, Katie."

"Hi, Miss Louisa." Kathleen let Blossom out and reached for a covered container of the oatmeal pecan cookies Louisa liked.

She took her boots off inside the front door. "Brought you something."

"Oh, you didn't have to do that," Louisa said, taking the container from her. She carried it into the kitchen, followed closely by Blossom. Kathleen saw her slip one cookie out from under the plastic lid.

"You've rearranged the furniture," Kathleen noted with some surprise as she hung her jacket and scarf on a hook.

"Aidan helped me move it to clean the floors, and we decided we liked it this way for now."

Kathleen smiled at the "we" references as she followed Louisa into the kitchen where two boxes of ashes sat on the kitchen chairs.

Bobby and Fred had brought Olivia's ashes with them on their ferry run the week prior.

"So it's working out, with Aidan?"

"Oh, yes. He's a lovely boy. Never much of a scholar. He always preferred to be fixing things. After he took them apart, of course. Tea? I was just heating the kettle up."

"Sure."

Louisa poured two cups of hot water and set them on the table with a selection of teabags. Kathleen joined her, choosing a bag and dunking it into her cup.

"I forgot, you would have taught all of them."

"Yes." Louisa plucked her glasses up from where they hung around her neck and peered through them to select a teabag for herself. "Up through Molly and Joey. When Matty and the youngsters his age came along, they started the boarding school business."

"It's too bad there isn't a teacher on the island any longer." Kathleen pried the lid off the container and placed a few cookies on each saucer.

"It is. We tried, but we couldn't find anyone who wanted to work here."

Kathleen looked up at the hitch in Louisa's voice. She suddenly seemed old and frail as her arthritic hands cradled her teacup.

"I worry for Little Sister," Louisa said. "If our young ones aren't raised here and then don't want to come back, what will happen?"

Kathleen laid a hand over Louisa's gnarled one. "Don't you think some will always come back? I did, eventually."

Louisa gave her a watery smile. "You're right, Katie. Let's have some of these cookies."

She closed her eyes as she chewed. "These remind me of Maisie. We were such good friends. How I miss her and Olivia."

Kathleen didn't know what to say. She nibbled on a cookie.

"Are you happy here, Katie?" Louisa asked.

Kathleen coughed a little at the unexpected question. "Yes."

Louisa eyed her over her glasses, fixing her with a stare that reminded her of Rebecca. "Are you really? Because we weren't so sure you were, when you first came back."

It was Kathleen's turn to grip her teacup as she thought. "I wasn't happy with my life, period, when I arrived here."

"That girl? The one who came here?"

Kathleen nodded. "Partly her. Partly... everything else."

"Does Molly make you happy?"

Kathleen stalled by eating another couple of bites of cookie. "Yes."

Louisa nodded and took a sip of tea. "I've often thought if we'd been born a generation later, Ollie might have been like you and Molly."

"Really?"

"Oh, yes. She was never one for the boys. But our generation just wasn't as open about such things. Still, the island has always been more accepting than the outside world. If there'd been the right girl, I like to think she would have settled down with her."

Kathleen tilted her head, regarding Louisa with new respect. "How about you? Didn't you ever fall for anyone? Want a family of your own?"

To her surprise, Louisa blushed furiously.

"What is it?"

Louisa pursed her lips firmly for a moment before saying, "There was one boy. A man, actually. When I went away to college. He was one of my professors. We..."

Kathleen gaped at her. "You had an affair with a professor?"

Louisa gave her a guilty grin. "You think I'm nothing more than a prim old spinster?" She sighed, and the grin faded. "I was young and romantic, and I loved him desperately, but he... There were others, you see. I was foolish not to guess that, not to realize I wasn't the only one."

"What did you do?"

Louisa sniffed. "What could I do? I finished my studies and came home, where I had an entire island of children."

She dusted cookie crumbs from her fingers. "How about we tackle this kitchen?"

⬥⬥⬥⬥⬥⬥⬥⬥⬥⬥

AN ANCIENT OIL-FILLED HEATER hummed nearby as Molly knelt on the deck of the boat she was working on. She carefully drilled a hole through a mortise and tenon joint with an antique hand drill. It took a little more time, but she liked the accuracy of the old tool. She backed the drill out and tapped an oak plug into the hole with some waterproof glue to secure the joint. She shaved away the excess peg with a flexible Japanese pull saw that gave her a nearly flush cut. Sanding patiently, she rounded the plug until it sat just proud of the surrounding board.

She sat back, humming with satisfaction as she inspected her work. She wished she could keep this boat after all the hours she'd put into her, but she wished that with every boat she restored. They each carried a bit of her with them when they sailed back to their owners.

She'd sent the rails and gauges away to be re-chromed. As soon as the weather warmed enough, she'd apply several coats of spar varnish, and this little beauty would be ready to sail.

Outside the boathouse, she heard the launch pull up to the dock. Now that it was winter, the boys were busy most days doing boat maintenance. They'd spent the day at Big Sister helping the marina owner there with some repairs. Voices and stomping footsteps echoed through the boathouse. Cap'n Jack shook his head at being disturbed from his nap.

The side door opened, and Matty came in.

"Hey, Mo."

He leaned over the side and whistled as he ran a hand over her woodwork. "Nice."

"Thanks."

She selected a new peg. "Good day?"

He shrugged. "Yeah. They've got some monster yachts over there. We'll probably be there for the next couple weeks." He dragged a stool over near her tool chest and sat down.

Molly read the signal that he wanted to talk and shifted to sit cross-legged on the boat deck. "What's up?"

Rather than answer, he leaned his elbows on his knees, rasping his thumbnail over a callus on his palm. She waited.

"Are you..." he began, but stopped. "You and Kathleen. Is this for real?"

Molly frowned. "What do you mean?"

He looked up at her. "Are you guys gonna get bonded? You moving in for good?"

Her shock must have shown on her face, because he grinned.

"What? You haven't asked her? She hasn't asked you? What are you guys waiting for?"

Molly shook her head. "Why are you asking me this?"

Matty's grin slid away. "Because, I'm gonna... I think I'm ready to ask Brandi."

Molly stared. "Ask her what?"

"To marry me."

"No way."

"Way." He grinned again, running his hands through his hair so that it stuck up all over. "I'm ready. I think."

"Really?" She climbed down off the boat and knelt facing him. "Are you sure? This is big, Matty."

His face split with an even bigger smile. "I know!"

He reached into his jeans pocket and held out his hand. Lying in a velvet box in his palm was a fine silvery chain with an intricate silver heart-shaped locket.

"It's white gold," he said. "Not silver, like the song."

She glanced up. "What song?"

He rolled his eyes. "You know." And he sang, "Brandy, you're a fine girl..." His voice trailed away. "Except I want her to be my lady, not the sea."

She laughed. "I had no idea you were so romantic."

He laughed, too, looking embarrassed. "I know it's not a diamond ring. But I hope she'll take this, and me, and wear my ring when we get married."

"Wow." Molly sat back on her heels. "You mean it."

He nodded. "Yeah. I do."

For a moment, she almost hugged him, but it just felt weird. So she punched him in the arm instead. "I'm happy for you."

"Honest Injun?"

She chuckled, knowing Rebecca would slap them both silly if she heard them. "Honest Injun. Where will you live?"

He shook his head. "Not sure. We haven't talked about it. Don't know if she'll want to leave the restaurant."

"She'll keep waitressing?"

"Her folks own the Lobster Pot."

"I didn't know that."

"Yeah." Matty scratched at his stubbly chin. "Might have to live on Big Sister. What do you think Mom and Dad will say?"

"You know they'll be happy for you, too."

"Thanks, Mo." He pushed to his feet, slipping the velvet box back into his pocket. He paused as he reached the door. "I think you should get a move on, before someone else steals your girl."

Molly listened to him walking away, trying to picture her baby brother married. She went back to work on the boat deck. She got another peg tapped and glued in place and was partway through sawing the excess off when she paused, thinking about what he'd said.

"What are you waiting for?" she muttered.

※※※※※※※※※

"NOW STOP FIDGETING."

Kathleen craned her neck to try and see her reflection in the glass of the kitchen door, but Jenny firmly repositioned her head.

"If you don't like this haircut, you don't ever have to come back to this barber," she said, snipping a little more off the top.

Kathleen's eyes widened as the auburn hairs fluttered down onto the white sheet wrapped around her shoulders in lieu of a hairdresser's drape. Her head snapped around again as the kitchen door opened and Molly came in.

"Not one word until I'm done," Jenny ordered her before she could say anything.

Kathleen tried to read the look on Molly's face, but the grin she wore wasn't reassuring.

"We might have a new Mo on the island," she said, fighting her laughter.

Blossom came out from under the table to greet her while Minnow meowed from where she was lying on the kitchen counter.

"Hush." Jenny pulled her comb through Kathleen's thick hair and snipped some more. "Don't tease her."

Molly composed herself and went to the sink to wash her hands. "Smells good."

Minnow hurried over to bat her paw at the stream of water.

"Ham and beans," Jenny said absently, continuing to snip here and there. She came around front and bent down to inspect her handiwork.

"I think one ear is lower than the other now," Molly quipped.

225

Kathleen grabbed an extra comb off the table and threw it at her.

"I think we're done," Jenny said, running her fingers through Kathleen's hair to let it fall in layers.

She pulled the sheet away and gathered it. Handing it to Molly, she said, "Go shake this out, please."

Kathleen reached up to feel her head as Jenny got the broom out of the cupboard. There was an awful lot of hair on the kitchen floor.

"I left some. Don't worry."

"It feels so much lighter," Kathleen said, going out to the living room to inspect her reflection.

It really was a nice cut, she realized as she turned her head back and forth. The layers framed her face softly. She smiled at herself.

When she went back into the kitchen, Molly did a double take. If Kathleen had any further doubts that the haircut flattered her, they were answered by the look in Molly's eyes.

She felt her cheeks burn and was only vaguely aware of Jenny saying, "Mo, why don't you set the table? Since you're both here, it's silly not to stay for dinner."

Joe came in with Joey and Matty. As everyone sat to eat, they talked about the day's work scraping and painting and varnishing hulls, but all Kathleen was really aware of was the pressure of Molly's thigh, firmly pressed against hers under the table.

She did note Molly exchanging a significant glance with Matty when Joe leaned over to kiss Jenny. The light, the laughter, the love around the table—here was everything Kathleen had ever longed for.

As if she could read her thoughts, Molly reached under the table to squeeze Kathleen's hand.

They stayed to help with the dishes and then drove back to the cottage.

"I'm glad this worked out," Kathleen said, shivering from the passenger seat. "I wasn't thinking about how late we might be leaving when Blossom and I walked to the house."

Molly cranked up the heat. "Me, too."

She sounded odd.

"Are you okay?"

Molly nodded. "I'm fine."

Kathleen didn't push as they arrived at the cottage. Molly cut the engine off, and Kathleen let Blossom out of the back seat. Before she could climb the porch steps, Molly caught her hand.

"What is it?"

They stood in the dark, no lights anywhere around them. Overhead, the stars were brilliant in an inky black sky. Kathleen tilted her head to gaze at it. Molly wrapped an arm around her shoulders and looked skyward as well.

A shooting star appeared.

Kathleen gasped. "Did you see it? Did you?"

"Yes," Molly said with a chuckle.

"I never saw any until I came here." Kathleen scrunched her eyes shut.

"What are you doing?"

"Making a wish," Kathleen said. "Shhh."

Molly waited until Kathleen opened her eyes. "What was your wish?"

Kathleen smiled. "I'm not telling. It might not come true." She angled her head. "What about you? Did you make a wish?"

Molly opened her mouth, but from inside the house, the telephone's jangle cut through the night. They both ran to the cottage. Ever since Olivia's heart attack, any phone call came with the dread that it might be bad news.

Kathleen yanked the receiver off the wall. "Hello?"

"Kathleen..."

She braced a hand on the wall. "Susannah." For one wild moment, she thought Susannah was back on Little Sister, but then she heard the sound of crying. "What's wrong?"

227

"My father..."

"What's wrong with your voice? You sound funny."

"He hit me," Susannah said, though her words were hard to make out. "He broke my jaw and tore my shoulder."

Kathleen dropped into a chair. Molly, she noticed, had stayed in the kitchen entrance. "Were the police involved?"

"Yes, but... they only make things worse."

Kathleen took her glasses off and pressed her fingers to her eyes. "You mean you wouldn't press charges."

"Can you come?"

Kathleen's hand dropped. Molly was no longer in the kitchen door. "Come?"

"Please. I need you."

"What about your sister?"

"She's with my mom, trying to calm him down—"

"So he doesn't hurt her," Kathleen finished for her. "Where are you?"

"I'm home, but I'm having a hard time taking care of myself with only one arm. I didn't know who else to call."

Susannah started sobbing. Kathleen listened, her eyes closed again, her sense of self-preservation battling her guilt. From the next room, she heard the sound of the front door opening and closing. She bit her lip to keep from hollering for Molly to stay.

With a resigned sigh, she said, "I'll have to get someone to bring me to the mainland. I'll be there by tomorrow night."

Chapter 15

ATRUCK ENGINE RUMBLED in the drive before cutting off. Molly sat propped on her bed, listening as the door slammed. A moment later, there were voices in the kitchen. Her mom, she knew, was warming up some dinner for Aidan. She looked at the bedside clock and was surprised to see it was nearly ten. She returned to her book, or tried to.

It had been a shitty day. Actually a shitty night and day—ever since she'd walked out of Kathleen's cottage last night. She'd reminded herself over and over that Kathleen was so kind-hearted, there was no way she could say no to what she'd heard enough to understand was Susannah's plea. With as few words as possible, she'd told her dad last night about Kathleen needing a ride to the mainland. Aidan had volunteered.

Blossom got up and put a paw on the mattress, whining softly. Joe had brought him that morning.

"Told Kathleen we'd keep him for her till she came home."

Home. Kathleen had started to call this island home, but would it still feel that way once she was back with Susannah, back among the people and in the city she'd lived in for so long? Molly felt a sensation like acid burning her stomach. She hadn't been able to eat more than a few bites all day.

She patted Blossom, and he lay back down.

About ten minutes later, heavy footsteps came up the stairs and there was a knock on her door.

"Come."

Aidan pushed the door open. "Okay to come in?"

"Sure." She closed her book and shifted to sit cross-legged on her bed as he dragged the desk chair over. Blossom went to him. Aidan absently gave his ears a rub.

"Got her there," he said. "Borrowed Bobby's extra car and took her to a car rental place. She should be close to Philly by now."

Molly nodded, tracing a finger over the title of her book embossed in its cover. "Thanks for taking her. I know this means a lot to her." She could feel Aidan watching her. "Why are you so late?"

"Stayed to take care of a few things. Wanted to talk to Bobby."

She glanced up. "What about?"

Aidan leaned forward, bracing his elbows on his knees. "I'm... I'm going to start training to be a ferry pilot, come spring. I spent today filling out all the paperwork."

Molly's mouth fell open. "Really?"

He nodded. "Yeah. Can't stay on Little Sister my whole life, renting a room from Miss Louisa. Been giving this a lot of thought. Couldn't have done it before... when I was drinking. My record's clean, thanks to you. Course, Bobby knows. We had to talk about that. Even one more drunk, and I'm out, he says. He won't take a second chance on me."

Molly nodded. "He wouldn't. But I don't think he'll have to worry about that."

Aidan lowered his gaze to his hands. "No."

A long, tense silence followed.

"Did she ever tell you," Aidan began hesitantly. "What happened that night? On the beach?"

"She found a letter from her dad to Maisie. Said her mom told her that she wished it had been her who died."

"Yeah." Aidan ran his hand through his hair. "Jesus, can you imagine Mom ever saying that to one of us?"

"No."

"It was her birthday," he said so quietly Molly wasn't sure she'd heard.

"What was her birthday?"

"The day Bryan... it was her tenth birthday. She said her folks haven't celebrated her birthday since. No one has. They only remember..."

Molly closed her eyes, dropping her forehead to her hand. "She didn't tell me that part."

"What about you?"

Molly lifted her head. "What about me?"

"No, both of you. You seem good together, Mo. Like this is the real thing."

"I don't know." She rested her elbows on her knees, frowning. "I thought... but now, with Susannah calling..."

"I don't think she really wanted to go."

She flicked a loose thread on her comforter. "You don't?"

He shook his head. "She was really quiet. Kept looking back. At the dock, before we shoved off... I think she was hoping you'd come."

Molly groaned. "I should have. I just..." She felt tears sting her eyes. Their gaze met and held.

"Does she know how you feel?" Aidan asked.

Molly shook her head. "I was trying to figure out how to tell her when... Maybe it's better this way. She'll go back and figure out she doesn't really want to be here."

"Bullshit."

"What?"

"I said, bullshit. This island is her home now. And you love her. Why can't you tell her that?"

Molly sat back, drawing her knees to her chest. "I don't think you're best one to be giving me advice on this. I don't recall seeing you laying your heart on the line for anyone."

Aidan dropped his head again, staring at his clasped hands. "I'm not sure I'm strong enough."

"What do you mean? You're one of the strongest people—"

"I'm not. I wasn't strong enough to deal with Bryan's death without drinking myself stupid. I'm not sure I'm strong enough to let myself fall for someone. I can barely keep myself together. But you are, Mo."

Her mouth opened and closed. She didn't know what to say.

"I watch Mom and Dad, and I'm kind of in awe," Aidan said. "They absolutely love each other. They love us, too, but nothing comes before the two of them, what they feel for each other. Jesus, that's scary."

"Scary?"

"Yeah. I think loving someone is one of the bravest things anyone ever does. Taking the chance of being hurt. Letting yourself need someone else, knowing how hollowed out you'd be if they weren't in your life. What's braver than that?"

She stared at him.

"She needs to know how you feel, Mo." He stood and put the chair back, giving Blossom a last scratch. "You owe yourself the chance at that kind of happiness."

He left, closing the door behind him. She turned to her reflection in the mirror over the dresser, wondering why she couldn't see what he did.

KATHLEEN FOUND A PARKING space on the crowded curb. Pulling her suitcase from the back seat of the rental car, she stared up at the lit windows of the second floor apartment she had shared with Susannah. She'd thought, when she left here five months ago, that she would never be back. She sighed and went to the entry, where she pressed the buzzer for apartment 2B.

"Kathleen?" came Susannah's muffled voice.

"Yes."

Susannah buzzed her through, and she climbed the stairs to the second floor. As she approached the door, Susannah opened it. Despite knowing of Susannah's injuries, Kathleen wasn't quite prepared for the sight of her black eye and the swollen bruising along the left side of her jaw, her right arm in a sling. She felt a seething rage at Susannah's father.

She stepped past Susannah and deposited her suitcase on the foyer floor.

"Thanks for coming," Susannah said, her jaw stiff, her lips barely moving.

"Have you eaten?" Kathleen asked, glancing at her watch and seeing that it was nearly eleven o'clock.

Susannah barked out a sound that might have been a laugh and led the way into the kitchen. The blender held a green concoction that she poured into a glass with a straw.

"Want some?" she asked, holding up the blender.

"Uh, no. I'm good."

They sat at the kitchen table.

"Is that all you can eat right now?" Kathleen asked, pointing to the green slush in the glass.

Susannah nodded. "Hurts too much to chew. If my jaw doesn't heal, they said they might have to wire it. Trying to avoid that."

An awkward silence filled the space between them.

"So what happened?" Kathleen asked.

Susannah took a sip through the straw and sat back, shifting her sling to try and get her shoulder in a more comfortable position.

"One of the neighbors told him she saw Mom talking to the postman, and he..."

Her voice trailed away.

"He went off," Kathleen supplied. "Let me guess, he waited until you were all there on a Sunday, and then, when he had a ready-made audience, he went off."

Susannah stared at her. Her lips moved, but no words came out.

"And you got in between them, so he turned on you." Kathleen shoved to her feet. "Nothing changes. And it never will unless you guys make it change. You do realize that, don't you?"

Susannah looked up at her, her eyes brimming with tears. "You know Mom will never leave him, and we can't leave her alone with him."

Kathleen crossed the kitchen and braced her hands on the counter, her head hanging. "It's late. Are you going to work tomorrow?"

Susannah shook her head. "Not looking like this. I'd have to explain..."

Yes, you'd have to explain that your father is an abusive monster, and you all put up with it, over and over.

Kathleen longed to say it, but instead, she said, "We should get to bed."

She picked up her suitcase and followed Susannah down the hall, stepping into the right-hand extra bedroom.

"I thought—" Susannah pointed at the master bedroom.

"No." Kathleen set her bag down, bracing herself. "I'll help you get ready for bed, but I'm sleeping here."

A short while later, with Susannah changed into a nightshirt and settled in the bed they used to share, Kathleen lay in the twin bed in the spare room. She'd never realized how noisy it was here—traffic and people talking out on the sidewalk and other tenants moving around upstairs.

She longed for the quiet of the island and her little cottage. She rolled over, wishing she were snuggled in Molly's arms with Blossom snoring nearby. How had life changed so much from just last night, when she'd been wishing on a shooting star? She closed her eyes, remembering the way the starlit sky had been reflected in Molly's eyes, as if she could see forever in their depths. A single tear leaked out.

She snorted into her pillow. "So much for wishes and happily ever after."

※※※※※※※※※※

MOLLY LASTED THREE DAYS. Three miserable days of trying to keep herself busy and not think about Kathleen, only to realize she wasn't able to think of anything else. *God, you were so stupid to let her go without telling her how you felt.*

Her mom had been agreeable to keeping Blossom at home with her during the day. The poor dog stuck to Molly like glue when she was home at night.

"You missing her, too?" Molly asked him when he followed her into the bathroom.

On the afternoon of the third day, Molly gave up. She went by the cottage. A quick search through a box of old bills gave her Kathleen's address in Philly. She drove home, where Blossom greeted her enthusiastically.

Jenny glanced up from where she was placing an apple pie in the oven. She pointed to a small, insulated food sack.

"I put together some things for you. Sandwiches, cookies, cold water."

Molly gaped for a moment. "How did you—?"

Jenny smiled and shook her head. "Molly, your soft heart is matched only by your stubbornness. Go pack an overnight bag."

Molly ran upstairs and threw some things into her gym bag. She tucked her wallet with her sheriff's badge into her back pocket and ran

235

down to the kitchen where her mom pushed the food sack into her hands.

"Promise me you'll stop and get a room if you get tired."

Molly grinned. "I will."

Jenny gave her a kiss and a shove out the door as she held onto Blossom's collar. "Tell your father I won our bet. And give Kathleen our best."

She hadn't made it to the Toyota when she heard a pitiful howling coming from the house. Giving up, she jogged back.

"I'll take him," she said, reaching down to rub Blossom as he danced around her.

"You're sure?" Jenny asked.

"I'm sure. Maybe he'll bring me luck."

She grabbed a second bag, filled it with dog food, and she and Blossom got in the Toyota.

Her dad had a boat fueled and ready for her. Blossom jumped in ahead of her, tail wagging as he paced.

"What was your bet?" Molly asked as she climbed in and stowed her bags.

"I bet you'd be ready to go after her yesterday," Joe said with a grin, untying the mooring line.

Molly looked back at him as the boat drifted away from the dock. "So, did you go get Mom?"

"You bet I did!"

He laughed as she pushed the throttle forward and waved.

It was a rough ride, with a steady north wind creating a sizeable chop to the water. She wrapped Blossom in a blanket and snugged her jacket under her chin, a knit hat under her hood. The boat settled into a regular rhythm of riding the swells. She forced herself to slow down enough to eat and drink a little, with just a little water for Blossom.

To the southwest, the sun sank below the horizon as an early February dusk settled. The sky darkened, and the stars came out. She watched them, the vastness and depth of those tiny, infinite points of light.

Damn, if only she'd gotten the chance to tell Kathleen her wish...

She steered into the lit-up marina and moored the boat before hauling her bags to the ferry office where she fed Blossom and called her uncle. She turned her back on Sadie, who was listening.

"Might be two or three days," she said.

"No problem," Bobby said. "No one else is planning on using it."

She thanked him. Sadie handed her the key, and she ran to where the blue Escape was parked. *What an appropriate model name.* She put her water in the drink holder, made sure she could reach the rest of the food her mom had packed. Blossom curled up in the back seat with a contented sigh.

Molly grinned at him. "Here we go."

Pulling out of the marina's parking lot, she began her trek to Philadelphia and, hopefully, the rest of her life.

⬛⬛⬛⬛⬛⬛⬛

"WHAT ARE YOU LOOKING AT?"

Kathleen glanced back over her shoulder into the dining room. "Nothing."

Standing on the little Juliet balcony, barely large enough for two small chairs, she stared sadly at the sky, where she could only make out a few of the brightest stars. There was Orion's belt and one or two of the other bright ones, but all the others, all the amazing stars she now knew were out there, they were invisible here, as if they didn't exist at all. It was beginning to feel as if her life on Little Sister didn't really exist, either.

"What do you want to watch on TV tonight?" Susannah asked.

"I don't care," Kathleen said.

"Come on in. You're letting cold air in."

With a resigned sigh, Kathleen stepped back inside and slid the door shut, remembering to flip all three locks.

"Sit here with me," Susannah said, patting the sofa.

Kathleen sat but kept a cushion between them.

"Don't you want to sit closer?"

Kathleen shook her head and positioned a fluffy sofa pillow between them. "The therapist said you should keep your arm propped up when you're sitting, remember?"

The last few days had been filled with chauffeuring Susannah to follow-up appointments and grocery shopping and writing checks to pay the bills and... *Everything I used to do,* Kathleen thought now. It felt as though every one of these tasks was another link in a heavy chain, tying her back down here.

There hadn't been a break long enough to do any of the work she'd brought with her. If they'd had other friends, Kathleen might have been able to get some things done, but friends were another thing Susannah had always refused for fear they wouldn't be discreet.

The hardest part had been earlier in the day when Susannah's sister, Darla, had come by.

"What are you doing here?" she'd asked when Kathleen answered the door.

"I asked her to stay for a while," Susannah had said quickly.

Not even bothering to hide her displeasure, Darla had pushed past Kathleen into the apartment. "You know what Dad would do if he saw her here."

"I wasn't anywhere around when he did that," Kathleen said, pointing at Susannah. "And none of you stopped it. Including not pressing charges."

She'd never spoken up before. Darla stared at her.

"You're sick," Kathleen went on, unable to stop now she'd started. "All of you. You keep up the pretense that he's some upstanding citizen, pretending you're protecting your mother, when all you're doing is letting him continue to get away with this."

She'd tried for over an hour to get them to see that the whole family needed help, but they wouldn't listen. "You don't understand," Darla said over and over, while Susannah kept silent.

Kathleen's nostrils flared now, just thinking about it. Susannah had clicked the channels until she came to some police drama she liked. *Now that's ironic*, Kathleen thought, as the detectives tried to convince a victim of domestic abuse to leave her situation. *Does she even see it?*

But one glance at Susannah confirmed that she didn't. Smothering a scream of frustration, Kathleen pushed to her feet.

"Where are you going?" Susannah asked as she reached the door.

"Just going to the car for something," Kathleen mumbled as she grabbed her jacket and wrenched the door open.

She nearly ran down the stairs and out onto the sidewalk. Pausing to take a breath, she coughed, choking on a cloud of diesel fumes as a delivery truck rumbled by.

"Kathleen, what are you doing here?" she grumbled aloud, echoing Darla's question from earlier in the day.

She shoved her hands into her pockets and walked toward her rental car. As she neared it, she saw a piece of paper fluttering from under the windshield wiper.

"No, no, no!"

She hurried the last few steps to the car. She'd made sure she parked legally—a difficult feat in this neighborhood. She snatched the paper from under the wiper. She had to angle it under the streetlight to read the writing on it: *Look inside.*

She whirled around, scanning the street to see if she was being watched—her city guard immediately up, something that hadn't been needed on Little Sister. Seeing no one, she unlocked the car.

Lying on the passenger seat was a small cloth bag secured by a ribbon. She got in, locking the door after her. As she picked the bag up, she realized the ribbon wasn't a ribbon at all. It was a dog collar, embroidered with pink and white blossoms. She unclipped it and tugged open the bag's drawstring. Reaching inside, she pulled out a small envelope and a black velvet box.

She opened the envelope first. Inside was a small card with neat handwriting.

> *We both miss you. Please come home.*
> *Love,*
>   *M&B*

Her eyes were so blinded by tears, she could scarcely see as she pried open the hinged lid of the velvet box. Lying inside was... "a shooting star," she whispered, touching a finger to a necklace with four small diamonds arcing toward a larger fifth one at the end of a graceful sweep. She placed a hand over her mouth, forgetting to choke back her tears.

She hurled herself out of the car, spinning in place. She searched the dark shadows between the cones of light from the streetlamps, hoping to see Molly and Blossom. Nothing.

She clasped the dog collar and the little velvet box. Hanging from the collar was a small tag she hadn't noticed before. Flipping it over, she read, *We're waiting for you.*

A window opened overhead.

"Kath?"

She looked up toward Susannah's voice. "Coming."

The window closed. She set the velvet box on the hood of her car and took the necklace out, fastening the chain around her neck. She slowly climbed the stairs to the apartment. Tomorrow. Tomorrow, Susannah would have to figure out how to be on her own again.

Outside the door, she paused, smiling as she touched her fingers to the shooting star on her chest.

❌❌❌❌❌❌❌❌

BLOSSOM LIFTED HIS HEAD and Molly lowered her book as they both listened to a new voice outside. Realizing it wasn't Kathleen, Blossom sighed and rested his head on Molly's thigh. She reached down to scratch his ears where they both lay on the bunk of the boat's small cabin.

"No bad memories of being here?" she asked him.

His tail thumped once in answer.

This waiting was murder. Had Kathleen found the note and the gifts she'd left? What if she hadn't gone to her car at all? Or worse, what if she didn't feel the way Molly did?

Molly felt only a small twinge of guilt over having used her sheriff's credentials to get the car rental company to release the make and license number of the car Kathleen had rented. As for the Slim Jim she'd used to open the car door, well lock-picking tools were necessary equipment in a place where people locked their keys in their cars with no locksmiths available.

She let her book flop onto her stomach. What if it didn't work? She really had to face the possibility that Kathleen might not come back. Molly closed her eyes and flung her arm over her face. Her brain, tired of this hamster wheel of speculation, shut down for a while. She drifted off.

She was awakened by a sudden rocking of the boat.

"Ahoy there!"

She sat up as Blossom bounded off the bunk. They both scrambled up the stairs to the deck, where Kathleen was standing. Blossom wriggled and jumped, trying to lick every bit of her he could get to.

Kathleen rubbed him and then flung herself into Molly's arms. Blossom stood on his hind legs to join in the group hug.

"How did you find me?" Kathleen asked, her voice muffled as she buried her face in Molly's neck.

241

"Well, being sheriff does have its advantages," Molly said. "I might have implied you were a person of interest in a case I was working and got your rental car info."

Kathleen pulled back, the necklace glinting at her throat. "You lied, didn't you?"

Molly's answer was in her kiss—passionate, hard, her arms holding Kathleen tightly, wanting never to let go. Kathleen kissed her back just as hard.

"Oh, I've missed you. Both of you." She planted a kiss on Blossom's head.

"You have?" Molly asked.

"Yes," Kathleen said, laughing and crying at the same time. "I have."

"How are you?" Molly asked. "How are things there?"

Kathleen pulled Molly over to sit down on a cushioned seat. "Things there are…"

Molly bit her lip.

"…such a good reminder of why I left."

"Really?"

"Yes, really." Kathleen bent down to hug Blossom again. He wagged his rump happily. "I can't wait to get home."

Now it was Molly's turn to get choked up.

Kathleen reached over to take her hand. "You really came to get me? Both of you?"

Molly lifted one shoulder in a careless shrug. "The island has been a little lonely without you. And the skies a little emptier."

Kathleen pressed her fingers to the diamonds. "A shooting star?"

"You never got to hear what my wish was," Molly said softly.

Kathleen leaned close and wrapped her arms around Molly's neck. "I think I can guess."

A serious expression settled over Molly's features as she deliberately unwrapped Kathleen's arms from around her neck and took her hands.

"I need to say this." She stared hard into Kathleen's eyes, trying to make certain Kathleen understood the impact of what she was about to say. "I love you. I've never said that to anyone other than my mom or dad. I love you, Kathleen Halloran. I want to spend the rest of my life with you. If you can't come back to Little Sister, I'll..." Her voice hitched a little. "I would leave to be with you. As long as we're together."

Kathleen stared wordlessly for a long moment. "You would leave Little Sister?"

Molly nodded mutely.

Kathleen's face split into a wide smile. "I love you, too, Molly Ahearn Cooper. And I want to live with you. On Little Sister. Forever. Watching shooting stars."

They kissed again, softly, slowly this time.

"I need to return the car," Kathleen murmured when they parted. "But then, can we go home?"

Molly glanced to the sky, already a deepening indigo as the sun tracked toward the western horizon. "We'll be sailing in the dark."

"That's okay," Kathleen said. "We'll navigate by the stars."

Chapter 16

K ATHLEEN SAT AT HER DESK, immersed in the manuscript she was editing. It really was a very good novel, but the author needed some help with developing the secondary characters. Blossom whined and rested his head on her thigh. She patted him absently and kept working. A moment later, he gave her a hard nudge with his nose.

She glanced down at him and then at the clock in the corner of her monitor. "Jeez, I had no idea what time it was. You probably need to go out, don't you?"

He barked and raced her down the stairs. When she opened the front door, he launched off the porch and raced to the nearest bush to lift his leg. She chuckled at his expression of relief and raised her face to the sun. The snow was nearly gone, and the air was mild, holding a promise of spring. It was warm enough to go without a jacket. She decided to stretch her legs and give her eyes a break from staring at the computer. She pulled the door shut and headed toward the bluff, Blossom galloping after her.

Small flowers were pushing up here and there, little white ones that she thought might be crocus. She paused, squatting to pluck one.

I really need to learn more about flowers, she thought. She stood and took a deep breath.

The shallow rays of the March sunlight bathed everything in golden light. She was struck again by how beautiful it was here on the island, and how lucky she was to live here.

"How lucky I am with everything," she said to Blossom, leaning down to ruffle his coat.

She got to the bluff and sat, gazing out over the ocean, the sky dotted with puffy clouds. Down below, the waves crashed against the base of the cliff.

She still felt a little guilty, being this ridiculously happy, but the guilt was slowly fading. It had been a lot stronger when she first got back to Little Sister with Molly. Her farewell to Susannah hadn't gone well. She'd forced herself to actually say good-bye this time, instead of just disappearing as she had in October.

"You're really going back?" Susannah had said in clear disbelief.

Kathleen had paused for a second. "You thought I was staying?"

"Yes. I mean, I hoped, once you were back here, you'd remember how good we are together, and you'd want to stay."

The warble in Susannah's voice had had the desired effect as Kathleen felt the onslaught of guilt. She turned away, gripping her necklace for courage.

"We're not," she said.

"We're not what?"

"We're not good together." Kathleen had braced herself to say what needed to be said. "We've never been good together. When we met, I clung to you for dear life, and you tolerated me."

"You don't mean that," Susannah said, her eyes wide.

"I do." Kathleen faced Susannah.

Whatever Susannah saw, Kathleen knew the instant that realization was reflected in her dark eyes.

"You don't love me anymore."

It wasn't a question.

Be kind, Kathleen thought as she took a deep breath. "Suze, things are not going to change. Your mother will never leave your father, and you will never leave your mother. You know it's true. I can't live like this again."

Susannah's tear-filled eyes hardened as her gaze flicked to the necklace visible through Kathleen's shirt. "There's someone else."

Kathleen shook her head. "This isn't about anyone but me. I'm just not willing to be last in your life anymore, your dirty little secret, and you can't tell me it will ever be any different."

"But we could—"

"No." As gently but firmly as she could, Kathleen looked Susannah in the eye. "We can't. I wish you happiness. I really do. But I need to leave."

And she had.

She pulled her knees to her chest now as the other wave of self-reproach washed over her—remorse that wasn't so easy to let go of.

She'd driven to her parents' house in Spruce Hill. Slowing as she neared the house, she'd realized her heart was pounding and her hands were strangling the wheel. She braked to a stop across from the circular drive where her father always parked his Land Rover or his Mercedes or his BMW—whatever the status vehicle of the month was—to make sure the neighbors could see it. The drive was empty. That most likely meant that her mother was home alone.

We could talk...

She'd snorted at that thought and sped away, ashamed at how relieved she felt.

Blossom jumped up onto the rock with her. The sun went behind a cloud, and a chill settled over them. She wrapped an arm around him, pulling him near for warmth.

247

"Come on," she said. "Molly will be home soon from the day's fix-it jobs. Let's see what we can rustle up for supper."

※※※※※※※※※※

MOLLY LAY AWAKE IN the dark, listening to Kathleen's deep breathing beside her. Her body still tingled from their lovemaking earlier. Blossom snored softly from where he lay in his bed nearby. Gently, she reached over to sift Kathleen's soft hair through her fingers, smiling as she remembered how Kathleen had straddled her, offering Molly a nipple to bite and lick as her fingers stroked until Kathleen had come, her breath catching as her orgasm shook her. She wasn't shy any longer about being naked or about letting Molly know when she was in the mood to make love.

She was so different from the buttoned-up, closed woman who had come to Little Sister just six months ago.

I'm different, too, Molly realized.

Never had she wanted more than a dalliance, just short jumps to the mainland to scratch an itch for sex. Not since college had she met anyone whom she had even thought about in terms of a relationship. That one relationship in college had ended badly, as angsty college relationships tend to, she supposed. But this... this felt so right.

Every day, she hurried home—she smiled in the dark at the thought that this cottage now felt like home—sometimes coming by mid-day for lunch as well. Of course, some days, they didn't bother with food at lunchtime, rushing upstairs to tear each other's clothes off and jump into bed. Evenings were spent reading or maybe watching a movie on one of Kathleen's computers.

Was this how her mom and dad felt? She wondered if this kind of happiness could really last decades. Maybe it was time to talk to Kathleen about the bonding ceremony.

She rolled over, snuggling a little closer to rest her cheek against Kathleen's shoulder. Soon. She'd talk to her about it soon.

"DO YOU KNOW WHAT'S going on?" Kathleen asked from the kitchen counter where she was stirring some mayonnaise into a batch of potato salad.

Molly frowned in concentration as she spooned a yolk mixture into two dozen deviled eggs. "I think so."

"Well?"

Molly shook her head. "You'll have to wait and see."

When they had everything packed up and ready to go, they loaded the food and Blossom into the Toyota and drove to the Cooper house. Aidan had just pulled in ahead of them and was helping Louisa out of her old Ford. He reached into the back seat and retrieved two boxes of ashes. He gave them a sheepish grin as he carried the boxes into the house.

Inside, the house had been decorated for Easter. Vases of wildflowers were scattered around on tables, and old stuffed bunnies were peeking out from behind the vases.

Kathleen picked one up. "Were these yours when you were little?"

Molly blushed. "Not all mine. They were ours. Can't believe Mom kept them."

Kathleen chortled and put it back. "I wouldn't have picked you out as the stuffed animal type."

Molly ignored her, carrying the basket of food into the kitchen. Rebecca was already there, along with Bobby and his wife, Laurie.

"When did you get in?" Molly asked him.

"Came over yesterday," he said. "Stayed in your room overnight. Hope that's okay."

Molly shrugged. "Sure. Nice to have you both here."

She looked around. "Where's Matty?" she asked, but she was pretty sure she knew.

Jenny was sautéing some shallots in butter. "He said he had something to do, but he'd be here for dinner."

Kathleen sent a puzzled look in Molly's direction, but Molly backed out of the crowded kitchen as quickly as she could. She found Aidan out on the front porch, playing fetch with Blossom, using an old tennis ball. She sat down beside him.

"You good?" he asked.

She nodded. "You?"

"Yeah."

Blossom brought the slobbery ball back to him. He threw it.

"You gonna say something today?" she asked.

"Yeah."

"Have you said anything to Miss Louisa yet?"

"Yeah."

She studied him. He had shaved, and his eyes were clear, his jaw firmly set. "She's okay?"

"Yeah."

Molly clapped him on the shoulder. "Good talking to you."

She got up and went to the garage. Her scull was lying upside-down on its rack, a layer of dust covering the hull. She took a rag and wiped it down. Silly really. If she just got it back in the water, it would be clean.

The door opened behind her, and Kathleen came in. She joined Molly, running a finger along the smooth wood.

"You miss it? Rowing?"

Molly nodded. "Always do through the winter. It's still a little early. Water will be wicked cold, but soon."

Kathleen wrapped her arms around Molly's neck. "You know I always enjoyed getting out for early walks. We've gotten kind of lazy through the winter."

Molly kissed her, savoring the softness. "I'm not complaining about how we've spent our mornings. But once the weather really warms up, I will want to get back out."

Kathleen laid a hand on the scull. "Would you teach me?"

"To row?"

Kathleen nodded.

"Sure I'd love to."

Another car door slammed outside.

Molly tugged on Kathleen's hand. "Guess we better get inside."

They left the garage to see Matty opening the passenger door of his truck.

Kathleen pointed. "Isn't that...?"

Molly grinned broadly. "It certainly is."

Brandi waved at them. Molly noticed she was wearing the locket around her neck. She urged Kathleen into a trot.

Matty beamed as he wrapped his arm around Brandi's waist.

"Ready?" Molly asked them.

They smiled at each other.

"Ready," Matty said.

⬚⬚⬚⬚⬚⬚⬚⬚

EASTER DINNER BECAME BOISTEROUS, even by Cooper house standards. When Matty made his announcement that he'd asked Brandi to marry him, and she showed off her white gold locket, gushing about how romantic she thought it was, with the whole song idea, Kathleen had turned to Molly with her fingers pressed to her own necklace.

Molly gave an embarrassed tilt of the head.

While everyone was noisily clapping Matty on the back and welcoming Brandi with hugs and kisses, Kathleen reached for Molly's hand under the table and gave it a squeeze.

When everyone finally settled again to their dinner, Bobby cleared his throat.

"While we're making announcements, Aidan has one."

Joe stopped with his fork halfway to his mouth, eyeing his oldest son. "What is it?"

Aidan set his own fork down. "I, uh..." He glanced at Molly, who nodded once. "I've been talking to Bobby. I'm going to start training to be a ferry pilot."

Unlike Matty's news, a stunned silence greeted Aidan's.

Joe leaned forward. "When? Where are you going to live? You won't be able to live here."

"No." Aidan looked his father in the eye. "I'll be leaving Little Sister. At least, I'll be here, but on a regular schedule. I've found a room to rent near the marina on the mainland."

When the silence stretched out, Bobby said, "I can't do this forever. Aidan's perfect to take over when I retire. We need someone from Little Sister in charge of that ferry."

Aidan raised his glass of ginger ale—he'd refused any wine—to Kathleen. "It's thanks to you that I'm doing this."

She felt her face burn as, all around the table, glasses were raised with murmurs of, "To Kathleen."

Jenny's eyes shone with tears, but she smiled as she nudged Joe and said, "We might be empty nesters yet, if we can just get rid of one more."

Joey took a big bite of ham, chewing slowly. "Nope. Not going anywhere."

Joe scoffed. "Then you're gonna have four times as many chores to do."

Laughter burst out, and then everyone was talking at once, asking Aidan and Matty and Brandi for more details.

At the other end of the table, Rebecca was speaking with Louisa, who was wiping her eyes with her napkin and nodding. Rebecca caught Kathleen's eye. In a flash, Kathleen had an image of Bryan—she suddenly remembered, he'd come to her in a dream. It was hard to recall the details, but something about a storm was coming. His hair had been blowing and he'd been trying to warn her about... She couldn't remember what. Kathleen blinked and looked back at Rebecca, but she was now talking to Laurie.

"You okay?" Molly asked quizzically.

Kathleen nodded. "Fine."

She went back to her dinner, but the memory of that dream stayed with her, like a cloud.

When dinner was over, Molly got involved in a conversation with Aidan while Kathleen helped clear the table. In the kitchen, she caught Rebecca.

"What was that look before?"

Rebecca pulled her out the back door, onto the porch. "What did you remember?"

"Bryan," Kathleen said. "He came to me in a dream, trying to warn me about something."

Rebecca nodded. "Maisie came to warn me."

"Warn us about what?"

"I don't know. But this didn't happen randomly, Kathleen. They both came to us for a reason."

She went back inside, leaving Kathleen alone on the porch. The warmth seemed to have gone out of the day. She gathered her sweater close and wrapped her arms around herself.

A moment later, Molly came out. "There you are. What are you doing out here?"

"Nothing." Kathleen pasted a smile on her face.

Molly's gaze wandered down to the diamonds hanging from Kathleen's neck. "When I left to go after you in Philly, I had no idea what I was going to say or do to tell you how I felt or convince you to come back. I pulled off the interstate to get something to eat and let Blossom out. Something made me keep driving along some small two-lane highway, and I found this little town with this little jewelry store run by a woman who makes all her own stuff. And there it was."

Molly stepped closer to wrap her arms around Kathleen. "I admit, I hesitated to copy my baby brother, but when I saw it, it had to be yours. I knew this was it."

Kathleen kissed her and leaned against her with a shiver. "Cold?"

Kathleen nodded against Molly's shoulder.

Molly held her more tightly, glancing toward the sky. "Think we might get one last winter storm."

"Really?"

"I feel something in the air."

⬚⬚⬚⬚⬚⬚

MOLLY CURSED UNDER HER breath as she jammed her shovel into the snow. When she'd predicted a last winter storm, she hadn't counted on another two feet. Every spring, she wondered how many more winters she could do this, but she knew she'd never go anywhere. Despite the damned snow.

Aidan's ferry apprenticeship had been delayed a few weeks by this storm, which was a good thing, as he'd been here to take care of Miss Louisa's shoveling, while Kathleen helped out at the cottage.

Molly paused to catch her breath, wondering where her aunt had got to.

Rebecca came out of the library holding a mug of hot chocolate. "Take a break. Come join me."

Molly was more than ready and didn't argue. She stomped the excess snow off her boots and joined her aunt inside where a second steaming mug was waiting. She dropped into a chair and closed her eyes.

"I think I'm getting too old for this."

Rebecca chuckled. "If you're too old, I'm ancient."

Molly peeled off her jacket and scarf and cradled the hot chocolate in her hands, savoring the warmth as she sipped the frothy liquid. "Oh, this is good."

They sat in silence for a bit, both enjoying their hot cocoa.

"Have you thought about a snow blower?" Rebecca asked.

"Thought about it, but they can't handle really deep snow, and I'd still have to haul it all over the island. Might look into a small tractor with a bucket, though."

Rebecca nodded. "That would be a good idea."

Molly cocked her head. "Has Matty talked to you about bonding?"

"He mentioned it. Sounds as if Brandi's family wants to host the wedding on Big Sister."

"Do you think they'll bond and live here?"

"I don't think he's spoken to her about it yet."

"Mmm." Molly drank her hot chocolate slowly.

Rebecca eyed her over the edge of her mug. "Was there some reason you were asking?"

Molly felt her cheeks warm. "I was just wondering if they'd picked a month."

"Because you'd like to pick one?"

Molly lowered her mug. "Well, there are only so many new moons."

Rebecca nodded. "Have you spoken to Kathleen about this? She hasn't said anything."

"Not yet."

When Rebecca remained silent, Molly set her mug down and leaned her elbows on the library table. "What?"

Rebecca pursed her lips for a moment. "This is awkward, Molly. I'm your godmother, and I couldn't love you more if you were my own. But this doesn't feel right."

Molly frowned. "What do you mean?"

Rebecca's brow creased as well. "I don't know. It just doesn't feel right."

Molly crossed her arms. "Matty and Brandi do, but Kathleen and I don't."

"Don't be daft." Rebecca waved a dismissive hand. "That's not it."

"Then what is it?"

Rebecca shook her head. "I wish I knew."

"You don't think she loves me?" Molly heard the challenge in her voice.

"No." Rebecca smiled. "I've no doubt how you feel about each other."

"Then what?"

Rebecca set her mug down and laid a hand on Molly's arm. "Kathleen came to us damaged. Damaged by her last relationship. Damaged by her brother's death. Damaged by her parents."

"I know that. She's over it."

"Is she?"

"Isn't she?"

Rebecca shook her head again. "I think she's over that woman. And I know her brother has come to her in dreams. But that's only two out of three. I have a feeling there's something more."

Molly remembered Kathleen's confession about what her mother had said all those years ago. She felt a chill steal through her. When her aunt had her "feelings", they usually turned into premonitions of things that came to be.

"Has she had any contact with her parents recently?"

"No. Not that she's said. And I think she would tell me."

Rebecca traced a finger around the rim of her mug. "I want to see you bonded, Molly. But you each have to come into it whole and unburdened..."

"And you think Kathleen isn't either of those," Molly finished.

Rebecca held her gaze. "Not yet."

IN THE KITCHEN, BLOSSOM raised his head with a small woof when the front door opened.

"Don't take your boots off," Kathleen called.

"Why?" came Molly's weary voice. "I am not shoveling one more inch of snow today."

Kathleen peeked around the door. "You don't have to shovel anything. We're going to the diner for dinner. Wilma called. I'm just wrapping up a pan of brownies to take with us."

Molly sank onto the small bench next to the door. Blossom wandered over to lick the snow off her boots.

A moment later, Kathleen came into the foyer with a towel-wrapped pan in her hands. She laid it in Molly's lap and kissed her.

"Tired?" she asked as she pulled her jacket off its hook.

Molly slid over to give her room to sit and put her boots on. "Exhausted."

"Well, Nels has made a huge batch of vegetable lasagna with the produce he's been growing in his greenhouse. Sounds good."

Molly let Kathleen tug her to her feet. "I'm so hungry, these brownies might not make it to the diner."

Kathleen chuckled and took the pan from her. "Want me to drive?"

"I'm not that tired."

"Hey, I'm a good driver."

"Under normal circumstances, yes. But this new snow is still iffy in places."

"All right," Kathleen conceded, secretly glad not to navigate in this, even with the Toyota's four-wheel-drive.

A lingering twilight helped illuminate the winding road as Molly drove them into town. Several trucks and SUVs were already parked at the diner, where the lights cast a welcoming glow into the deepening dusk.

Wilma called out a greeting as soon as they entered. Kathleen went to set her brownies on the counter, making space between Louisa's orange-cranberry bread and one of Jenny's creamy pumpkin pies. Aidan, Matty, and Joey were all seated at counter stools.

"Don't even think about it," she said sternly as they eyed the desserts.

Molly sank into a chair, her chin cradled in her hand, her eyes drooping. Blossom curled up under her chair.

"Poor thing," Wilma clucked. She poured a cup of coffee. "Here, Mo. Drink this down or you'll be falling asleep in your supper, like you did when you were three."

Louisa joined her. Kathleen, convinced that Molly would be kept awake by having to converse with Louisa, set about helping lay out stacks of dishes and silverware.

"So the greenhouse is a success?"

"Oh, it's been wonderful," Wilma said. "The solar panels Molly installed have meant we can keep the greenhouse warmer without using the island's electricity at all. And the batteries store enough energy to run the heating and lighting even on cloudy days. Nels says it makes all the difference."

Miranda sidled over. "Tim is convinced. We're ordering a greenhouse and solar panels for the market and the house. And the chicken coop."

Kathleen pointed to a platter of baked chicken. "Is this—?"

"No," Miranda said with a chuckle. "Once we've given them names, we can't eat them. Eggs only."

"Good," Kathleen said. "Maybe I should think about solar for Nanna's cottage."

"Don't you mean your cottage, Katie?" Wilma asked.

Kathleen stopped and smiled. "I guess I should start thinking of it as my cottage, shouldn't I?"

"I think it's something we should bring up to the island council," Miranda said. "If we added wind turbines, and if everyone on the island added solar panels, we might be able to cut our fuel bills considerably and not rely on the tankers getting out here."

"When does the island council meet?" Kathleen asked.

"May first, the traditional day of Bealtaine," Wilma said. "More often if we need to."

"Supper's ready," Nels called, carrying an enormous pan in his oven-mitted hands.

He dished out generous portions onto plates that were passed out to everyone there. They went down the counter, adding rolls and meatballs from other bowls.

Kathleen brought plates to Molly and Louisa before joining them. Jenny and Joe squeezed in at their table.

"I'll need to fill the oil truck tomorrow," Molly said. "Got a few people need deliveries."

Joe shook his head. "Tanker hasn't come. We're down to our last two hundred gallons. Better ration it till they get out here."

Molly frowned. "They were supposed to be here last week. What's up?"

Joe shrugged as he chewed. "Don't know. I'll call tomorrow."

"I'll turn our thermostat down," Louisa said quickly.

"We better tell everyone to go easy with the heat," Jenny said. "If we don't get a delivery soon, it's going to get cold pretty quick."

Molly yawned as she finished her lasagna. Kathleen smiled and took her plate.

"Let me help wash up, and we'll head home."

"You go," Jenny said, pulling the plates from Kathleen's hands. "We'll take care of things here."

"Thanks, Mom." Molly stood. "Night, everyone."

They left to a chorus of good nights from everyone still at the diner.

"Are you okay to drive home?" Kathleen asked.

Molly yawned again. "Mmm hmm. Better sing to keep me awake."

Kathleen laughed. "That would keep you awake, believe me."

Molly grinned. When she turned the ignition, she found an oldies station on the radio. There was a lot of static, but she cranked the volume up. They drove home, singing along to Roy Orbison and "Pretty Woman."

Chapter 17

KATHLEEN SAT AT HER DESK, a blanket wrapped around her legs and fingerless mittens on her hands as she worked. She wore a T-shirt under a thermal long-sleeve under a wool sweater. Next to her, Blossom lay curled up in his bed. She'd taken to carrying it anywhere she was so he'd have a warm place to rest. Currently, he had the additional warmth of burrowing under an old towel she'd draped over him, so that all she could see was a spotted rump.

Outside, the weak April sunshine held the promise of warmth, but it didn't really deliver.

Molly had cautioned her to keep the furnace only warm enough to keep the pipes from freezing during the nights, which still dipped into the low thirties.

Their nights in bed had become decidedly less romantic.

Kathleen paused as that thought crossed her mind. They weren't less romantic at all. They were definitely less sexual—getting naked, even under two blankets over top of the electric one, was not appealing—but they had cuddled together most of the night. She couldn't decide now which was nicer, the shared warmth or the touching.

Lost in those thoughts, she heard the oven timer go off downstairs. Blossom scrambled out from under his towel as she got stiffly to her feet.

She'd never minded cooking when she and Susannah lived together—she was certainly better at it than Susannah was—but she'd found here that she really enjoyed it. The little cottage felt so much homier when it was filled with the scents of a hearty stew or soup, or better yet, bread or pie or cookies.

She made a face as she grabbed the spare tire that had started to inflate around her waist.

"Too many cookies and pies," she said with a sigh. "Not enough walking."

Blossom turned circles near the back door. She let him out and opened the oven to take out the loaf of orange-cranberry bread she was trying for the first time. She'd talked Louisa into giving her the recipe. Sniffing deeply, her eyes filled with sudden tears, as the scent brought back the memory of the first time she'd had this bread when Olivia and Louisa had come over to welcome her by helping her to clean the cottage.

She slid the fragrant loaf onto a cooling rack.

Back upstairs, she decided that neither her butt nor her eyes could take any more time at her computer. She quickly peeled off some layers and changed into others that could wick if she actually managed to work up a sweat—a prospect that seemed unlikely, considering she'd have to thaw out before she could generate any excess heat.

Blossom was sitting on the front porch.

"Were you waiting for me?" she asked. "Come on. Let's get some exercise."

Blossom led the way out to the road, and she willingly followed. Without any plan, they walked quickly, Kathleen out of breath way too soon.

"I am out of shape," Kathleen huffed.

She found herself heading toward the cemetery. Car tires crunched behind her, and she automatically moved to the side. An old Ford pulled up beside her.

"Miss Louisa."

"Hello, Katie. Where are you headed?"

"Nowhere special. Just out for a walk. What about you?"

"Going to the cemetery to clean up. Want to join me?"

Kathleen hesitated. Getting in the car would effectively spell an end to her walk, but... "Sure."

She opened the back door for Blossom and saw the two boxes of ashes secured by their seatbelts.

"He can't hurt anything," Louisa said.

He jumped in, settling between the boxes while Kathleen got into the front seat.

"I'll need a taste tester later," Kathleen said.

Louisa glanced over. "You made the orange-cranberry bread?"

"Yes. I know it won't be as good as yours, but—"

"We need someone else who can make it after I'm gone."

Kathleen didn't know what to say to that.

An awkward silence filled the car.

"Aidan left?" Kathleen asked.

Louisa nodded. "Two days ago. This will be just what he needs. Bobby will be a good mentor, and he'll have a goal to work for. He hasn't had one since that terrible summer."

Kathleen fastened her own seatbelt, though they had less than a mile to the cemetery. "What was Aidan like? After?"

Louisa steered around a curve in the road. "He never was one for school and studying, but he was only fifteen. Too young to quit school. He struggled through those next few years. He wasn't drinking then, of course. But he picked fights, snuck out of the house. I believe Jenny and Joe had a hard time with him. He wouldn't talk to anyone about what happened."

263

She arrived at the cemetery a moment later and parked. When Kathleen let Blossom out, he immediately chased a rabbit into the trees. Kathleen was surprised to realize Louisa was wearing a pair of Olivia's old dungarees—the first time she'd see her in pants—tucked into her rubber boots.

Louisa opened the trunk, and they retrieved a few things she had stashed there: a small rake and a couple of trowels.

"How are you doing, with your oil?" Kathleen asked, noting Louisa's heavy jacket and scarf and gloves.

"I'm not sure I can remember worse, but Daddy talked about the war, when we didn't get oil for months at a time, so I try not to complain."

Kathleen, who had a bitter complaint on the tip of her tongue, swallowed it.

Most of the snow had melted, leaving only small clumps of white in the shadows of the trees and headstones.

They went first to Nanna's grave, where the little rose bush sat, looking forlorn against the granite. They both knelt, clearing away the fallen leaves to reveal tiny flowers poking through the grass.

Kathleen gasped. "I didn't know these were here. The white ones are crocus, right?"

"Yes. And this," Louisa cradled a little purple one, "is hyacinth. I planted these last year, hoping the squirrels wouldn't get them."

"They're lovely."

Kathleen worked, tenderly raking the grass over the gravesite. She lifted her hands to her face, inhaling the scents of dirt and flowers and spring. "I miss her."

"So do I." Louisa sighed and used Kathleen's shoulder to help push to her feet.

They walked to another part of the cemetery, to an older stone.

"Máiréad Woodhouse," Kathleen read. "What a pretty name."

"Mama was pretty," Louisa said softly. "A tiny thing, but tough as nails. I favor her. Ollie favored Daddy."

Reading the dates on the marker, Kathleen said, "She died young. Only fifty-four."

Louisa nodded. "Cancer. We don't get it often here. The doctors said there wasn't anything they could do for her. She didn't want to die in a hospital so far from home, so we took care of her best we could."

They swept away the leaves and sticks from her grave, finding more small flowers scattered over the site.

"Family is important," Louisa said as they worked.

Kathleen bit her lip and kept working. "I agree family is an important influence. But not all families are healthy or good for you."

She felt Louisa's gaze, studying her.

"I suppose you're right," Louisa said softly.

They both looked up at the sound of another vehicle, approaching fast. A cloud of dust followed as it pulled to a hard stop and Jenny got out.

"Emergency meeting. In town. Now."

She got back into her SUV. Kathleen helped Louisa to her feet, and they hurried back to the car. Kathleen called to Blossom, who came bounding out of the woods.

"You drive, Katie," Louisa said, getting in the passenger side.

Kathleen adjusted the seat and drove as quickly as she could down into town, where it seemed most of the islanders were already gathered, tightly packed inside the diner.

She and Louisa crowded in. Someone got up to offer his seat to Louisa, but Kathleen remained standing as she scanned the crowd for Molly. She saw her on the other side of the diner, a somber expression on her face as she nodded in Kathleen's direction.

Joe called for quiet. "I found out why we haven't had any oil delivered for over a month."

An ominous silence followed.

"Our oil company has been bought out, and we've been cut off."

An angry buzz broke out, like a disturbed hornet's nest.

"Who?" someone called out.

It seemed to Kathleen that Joe was deliberately looking anywhere but in her direction.

"Michael Halloran."

As one, every person in the diner turned to stare at Kathleen as the floor tilted under her feet.

✖✖✖✖✖✖✖✖✖✖

VOICES CONTINUED TO BUZZ around her. Someone lowered Kathleen into a newly vacated chair.

"Land sakes, she's white as a ghost," Wilma clucked, pushing a steaming cup of coffee into her hands.

"We need to hear what she has to say," someone called out, and several people echoed that sentiment.

Kathleen was guided toward the counter, where Joey and Matty each took her by an elbow and hoisted her up to sit on the counter. From there, she felt like a specimen on display for the assembled islanders.

Joe pushed through the crowd and laid a hand on her knee. "Did you know?"

Mutely, Kathleen shook her head.

"Of course she didn't know," Molly said, elbowing people aside to get to Kathleen.

"We have to ask, Mo," Joe said.

"It's okay," Kathleen managed to say, clasping Molly's hand. She looked down at Joe. "I haven't spoken to my father in months. I had no idea."

"Why would he do this?" someone else asked, Kathleen couldn't tell who.

She shook her head again. "I don't know. The only thing I can think of is..."

She scanned the sea of faces, most of them familiar now. "He never forgave my grandmother, or the island, for my brother's death. When I

266

came here, I think that may have been the thing that pushed him to do this."

She blinked rapidly. "I'm sorry."

The murmurs this time were sympathetic rather than angry.

"It's not your fault," Rebecca said loudly enough for everyone to hear. "Those of us who grew up with Michael know he's more than capable of this."

"How bad is it, Joe?" came a voice from the back of the diner.

Joe gave Kathleen's knee a squeeze. Turning to the others, he said, "It's not just heating oil. The generators for our electric are still half-full. We filled them when we got our last shipment of diesel, but it won't last long. We have enough fuel for another couple of weeks for the fishing boats. And gasoline for cars, we have maybe enough to get us through the end of the month, based on our typical usage. We'll all need to conserve as much as we can. Carpool or bike if you don't have to drive. Turn off everything electric that doesn't need to be on."

He shifted onto a counter stool. "I've contacted another oil company, down the coast. They can get a delivery to us sometime in the next couple of weeks, if the weather holds. It'll cost more, as they're having to ship it farther."

Another angry hum rose.

Joe spoke over it. "We won't charge any mark-up on that shipment. You'll pay what we pay."

The hum died down.

"That's good of you, Joe," said Tim.

Joe shrugged. "We're in this together. All of us or none of us."

Miranda climbed onto a chair and held up her hand to quiet everyone. "This is exactly why we need to make a real commitment to becoming self-sufficient. Solar and wind and waves are all things we've plenty of and can make use of. We always complain about the wind. We can turn it to our advantage."

"That won't help with the boats," Joey said.

"True," Miranda agreed. "But it's a start."

"How do we start?" Wilma asked.

Kathleen raised a timid hand. "I... I've been doing some research on that."

⬚⬚⬚⬚⬚⬚⬚⬚⬚

MOLLY GAVE A WIDE yawn as she drove the empty tanker truck back to the marina. She'd spent the day delivering load after load of heating oil to various houses around the island. The islanders had all agreed to cap deliveries at no more than one hundred gallons each until the oil company could get back to them with another tanker of oil and gasoline.

"We still have to conserve our heat and electric," she'd warned each one. Some of the houses had required a restart of their furnace as well, since they'd run completely dry.

She parked the truck and went to the office where her father was bent over a logbook.

"Thank goodness spring is here, and it's been mild," she said as she dropped into a vacant chair.

"Go home, Mo," Joe said.

He and the boys had spent the day refilling the diesel tanks for the electric generators and doing some overdue maintenance on them while they were there.

"In a minute," she said. She pulled a different logbook out, transferring notes on each delivery she'd made before she forgot. "Everyone said to thank you again for not charging extra."

Joe grunted.

Molly glanced in his direction, noting the hard line of his clenched jaw. "She feels horrible about this."

Joe looked her way, his expression softening. "Kathleen has nothing to feel bad about. She's not responsible for what Michael does. But I'd like a few minutes alone with him."

Molly grinned, but then her grin faded. "Did Aidan ever tell you and Mom what Kathleen told him the night she hit her head?"

Joe laid down his pencil and turned to face her. "Not exactly. Only that it made him realize he needed to make a change."

Molly studied the grease under her fingernails. "Bryan died on Kathleen's tenth birthday. The next summer, on her eleventh, her mother asked why it couldn't have been her."

Joe shoved to his feet, pacing the small office with his hands fisted. "What is wrong with those people?"

He ran his fingers through his hair. "When I thought we'd lost Aidan that day... Your mom and I would have held on to the rest of you and never let you out of our sight."

Molly blurted out the thing that had been eating at her. "Rebecca thinks Kathleen isn't ready to bond. That there's something she hasn't dealt with. What if..."

"Mo," Joe said, laying a hand on her shoulder. "Kathleen loves you. That much is clear. But this... If she's never confronted Michael or Christine about this, she won't be whole until she does."

Molly looked up at him. "Yeah, but now, with him doing this. It feels like another wedge between us."

He squeezed and then gave her a shove toward the door. "Go home. Somehow, we'll get through this. It'll all work out."

Molly didn't argue. She got into the Toyota and yawned some more on her way to the cottage, which was dark when she pulled up.

Blossom greeted her at the door, but there was no sign of Kathleen. A light shone from upstairs. Wearily, she climbed the stairs to find Kathleen hunched over her keyboard.

"Sorry," she said before Molly could speak. "Let me just finish this."

Molly kissed the top of her head and went to the bathroom to scrub her hands with a nailbrush. A couple of minutes later, Kathleen came in.

"Had to finish that while the thoughts were in my head."

"Afraid they might leak out?" Molly asked, glancing at Kathleen in the mirror.

"Afraid they won't be good enough."

Molly checked her hands, decided they passed inspection, and dried them off. "I'm starving. Let's rustle up some supper."

"Leftover soup and bread okay?" Kathleen asked, taking Molly's hand and walking her toward the stairs.

"Sounds wonderful."

Kathleen flipped on one light in the kitchen. "I'm trying to keep my electric usage to a minimum."

"Thanks. It helps. Dad and the boys got the generators filled today, and I spent the day filling oil tanks."

Kathleen got a large ceramic bowl out of the fridge and ladled thick potato soup into a pan to warm it. Molly got a bread knife and cut thick slices from a loaf Kathleen had baked yesterday.

"What were you working on?"

Kathleen adjusted the heat under the pan. "Grants. I've never written grants, but I have friends who have. So they've been giving me advice and proofreading what I've prepared so far. There are all kinds of grants for renewable energy projects from universities and green manufacturers. I've also been emailing the people who spearheaded the green initiative on Eigg."

Molly glanced up. "The island off the coast of Scotland?"

"Yeah. And Kodiak in Alaska. They managed to do it. Completely green with only diesel backup. If they can, we can."

Molly heard the hard edge to Kathleen's voice. She set the bread knife down and stepped close to wrap her arms around Kathleen.

"It isn't your fault," she murmured.

Kathleen held her tightly. "I know you and the others keep saying that. But it feels like my fault. He wouldn't be doing this to you if I hadn't come back here."

Molly pulled back enough to look into Kathleen's eyes. "Maybe. But if you manage to help us make this conversion to renewable energy—something Rebecca has been pushing us to do for years—that'll really burn your father. I know that's not your goal, but this move of his was pretty cruel. In a way, he may end up doing us a favor. That's the best revenge of all."

Chapter 18

THE SUN, BARELY PEEKING over the horizon, threw long shadows across the beach to the rocky sea wall. Kathleen shivered in the early morning chill.

"Why are we out here so early?"

"Because," Molly said, grunting a little as she pulled the first of two sculls off the Toyota's roof rack, "this is the time of day when the water is the calmest."

Kathleen looked back out at the ocean and saw that the waves barely made a ripple, washing gently onto the sand.

"Get the oars, will you?" Molly asked as she pulled the second scull down and carried it to the water's edge.

She secured the oars Kathleen brought to her and turned to inspect Kathleen. She checked the straps on Kathleen's life vest.

"Why aren't you wearing one of these?" Kathleen asked. "And why are you wearing suspenders?"

Molly grinned. "These aren't suspenders. It's my life vest, inflatable if I need it."

"I feel like a five-year-old," Kathleen grumbled, looking down at her bright orange vest.

"You haven't been on the ocean in a quarter century. You're wearing it," Molly said flatly.

Kathleen decided she couldn't argue with that logic.

"Get in and I'll push you out," Molly said.

She steadied the scull while Kathleen clambered in, feeling very clumsy as the boat rocked a little. She crouched, gripping the sides.

"You have to let go and turn around to sit," Molly said gently. "I've got you. You're not going to fall in."

A nervous giggle burst out of Kathleen's mouth. "I'm not even in the water."

"I wasn't going to point that part out. Yet."

Taking a deep breath, Kathleen let go and turned to sit on the scull's seat.

"Secure your feet and feel how the seat glides on the tracks," Molly said, still holding the scull securely so it didn't rock.

"Okay, just hold the oars out of the water, and I'll push you out. Sit still until I'm with you."

Kathleen maintained a stranglehold on the oars as Molly gave the scull a hard shove. A minute later, Molly rowed out to her.

Back on the shore, Blossom barked frantically from where he was tethered to the Toyota's bumper.

Patiently, Molly coached her on how to drop the oars—not digging too deep and not skipping along the surface—and pull with long, even strokes.

"This is harder on the ocean than on a river or lake," Molly reminded her when Kathleen got frustrated. "The water level keeps changing under you. But you'll get the feel for it."

And she did. Slowly, Kathleen settled into a rhythm of breathing and pulling, breathing and sliding, breathing and pulling. It was hypnotic.

WHEN THE STARS SANG

"I think I understand why you like this," she panted.

"It's kind of like meditation," Molly said. "Once you don't have to think about it any longer. Stop and rest now."

They let the sculls drift. Kathleen's breathing slowed as she looked around. Little Sister looked really far away.

"How far is the buoy?" she asked.

Molly hesitated a moment and then pointed behind them, toward the horizon. "Still out of sight and hearing. We haven't gone that far."

"This feels far to me," Kathleen said, twisting around carefully, her hands tight on the rocking scull.

"It was. They never should have done it. It was already blowing. When the waves are even three or four feet, you drop out of sight. It's easy to get disoriented. You don't know which way is back. And you can never, ever outrace a storm."

Kathleen pulled on one oar, turning the scull, thinking about how scared Bryan must have been. When she was a child, especially here on the island with Nanna, she'd always kind of enjoyed storms, tucked cozily inside the warmth and shelter of a house. But after the horrible storm that stretched on into the night while they waited and waited... She'd often wondered what it had been like for Bryan, out on the ocean. She shivered now.

"Let's go back," Molly said.

Kathleen didn't argue. She mimicked Molly's technique to turn the scull completely, and they began the return trek to the island.

⁂

BLOSSOM SAT, HIS HEAD swiveling from Kathleen to Molly at regular intervals as they chopped carrots and potatoes and onions and celery for a pot of stew.

"Here you go," Molly said, handing him a chunk of carrot. "Now stop begging."

275

He meekly accepted the carrot and took it under the table to gnaw on it.

"He begs because you give him stuff," Kathleen said, glancing up from her onions with tear-filled eyes.

Molly grinned. "I know. But he had such a tough life before you took him in."

Kathleen snorted. "I think he's learned to use that excuse." She pushed her chopped onions aside and started to peel a potato. "Can't wait to be getting these from our own garden soon. Thanks again for helping me. I never had a garden before."

They went back to work, a companionable silence filling the air between them. Outside, rain pelted the windows, and the trees groaned in the wind.

"It's going to blow hard tonight," Molly said. She saw Kathleen roll her shoulders. "Still sore?"

Kathleen gave a half-shrug. "A little. It's been three days. Thought it'd be gone by now."

"But you're not used to rowing. I was sore, too. I haven't rowed on the water since November."

A hard gust rattled the windows.

Molly glanced over as Kathleen paused, looking out into the darkening afternoon. She'd been quieter, more pensive since their rowing excursion. And she'd been dreaming, sometimes waking Molly as she whimpered and twitched in her sleep. Molly was pretty certain the dreams were all of Bryan.

Molly opened her mouth to say what had been on her mind, but she turned back to her carrots. Kathleen had faced so many things: coming back here alone; confronting Susannah and even going to take care of her; overcoming her fear of the ocean enough to get out on it in a scull.

But she'd avoided any discussion of her parents, of talking to her father about his buyout of the oil company and what he'd done to the island. She was working harder than anyone to come up with lists of wind and solar contractors and suppliers to help Little Sister become less dependent on outsiders but, on this one topic, Kathleen had kept her thoughts and feelings to herself.

They scooped the vegetables into the pot with the roast and a thick broth.

Kathleen adjusted the burner and stepped out onto the back porch, watching the rain lash the trees. Molly followed her outside, where the wind blew cold. Kathleen shivered.

"What must it have been like?" she whispered.

Molly wrapped her arms around Kathleen from behind. She didn't need to ask what she was talking about. Kathleen turned and buried her face in Molly's neck.

Molly held her tightly. "Come inside," she murmured. "I'll light a fire."

"That sounds nice."

Kathleen curled up in her chair while Molly laid a fire and got it lit. They sat in the twilit room as the flames crackled. Molly shifted the ottoman aside to sit on the floor with her back against the chair. Kathleen reached out to sift Molly's hair through her fingers. Molly leaned into Kathleen's hand. Turning, she pressed a kiss to her palm.

"Does Rebecca do weddings?" Kathleen asked.

Molly stilled at the question. So unexpected and so hoped for. "In a manner of speaking."

"What do you mean?"

Molly swiveled to sit sideways to the chair so she could see Kathleen's face. "She can do weddings, of course. And does for tourists or islanders who don't live here anymore. But for us, it's different. She does the bonding."

Kathleen's face in the firelight was impossible to read. Molly saw something flicker across her eyes.

"This doesn't involve more blood, does it?"

Molly smiled. "Actually, it does."

277

Kathleen threw one hand up. "What is it with you people and blood?"

Molly hesitated a moment and then reached out to take that hand, holding it in both of hers. "Blood is powerful. It binds us. To each other. To the island. It's something that came down to us from the First Ones. This is why people here don't get divorced. Once we bond, it can't be undone."

"How does it work?"

"It can only be done at a new moon, naked, standing just where water meets earth."

Kathleen narrowed her eyes. "You're serious. Naked on the beach under a new moon."

Molly nodded.

"Who else is there?"

"Anyone who is invited. Usually family and a few close friends. The Keeper does the ceremony."

Kathleen's focus shifted to the fire. Molly held her breath, wondering if she should ask, but Kathleen returned her gaze to Molly's.

"Will you bond with me?"

Fighting the urge to leap into the chair with Kathleen and kiss her, Molly considered the concerns her aunt and father had voiced. "Remember what I said. This is forever. Are you sure?"

Kathleen slid down from the chair to kneel in front of Molly and take both of her hands. "Molly Ahearn Cooper, will you bond with me?"

Molly kissed each of Kathleen's hands. "I will. Kathleen—" She paused. "What is your middle name anyhow?"

"Anne. With an 'e'."

Molly smiled. "Kathleen Anne Halloran, will you bond with me?"

Kathleen nodded.

Molly laughed and pulled her down to lie on top of her. Kathleen lowered her head, brushing her lips over Molly's. Molly raised her face to meet Kathleen's mouth, lips and tongue asking, seeking. Kathleen answered, opening to her.

When Blossom's wet nose suddenly nudged Molly's ear, she broke the kiss.

"So much for a romantic interlude in front of the fire."

Blossom squirmed nearer, his tail thumping the floor.

"Fur-kids." Kathleen reached over to pull him close to them.

Molly laughed. "I guess."

"So how do we schedule this with Rebecca?"

"Bealtaine is Saturday. We'll talk to her then."

Kathleen sat up, pulling Molly with her. "I guess we have a bonding to plan. That's something I never thought I'd say."

"Not getting cold feet already, are you?"

Kathleen kissed her tenderly. "No cold feet. This is forever."

⬚⬚⬚⬚⬚⬚⬚⬚⬚

THE FIRST OF MAY dawned with a spectacular sunrise. Molly left early to row, and Kathleen decided to go for a long walk. Blossom was ecstatic at the opportunity to get out and chase rabbits and squirrels. He romped ahead, checking frequently to make sure Kathleen was still coming.

She huffed along the trail through the woods to the bluff, pausing there to catch her breath and admire the rose and lavender hues in the sky. She'd been tempted to roll over and stay in bed, but the prospect of being naked on the beach in front of Molly's entire family pushed her to get up.

She patted her butt as she panted. "Nothing like a little incentive."

She'd done some reading about Bealtaine to help prepare her for the evening's celebration. This island was such a wonderful, curious mixture of old Celtic and First Ones' traditions. It seemed they'd chosen the best of both to hold on to and pass down. Even if they did involve blood and nudity.

Molly had told her that they rarely had tourists as early as this. Bobby usually found ways to delay the ferry so that the islanders could have the beach to themselves tonight. But Kathleen wasn't quite sure what to expect. Molly had been vague about the details. She knew it would involve another bonfire and, like Samhain, blessings on each house by relighting the fires from the bonfire.

She walked on, doing a wide loop that brought her back to the road. By the time she and Blossom got back to the cottage, they were both winded. It felt good. She showered quickly and had coffee brewing by the time Molly got home.

"Oh, that smells good," she said as Kathleen handed her a mug. "Good row?"

"Mmm hmm." Molly took a sip, her eyes closed. "Good walk?"

"Yes. Pancakes or eggs?"

"Pancakes."

Kathleen got a griddle and bowl out while Molly fed Blossom.

"So," Kathleen said as she mixed some pancake batter, "are you going to tell me more about tonight? Does it involve drinking more of that... What was it at Samhain?"

"*Poitín*," Molly said. "And yes. It usually does."

"Blood? Getting naked on the beach? Because I am drawing the line at both of those."

Molly laughed. "There's no bloodshed, unless someone gets drunk and falls down. And not typically any nudity these days, though you know Siobhan does like to go skyclad."

Kathleen poured some batter onto the griddle.

"Of course, there was the year Miss Louisa and Miss Olivia both got tipsy and ran naked on the beach."

Kathleen turned to her, open-mouthed. "No."

Molly grinned and got two plates down. "Yeah. I was about thirteen. It was hilarious. Of course, you have to realize, people here don't look at nudity like mainlanders do. It's not usually a big deal, but when you have to step into a schoolroom full of kids after they've all seen you naked under the moon... Well, I think Louisa realized that probably wasn't the best image for us to have of our teacher."

Kathleen was laughing so hard, she almost let the pancakes burn.

"I'll lay a fire in the grate," Molly said once they were seated. "We have to light the fire from the bonfire. That's very important."

Kathleen tilted her head. "I remember when you accompanied me back here to make sure I lit the Samhain fire. To protect the island."

Molly blushed as she laughed. "Yeah. I guess that was pretty transparent."

Kathleen stabbed at her pancakes. "Not as much as I guess it would normally have been. I was still so wrapped up in my own worries."

Molly reached for her hand. "And I was still convinced you'd run at the first bit of trouble. I'm glad I was wrong."

"You weren't wrong then." Kathleen raised Molly's hand and brushed a kiss over her knuckles. "If Susannah or this stuff with my dad had happened back then, I might have left."

Molly squeezed her hand. "But not now."

Kathleen smiled. "Not now."

<hr />

THE SUNSET PROMISED TO be as beautiful as the dawn had been. Molly and Kathleen decided to walk to the beach. Molly carried a basket filled with food.

"Feasting is as important as anything else," she'd insisted as she wheedled Kathleen into making her lasagna and Maisie's oatmeal pecan cookies.

A number of others were already gathered on the beach when they arrived. Joey and Matty were stacking wood for the bonfire that had been prepared.

"Where's Rebecca?" Molly asked her mom as Kathleen made room on the makeshift table for the lasagna.

Jenny looked around. "I'm not sure. We spoke earlier about what we were bringing. Thought she'd be here by now."

Louisa sat in a beach chair, Olivia's ashes on one side, her father's on the other. Kathleen went over to sit with her while Molly went to find Joe.

She came back to Jenny a few minutes later. "Where's Dad?"

Jenny straightened and put her fists on her hips. "He was just here a little while ago. We came together. Where did that man get to?"

"Something's up," Molly said.

Another car pulled up near the sea wall, and Wilma got out. She stood at the rocks and gestured to Molly, who clambered over the barrier.

"What's wrong?"

"Joe says you're to come," said Wilma. "There's a man. At the hotel."

"What man?" Molly demanded. "Bobby and Aidan aren't due until Tuesday. They didn't come today, did they?"

"No, no." Wilma wrung her hands. "He came by himself on his own boat. Asked for a room. Don't like the look of him."

Jenny climbed over the rocks and hurried over to them.

"Dad wants me to come. A stranger at the hotel. Stay here. We'll be back as soon as we can."

She got into the car. As Wilma pulled away, she looked back to see her mom huddled with a knot of islanders.

She and Wilma found Joe and Nels in the hotel diner's kitchen where they could watch the stranger sitting at the counter.

"Any idea who he is or why he's here?" Molly asked.

"No." Wilma put some fresh coffee on to brew.

Nels sloshed a little olive oil in an omelet pan and cracked three eggs into it. "Why are we so worried about this guy?"

Molly craned her neck to study him. He appeared to be fortyish, neatly trimmed salt and pepper hair, wire-rimmed glasses. He had the look of money about him. Freshly ironed button-down with a telltale logo on the chest. "Because we don't get many people so eager to visit us that they come in their own boat, especially after all the fuel oil kerfuffle."

She turned to Wilma. "Did you get a name?"

Wilma gave her a nervous giggle, her eyes wide with her own daring. "Did better than that. I copied his driver's license."

Molly grinned. "Good for you. Let me have it. I'll see what I can find out. Meantime, you go ahead and serve him. Try to keep him busy here."

"I'll go back to the beach," Joe said. "Make sure everyone's on guard."

Molly followed Wilma to the hotel office where Wilma handed her the copy of the stranger's driver's license.

"Be right back."

Molly slipped out the back door and made her way to the island's sheriff office, a tiny office space on the town's main street. She didn't spend much time here, but it was a place summer tourists could go if they had a problem, and she suspected the mere presence of a sheriff's office on the main street was a deterrent for some people who might be tempted to do something stupid.

She picked up the phone and called a buddy of hers who was a police officer on the mainland. They'd gone to the academy together, and he'd tried hard to recruit her as he rose in the ranks of his department.

"Hey, Gary," she said when he answered. "Molly Cooper over on Little Sister. Need a favor. See what you can find out about..." She squinted at the copied driver's license. "Stanley Hirschman." She read off his address in Philadelphia.

She listened to him clicking away on his computer and jotted down the information he found for her.

"This is helpful," she said. "Keep checking. If you find anything else, give me a ring."

Just as she hung up, Rebecca knocked and opened the door. "Figured you'd be here." She pointed to the paper lying in front of Molly. "What did you find out?"

"He's an attorney in Philadelphia."

Rebecca nodded. "We can guess who sent him here."

"What does Michael want now?"

Rebecca's eyes narrowed. "I think I know."

※※※※※※※※※

THE ATMOSPHERE ON THE island was almost telepathic. Every islander knew this attorney was there, even if no one knew for certain why he had come.

Kathleen drove into town to do some marketing. The main street was nearly deserted. She peered through the diner window as she went by. It was empty. She and Blossom entered the market to see Miranda whispering with Louisa. They both jumped as the bell tinkled.

"Oh, it's you," Miranda said.

"Where is everyone?" Kathleen asked.

"They're all laying low," Louisa said. "Out on their boats early. Doing all their errands as soon as the sun's up and then staying home."

"So what's up with Stanley?" Kathleen asked in a low voice.

"Wilma said he asked where the library is," Louisa whispered, as if Stanley Hirschman might overhear her.

Kathleen perked up, thinking immediately of all the island's genealogy books. "Did Rebecca know?"

"Yes," Louisa said. She winked. "He can access half the library."

"Good." Kathleen leaned closer. "But what does he want?"

"No one knows," Miranda said.

"But," Louisa said, "Siobhan said he was in her shop asking about houses for sale. When she told him there weren't any, he didn't believe her. Word is he was asking others the same thing."

284

"What's he want a house here for?" Kathleen asked.

Miranda shrugged, but Louisa said, "I don't think he wants a house. He's digging."

"For what, though," Kathleen wondered.

⁂

"SHERIFF."

Molly froze. *Damn.* She'd been keeping herself busy all over the island, staying out of sight, but she'd come to check the answering machine in her office and see if Gary had any more information for her. She turned.

"Mr. Hirschman."

A flicker of surprise shone in his eyes.

She smiled. "Small island."

He smiled, too, but it wasn't a pleasant expression on him, revealing long, yellowed teeth.

She decided to press her advantage and dispense with the niceties. "What can I do for you?"

He pointed toward the office. "Can we talk?"

"Sorry. I've got a few more calls to make. I've only got a minute."

His smile faded as he reappraised her. "Okay. I'll get to it. There are no houses for sale on this island. I've been looking for real estate records and can't find any. That's highly unusual."

She crossed her arms. "That would be because there are no houses for sale on Little Sister. People who grew up here tend to want to stay."

"And the real estate records?" His voice was nasal and irritating. "Even if we have to go back several years, there must be some records. I couldn't find any listings at the library, and there doesn't seem to be any kind of town hall."

He nodded toward her office. "I thought maybe you have the records."

"And what is your interest in them?"

He smiled again. "Just doing a bit of research for a client."

"Michael Halloran?"

The smile slid away immediately. "Sheriff Cooper, those records are public. You can't keep them from me or Mr. Halloran."

"Go home, Mr. Hirschman. Tell Michael if he has something to say to us, he can come and say it himself."

She turned on her heel and walked to the Toyota, roaring the engine to life before pulling away. In the rear-view mirror, Stanley Hirschman watched her.

"We haven't seen the last of you, have we?" she muttered.

Chapter 19

THE WEATHER WARMED AND gentled. Molly got back into a regular rhythm of rowing almost every morning. Kathleen joined her occasionally but knew she held Molly back, so most mornings, she and Blossom went for a walk that bumped into a jog every now and then.

To her delight, her editing and cover work had remained steady.

"Who knew all I needed was an Internet connection, and I could make a living?" she said to Rebecca one day when she arrived at the library. "I should have done this years ago."

She knew she'd never get rich doing this, but living on the island had changed her perspective on money. "And everything else," she could have said.

Growing up, her parents had been driven by social status and getting ahead. And making it as ostentatious as possible, she realized now. Even with Susannah, that carefully crafted façade of respectability, designed to shield her family from the taint of her father's abusiveness, had dominated their lives together.

But here, no one was obsessed by the need to make as much money as possible. There was no social ladder to climb. Climbing up to the Head was the summit, literally, of life on Little Sister, and that would soon be occupied by four wind turbines. One of Kathleen's grants had come through, enough to begin the wind portion of the island's transition.

Molly and Joe and a handful of the others were working with the contractors to figure out how to connect the island's small power grid to the turbines and a bank of batteries. Most of the islanders were already installing solar panels on their own roofs with battery backup to hold the energy.

"When is Molly going to get to your house?" Rebecca asked as they prepared to resume Kathleen's training on the island families.

"Not sure. She's so busy getting everyone else's panels installed, we'll probably still be waiting next winter. Like the mechanic who never gets his wife's car fixed."

Kathleen realized she had just basically called herself Molly's wife. Rebecca seemed to have realized it, too. Kathleen glanced up to find Rebecca staring at her. Kathleen felt trapped, hypnotized by those blue-green eyes.

She cleared her throat. "I've been meaning to talk to you."

Rebecca waited.

Kathleen squirmed. This was harder than she'd expected. "Molly told me about the island's bonding ceremony, and I was—"

"No."

Kathleen was caught with her mouth open, ready to utter her next words. She closed it for a moment and then said, "Excuse me?"

"I can't bond you." Rebecca's voice was firm, but her eyes were soft. "I'm sorry."

"But... why?" Kathleen's nostrils flared. "It's because of my father, isn't it? First the oil company and now this lawyer."

"Yes... and no."

Kathleen slumped back in her chair. "What does that mean?"

Rebecca kept her voice even as she said, "We don't hold you responsible for what Michael does, but I can't and won't bond you with Molly while you're still bound to him and your mother."

Kathleen frowned. "What does that mean? I haven't had anything to do with them for years."

Rebecca reached across the table to squeeze her arm. "I'm sorry for you both." She stood. "I really am."

Kathleen was left sitting alone, staring at the door. "What the hell?"

※※※※※※※※※※

THE FIRST TOURISTS BEGAN to arrive on the weekly ferry, and Molly was amused, listening to Kathleen complain about them.

"The ferry came in today," she grumbled when she got home with groceries one afternoon. "I've got to remember to stay away from the market on ferry day. It was full of tourists. They're really annoying."

"They can be," Molly acknowledged as she helped put the groceries away.

"Now I understand how everyone in the diner the night I arrived knew I didn't belong here."

Molly smiled. "It's not that you didn't belong, it's just that we know the regulars, you might say."

"Well, it feels strange after all these months to walk into the market or down the street and see faces I don't know."

"The big rush will start next week," Molly said from the pantry. "After Memorial Day. The ferry will start to run daily until Labor Day. You won't be able to get away from them, but some of us depend on them, so be nice. Wilma and Nels make enough during the tourist season to get by the rest of the year. And I don't know if Miranda told you, but we get a discount."

289

She emerged from the pantry to see Kathleen snatching the receipt from her bag.

"I just thought things were on sale."

"No. They lower their prices during the winter, and bump them a little for the summer, but they don't like to make us pay more."

Kathleen shook her head.

"What?"

"It just still surprises me that people here are so kind to one another."

For some reason, she sounded sad as she said it.

Molly wrapped her in a hug. "Kindness shouldn't be a surprise."

Kathleen held her tightly. "But it is. Sadly. There seems to be less and less of it out there."

She pulled away. "What are you doing here, by the way? Don't you have any jobs to do this afternoon?"

"Nope. All done." Molly's mouth tugged into a grin. "What did you have in mind?"

Kathleen blushed. "Well, that wasn't what I was thinking, but I could be persuaded."

"What were you thinking?"

Molly reached up to tuck Kathleen's hair behind her ear, running her fingertip along the sensitive skin of her ear lobe. She got the reaction she was aiming for as Kathleen's eyes slid out of focus and she seemed to forget what she was thinking.

"I think I could put you to sleep doing this."

Kathleen shook her head. "Um, picnic. Maybe with Miss Louisa and your mom and dad if they can come? It's a beautiful day."

"Where?"

Kathleen thought. "Some place no tourists will interrupt us. The bluff?"

"Sure. It's far enough away from town and tucked back in the woods. Should be quiet there. Want me to see if Rebecca can join us?"

An immediate shadow fell over Kathleen's face, but she only said,

"Let's keep it small. Why don't you give your mom a call? I'll start making some chicken salad."

Blossom stood suddenly, his hackles up, a low growl rumbling from his chest as he stared toward the front of the cottage. Molly went to the door.

Kathleen hurried after her to see a sheriff's car parked in the drive. A man in uniform got out from behind the wheel while Rebecca got out of the passenger side.

"I think the picnic is going to have to wait," Molly said.

⁂

NIGHT HAD FALLEN BY the time the telephone jangled. Kathleen had been pacing anxiously since Molly had left almost three hours earlier with the sheriff's deputy from the mainland and Rebecca. She ran to the kitchen to answer.

"Come to the library," Molly said curtly.

"What is going on?"

"We'll explain when you get here."

Kathleen's heart thudded with dread as she drove to the library where Joe's truck and Louisa's Ford were already parked.

Molly came out to greet her.

"Why is it dark if we're all meeting here?" Kathleen asked.

"Shhh." Molly gestured her inside.

Confused, Kathleen followed Molly's lead, closing her door softly and stepping up onto the library's porch. Blossom seemed to sense the need for secrecy and tiptoed across the wooden boards so his nails wouldn't click.

Molly opened the door quietly, locking it behind them.

Rebecca peeked through the doorway from the genealogy room. "Come to the back."

Kathleen and Molly entered the back room to find Jenny, Joe, and Louisa already seated around the table. An oil lamp burned with a low flame, and the curtains were drawn. Rebecca closed the door after them, locking it as well.

Wondering what in the world was going on, Kathleen sat and waited. Blossom lay down under the table where she could feel his chin resting on her foot.

Molly slid a thick envelope onto the table. "That deputy came to serve a summons. We're being sued."

"Sued?" Kathleen asked when she found her voice. "By whom? For what?"

Rebecca leaned forward from where she sat at the end of the table. "By Michael."

"What?" Kathleen felt as if someone had punched her in the gut. She couldn't meet Rebecca's gaze.

Jenny laid a hand on her sister's arm and said gently, "He's suing us for ownership of Maisie's cottage."

"And for access to all of our real estate records," Rebecca said.

"But..." Kathleen's mind churned but no words came.

Molly took her hand protectively. "He's probably angry that we found a way around his little oil embargo, and he's looking for another way to make trouble."

"How do we respond?" Louisa asked. "We've had other offlanders ask about this sort of thing in the past, whether they could inherit a family house, but no one has ever gone so far as to sue us."

"We'll probably have to hire an attorney to represent us," Joe said.

Louisa tsked. "But that might mean having to divulge everything."

"If I'd gone on to law school—" Molly said.

"Don't be stupid," Rebecca said. "You'd have been miserable as a lawyer."

"How... how does the island pay for an attorney?" Kathleen asked timidly. "Do we take up a collection? I've got some money in savings."

"We won't need to go that far, but thank you, Kathleen." Jenny patted her hand.

"Then how...?"

A heavy silence filled the room. Kathleen looked from one of them to another as they all glanced around as if waiting to see who would speak first.

"What is it?" she asked. "What did Miss Louisa mean, 'divulge everything'?"

Rebecca stared hard at her. "What we're about to tell you cannot go any further. Your word on that."

Kathleen nodded. "My word."

Molly squeezed Kathleen's hand. "When the ship wrecked, it wasn't just carrying Irish peasants. It was carrying a heavy load of treasure."

"Treasure." Kathleen's mouth quirked into a disbelieving grin.

But no one around the table was sharing the joke with her.

"You're serious," she said faintly.

Rebecca and the others stood. Kathleen shuffled her chair back, and Blossom jumped out of the way as they picked the table up and moved it to the wall. The rug underneath, woven in a primitive pattern of trees and animals that Kathleen had never noticed before, was rolled aside.

Joe pulled an old iron tool out of his pocket and slid it between two floorboards. Up popped a trap door so cleverly built into the floor that, until its clasp was triggered, it was impossible to see.

Rebecca took the oil lamp and led the way down a set of wooden stairs into a yawning chasm below. The others followed. Kathleen found herself standing in a kind of cavern—half rock, half dirt—supported by stout timbers.

"In the years after the shipwreck," Louisa said, "the First Ones, who were excellent swimmers and divers, brought up all of this, piece by piece."

Kathleen's mouth gaped at the array of old wooden tables covered with stacks of dishes—gold and silver and bone china glazed in intricate patterns. There were a couple dozen or more leather sacks sitting about, and gilded frames stacked against the wall. Leather cases held heavy silverware and serving pieces.

"This weight probably helped sink the ship," Rebecca said. "Of course, the Irish knew nothing about it until the ship went down."

"These are full of coins and jewels," Molly said, untying one of the sacks and reaching inside to pull out a handful of stamped gold coins.

"The island has been sitting on this, all this time?" Kathleen asked.

"We've been its protectors, all this time," Rebecca corrected.

Something clicked in Kathleen's mind. "This is why Molly was gone for hours, isn't it? You were trying to decide whether I could be trusted with this."

Joe shuffled his feet and Jenny looked abashed, but Rebecca frowned. "Can you blame us?"

"No. I don't blame you at all. Especially considering what my father is trying to do."

She swept a hand around at the accumulated wealth. "What do you do with this?"

"A few pieces were sold long ago, and the money invested," Rebecca said. "That's what pays Molly's and my small salaries. It pays for regular upkeep on things we all use, like the power station. The rest we keep secret and safe for the day when it's needed. I'm not just the Keeper of the Record. I'm Treasure Keeper as well."

"A few people are always designated guardians," Jenny said. "As a safeguard, we keep the investment records and pay the sheriff and the Keeper from an island account so no single person is the only one dealing with it."

"We've also used it a few times when someone had a fire or bad storm damage that wasn't covered by insurance, to help them rebuild," Joe said.

"I take it the other islanders don't know about this?" Kathleen asked.

"They know there's a fund somewhere," Jenny said. "As much as we trust and rely on one another, this would strain the relationship we have with the ones who leave."

"Prodigals," Kathleen murmured.

"Exactly." Jenny nodded. "They would ask for their share of the island inheritance, when it's not ours to give them."

"My father certainly would."

"If he knew about it," Rebecca said. "Which he cannot ever know."

"No." Kathleen glanced around at all of them again. They had trusted her, despite all, and it meant everything. "He can't."

⬛⬛⬛⬛⬛⬛

LYING IN BED LATER that night, Molly heard Kathleen huff as she tugged on the covers.

"Can't sleep?"

Kathleen rolled to face her. "You, either?"

"No." Molly reached for Kathleen's hand. "What's wrong?"

Kathleen snorted. "Everything is wrong. My father is doing his best to injure this island and everyone on it."

They were quiet for a moment.

"I should call him. Try to talk to him. Why didn't they ask me to do that?"

"They talked about it," Molly said.

"When you were all trying to decide whether you could trust me with the knowledge of the treasure?"

Molly bit her lip.

"What did you want to do?"

Molly squeezed her hand. "That's a silly question. You know I trust you."

"I'm sorry." Kathleen shifted to rest her cheek against Molly's shoulder. "I do know that."

Molly pressed a kiss to Kathleen's forehead.

"What about the others? Rebecca didn't want to tell me, did she?"

"It wasn't Rebecca."

Kathleen lifted her head. "Who, then?"

"Louisa."

Kathleen sat up in bed. "Louisa doesn't trust me?"

"Louisa doesn't trust your father," Molly corrected. "She remembers what he was like with Maisie. And she's afraid there's something that's keeping you from confronting him. Even my mom agreed. Not that we shouldn't trust you, but that Michael will try to manipulate you. She and my dad and my aunt said he was pretty ruthless. They're not sure you'll be able to defy him face to face."

Molly couldn't read Kathleen's features in the dark but, after a moment, Kathleen lay back down beside her.

"Maybe they know my father better than I do."

Molly wrapped an arm around her. "But I know you."

※※※※※※※※※

"DAD, YOU NEED TO drop this lawsuit."

Kathleen knelt in the garden, trowel in one hand, a clump of weeds in the other, as she rehearsed how to confront her father.

The soil, black and enriched by a winter's worth of compost, was yielding a wide array of produce: three kinds of beans, carrots, turnips, tomatoes, onions, beets, radishes, potatoes, strawberries. Only the strawberries were ready to be picked, but everything was coming up. At least the parts the rabbits and squirrels hadn't eaten.

Nearly every time Blossom went out, he managed to chase a couple of critters out of the garden. It had become his favorite sport.

Kathleen moved along the row, digging more weeds, trying to figure out how to address this issue.

Rebecca had contacted an attorney to draft a response, but no one knew if the islanders might have to actually appear in court.

"Who does own the houses?" Kathleen had asked in the library the night they showed her the treasure.

"A trust," Rebecca told her. "That's why you signed a lease when you came here. You'll never own that cottage or the land it sits on. None of us do. It's what protects us from someone like—"

She'd stopped abruptly.

"It's okay," Kathleen said. "You can say, 'like Michael'. It's true."

"Okay. Someone like Michael deciding he wants to sell to an offlander. If we allowed that, we would have been like Big Sister long ago. And none of us would be able to afford to live here now."

"I wonder if he knows that, though," Jenny had said.

"What do you mean?" Kathleen asked.

"Well, he left here when he was young. Maisie still lived in the house. I assume he didn't discuss what would happen to it when she died. And after Bryan... well, he never talked to Maisie again. Maybe he honestly doesn't know how things are done here."

Rebecca's mouth had tightened. "He's about to find out."

Kathleen finished her weeding. She put her tools away and sat on the back porch with a glass of iced tea. Blossom came to lie down beside her, his chin resting on her thigh. Out on the road, there was more noise as cars and trucks drove by in both directions. Ever since Memorial Day weekend, as Molly had predicted, there were a lot more tourists.

Plus all of the island's school-aged children were now home for the summer. Most of the island businesses—Wilma and Nels, Miranda and Tim, Siobhan—had hired teenage help for the summer.

Kathleen had made a habit of doing her errands early and then staying home, but Molly had to be visible. Plus, her fix-it work didn't take a holiday, though most of that work now consisted of installing solar panels for the island houses and working with the crew who were constructing the wind turbines.

Up on her own roof, the new solar panels gleamed—"so we're not the last ones," she'd teased—providing all of the energy for the hot water and the house's electricity. It felt good to know the island would be in better shape this coming winter, no matter what happened with her father and this lawsuit.

She knew the islanders didn't exactly blame her, but she still felt self-conscious when she stepped into the diner or the market and conversation ceased. It wasn't hard to guess they'd been talking about her dad. She understood and was grateful that they were able to separate her from him, and she was determined to prove herself an islander, no matter what.

"Well," she said to Blossom. "If I'm going to talk to him, I might as well get it over with."

She went inside and lifted the handset off the hook. She had no idea if he was at the office or at home. Taking a deep breath, she dialed his cell phone.

"Dad," she said when he answered.

"Thought I recognized that number," he said.

Long seconds ticked by as they both fell silent.

"Why are you doing this?" Kathleen blurted at last.

"Because those bastards deserve it."

"You can't win."

He laughed. "It doesn't matter. I don't have to win. All I have to do is tie this case up in the courts for years, cost them so much in attorney fees that I'll break them. I'll break that damned island and every single person who lives there. Every last one who ruined my life, who took the life of my son."

"You might want to remember you have a daughter, too," Kathleen longed to retort, but the words stuck in her throat.

She paused and tried a different tack. "You grew up here. You knew these people. All our family comes from here. You used to want Bryan and me to have a good time." She squeezed her eyes shut, hoping that appealing to his childhood memories on Little Sister would work.

"I hated that goddamned place when I was a kid," he snapped, immediately dashing her hopes. "Stuck on that tiny rock in the middle of the ocean, nothing to look forward to except a life of smelling like fish guts or working for pennies catering to tourists. Being there for a summer was one thing. Living there was another."

Kathleen pressed her fingers to her forehead and paced, the phone cord trailing behind her. "Okay, so you didn't like it. You got away. Made a life for yourself. You don't have to do this."

A pregnant pause hummed over the telephone line.

"Leave. And I'll drop it."

Kathleen's knees buckled, and she fell into a kitchen chair, feeling as if someone had knocked the air from her lungs. "What?"

"I said, if you leave Little Sister and never go back, I'll drop all this."

"Why would you ask me to do that?"

"Because I'll never let them have anything else that is mine!" His voice was almost a snarl. He waited a beat. "Think about it, Kathleen."

He hung up. Kathleen stared at the receiver in her hand.

Chapter 20

THE WIND TURBINES WHIRLED, looking deceptively slow from a distance, but up close, Molly heard the huge *whoosh* the blades made as they swept by, driven by the ever-present wind on the island. The island's power grid was now being supplied more than fifty percent by the turbines. In the off-season, when the electric usage fell again, the percentage would be higher, but for now, with the tourist demand, it wasn't quite enough. Next year, when the solar installation was hopefully complete and they could get started on hydroelectric as well, things would be even better.

"Screw you, Michael Halloran," she muttered, getting back in the Toyota.

She thought about swinging by the cottage, but the argument she'd had that morning with Kathleen still stung. All Molly had done was to ask her if she wanted anything from the market for supper that evening, and Kathleen had snapped back that she had a huge stack of work to catch up on and that Molly could grab supper for herself at the diner.

Molly had stormed from the cottage but, thinking back now, it didn't make sense. Just a few days ago, Kathleen had talked about how she'd gotten caught up on all of her book projects. She wondered if Kathleen could be PMSing, but it wasn't the right time of the month for that.

And it wasn't just this morning. Kathleen had been crabby for the last few days. Just the other day, Molly had seen her out for a walk while she was up on someone's roof doing a chimney repair. Molly paused to watch her, walking with her head down, legs churning, much as she used to when she first came to Little Sister, back when she reminded Molly of a sandpiper. Back when she was all closed up inside herself.

It wasn't like her, Molly realized now. Something was up.

She drove into town, having to slow down as a group of tourists on bikes clogged the road. They shifted over to single file so she could pass them with a wave.

"Gotta be friendly," she reminded herself for the tenth time that day.

Town was lively. Wilma and Nels had quickly filled the five rooms the wind turbine contractors had vacated after weeks when the construction was happening. Molly went to the marina where her dad was busy fueling a private boat for someone who had decided to make the trip out to Little Sister. She went into the boathouse to inspect her winter project—the rich wood with its spotless varnish, seats newly upholstered in a red that matched the original, gleaming chrome on the rails and gauges, all ready to be delivered. It made her a little sad.

"Want to take her for a spin?"

She whirled around to see Aidan coming in behind her. "Hey, you." Her face split into a wide grin, and she punched him in the arm. "How are things?"

He nodded. "Things are good." He pointed to the wooden beauty. "Really. Let's take her out."

"You have time?"

"Yeah. We don't shove off for an hour. We're all loaded with the cargo we're taking back."

She didn't need to be asked twice. They unhitched the mooring lines and climbed in. The engine purred as Molly backed the Runabout out of the boathouse. Joe saw them and gave them a wave. Molly sat at the wheel and lowered her sunglasses from the top of her head.

Aidan sprawled on the bench seat at the back of the boat, his face tilted to the sky, his eyes closed, letting Molly steer them through the harbor and out to the open water. She cranked the throttle, and the sleek boat nearly flew over the water. The wind whipped their hair, and Molly let out a whoop. Behind her, Aidan laughed.

"God, it's been so long since I've been out on the water in something I wasn't rowing," she yelled.

"That's something I can't say," he hollered back.

She pulled back the throttle, letting the Runabout cruise at a speed that made for easier talking.

"So it's really going well, with Bobby?"

He sat up. "Yeah. I'm learning loads. I've lived on Little Sister my whole life, and I never realized how much stuff has to be hauled back and forth. And believe me, we do way less than other islands."

Molly eyed him. "And... everything else? When you're not working?"

"You mean, am I drinking?" He shook his head. "No, Mo. I'm not. To be honest, most nights, after working sixteen hours, I'm so tired, all I can do is fall into bed. That's a good thing."

He nodded his head toward the island. "How are things here?"

"Good. Mostly."

She filled him in on the legal shenanigans.

"That shit," Aidan said.

"I don't really remember him," Molly said. "But I agree. He is a shit."

"How's Kathleen with all that? Must be hard for her."

Molly frowned at the ocean. "I guess."

"You guess. What's up? Trouble in paradise?"

She started to reply a couple of times, but wasn't sure what to say.

"She been acting weird? Kind of distant and angry?"

Molly turned to face him. "How would you know that?"

He leaned forward, his elbows braced on his knees, his dark eyes focused intently on her. "Mo, don't you know what time of year it is?"

Molly's mouth dropped open.

"It'll be twenty-five years week after next," he said softly.

"I forgot."

He dropped his head to look down at his hands. "Lucky you."

"Oh, no, Aidan." She shifted the throttle to neutral, letting the boat drift as she joined him on the bench seat and draped an arm over his shoulders. "I never... I just forgot the date."

"I promise you, she hasn't." He sat up, scrubbing his hands over his face. "But it's also her birthday."

"Yeah, it is." Molly thought. "Do you get days off?"

"I haven't asked for any. It's our high season."

"I know, but just an overnight on Little Sister. Bobby and Fred can handle that without you."

He blinked. "Sure I think that would be okay. Why?"

Molly slapped him on the back and returned to her seat. "Because we're gonna have a *céili*. It's time for her *tar abháile*."

❈❈❈❈❈❈❈❈❈❈

THE WINDOWS WERE THROWN open and a wonderful breeze drifted through the screens. Even from outside, Kathleen could smell the aroma of Louisa's orange-cranberry bread as it cooled. It was one of Molly's favorites. She cut some of the green leafy lettuce, and picked a bowlful of strawberries along with a couple of small onions and radishes for a salad. Blossom lay nearby, gnawing on a stick.

She'd been such a bitch to Molly the last few days, and this morning had capped it off.

I should just tell her. Tell her what Dad said. Why am I keeping it a secret?

But it wasn't that easy. She knew what Molly's answer to Michael's ultimatum would be, but she needed to think this through on her own. Molly and Rebecca and the others seemed confident his lawsuit had no chance of winning, but even so, what if it did what he said, broke the island after years of court battles? Or forced them to reveal the existence of the treasure? What if she could have prevented it by simply leaving?

She carried her harvest into the kitchen and plopped into a chair. *Simply leaving. Except it isn't simple at all.*

Maybe Rebecca had been right about refusing to bond her to Molly. The damned woman could read the future.

She looked around. Everything about this cottage, this island, felt like home now. More of a home than any she'd ever known, at least since she was ten. For what felt like the millionth time, she forced herself to consider what she would do, where she would go, if she were to leave Little Sister.

Going back to Susannah was unthinkable. Going back to her parents' house was even more unthinkable. She couldn't even remember the last time she'd actually spoken with her mother.

A grinding noise distracted her, and she bent over to see Blossom, lying under the table, still chewing on his stick.

"You silly dog."

She pulled the stick away from him and tossed it out the back door. He glared up at her, his expression of indignation clear. She got a large carrot out of the fridge and snapped it in half.

"Chew on this."

He accepted it and turned three circles under the table before lying down to munch on the carrot instead.

"And you played me perfectly, didn't you?"

She washed the vegetables and made a salad, chopping up the other half of the carrot, then cleaned and cut the strawberries into the salad as well. She had chicken marinating in the fridge to bake later. Glancing at the clock, she realized she had no idea where Molly was or when she would be home. Times like this, she missed cell phones, and she understood why Jenny had gotten in the habit of making things that could be kept warm for hours if need be.

She stopped abruptly at the comparison, at the thought that she was becoming so domestic. That was something she'd never wanted to be, but this felt... good. Making food for someone she loved. Working at home where she could throw a load of laundry in the washer in the middle of an edit or go for a walk to clear her mind and come back to her work when it suited. This was the life she wanted, and she was furious with her father for trying to take it away from her.

The familiar rumble of the Toyota sounded from the driveway, and Kathleen quickly wiped her wet cheeks.

Hurrying to the front door, she watched Molly get out, admiring her long, lanky body and tanned face. She found herself the last few days looking at things as if she might never see them again.

She stepped out onto the porch and, the instant Molly climbed the steps, wrapped her arms around her.

"I love you so much," she murmured.

Molly held her tightly. "I love you, too."

"I am so sorry about this morning. I wouldn't have blamed you if you hadn't come back at all. I thought you might not."

Molly pulled away and looked at her. "That'll never happen. But I'm sorry I haven't been more aware of things."

Kathleen's eyes widened. "Things?"

"Yeah. Aidan reminded me what time of year it is."

"Oh." Kathleen backed away. "That."

Molly frowned. "Isn't that what's been bothering you?"

"Well, yes, of course."

Kathleen turned to go back inside, but Molly grabbed her hand. "There's something else."

"I've got to get the chicken in the oven."

Molly let her go, but when Kathleen went inside, Molly didn't follow. Kathleen glanced back to see her sitting on the porch. With a resigned sigh, she slid the pan with the chicken into the oven and went out to sit beside her.

Molly waited.

"I talked to my father." Kathleen kept her gaze fixed on a butterfly flitting about one of the azalea bushes. From the corner of her eye, she saw Molly turn to her but, still, she said nothing, waiting for Kathleen to continue. "Last week. I asked him why he was doing this to the island." She bit her lip for a moment. "He said we deserve it."

She leaned forward and rested her elbows on her knees, staring down at her sneakers. "He said if I left Little Sister, he'd drop the lawsuit."

A definite chill emanated from Molly's direction. "And you're thinking about it?"

"How can I not?" Kathleen took her glasses off and pressed the heels of her hands to her eyes. "If I left, you'd all be safe."

"Bullshit." Molly shoved to her feet and stomped down the steps. She picked up a stick and snapped it, but Kathleen had the feeling she was envisioning breaking something else.

Blossom, thinking this was a game, danced around, racing away from her a few steps and then twirling circles. Molly threw one piece of the stick, and Blossom raced away to seize it, but then flopped down to chew on it.

Molly turned to face Kathleen, her fists on her hips. "What do you want to do?"

Before Kathleen could answer, she held up a hand. "Not what do you think you should do, or what does anyone else want you to do. What do *you* want to do?"

Kathleen slid her glasses back in place. "I want to stay. With you. In our cottage. In the home we've made here."

Molly dropped her fisted hands and climbed the steps to sit again. She reached over to take Kathleen's hand.

"Okay then."

Kathleen held Molly's hand, their fingers intertwined. "That's it?"

Molly squeezed. "He has no power here. None except what you give him. Remember that."

Kathleen raised Molly's hand to her lips. "I don't deserve you."

"Hey." Molly touched her other hand to Kathleen's cheek. "That's not how it works. Love that has to be deserved or earned was never love to begin with."

Kathleen stared into those beautiful eyes and saw in them Molly's faith—a quiet, unshakeable faith that was as much a part of her as the swirling colors in her eyes, the part of her that had been instilled and nurtured by Jenny and Joe and the people of this island. Kathleen knew its roots were as deep as the island itself.

She buried her face in Molly's neck, letting herself sink into Molly's strong embrace. She felt the truth of those words but wondered if she could ever make herself believe them.

<hr />

SUDDEN LIGHT FILLED THE bedroom as Molly slid the curtains open. Kathleen scrunched her eyes shut, rolled over, and tried to pull the covers over her head.

"Oh, no you don't." Molly yanked the covers back down. "Time to get up. Got things to do."

"What things?" Kathleen mumbled.

"You'll see. Get showered. Quick. I'll get coffee started."

Molly gave her a light swat on the butt. She and Blossom hopped down the stairs. Outside, he ran into the trees while she breathed deeply of the morning. It was going to be a beautiful day. Perfect.

When they went back inside, there was no noise from upstairs.

"Go jump on her," she said.

Blossom raced up the steps. A second later, Molly smiled as she heard a startled "Shit!" Blossom trotted back downstairs, looking very pleased with himself.

"Good boy," Molly said, giving his ribs a thump. "Let's get breakfast."

A half hour later, Kathleen was still grumpy, clutching her travel mug as Molly drove to the marina.

"Are you going to tell me where we're going at the butt crack of dawn and why Blossom isn't coming?"

"It's way past dawn, and we're going to Big Sister. I have to deliver the Runabout. And after forty hours of work sanding and varnishing that boat, I don't want any dog claws on it. He can spend the day tormenting Minnow."

Kathleen perked up a little. "We're going to Big Sister?"

"Yup. You packed your backpack for the day like I told you?"

"Yes, but we're going to be there in a couple of days for the wedding."

"I know." Molly grinned. "We haven't been off the island for months. And the wedding day will be all about Brandi and Matty. We're going to make a one-day holiday of it."

Joe was waiting for them at the marina. The little boat, her rich wood gleaming, bobbed gently as if she were eager to be off.

"I'm gonna miss this one," Molly said. "She's a beauty."

Joe held the keys out. "They paid half in advance. If they don't pay you the rest today, they don't get these."

"Right." Molly flashed her wallet with her sheriff's badge. "I don't usually have any trouble collecting."

"That's my girl." Joe offered Kathleen a hand as she climbed in. "Have a good day. See you tonight."

Joe and Molly exchanged a look. She hopped down into the boat and settled herself in the driver's seat. She turned the key, and the engine purred.

"Love that sound," she called back to her dad. "Might have to get me one of these."

He shrugged as he untied the line from the cleat and tossed it in. "Find one that needs fixing and make them an offer."

She pushed the throttle, and the little boat began to ease away from the dock.

"Don't forget to pick up the cruiser!" he yelled.

Molly gave a wave over her shoulder.

"What's the cruiser?" Kathleen asked from the passenger seat while she secured her life vest.

"Our next project and our way back here. As if I could forget."

She kept to a slow speed that didn't create a wake as they made their way through the island's harbor.

Kathleen ran her hands over the new red leather upholstery. "This is beautiful. You and your dad did all this?"

"Yeah. Most of it. The boys helped some." Molly patted the console. "Not bad for a boat built in 1937, huh?"

Once out on open water, Molly snugged her sunglasses on her face. "Hold on."

She pushed the throttle forward, laughing as the boat's engine roared and the sleek craft shot forward.

"You okay?" she asked over the noise of the wind.

Kathleen nodded, the cords on her neck rigid. Molly reached for her hand. Kathleen held it tightly at first, gradually relaxing.

"You put both hands on the wheel," she said.

Molly laughed again and released her hand. Kathleen settled more comfortably in her seat, looking around and seeming to enjoy the speed as the Runabout cruised over the water.

It felt like no time at all before they were pulling into a private boathouse below an enormous mansion on Big Sister. Molly eased up to a new-looking dock and moored the boat. She held it steady while Kathleen got out. With one last lingering inspection, Molly climbed out and reached for a phone mounted on the wall.

"I'm sure going to miss this boat," she said with a sigh as she dialed the house.

By the time the happy owner had looked the boat over and written her a check—which Molly accepted with an ostentatious display of her badge when she tucked the check into her wallet—the sun was well up in the sky.

Kathleen and Molly peeled off the light jackets they'd worn and stuffed them into the backpack.

"Where are we going now?" Kathleen asked.

"You'll see."

"Why are you being so mysterious?"

But Molly just grinned and led the way through the beach castle's landscaped yard and out to a cul-de-sac beyond, where a yellow Jeep was waiting. She fished around under the running board and found a magnetic key-holder.

"Get in."

"What is all this?" Kathleen asked as she climbed into the Jeep's passenger seat to see an insulated cooler in the back seat.

"Picnic."

"A picnic? How did you—?"

"Brandi." Molly grinned as she put the Jeep in gear. "Nice to have connections."

She drove out of an impossibly expensive community of other beach mansions. In a few minutes, they were in an area of dunes devoid of houses.

"They haven't built here?" Kathleen asked, her head swiveling as she looked around.

"Not yet." Molly shook her head. "This has been designated a bird sanctuary, the only protected area left on this island. But there are some people who keep trying to get permission to build. We'll see how long it is before they cave to the money."

She stopped to put the Jeep into low four-wheel-drive. "Hold on."

Kathleen gripped the handles inside as the Jeep bounced over a dune creased with other tire tracks and out onto the beach.

"You can only get to this stretch with real four-wheel-drive," Molly said. "Even then, it's easy to get stuck."

She steered the Jeep nimbly along the beach, staying out of the softer sand, and arrived at a point that was completely isolated.

"Look at this view," Kathleen said as they got out.

Molly leaned against the Jeep and watched her—the wind playing with her auburn hair, the huge smile on her face as curious gulls circled. "I'm looking."

THE SUN WAS HALFWAY to the horizon by the time they chugged out of the marina.

"The lunch was wonderful," Kathleen had said to Brandi when they brought the Jeep back. "Thank you so much."

Brandi beamed. "I'm so glad you liked it. I packed it myself."

She showed Kathleen a photo of her wedding dress while Molly ran to the bank to deposit the check.

"You're going to fit right in with this family," Molly said with a quick hug when she returned. "We'll see you in a couple of days."

Brandi had sent them off with a wrapped pie. "For tonight."

Kathleen glanced back at the pie, sitting with her backpack on the floor of the boat now as Molly steered the launch past a line of buoys. "What did she mean, 'for tonight'?"

Molly shrugged. "Guess she was just sending something home for Mom to serve with supper tonight."

"Oh."

Kathleen turned around, facing the ocean stretching out before them. Little Sister was barely a dot on the horizon.

The only shadow on the entire day—other than being awakened too early—was that Molly hadn't acknowledged once that she remembered it was Kathleen's birthday.

The day was wonderful, she reminded herself. *Stop being stupid.*

But there it was, a little gnawing remnant of the hope that someone would finally remember this day for something other than the only thing anyone ever did remember. Twenty-five years. How was that possible? She felt guilty even wanting this day to be more about her than Bryan. A birthday couldn't compare with his death.

She settled into the cracked vinyl seat of this boat, her jacket pulled close against the cooling air.

"What's wrong?" Molly asked.

"Nothing." Kathleen heard the grumpiness of her voice and forced a more cheerful note. "Are you sure this thing will get us back?"

Molly grinned. "Not completely. But I made sure the radio works. Just in case. And if we have to drift around out here for a while under the stars, I'm sure we could find something to do."

Kathleen felt her cheeks warm. "One track mind."

"Not one track, but it's the main track."

Kathleen chuckled. "Thanks for a nice day."

Molly opened her mouth to say something but seemed to change her mind. She just smiled. "You're welcome. Settle back and enjoy the ride."

Kathleen hunkered down in the seat. As the cruiser chugged along, the wind grew cooler. Molly was still in slim-fitting shorts and a T-shirt that showed off her back and arm muscles. Kathleen tilted her head as she reconsidered the whole getting stranded under the stars thing.

Her stomach rumbled. Their picnic was hours ago, and there had been a lot of hiking and shopping since then. That pie back there was calling to her.

Although it sounded as if it were on its last leg, the cruiser brought them safely into Little Sister's marina, where lights strung above the dock weren't the only thing to welcome them.

The ferry was still there, a queue of people waiting to board.

Molly eased the boat up to the dock and jumped out to secure the line to a cleat. The office was dark, too.

"Where is everyone?" Kathleen asked as she handed over the pie and the backpack and then climbed out of the boat. "What's the ferry still doing here at this hour?"

"I don't know."

Sudden footsteps thumped in their direction as Fred jogged toward them as fast as he could.

"What's going on?" Molly asked. "Where's Dad? Why's the ferry still here?"

Fred held up one finger, gasping for air after his short sprint. "Bobby delayed gettin' here so long's he could," he wheezed. "We pretended the engine broke down halfway here. To give you time to get back."

"Why?"

He leaned over, his hands braced on his knees, trying to catch his breath. "Katie, your mom and dad are here."

Chapter 21

KATHLEEN NEVER DID REMEMBER much about the drive to the cottage. She imagined her heart was pounding and her hands were shaking but, honestly, she couldn't recall. She only remembered the pressure of Molly's hand, holding tightly to hers, anchoring her.

A shiny, black Land Rover was parked in the drive, along with Joe's truck. A small group of people was gathered on the porch. Blossom came bounding to Kathleen when she got out of the Toyota. He wagged his whole body as she rubbed him. She took a deep breath and straightened to face her parents.

Kathleen nearly didn't recognize her mother. Under her perfectly coifed hair—blonde now—and makeup, her eyes and cheeks were sunken. Her expensive clothing couldn't hide the angularity of her thin frame. Only her ever-present cigarette was the same. Her father looked as he always did, handsome, with more streaks of gray in his auburn hair than Kathleen remembered. His eyes, though, were hard.

"Mom, Dad."

"It's about time you got back," Michael snapped.

Kathleen felt a stir of irritation. "Well, I didn't know you were coming, did I?"

"That's what we told him," Joe said.

For the first time, Kathleen realized that Jenny, Joe, Rebecca, and Louisa were all gathered there, standing like some kind of barrier between her parents and the front door.

"What are you doing here?" she asked them.

"That's what I want to know," Michael said. "I'd like to get into my house."

Rebecca stepped forward. "It's not your house. It never was."

Michael visibly bristled. "It was mine as soon as my mother died."

Rebecca deliberately turned her back on him to face Kathleen. "It's time to go."

"Go?" Kathleen stared at her. "Go where?"

"You'll see," Molly said. She tugged on Kathleen's hand and led her back toward the Toyota. Louisa and Rebecca joined them while Joe and Jenny headed to the truck.

"Where are you going?" Michael demanded.

Jenny called over her shoulder, "You and Christine are welcome to join us."

Kathleen's head was spinning so fast, it felt as if she were in some kind of bizarre dream in which she was being shunted from one surreal scenario to another.

Molly pulled out of the drive and turned away from town.

"Where are we going?" Kathleen asked.

Louisa leaned forward and laid a hand on her shoulder. "You'll see in a minute, Katie."

The sun was below the trees and an indigo twilight was falling as Molly pulled into the cemetery. Kathleen's heart sank. She should have known. Twenty-five years. Of course they'd all be thinking of

Bryan. Molly parked, and they got out.

"What are all these other cars doing here?" Kathleen asked.

Behind them, the Land Rover ground to a halt.

"Come with me." Molly took her by the hand again and led her past the chapel to the stone ring.

The interior glowed in the gathering darkness. They ducked under the low stone lintel to find the space lit by at least a hundred candles.

"Happy Birthday, Katie," said Louisa.

Kathleen found herself engulfed in hugs and kisses from Wilma and Tim and Miranda and Siobhan and more than a dozen others.

"Aidan!"

Wordlessly, he wrapped his arms around her and held her tightly.

"What the hell is this?" Michael demanded as he and Christine stepped into the flickering light inside the stones. "What are you doing?"

"Celebrating," Rebecca said.

"How dare you."

Kathleen turned as her mother spoke for the first time.

Christine's face was wraithlike in the candlelight. Her sunken eyes burned. "It's the anniversary of my son's death, and you're celebrating?"

Rebecca's nostrils flared, but her voice remained steady. "We're celebrating life."

Michael looked around. "Life? What life?"

Jenny stepped nearer to face them. "Do you even remember, have you ever remembered that this isn't just the day Bryan died? It's also Kathleen's birthday."

Michael's mouth was already twisted with a retort which he never uttered as he stared at Kathleen, his eyes wide.

Jenny smiled. "That's what we're celebrating. We're choosing to celebrate the gift of the person who is still with us while we honor the memory of the one who went on."

Rebecca scowled. "He'll never understand. He never did."

Jenny, though, placed a gentle hand on his shoulder. "It's time you stopped blaming Kathleen for living."

"Blame her? Of course we don't blame her for living."

Jenny's gaze moved beyond him, to where Christine stood. "She does."

"No, she d—" One look at his wife's face silenced him.

Christine's features remained a mask. Kathleen waited to see if her mother would look at her, would finally see her standing there, alive and breathing, and be glad for it, but...

Aidan shouldered his way past his mother, gently nudging her aside. "If you want to blame someone, blame me. I'm the one who dared him. I'm the one who went out with him. I'm the one who came back when Bryan didn't."

Michael looked as if he'd like nothing more than to plant his balled-up fist in Aidan's face. Aidan must have sensed it, because he stood still, offering himself to Michael's wrath.

"No."

Kathleen felt as startled as everyone else looked. For a moment, she searched, too, for whoever had spoken before realizing it had burst from her. She stood frozen for a second when her father fixed her with his icy stare, but then she took Aidan's hand.

"Bryan was being stupid that whole summer. He was sneaking out at night, climbing out his window and doing all kinds of risky things. He could just as easily have fallen and broken his neck climbing down that tree. He asked me not to tell Nanna, and I didn't."

Her chin trembled. "I could have stopped it, but I didn't. It was an accident. It's not Aidan's fault."

"And it's not yours," Aidan said softly.

"Bryan did what we all did, Michael," Joe said. "You and I, all the other kids our age, we all did the same foolish stuff growing up here. But we got away with it."

He laid a hand on Aidan's shoulder. "Part of me would have died if Aidan had been lost in that storm, too, but I wouldn't have loved my other children any less."

A heavy silence followed.

Louisa took Kathleen by the hand. "Come, Katie."

She led Kathleen to the center of the circle with the others gathered round.

"If Maisie were alive," Louisa said, "she would be the one to do this, your first birthday after deciding to make your life here. As the oldest one here, and her friend, I'm chosen."

Rebecca handed her a small pine branch. Louisa held it in the flame of one of the candles until it ignited, flaring brightly in the darkness. She let it burn so that the glowing ashes dropped into a bowl that Rebecca held. She mixed the ashes with some oily substance in the bowl.

Rebecca pulled out her knife, smiling at the expression on Kathleen's face. "Just a couple of drops."

Kathleen held her hand out and let Rebecca stab her finger, squeezing a few drops of blood into the oil and ashes. She stirred the mixture with her knife.

Using her thumb, Louisa daubed a smear of oily ashes on Kathleen's lips. "May you speak only truth."

"Take your glasses off and close your eyes," Rebecca whispered.

Kathleen did as she was told to let Louisa daub more of the ashes on her eyelids. "May you see only beauty."

Next, her forehead. "May you know your soul's purpose while you walk in this world."

She tugged the collar of Kathleen's shirt down and painted a swatch of ashes over her heart. "May you always give and know love."

Kathleen opened eyes that shimmered with tears. "Thank you."

Louisa bent to scrape what remained of the mixture into a hole Rebecca had dug with her knife. With the dirt tamped back in place,

Louisa stood and enfolded Kathleen in an embrace. From the corner of her eye, Kathleen saw her mother leave the stone ring. She closed her eyes again. When she opened them, her father was gone, too.

⬛⬛⬛⬛⬛⬛

A LIGHT BREEZE BLEW through the screen, bringing the smell of a storm. It would be here before morning. Molly eased out of bed without disturbing Kathleen. Blossom lifted his head to watch as she crept to the hall. She waggled her fingers at him, and he followed. Together, they went downstairs and out onto the front porch. She sat on the edge of the porch, and he sat, too, leaning against her.

Overhead, heavy clouds had moved in. The wind teased Molly's hair as she swiveled her head, listening. For what, she wasn't sure.

Something had shifted last evening. Standing in that circle, when Aidan and then Kathleen had stepped up to face Michael, something like a whisper had rippled through those ancient stones, bringing goosebumps as Molly watched them.

The rest of Kathleen's birthday celebration had been perfect, just as planned. From the stone circle, they had all gone into the chapel where food waited. Wilma had brought a cake, beautifully decorated by Nels, with icing flowers in blues and greens. It looked like one of Kathleen's paintings.

Molly recalled her own *tar abháile*–her homecoming. The boys had all followed tradition and done theirs the first birthday after they graduated from school, even though they hadn't actually gone anywhere. But Molly had gone away, to college and then the academy. Even after she'd come back, she'd been so unsettled that Rebecca had refused. Not until the next August, with Molly resigned more or less to doing the sheriff's job and starting to establish her fixit work, had Rebecca taken her to the circle on her twenty-third birthday and anointed her. Molly smiled now, remembering how instantly it had felt as if a huge weight had been lifted. This island was exactly where she wanted to be, and that ancient ceremony—one blended from the First Ones and the Irish—had confirmed it for her.

She'd wanted the same for Kathleen. She'd wanted her first birthday celebration in twenty-five years to be the thing that anchored her here, on Little Sister. But then her parents had to show up. Molly didn't really believe in coincidences. Michael and Christine just happening to show up on this particular day was no accident.

All evening, Molly had kept a close eye on Kathleen, waiting for some break in her composure, but it hadn't come. When they got home—both relieved to find that Michael was not waiting there for them—Molly had expected Kathleen to dissolve into tears once they were alone. But there'd been no tears.

"Thank you. For the best day I can remember in forever," Kathleen had said, wrapping her arms around Molly's neck to kiss her.

"I wanted it to be perfect," Molly said morosely.

"It was perfect."

Molly had been ready to argue, but Kathleen's soft lips silenced her, and they hadn't spoken of it again as they lost themselves in lovemaking.

She glanced up to where Kathleen lay sleeping, wondering if she was as okay as she seemed. She gave Blossom a rub.

"Let's go back to bed. Maybe even sleep a little."

<hr/>

KATHLEEN STOOD, A MUG of coffee cradled in her hands, as she watched the storm from the shelter of the back porch. The rain fell in gray curtains, gusty winds bent the trees, and black clouds filled the sky. There was little likelihood the ferry would make it to Little Sister today, which meant there was little chance her parents would just disappear.

She sighed and took a sip of coffee.

"What did you expect?" she muttered. "For her to break down in tears? Beg your forgiveness and declare she never meant what she said?"

For years, she'd wondered what it was about her that made it impossible for her mother to love her the way she'd loved Bryan. She'd tried to do little extra things—clean the house without being asked; bake her mother some cookies; bring home fresh flowers—but none of those things had worked. They hadn't even been acknowledged. And always, *always*, Kathleen had secretly thought it had to be something lacking in her.

But last evening, everything had shifted.

For the first time, Kathleen had seen her mother, not as her mother, but as a broken, bitter woman, unwilling or unable to rise above her grief.

"Hey."

She roused herself at the sound of Molly's voice and went into the kitchen to find her pouring herself a cup of coffee.

"You were up early," Molly said. "You okay?"

"Yeah."

"That sounded convincing." Molly set her cup down and sat.

Kathleen joined her at the table. "I'm fine. Really. Just thinking."

"Probably hard not to, after last night."

Kathleen nodded. Molly reached for her hand and frowned at their intertwined fingers.

"Are you going to go into town to see them?"

Kathleen didn't need to ask who "them" was. "I don't know. Probably. I still have to talk to my father about the lawsuit."

"It's not your responsibility to stop him, you know. That's why we hired an attorney."

"I know, but I need to do what I can. If I don't at least try..."

Molly nodded.

Blossom jumped up and trotted toward the front of the house, growling. Molly and Kathleen followed.

"Crap."

Kathleen reached for Molly's hand at the sight of the Land Rover pulling to a halt in the drive. A black umbrella speared the air when the driver's door opened. Michael splashed his way to the porch, flapping his umbrella as he jogged up the steps.

He propped the umbrella against the wall and pulled the storm door open before skidding to a halt when he found Kathleen and Molly standing shoulder to shoulder.

"Oh." He took a step back off the threshold and cleared his throat. "Never had to knock to come into this house before."

"Things are different now," Molly said coolly.

He ignored her and stared at Kathleen. "I'd like to talk to you."

Kathleen stepped aside. With a small nod at Molly, she signaled her willingness. It had to be done and this saved her a trip into town.

Molly hesitated a moment and then said, "I'll be at the house, working with Mom today."

Kathleen caught her by the hand as she headed out the door and deliberately kissed her. "See you for supper."

She led the way back to the kitchen. Michael took his time, looking around.

"Not much has changed here," he commented as he followed her.

"Some things have changed."

"What?"

"Nothing." Kathleen got another mug down. "Coffee?"

"Sure."

Michael sat at the kitchen table while Blossom watched them from the safety of his position under the dining table and chairs.

Kathleen refilled her own coffee, careful not to drop the two mugs from her suddenly sweating hands, and joined him at the table. An awkward silence filled the kitchen.

"I... I didn't realize," Michael began. "I never meant to ignore you or your birthday after..."

Kathleen gripped her mug hard, steeling herself. *I will not cry.* "I guess it's understandable that everyone only remembers Bryan on that day. But it's been kind of hard."

She forced herself to meet her father's gaze and was pleased when he had to look away. He stalled, sipping his coffee.

She decided to press her advantage. "Why did you come here?" she asked. "It clearly wasn't to wish me a Happy Birthday."

Michael's jaw clenched, but he absorbed the verbal punch. "Twenty-five years. It felt like a milestone, of sorts."

Kathleen nodded. That she understood. "I think that's part of what drew me here."

Michael sat back, his eyes hard. "But it's more than that. You've been here for months."

Kathleen braced herself. "I'm staying. This is my home now."

His mouth compressed. "Why? Why would you throw away the life you had for this godforsaken rock?"

Kathleen smiled. "I've found the life I always wanted. I've found people who welcome and accept me for me."

Michael angled his head. "This cottage doesn't belong to you."

She recognized that expression, the one he reserved for his business deals, for when he gloated about defeating his opponents.

"No. It doesn't."

Whatever he had expected her to say, whatever counterarguments he had prepared for her protests, he apparently hadn't expected this simple admission. He stared at her.

"It doesn't belong to anyone."

He frowned. "It was my mother's. She died without a will. That makes it mine."

Kathleen eyed him over the rim of her cup. "It never belonged to Nanna."

"Of course it belonged to her. Christ, she lived here for almost seventy years. The mortgage must have been paid off decades ago."

Kathleen shook her head. "No house on this island belongs to anyone. Neither does the land. It all belongs to an island trust. It's only leased to us. Nanna was a tenant. That's what I am. A tenant. I'm nothing more than a caretaker."

The look on her father's face as he absorbed this was priceless, Kathleen thought.

"Of course, you do have first dibs," she continued. "If no one from our family had claimed it within a year of Nanna's death, then it would have become available to the other islanders in a lottery. That's how it works here. I didn't know that, and I arrived just a month before that deadline. But I will move out if you or Aunt Moira want to live here."

Michael's face went white. "What do you mean we don't own it? We have to!"

Kathleen fought a sudden urge to laugh at his inability to let that go. "Our ancestors took precautions generations ago. I'm pretty sure your lawyer will tell you that the trust is unbreakable."

He shoved to his feet. She let him stomp around the kitchen as she calmly sipped her coffee.

"I'll still break this island," he spat.

"The oil company?"

He stopped to stare at her.

"It won't work. We've found another oil supplier for what little we need now. And we're in the middle of converting the entire island to wind and solar. Soon we'll have hydroelectric, too. Either tidal or wave energy. We'll be self-sustaining. In a way, you did us a favor by forcing us to look at other options."

For one awful moment, as he stood there, trembling in his fury, she thought he might actually hit her. Blossom growled from the dining room. Michael's gaze flicked in his direction.

She felt a stirring of something completely unexpected—pity. "Dad, none of this—not the lawsuit, not the oil company—nothing will bring Bryan back to you. I'm sorry I wasn't ever enough for you and Mom, but that's something you're going to have to figure out how to live with. Isn't twenty-five years long enough to punish the world?"

⬡⬡⬡⬡⬡⬡⬡⬡⬡⬡

"ARE YOU GOING TO actually weave that up, or just sit and stare at it until it weaves itself?"

Molly jumped a little and grinned sheepishly at the reeds in her hands, half-plaited in a St. Brighid's cross. She started weaving again, fully aware of her mother's penetrating gaze.

"I can feel you staring."

Jenny chuckled. "And I can hear the wheels turning in your head." She laid a hand on Molly's arm. "Do you want to go back to the cottage and check on her?"

Molly shook her head. "It'll look like I don't think she can handle her father."

Jenny tied a white ribbon around a small nosegay of one white sweetheart rose surrounded by baby's breath and added it to the basket in front of her. "You think she can? Michael can be pretty forceful."

Under the table, Minnow lay on her back, playing with a length of frayed ribbon Molly had tied to the table leg and left to dangle.

Molly bit her lip as she plaited the reeds into a square pattern. "I think," she said carefully, "she needs to do this."

"And if she doesn't?"

Molly didn't answer as she completed the knots tying off her cross, adding it to the stack she'd been making.

"Then I'll have my answer," she said at last.

"About bonding?"

Molly nodded. "Rebecca thought something was holding her back."

"Yes." Jenny sighed when Molly glanced at her. "We've talked. I shared what Kathleen's mother said to her. It makes my heart ache to think what that poor girl has been dealing with on her own all these years."

"She's not on her own anymore."

Jenny smiled. "No. But she still has to figure out how to come to terms with her parents, and that's something no one else can do for her."

The telephone rang. Jenny got up to answer.

"Oh, hello, Wilma."

Molly paused her weaving.

"Really? Okay. I'll tell her."

Jenny hung up and came back to the table.

"Well?" Molly prompted when her mother didn't say anything.

"Michael just came back to the hotel and told Wilma they'd be checking out tomorrow."

"Ferry's coming for sure?"

"It better. Storm'll blow through tonight, and we've got to get to Big Sister."

Molly jumped up and ran to the door before she remembered. "Shoot." She ran back to the table to kiss her mother on the cheek. "I'll be back to finish the crosses. I know the wedding's tomorrow."

"Go," Jenny said, laughing. "And give Kathleen a hug for me."

※※※※※※※※※

KATHLEEN DID A QUICK calculation. The ferry usually arrived by noon, and was scheduled to depart at four. That meant her parents would be off the island by the time they got back from Big Sister.

But they're still here now.

"You ready?" came Molly's voice from downstairs.

"Just about."

Kathleen carefully draped a garment bag with her wedding clothes over her arm and picked up another bag holding shoes and hairbrushes and other essentials. Practical considerations.

"You don't want to be in a boat, in wind and salt spray, wearing your good things," Molly had warned her.

"What about you?"

"I'm wearing jeans and a T-shirt."

Kathleen still wasn't sure whether Molly was joking. She dubiously checked her own shorts and polo in the mirror and hurried down to where Molly and Blossom were waiting.

"All set?" Molly asked, taking the bags from her.

"I guess. You're still not telling me what you're wearing? Some floofy bridesmaid dress?"

Molly only shrugged. "You'll have to wait and see."

They hurried to the Toyota and drove into town, splashing through the puddles left by the storm. Molly parked at the marina, where the rest of the Coopers were gathered, along with Rebecca and Louisa, each holding a box of ashes.

Jenny stood with her hands on her hips. "Joseph Ryan Cooper, we are not taking the fishing boat."

"But it's the biggest," Joe said, looking perplexed. "We'll have to take two boats otherwise."

"I am not arriving at my son's wedding smelling like a lobster."

Joe sighed and gave Joey a nudge. "Let's fuel up two others."

"And wipe down all the seats," Jenny said.

Kathleen glanced toward the hotel. As if she'd read her mind, Molly said, "This is going to take a few minutes. Go."

Kathleen jogged to the hotel. Peeking into the diner, she saw her parents sitting at a table over their breakfast. Her heart thudded in her chest.

"Morning, Katie," Wilma sang from behind the counter.

Kathleen smiled in her direction.

Michael stood as she neared.

"Morning," she said. She gave a wave toward the marina. "I've got a wedding to go to today, so..."

Her mother hadn't looked up from her plate of barely touched food, but Kathleen saw that her hand trembled as it gripped a fork.

She gazed into her dad's eyes and, for a moment, saw the man she once knew—the one who waved and waved from the ferry as he left her and Bryan here for wonderful summers with their grandmother, the one whose arms she leapt into when he came back to collect them at the end of the summer, the one who couldn't wait to hear about all their adventures. His eyes reflected a puzzlement, as if he, too, had a distant memory of those days.

She flung her arms around him. "I love you."

He awkwardly patted her back, as if he no longer remembered how to do this, but he didn't say anything.

Kathleen leaned down and kissed her mother's cheek. "I love you, Mom."

Without looking back, Kathleen hurried out of the diner.

Molly was watching for her. Wordlessly, Kathleen moved into her waiting arms.

"You okay?" Molly asked.

Kathleen nodded. She sniffed and pulled back. "We all set here?"

They got into two smaller boats, Louisa, Kathleen, Rebecca, and Blossom riding with Molly, while Jenny, Joey, and Aidan rode with Joe.

"Aidan got another day off?" Rebecca asked, securing the two boxes on a seat as Molly steered through the harbor.

"He'll catch a Big Sister ferry when they make the return trip this afternoon," Molly called over her shoulder.

The sky was overcast to the east, the remnants of the storm that had battered them, but overhead, the clouds were light and wispy, promising a clear day for the wedding.

The two boats docked at the Big Sister marina, and everyone made their way to the island's church, which was beautifully decorated with fresh flowers.

Kathleen went with Louisa to the women's restroom to help her get changed while Molly disappeared with Joey and Aidan.

"You look beautiful, Katie," Louisa said when Kathleen stepped out of the bathroom stall wearing a dark green sleeveless silk blouse and white slacks. "That color goes wonderfully with your hair."

"I hardly ever wore dresses," Kathleen said. "And I didn't keep any when I moved here. You sure this is okay?"

Louisa chuckled and said, "On the island, we don't set much store by things like clothing. You could have worn a swimsuit for all they would care. Matty and Brandi just want you to share their day."

Kathleen thought about the ostentatious mansions she'd seen. "Maybe that's true on Little Sister, but I doubt the people on Big Sister feel that way."

Louisa let Kathleen brush her fine silver hair before tucking it back up into its bun. She brushed out her own hair, still looking decent from Jenny's last cut. Standing side by side with Louisa, they inspected their reflections.

"You're beautiful, Katie."

Kathleen laughed. "Thanks for being my date."

Louisa took her by the hand and led her out to where Blossom was waiting for her, now bedecked by flowers woven around his collar. Two baskets sat at the back of the chapel, one containing the tiny white nosegays and the other, dozens of woven St. Brighid crosses. Kathleen took a cross while Louisa plucked a nosegay.

Joey and Aidan, both wearing dark suits and ties, walked them to an empty pew near the front.

"You both look so handsome," Louisa said, patting Joey on the cheek.

"Miss Olivia and Mr. Woodhouse are in that pew with you," Aidan said.

Kathleen smiled at the thought of how normal that seemed now. He gave her a wink and went to escort more people to seats.

They sat, listening to the hushed voices around them. Kathleen inspected the intricate knots of the reeds, knots made by Molly's hands.

"You take that cross home and hang it on your wall," Louisa whispered. "It's a blessing on the house."

The church filled quickly. Kathleen craned her neck, hoping for a glimpse of Molly. She'd been very mysterious about this whole wedding thing.

Rebecca, Jenny, and Joe all came to sit in the pew in front of them. Kathleen was just about to ask about Molly when the music started.

Everyone stood as the first bridesmaids appeared from the church vestibule. Kathleen nearly laughed out loud, trying to picture Molly in one of the pretty, but very feminine, gowns. But the bridesmaids were all blonde, clearly related to Brandi, most likely her sisters.

While everyone else sighed when Brandi stepped into view, accompanied by her father and looking very pretty, Kathleen turned toward the altar to see Matty standing with a stupid grin on his face at the sight of her. Next to him were Aidan and Joey... and Molly. All wearing suits and ties.

Molly caught her eye while Kathleen caught her breath. The bride might have been everyone else's focus but, to Kathleen, no one in the entire church was as beautiful as Molly Cooper.

Chapter 22

SWEAT POURED FROM KATHLEEN'S nose in a steady drip as she dug her pitchfork into the ground and uprooted the brown lumps below. Inspired, Blossom dug until he unearthed his own potato. He carried it into the grass and plopped down to chew on it. Kathleen took it from him and substituted a carrot instead.

"Aren't they lovely?"

Louisa, protected from the sun by her floppy straw hat, came along next to her, plucking the potatoes from the dirt, giving them a light rub to loosen clumps of soil, and then placing them in an old bushel basket. She raised one to her face and inhaled.

"I just love that smell."

Kathleen paused to lean on her pitchfork. "It does smell good. I never would have guessed that things fresh from a garden could smell and taste so different from what I always bought from a store."

Louisa chuckled. "I remember you saying that when you were little, and you picked your first strawberries from Maisie's garden. She declared you should have turned pink, you ate so many."

Kathleen lifted her T-shirt hem to blot the sweat getting into her eyes.

"I so appreciate you helping me with this, Katie."

Kathleen gazed fondly down at her. "You know it's no problem, especially since Miss Olivia is being so lazy, just soaking up the sun."

Louisa cackled, glancing at the two wooden boxes sitting in the grass beside the garden. "Ollie hated digging potatoes. She's probably laughing at us."

"Well, this is payment for you teaching me how to can."

"Oh, you'll love having things from your own garden all winter long."

Kathleen resumed digging down the row. "I can't believe we're preparing for winter. Where did the time go?"

"It only goes faster, the older you get," Louisa said. "The children will leave to go back to school in a few weeks, the tourists will all go home, and we'll have Little Sister to ourselves again. Almost a year from when you came to us."

Kathleen paused again. "Almost a year. That seems impossible."

"Life is a wonder."

They reached the end of the row, and Kathleen carried the basket of potatoes to the cellar. She gently dumped them into the old, wooden potato bin and climbed the steps to find Louisa sitting in the grass between the two wooden boxes.

Kathleen hurried over. "Miss Louisa, are you all right?"

She dropped to her knees beside her.

The hat flopped as Louisa nodded. "I'm fine." She wiped her tears dry. "Just being a sentimental old woman."

Kathleen helped her to her feet. "Let's take a break."

They carried the ash boxes inside, leaving their dirt-encrusted shoes on the back porch. Louisa poured them both tall glasses of lemonade and brought them to the table.

Kathleen watched her anxiously.

Louisa smiled and patted her hand. "I'm fine, Katie. Just suddenly missing everyone. Silly of me."

"I don't think it's silly at all." Kathleen flipped her hand over to squeeze Louisa's. "I miss Nanna like crazy. I still blame myself for staying away so long."

"Don't. She knew why. And she always knew you'd come back."

Kathleen swallowed hard. "Then she knew more than I did." She stared down at her young fingers intertwined with Louisa's gnarled ones, imagining what it would be like to hold Nanna's hand one more time. "I always thought she'd remember."

"Remember?"

Kathleen closed her eyes, knowing it sounded childish, but she couldn't help it. "My birthday."

"But she did."

Kathleen opened her eyes.

"She wrote to you and sent you a birthday card every year. And Christmas presents. She wondered why she never heard back from you."

As Kathleen absorbed this news, a missing piece clunked into place. "My mother."

"Your mother kept them from you?"

"No." Kathleen was certain. "She destroyed them. That's why Nanna's letters stopped."

"Oh, Katie. I'm so sorry Christine would do that."

But Kathleen beamed. "It doesn't matter."

Louisa looked bewildered. "It doesn't?"

"No. My mother is trapped in her own misery, and she won't rise above it. But this means everything to me. Just knowing that Nanna didn't forget me."

"You thought that? All these years?" Louisa squeezed Kathleen's hand between both of hers. "No, no, no. She never did. She never gave up hope that you would find your way back here."

Kathleen took a deep drink of her lemonade. "I did. It took me twenty-five years, but I did."

⬚⬚⬚⬚⬚⬚⬚

MOLLY TUGGED ON THE oars, lost in a world shrouded in mist. She was soaking wet, covered in tiny droplets of fog that had condensed on her arms and her tank top, dripping from her hair onto her bare shoulders as she leaned into her strokes.

Behind her, the sun was only a diffuse light through the swirling haze but, as it rose higher, it began to burn off the fog. She kept pulling—long, even strokes in sync with her breathing, reveling in the burn in her arms and back and thighs. In the past, she used to imagine herself just continuing on this trajectory, straight on till she hit the southern tip of Nova Scotia. Or beyond. Away from Little Sister. Away from her life here. That was mostly when she'd first come back here after college, that first year when she still wasn't sure this was where she wanted to be. Back in those lonely days, the days she and Siobhan comforted each other. Over the years, she'd settled more serenely into the notion that she would spend her life here on this island, alone, but content.

The sun's warmth sank into her back like a tonic. On either side, the water droplets that sprayed from her oars sparkled like miniature diamonds as the scull glided over the ocean.

Like something from a fantasy book, Little Sister slowly appeared, seeming to rise out of the water as the fog lifted. From this distance, the tips of the wind turbines were visible, still now. Soon, the winds would pick up, and the blades would churn.

It had been a long time since she'd felt this stir of restlessness. She paused her rowing. The scull slowed, bobbing on the sea. It was more than restless, if she was honest.

Ever since the wedding, ever since Matty and Brandi had started their life together, this feeling had been growing, bubbling and festering. All sense of contentment seemed to have evaporated.

Kathleen loves me. We're living together. It should be enough.

She kept telling herself that. It shouldn't matter that they weren't bonded. It was just a ceremony, like a wedding was just a piece of paper. Except it was more than that.

She dropped the oars and propped her elbows on her knees, resting her head on her hands.

She wanted that ceremony, that tie to their ancestors. She wanted her family to acknowledge—formally—her bond with Kathleen. She resented that Matty had that recognition.

That's not true. It's not him.

She resented Rebecca for refusing them. She knew her aunt meant well, but...

"Goddammit!"

She slapped her oars into the ocean. Almost immediately, she got an answering splash as a pod of dolphins suddenly surfaced all around her. One stopped to eye her, lolling on its side, chattering and tossing a splash of water in her direction with its flipper.

She laughed. It was impossible not to. Accepting the challenge, she pulled on the oars, and the race was on.

The dolphins easily beat her as she rowed back to Little Sister, but their company was just what she needed. By the time she waved goodbye to the pod and dragged the scull onto the beach—already occupied by a woman tourist doing yoga on the sand—she'd made up her mind. She was going to have a little talk with Rebecca.

FOR ALL HER MONTHS on the island, Kathleen realized she'd never been to Rebecca's cottage. It suited her—pristine white shutters against dove-gray clapboards, beautiful flowering shrubs carefully laid out around the neat little house.

"Are you sure about this?" she asked as Molly parked the Toyota.

"I'm sure," Molly said with the same determination she'd had when she came home from her row.

She'd taken only enough time to shower before announcing they were going to talk to her aunt.

Kathleen hung back. "Isn't it too early? Shouldn't we have called?"

Molly took her by the hand. "She's an early riser, and there's no need to call."

She did at least knock on the screen door, though the front door was open.

Kathleen hissed at Blossom, who was cocking a leg over one of the hostas. "You go pee on a tree."

He obliged, trotting into the surrounding trees to do his business.

In the meantime, Rebecca came to the door. "Well, come on in."

Molly held the screen door for Kathleen and Blossom.

"Coffee?" Rebecca asked over her shoulder as she headed back to the kitchen.

Kathleen took in the immaculately clean living room, with floor to ceiling bookshelves lining the walls, the comfortably arranged chairs with matching ottomans near windows and lamps for plenty of light.

She followed Molly back to the kitchen, also spotless, with everything seemingly in its place. The walls were a cheerful apple green, contrasting nicely with the white cabinets and soapstone counters.

Rebecca poured two big mugs of coffee and set them on the table with a plate of cookies. She joined them with her own cup—fine china with a saucer—and offered Blossom a cookie.

"Wondered how long it would be before I saw you."

Molly, whose mouth was already open to say something, hesitated. "You were expecting us?"

"Well, not this morning, but yes." Rebecca took a sip from her cup, those curiously pale eyes scrutinizing Kathleen over the rim. She set her cup down delicately on its saucer. "You haven't spent much time at the library lately."

Kathleen felt herself blush. "I've had a lot of work to do."

"I see." Rebecca nodded. "And it had nothing to do with the fact that I wouldn't bond you?"

Kathleen stared at her coffee cup for a moment, watching the steam rise in swirls.

Haven't you learned anything in your time here?

She forced herself to meet Rebecca's gaze. "Yes. It hurt when you said you wouldn't bond us. But you were right not to."

Molly gaped at her. "She's not right!" She rounded on Rebecca. "None of this is right. We deserve to be bonded."

Rebecca's face broke into the tiniest smile. "All right."

"You—" Molly stopped abruptly, her eyes narrowed. "All right? Just like that?"

Rebecca's mouth tightened. "If you don't want it enough to fight for it, I'm not going to just hand it to you. This is too important to be tossed around frivolously."

Molly sat back, chastised. "Fair point."

"But," Kathleen looked from one of them to the other, "what about my father? What about the lawsuit?"

"That doesn't matter," Rebecca said.

"What do you mean it doesn't matter? He's my father. He's doing it because I'm here. How can it not matter?"

Molly was watching her aunt closely. "Because you've faced them. You've forgiven them."

"Yes. And no." Rebecca set her cup down. "Michael wasn't the one holding you back, Kathleen. You can't control what he does, but you have faced him and your mother. I watched you with Michael and Christine the night of your *tar abháile*. And Wilma told me about the morning of the wedding. Their inability to let Bryan go, to move on, is their burden now. The weight you've been dragging around all these years is gone. You're free of it. This is why I wouldn't bond you before. It wouldn't have been fair to Molly."

She stood, laying a gentle hand on Kathleen's head. "It was never your parents you needed to forgive."

⬛⬛⬛⬛⬛⬛

"IS KATHLEEN NERVOUS?"

"A little."

Molly was on her hands and knees, helping put a fresh coat of paint on the front porch floor of the Cooper house. Jenny painted from the other end as they worked toward the middle.

"Where is she?"

"Working at home."

Jenny paused, focusing off in the distance. "We haven't had a bonding since... Miranda and Tim."

"I know. Do you think Matty and Brandi will?"

"Only if they decide to move here." Jenny slid her container of paint over a couple of feet and started on a new swath of floorboards.

"I saw Joey going out yesterday."

"Yes. Matty's boating out to meet him. Not sure how long they'll keep doing that."

Molly sat back on her heels. "I feel kind of guilty. With Aidan gone, I could go with them."

"You've never wanted to fish. You've got plenty to do here." Jenny dipped her brush in the paint, a pretty blue-gray. "To tell you the truth, I kind of hoped this would spell the end of fishing for Joey and Matty. Sometimes, it feels I've spent half my life waiting for them to come back safe."

"Really? You never say much."

Jenny shrugged. "What could I say? When your husband and sons fish for a living, you learn to live with the uncertainty. But every time they're out when it blows, I pray."

340

"You think Matty will come back?"

"I think he'd like to. But he'll have to talk Brandi into it. Little Sister is so much quieter. Not sure how she'd handle the off season here."

Molly swiped her paintbrush along a couple of boards. "Big Sister would drive me crazy. All those rich people, and so many more tourists than we get. I'll be glad to see ours leave next week after Labor Day."

They worked in silence for a few minutes. Molly shifted her paint container again and glanced over to find her mother watching her.

"What?"

Jenny's eyes shimmered. "I just can't believe how the time has passed, how much has changed. Maisie and Olivia both gone. Matty married, Aidan working with Bobby, now you getting bonded. It flies by so fast. Enjoy every minute, Molly."

Molly set her brush down and shuffled over to sit beside her mother. "We haven't really talked about this, but will you stand for me?"

Jenny stared at her for a moment and then flung her arms around her. "I'd love to! Who's standing for Kathleen?"

"She said she'd like Louisa to do it."

Jenny drew back. "Oh, that's lovely. That will mean the world to Louisa."

Her gaze focused on something over Molly's shoulder. Molly turned around to see Minnow traipsing over the freshly painted floorboards, leaving telltale paw prints in her wake.

"Darn cat."

Molly shifted to get her paintbrush and repaint, but Jenny caught her arm. "Don't. Leave them. In fact..."

She tugged on Molly's hand. "Let's press our hands into the paint, too."

"Are you serious?" Molly frowned at her work, itching to fix it, make it perfect.

"Sure I'm serious. Come on."

They knelt side by side—Molly pressing her right hand, Jenny her left—leaving a pair of perfect handprints in the paint.

Jenny sighed. "Every time I see these, I'll remember this day."

Chapter 23

FOR THE RESIDENTS OF Little Sister, the week after Labor Day was an island-wide celebration. The last daily ferry of the high season had left with the most of the tourists earlier in the week. It felt as if the island heaved a sigh of relief, tinged with a bit of sadness, as the children had all left as well, to return to school on the mainland.

"I can't believe I'm the only one in here," Kathleen said to Miranda when she walked into the market.

She snatched up Ellis, who was toddling toward Blossom, making a grab for the wagging tail.

"I know." Miranda handed Ellis a teething ring. "It always feels so quiet after they leave."

She tilted her head. "You all set for the new moon?"

Kathleen's eyes widened. "Is there anything I need to do to get set? I mean, it's just the ceremony on the beach, right?"

"Yes, of course." Miranda pulled her into a tight hug. "I'm just really happy for you two."

"You're smirking," Kathleen said when she pulled back from the embrace to look at Miranda. "Why are you smirking?"

"No smirking. Just happy."

But as Kathleen checked out and picked up her bags, Siobhan came into the market, her long hair pulled back with a tie-dyed scarf.

"Ready for tonight?" Siobhan asked.

"Why does everyone keep asking me that?" Kathleen demanded.

But Siobhan shared a wink with Miranda. Kathleen heard them both chuckling before the door swung shut behind her.

On her way home, Kathleen reviewed everything Molly had told her about the ceremony. There would be the whole naked thing and the blood thing, but she couldn't recall anything else worthy of that reaction.

She took a detour to the Woodhouse place and found Louisa outside, trying to mow the grass with an old-fashioned push mower.

"Let me do that for you." Kathleen jumped out of the car and took over despite Louisa's objections.

Blossom chased bumble bees while Kathleen mowed. It didn't take long, but she quickly worked up a sweat. Louisa met her on the porch with a bowl of water and an icy glass of lemonade as she finished. Blossom lapped up the water and plopped down in the shade, his tongue lolling.

"Thank you, Katie."

Kathleen took a long drink. "Oh, that's good." She swiped her forehead with her shirtsleeve.

Louisa held her hand and patted it. "Thank you again for asking me to stand for you. It should be Maisie, but I'm happy to be there in her place."

Kathleen smiled. "I can't think of anyone I'd rather have."

"I'll come by myself. I know I'm a silly old woman, dragging Daddy and Ollie with me everywhere."

"Absolutely not!" Kathleen turned to face her. "They're as much a part of Little Sister as Nanna. I'd be very disappointed if they weren't there."

"Really?" Louisa's watery eyes lit up.

"Really."

⣿⣿⣿⣿⣿⣿⣿⣿

MOLLY SHIFTED RESTLESSLY IN her new recliner while Kathleen pretended to read. Up on the mantel, the clock ticked glacially. When the eleven-thirty chime sounded, Molly turned to her.

"We should go now."

Kathleen nodded mutely and closed her book.

Blossom, who had been snoring in his bed, leapt up, immediately wide-awake.

"Drive or walk?" Kathleen asked.

"Walk, I think."

Outside, the September night had cooled. They headed to the trail that meandered through the woods down to the beach.

"No need for a flashlight tonight," Molly said as faint star shadows rippled over them.

Kathleen didn't respond. They descended the trail, but before they got to the beach, she reached for Molly's hand and pulled her to a halt.

"I know, when I first came here, you had your doubts about me. And since then... Susannah and now my father—"

"Stop." Molly reached up to cup Kathleen's face in her hands. "I stopped having doubts about you a long time ago."

"I know, but..." Kathleen looked deep into her eyes. "This is forever. I just want to say, before we get down there, that if you want to change your mind, or—"

Any further words were silenced by Molly's mouth on hers, a kiss so tender, so passionate, so strong that it left Kathleen's knees weak.

When the kiss ended, Kathleen pressed her forehead to Molly's.

"Any more questions?" Molly murmured.

Kathleen just shook her head.

Molly smiled. "Good."

They continued down the trail.

"There are still a few tourists here," Kathleen said. "How do we know they won't show up?"

"If they get past Wilma, there are others standing guard who will keep them from getting to the beach."

Overhead, the dark disc of the new moon rode in a sky blanketed in stars.

"Glad we didn't wait until November to do this," Kathleen said.

Molly chuckled. "I know. This is chilly enough in September."

"Are you going to tell me why Miranda and Siobhan were laughing this morning?"

Molly grinned. "I have a feeling we'll be coming home to find the house will have a few additions."

"Oh." Kathleen breathed a sigh of relief. She'd been nervous all day that there was some other part of this ceremony that she didn't know about.

Blossom romped ahead of them to greet the people already gathered at the beach. Joe and Jenny stood with Rebecca and Joey. Matty and Brandi held the wooden boxes of ashes.

Louisa came to meet them, taking Kathleen and Molly each by the hand. "I'm so happy for you both."

She led them to Rebecca.

"It's not too late to change your minds," Rebecca said. "This is not a commitment to be taken lightly. Once you do, this is forever."

Kathleen turned to Molly. "We've already had this discussion."

Molly simply nodded.

"All right. Molly, you go with Jenny that way." Rebecca pointed to the south end of the beach. "Kathleen, you'll go with Louisa."

Louisa took Kathleen by the arm and guided her to the north end of the beach while Joey kept hold of Blossom's collar to keep him from following.

"Undress here, Katie," Louisa said. "Go naked into the water to meet Molly."

Kathleen looked dubiously at the waves lapping onto the sandy beach. "How far out do I need to go?"

"Waist-deep should do it." She reached up to pat Kathleen on the cheek. "We'll be waiting for you."

She left her. Kathleen's heart was pounding as she slowly undressed, feeling very self-conscious. She folded all of her clothing neatly, laying everything on top of her shoes. She hesitated a second and then took her glasses off, leaving them atop the stack. She couldn't help wrapping her arms across her chest, suddenly glad the other people gathered on the beach were no more than a blur as goosebumps covered her skin.

She waded into the water, sucking in a breath. The September days might have been mild, but the water was freezing.

"Tradition, my ass," she muttered through chattering teeth. She forced herself to wade deeper, feeling the sandy bottom with each step before committing her weight. She had no idea if there was any kind of drop-off.

When she got waist-deep, she turned parallel to the beach, hoping Molly was headed in her direction. To her relief, a blurry figure moved toward her.

"Wow," she said when Molly got close enough to come into focus.

Starlight gilded her shoulders, the curve of her breasts and hips, her face. Kathleen stared, wobbling a little as the waves pushed against her.

"You are so beautiful."

Molly smiled and reached out to touch the shooting star necklace, the only thing Kathleen was still wearing. "So are you. If I'd known this would feel so erotic, we'd have been out here months ago."

347

Kathleen giggled nervously. "What now?"

"We go under."

"Under?"

Molly nodded. "Like a baptism. Together. Ready?"

Kathleen held her breath and dropped, letting herself sink under the water. For a moment, she gazed up at the rippled sky above. They came up together, pushing wet hair back off their faces. Hand in hand, they returned to the beach.

Jenny and Louisa were waiting for them, holding a blanket of some kind. When Kathleen and Molly waded out of the water onto dry sand, they wrapped the blanket around them. Kathleen saw that it was a quilt.

Rebecca and the others all gathered round as Molly and Kathleen stood shoulder to shoulder with the quilt's welcome warmth covering them.

"This quilt," began Rebecca, "made from the clothing of our ancestors, reminds us that individual things can become one. So, too, can two people become one, bonded to each other, bonded to this island, bonded to all who came before or will come after."

Kathleen glanced down and saw that the quilt was indeed sewn together from patches of cloth and leather. She recognized a familiar patch of red-and-black-checked flannel.

"Kathleen, standing here as you are, knowing that all any of us ultimately has to offer to another is heart and body and soul, do you take Molly to be your bondmate, to love her and stay true to her only, caring for her through all life has to offer, its challenges and its joys, for the rest of your days in this realm?"

Kathleen looked into Molly's eyes. "I do."

Molly repeated the pledge.

Rebecca pulled her knife from a sheath on her belt. She gestured to them, and Molly held out her hand, palm up. After a heartbeat's hesitation, Kathleen did the same.

Quickly, Rebecca slid her blade over each palm. Kathleen bit her lip against the sharp pain. Rebecca pressed their bloody palms together, squeezing them between both of hers, letting drops of blood fall to the sand below. She squatted down and used the knife to bury the bloody sand.

"Your blood, mingled together, is now part of Little Sister. For all time, you are bound to each other and to this island. No matter where you roam, you carry us with you. We will sustain you in times of trouble and celebrate with you in times of joy. When your life in this plane ends, you will become part of this island, sustaining the generations to come. Bright blessings on you, Molly Ahearn Cooper and Kathleen Anne Halloran."

Louisa clasped them each in a tight hug and kissed them on the cheek. Rebecca offered them two handkerchiefs to wrap around their hands and stem the bleeding.

Joe embraced Molly. "We're proud of you, Mo."

"Thanks, Dad."

He kissed Kathleen on the cheek. "You were already part of the family. This just formalizes it."

Matty grinned at them. "Nice birthday suit, Mo."

"I wouldn't go there," Brandi said. "At least for them, nothing shrank."

"Ouch," said Joey, doubling up in laughter.

Molly shook her head. "Boys."

Blossom pulled loose from Joey's grasp and wriggled under the quilt to sit between them.

"We'll leave you alone now," Jenny said. She pushed Joey and Matty toward the sea wall. "Come on, you two."

Still wrapped up together, Molly and Kathleen sat on the beach. Blossom lay down across their feet, determined to stay close.

"That was beautiful," Kathleen said.

"It is a beautiful ceremony," Molly said. "I was so nervous, I thought I might pass out."

Kathleen clasped Molly's bandaged hand in hers.

Molly tilted her head. "The sky is so incredible tonight. It's perfect. The stars are amazing."

Kathleen looked up, squinting.

"You can't see. Where are your glasses?"

But when Molly started to get up, Kathleen pulled her back down. She knelt in front of her, letting the quilt slip from around her shoulders. Kathleen bent to kiss her, a soft, lingering kiss. When she pulled away, Molly gazed up at her.

"I don't need my glasses." Kathleen tilted her head, looking into Molly's eyes where she saw galaxies in perfect focus. "I can see everything I need to. Right here in your eyes."

THE END

About the Author

CAREN WAS RAISED IN Ohio, the oldest of four children. Much of her childhood was spent reading every book she could get her hands on, and crafting her own stories. She was influenced by a diverse array of authors, including Rumer Godden, J.R.R. Tolkien, Ursula Le Guin, Marion Zimmer Bradley, Willa Cather, and the Brontë sisters. She has lived in Virginia for over twenty-five years where she practices physical therapy, teaches anatomy and lives with her partner and their canine fur-children. She began writing creatively again several years ago. Her first novel, *Looking Through Windows*, won a Debut Author award from the Golden Crown Literary Society in 2009. Since then, she has published several more novels, winning multiple Rainbow Awards and a 2014 GCLS Award for *In This Small Spot*.

46301333R00224

Made in the USA
San Bernardino, CA
05 August 2019